DAMSEL

TRACY BROEMMER

Damsel

by

Tracy Broemmer

Women's Fiction

Published by Tracy Broemmer

Edited by Lexie Broemmer

Cover by Hell Yes Designs

All Rights Reserved

For victims
& survivors
& their families

And also
for the boys
& men who are
falsely accused
& their families, too

A NOTE TO READERS

Dear Readers,

When I start a book, I am writing a story that is inside me, burning to get out. I don't write to teach lessons or push an agenda. I write because there are people in my head, telling me their story, making me laugh or cry with them, and I desperately want to share those stories with you.

Sometimes you ask me where I get my ideas. (I am always lost in my head, but I still wonder the same thing about the authors I love to read.) The question sort of terrifies me... because of course I want to talk about my ideas and my characters because they're as real to me as you are. But also, I know I could rattle for hours on end about fictional people who are born in my head and live their lives on paper or in e-books, and if I spend too much time talking about fictional people, you guys might decide I'm crazy.

I take some ideas from news stories. I don't try to write actual news events as stories, but I do pick up plot ideas from things I hear when I pass the TV or things I see in papers or on magazine covers. Even then, I'm not suggesting any of you take sides on an issue, let alone asking you to see something my way. Maybe you can argue that I'm at least posing an idea and asking you to think about it. But for me, even then, what I'm doing is sharing a story that might make you laugh a little and cry a little and maybe even think, *I'm not alone. Somewhere out there, someone else is dealing with his or her own struggle.*

As a reader, I want to find books that I will devour. I want to be *entertained*. I want to fall into a fictional world that might be very similar to mine, but still takes me away from my world for a while.

Most of my books start with characters—people in my head who live and love and laugh and cry, the way I do. And those characters tell me their stories. I rarely focus on a plot idea first. Maybe that's because I'm a people watcher, and when I see sisters or friends or romantic couples laughing or crying or arguing, I want to know THE WHY. I want to know their hearts and minds and HOW they live.

Most often in my writing process, I walk around with these new people in my head, and I listen for a while to what they're saying and what they want me to know. Once I see them clearly, I start writing with a general idea of where I'm going. The title usually comes next—early on—which helps me to pull the whole idea together and focus, and when I'm lucky, the characters take over, and the book writes itself.

Last fall, I woke up on the last morning of a trip to Aspen,

Colorado. My husband was already downstairs at his work-shops. I climbed out of bed to take on the day, which would include packing up and flying to Phoenix, Arizona for a book conference. I was writing Always, Jess, book 3 of The Mississippi Queen Trilogy, and loving the book and the series and the Queen. As I got out of bed, the words to start *this* book—Damsel—were in my head. Not an idea. Not a family. Not a character. THE WORDS...*You hear a knock on the door*...I'm pretty sure I've never started a book this way, but before we left Aspen that morning, I was ten pages in on something new and very dark and disturbing, and having to shut down the laptop to go the airport was PAINFUL.

I didn't start the book as any sort of political or social state-ment. And no, I did not write this based on any sort of personal experience. I started the book because I couldn't NOT start the book. I was compelled to tell a story, period.

Somewhere around ten chapters into the book, it became a little something more, though my intention was and is, still to tell a story and make you feel something. This book is about rape. The assault scene is not explicitly detailed, but it is several pages long, and it's gritty and maybe very painful for some to read. I didn't write it to be salacious or gratuitous, but because I got caught up in the story and I had to write it as I did. This book also addresses the #metoo movement, though not in a big political setting. It's simply—and complexly—the story of a woman who has two sons and a husband, who struggles to move on after she's sexually assaulted.

I have a son I'm very proud of. He's a smart, kind-hearted young man who's been taught right from wrong. He is thoughtful and compassionate, and he respects people: me, his father, his elders, professors, people in authority, women, girls, and his peers. I worry just as much for him now when he's out in any social situation as I do when my daughter is out with friends.

I wrote this book with absolute respect and love for victims of sexual assault. I believe in justice. I believe that women are strong and deserve the same respect men do. But I don't believe that every boy or man accused of sexual harassment or sexual assault or rape is guilty. I'm not pushing an agenda with this book. I'm not hoping to teach any lessons. I don't want to hurt anyone. I just wanted to tell a story about a strong woman who overcomes a devastating life experience and has to bounce back for other people in her life.

I don't stereotype people, so I can't make a blanket judgment that every man or boy accused is guilty or innocent.

Respectfully,
    Tracy

*There is no significance to the actual assault happening in Aspen. I chose Aspen simply because it's where I was when I started the book. The scenery is breath-taking, and the people we met there were all very welcoming.

CHAPTER 1

*Y*ou hear a knock on the door, and you figure it's your husband, so you go to answer it. You don't pay attention to the peephole, because you're in a hotel room, and it's early morning, and he just left not even five minutes ago, so you assume he forgot something. He's going to a workshop session, and you have the morning for fun, so you're not showered or dressed yet. But since it's your husband at the door, you grab the handle absently and push it down. The door starts to open, and you're looking back over your shoulder at your bag open on the luggage rack.

"What'd you forget?" you ask, head still turned the other way, but no one answers so you look back as someone who apparently isn't your husband pushes hard at the door to shove it open. A stranger eyes you coldly as he reaches back to close the door. He's dressed in normal clothing; he's not a hotel employee, and he doesn't look like a thug.

Except why is he busting into your room at seven in the morning, and why are his eyes crawling over you leaving you feeling cold and clammy and dirty? Terror isn't here yet, because you're still putting it together—the whole scene. Daylight pushes at the heavy curtains at your back, and you smell coffee—even though there's none brewing in your room. The man watching you wears stylish jeans and a brown leather jacket, and the toes of his brown leather shoes are scuffed and worn.

He's sort of good-looking, and that's another thing you can't piece together with what's going on. This man is a complete stranger, and he's now in your hotel room with you. He's between you and the door, and his icy blue eyes —you guess there might be a name for that specific color, but you've always just thought it was creepy and cold—are all over you, and for the first time, a shiver of fear tiptoes up your spine.

He doesn't speak, and suddenly you realize the only sound in the room is heavy breathing. It's you, because something isn't right here. You're not a small-town girl, but you're not big city, either. You know crime, but only what you see on TV. World news, national news, local news, all of the above. There's a widespread drug problem where you're from, and now and then someone is murdered, maybe an errant bullet in a bar fight gone too far or even a drive-by shooting. You're not naïve, and you know there are women who are assaulted everywhere, but you don't hear much of that in the local news.

What you do hear seems to happen on the other side of town. It's rare for something big to hit the news east of 10th Street, and so your closest brush with crime is so distant you still don't believe this is happening.

You're intelligent. Well-educated. Reasonably attrac-tive, though you know sexual assault has nothing to do with looks and appearance, and it's all about power.

The stranger in your hotel room flexes his fingers now

and balls them into fists. You're still studying him, looking at the navy shirt under his coat. The gold chain around his neck. The graying stubble on his face. Ordinarily, you would find that attractive. But he's leering at you now, and you remember you're in the skimpy nightgown you purchased and packed special for this trip.

You and your husband travel together now and then, and it's always a nice little get away from real life. Your kids are your entire world; Matthew will be heading off to college next year with a nice academic scholarship, and fourteen-year-old Jordan is an up-and-coming soccer star. But they're kids, and the world still revolves around them— or so they believe—and you and your husband rarely get any time together for a glass of wine without one of them barging in to crash the conversation or having to discuss Matthew's English term paper on Keats or where Jordan is spending the night next weekend. If there's no time for a glass of wine together, making love has become nearly impossible, because your schedules never click.

When you're home and wishing your husband were around, he's out of town or working late, and when he's home and wants to love you, you're exhausted because you worked a twelve-hour day and finished three loads of laundry and fixed dinner. You're asleep before your head hits the pillow, and if your husband wakes you then to make love, there's no pleasure in it.

So when you planned this trip, you went to the boutique on the corner of Mills and Ray, and you purchased a thong in a dusty-rose color, and you picked out this tiny, satin slip of a nightie in crème, and last night you wore it for your husband. He had responded like a love drunk fool as you knew that he would, and the corners of the sheets are untucked and the comforter is draped half over the bed, and your inner thighs burn from the delicious scruff on your husband's face, and the tenderness in your sex from hours of lovemaking doesn't matter because he made you purr with content, and the orgasms were so intense that there were tears, and after twenty years of marriage, you're so in love with him—

It's hard to comprehend the evil in the world.

You know it's out there, because you're intelligent, and you're street smart. Or you thought you were, but what does street smart have to do with a stranger barging into your hotel room in broad daylight?

He moves suddenly, and your heart pounds so hard, you think it will explode. But he only twists around to flip the deadbolt on the door. If your husband would come back now, he could not get in. Not even with his key.

"What do you want?" Your voice does not sound right, but it's not octaves higher with fear yet, either. The stranger shrugs out of his jacket as he saunters toward you. His navy shirt is pressed to perfection, right down to the creases in his sleeves. He meets your eyes with a heavy, intense stare, and terror ignites flames in your belly. Like a snake, he strikes fast, and his fingers are tightly coiled around your wrist. His skin is warm and dry. Up close to him you smell cologne, and you wonder who on the seventh floor of the hotel brewed coffee and if he or she is drinking it while getting ready for the day or while reading the paper.

The stranger cups your chin in his other hand, and you try to wrench free of his grasp, but he only squeezes his thumb and fingers hard enough to hurt you. To bruise you. Desperate to get away from him, you take a step back and then your bare foot is caught up in the comforter.

The bed reeks of the sex you had with your husband, and the stranger's nostrils flare as if he smells it, too. His eyes darken, and he drops his hand from your face to rub his crotch suggestively.

This is real. Your heart is thundering in your chest now, and you whip your head around, hoping to find something you can use as a weapon. The lamps are screwed into the walls, and your curling iron, your hairspray—anything you might use to defend yourself—are in the bathroom and completely out of your reach.

The stranger steps into you, and you have nowhere to go with the bed at the back of your legs. With a hard push —his hand between your breasts now, his fingers brush the diamond pendant your husband and your boys gave you for Christmas seven years ago—you fall to the bed, and he is on top of you before you can move. His erection presses hard into you as he leans up a bit to reach for something, and then his lips tip up in a cold smile as he shows you his find. Your thong hangs from his fingers. When he lifts it to his face and buries his nose in it, your body clenches with the need to scream and voice your rage and your sudden panic.

Don't give him the satisfaction, you tell yourself. But the flames of terror rage inside you, and your chest is tight, and he scoots up over you now and straddles you—his thighs pressing into your breasts—and you can't help the little sob as you gasp to breathe, and you want to scream, but he clamps his hand down over your mouth. When you try to bite him, he presses harder, so hard it hurts your neck.

"I'm not gonna hurt you," he says, and his voice is pleasant. Like you could almost imagine bumping into him in the hotel bar the night before. With his immaculately pressed shirt and his casual loafers and his warmish voice, you could almost think his name might be Ed, and he might have kids of his own, and he might like the Jason Bourne movies. Because he seems so normal.

Except that he's going to rape you.

"Just keep your mouth shut, and I won't hurt you." He presses again on your face, and he arches his eyebrows as if you're a five-year-old, and he's making a deal with you that if you behave, he'll buy you candy. Or if you don't—if you make a scene—he'll punish you.

Does he think forcing himself on you like this isn't hurting you?

"Do you hear me?" He sort of shakes and twists your chin for emphasis, and it hurts, so you nod. You wonder where your thong is now. You don't want it. You'll never touch it again, but the thought of this stranger walking out of your hotel room with something so personally yours makes you throw up in your mouth. His hand is still clamped over your lips, and you struggle beneath him to breathe.

How can he rape you and not hurt you? This is a violation, and even if he were to change his mind now and scramble away from you, afraid of getting caught, you are probably bruised, and you'll carry scars inside that forever mark you as his victim.

How can he let you look at his face, look into his eyes, if he's going to assault you and then walk away? You could identify him. You could call the police and give them his description, and he could be arrested for rape.

What if he's going to kill you?

He scoots back down enough to press himself into the v of your thighs again. Slowly, he lifts his hand from your face, but the warning in his eyes is lethal, and you press your lips together to hold in the screams and the cries and the whimpers.

When his big hand covers your breast, you swallow

another mouthful of vomit and squeeze your eyes closed. He gropes you hard, and then he pinches your nipple so hard it brings tears to your eyes. You hear the rasp of his zipper, and you chant inside your head that he can't get to you. He can't hurt you.

He's rough, and it hurts, but it's fast, thank God, and when he finishes—inside your body—he climbs off you and pulls his pants back up over his hips. Silent tears streak your face as he zips the jeans. His eyes still watch you like you are prey, even though you are dead inside.

When he backs away from you, he picks up his coat and puts it on. Your thong is stuffed in his hip pocket. His semen is cold and sticky between your legs. Your heart does not thunder anymore. In fact, you barely feel it beating.

He turns away as if to leave, and you roll to your side and curl into a tight, little ball. The thermostat is set at 70, but the sheets are cold, and your skin is cold and clammy. You hear his footsteps, but instead of leaving, he's come back to stand by the bed. He smacks your ass cheek, and the sting lingers when he pulls his hand away.

You refuse to react. Maybe you are playing dead. Maybe you wish you were dead. You wonder what Matthew and Jordan are doing right at this moment. They should be at school. Matthew would be in first hour at the high school, senior English. Jordan would be in PE. As an athlete, it's his favorite class, but he hates that it's first. You agree; stupid scheduling on the teacher's part. Who wants a room full of sweaty eighth graders for an entire school day?

You aren't dead after all, because when you hear the click back of the lock, your heart whooshes to life again. You lie still, marveling at the crazy galloping in your chest. The door opens, and you hear voices out in the hallway.

Someone asks for the USA Today because it wasn't delivered this morning, and you think that now *you* are news. You are a statistic. You hear that voice that said he wouldn't hurt you wish a good morning to someone as the heavy door finally closes. Your heart is straining now inside you, and you wonder if you are having a heart attack.

Your husband is probably in the Ironhorse Ball Room right now, schmoozing with his colleagues. One hand is tucked in the hip pocket of his charcoal gray suit pants and the other holds either his phone or a cardboard coffee cup with expensive coffee that probably tastes like tree bark.

Paralyzed, cheek pressed to the cool white sheet, your mind whirs through the things you had planned to do today. After a shower, you were going to pack up your laptop and walk two blocks to the coffee shop on the corner. You'd gone there yesterday, and it had been cozy and inviting, and you had worked there for hours—

Is that where he saw you first? Did he notice you there at the two-top table by the window? You were so involved in your files on your laptop and then on the phone call with Anna back at the office. People had come and gone all morning, but you barely looked up, and he could have been watching you. He could have followed you back to the hotel.

Your fingers hurt, and the stale air in the room blows over your nearly nude body. When you move, your back hurts, and your thighs hurt, and you think it's a little like when you were in a wreck just out of college. You were driving five miles per hour over the speed limit, Boston blaring on the radio, and wham! out of the blue, an older model station wagon T-boned you, and at first the shock blanketed you from the pain. Your hands were icy cold, and you were pinned in the car, your leg jammed under the steering wheel. You watched dry-eyed as rescue workers cut the door of your car open to get you out.

When you were safely inside the ambulance, when there were people around you to care for you, your body started to shake, and your skin was cold, and a paramedic covered you with a blanket. Tremors still racked your body; even your chin quivered with the fear, the knowledge of how lucky you were to be alive. When the ambulance stopped in the bay at the hospital, the pain roared to life.

Now, alone in your hotel room, your body tells you it hurts. Your body—every inch of your body—hurts, and suddenly, you shake so violently, the sheets rustle as they had last night with your husband, and you need to vomit.

Moving is a struggle, because your muscles have tightened up in the few minutes since the stranger left you alone. You're stiff, and each time you shift on the bed, something else screams with pain. But you can't scream. If you scream, someone might hear you. Someone might come to help you now, and it's too late. You're not afraid that the stranger will come back. He is probably already heading out the main doors of the hotel, maybe speaking pleasantly with the valet who stands at the podium, the one who greeted you and your husband three nights ago when you drove in.

If you scream, someone might hear you. And they might come to help, and they can't. There's no helping you now. You scoot another inch toward the edge of the bed, and the sheets scratch your sensitive skin, like when you have the flu. The desperate yelp that escapes your lips startles you, because the silence in the room is now oppressive and overbearing. If you don't close your mouth now, you will cry. That big, ugly gut-wrenching cry that will come from deep and low in your belly, maybe deeper even than that. From the spot the stranger violated. If those sobs start now, they will never stop.

So as you slide off the edge of the bed, and the sheet and comforter fall completely to the floor, you press your fingers to your lips to hold it all in. Ashamed of your body now in the skimpy nightie, wishing you had a book of matches because you would burn it and maybe the bed, too, you hunch your shoulders and shuffle to the bathroom.

The gray floor tiles are cold on your feet, and the light you had turned on before the stranger burst into the room is garish and bright. You look up with a squint, but you are careful not to look at yourself in the mirror. The frosted glass door to the alcove for the toilet is heavy, and your arm quivers as you yank it open.

The tip of your index fingernail is ripped off and bloodied, and you wonder if you fought him. Did you scratch and claw at him when he pressed his hand over your mouth? Or was it when he shoved his penis inside you and squeezed his hands around your neck and you panicked because you were suffocating?

You can't remember, and trying to remember is like your drunk brain is flying down the highway one hundred miles an hour, windows down, and sirens blaring some-where behind you. You tell yourself to stop trying to remember. It's best to just forget it. Blood still oozes from the nail tip, and your hand is curled around the lid of the toilet.

His semen is still sticky and wet on your inner thighs. Standing still in front of the toilet, you imagine you feel it again, his body moving inside yours. A violent wave of nausea rips up from your belly, and you duck over the bowl to get it out. To get him out.

But you can't. You haven't eaten. You haven't even had

coffee, though someone on this floor has. Your body heaves, but you're dry, and you sink to your knees at the toilet. Your hand is pressed against the toilet lid, and with the other, you tuck your sweaty tangled hair behind your ear. The light catches on your wedding ring, and you don't know how you can keep this from your husband.

But you know you can't possibly ever tell him.

He can't possibly know that you've been violated like this.

CHAPTER 2

*T*he flight attendant is too friendly, and she lingers in the aisle close to where you and your husband sit. Distracted as usual, Ben glances at her now and then with his trademark smile and says something to her. You want to hit her. You flex your fingers into a tight fist and imagine what it would feel like to ram it—knuckles first—into her face. You imagine the pop, maybe you would connect with her nose or her mouth. Her flashy pink lipstick would cake your knuckles, and her lip might bleed. The thought horrifies you. Violence is something other people resort to when they are angry or impatient. Then again, rape is something that happens to other women.

The woman hedges down the aisle away from you, away from Ben, but now and then she looks back at you. You grind your teeth together and wonder if she's seriously flirting with Ben when you are sitting right beside him, or if she's just doing her job, and you've become ridiculously oversensitive.

Ben lifts his gaze from his laptop when you shiver. He

watches you tug your sleeves down over your hands; when you meet his eyes, he quirks his eyebrows in question.

"Are you cold?"

You aren't. But you don't know what you are, and you can't discuss it with him. You nod and flash him a quick, insincere smile. When it placates him, and he's concentrating on his laptop again, you wonder if you should be annoyed that it's so easy to fool him. Shouldn't the man you've lived with for years just know something is wrong?

You look away and turn your head to the window. It's not fair to blame Ben. Intellectually, you know that, but your heart doesn't want to listen. He loves you. Life has become so fast-paced that now and then it makes your head spin. But you have never doubted that he loves you.

The windows on planes are small, and you feel squished into your seat. Your carry-on bag is stowed under the seat in front of you. Normally, you would have your laptop out, too, or you would turn your iPad on and read something. On the flight to Colorado, you were reading a Kate Carley romance novel. The thought of reading a sensual scene now makes you gag. To cover it up, you cough a bit.

You keep your eyes on the clouds just outside the window. Your forty-four-year-old knees ache with the need to stretch, but you have nowhere to put your feet. Earlier, after you soaked in the tub and then scrubbed your skin—head to toe—raw, you stood in front of the mirror and forced yourself to see your reflection.

Too late to call the police, because you bathed. Any evidence the stranger had left inside you was now gone. As you looked yourself in the eye, you told yourself it was okay. It was better this way, because reporting it makes it important. You don't want to give the son-of-a-bitch the satisfaction of making him important. You survived the contact. You survived a stranger forcing you down and putting his body inside yours.

As you backed away from the mirror, eyes downcast because you didn't want to see the lies and the fear looking back at you, you admitted to yourself it wasn't bravery or determination that made you forego reporting the assault. It was terror. How could you possibly sit in your hotel room, in that skimpy piece of silk you'd worn for Ben, and tell a police officer that a stranger waltzed in and raped you?

What if the police didn't believe you? What if they said it was your fault?

You'd dressed slowly, careful with the bruises and the sensitive skin. Thankfully, you'd packed all long sleeves— even turtlenecks—so you could hide it all from Ben. You'd plastered on cover-up makeup over the marks on your neck. With your hair down and the cover-up and turtle- neck you chose to wear, you feel confident that Ben hasn't noticed anything different. With your suit of armor— camouflage, because you've chosen to hide, not strike back —you packed and ignored the bed, because you refused to remember what just happened there.

Ben found you posed demurely on the small leather sofa by the window. Legs crossed, you held the USA Today paper—how many times had you relived that moment when the stranger left your room and you overheard someone in the hall complaining that his had not been delivered—though you hadn't read a word.

Between the rape and the lengths you went to to hide it, you perched on the edge of the tub, careful not to sit in any splashes of water left behind. You debated the phone call you knew was necessary, and each second that passed by made it bigger and scarier in your head and your belly.

When the receptionist at your ob-gyn's office answered,

you asked to make an appointment, and you used the word *emergency*. But when she transferred you to the nurse, you chickened out and said it was *important*. What was the emergency now, anyway? The worst had been done. And you had compounded that by washing away the evidence.

Laurie—Dr. Ambern's nurse—asked you twice what sort of problem you were having, why it was important to get in so quickly. You know Laurie well; you've been a patient with Dr. Ambern since just after Matthew was born. Still, sitting alone in the hotel bathroom, with the toxic memories playing in your head, you couldn't bring yourself to say it. You couldn't force the word out. Instead, you had said again that you needed to see Dr. Ambern, and the third time you said you had something *urgent* to discuss with her.

Maybe Laurie had another call holding. Maybe she heard the desperation in your thin voice. Maybe a cancellation happened on the computer screen right in front of her eyes. Whatever the case, she put you down for ten o'clock tomorrow morning.

Now, you wonder how you will be able to sit in Dr. Ambern's office and tell her what happened. The woman is probably just on the far side of sixty. She's very mild-mannered and pleasant, and you've become friendly with her as much as a woman can be friendly with her ob-gyn. She delivered Jordan. She asks after both of your sons at every visit. She remembers the time Matthew had strep when he was seven. She gave Jordan a soccer jersey from Spain.

She is kind and understanding, but you would bet money that she's never been raped. And you worry that she will wonder how you were so stupid, so weak.

The stiffness in your knees makes you wiggle again in your seat. You glance at Ben again. His hair is still thick and black, and you often tease him that he must have it colored somewhere secretly, because there's not a thread of silver in it. He always laughs and promises you it's because he's young at heart. The thought brings a cringe, because usually when he says that, he chases you around the house and when he catches you, he throws you over the bed to *tumble* you. When you laugh at his intentions, he flashes you that delicious, ornery grin, and he's got you. That grin—and the sparkle in his midnight eyes—has always been your poison.

At the airport earlier, you had nibbled on a toasted bagel and fresh fruit. Ben had marveled at the fact that you weren't hungry as he crushed a bacon cheeseburger and a plate of fries. Now your bagel and fruit and your poison—and the fact that you think you don't want it ever again—make your stomach twist uncomfortably. You swallow hard and hold yourself still for a moment and take that time to study the slate-gray rims of Ben's reading glasses. Perhaps the glasses are the only sign of his aging.

That's not true, but you do admit that at first glance, he appears much younger than forty-six. Because you know him, because you've loved him through years of marriage —ups and downs and plain old days—and his years on his job and the responsibilities of aging and sick parents, you can look at his face and remember the way life had settled into his skin and marked him as mature and maybe wise.

He doesn't look at you, but he knows you're watching him. When he takes his hand from the laptop and reaches for yours, you brush his fingers with yours and then pull your hand away again. Turn back to the window and wonder why the oxygen masks don't drop down from above you, because there's something wrong with the air pressure in the cabin, and you can't breathe.

Dr. Ambern's gaze is both patient and expectant as she watches you from across her desk, and your chair squeaks when you squirm uncomfortably. Her silver hair is cut in a bob; the last time you saw her it was longer and a bit unruly. Your eyes slide now to her hands, folded on her desk, and you study the simple gold band on her ring finger. She knows so much about your life, and all that you know about her is that she and her husband went to Spain once a few years ago.

"Delilah." Her voice is soothing, and she tips her head just so, and like she's flipped a switch, your eyes glaze with tears.

You're wasting her time. She would never prod you along with those words, and yet, it's true. There are other patients in her waiting room, eyes on the talk show or game show on the TV as they wait impatiently for their name to be called so they can get this uncomfortable business out of the way for the year—or month, for those who are pregnant—and go on about their days.

You nod, because you have to speak, and the longer you take to spit it out, the bigger the words become and the harder they are to speak, to shove out of your mouth.

"Ben and I were just out of town," you start, and you hate the way your voice falters just with those words.

"Where did you go?" Her face lights with interest, and you wish this was a friendly visit over a cup of coffee and you could tell her about the wonderful views and the mountains and the streams.

"We were in Colorado." Your whisper is hoarse, and you clear your throat as you meet her eyes. She nods and waits silently for you to continue. You don't want to go through the whole story, the whole ugly story about a man knocking on your door and you assuming it was Ben and not paying attention as you opened the door.

"What happened?" Her voice is still gentle, but she looks grim now, as if she knows you are here to tell her something bad.

You close your eyes, because you think it might be easier to say it if you aren't looking at her.

"I was raped."

You deliver the words in a steady, quiet tone, and you are parts relieved and parts horrified that you spoke them so easily. You hear Dr. Ambern take a sharp breath, so you blink your eyes open and watch her as she regards you with concern.

"Okay." She finally nods. "You did the right thing to call me."

You nod, but you sit silently and wait for her to take charge.

"Did you call the police? Did the emergency room do a rape kit?"

Tears slide over your face, and you shake your head. "I didn't..." When it is impossible to speak, you clear your throat and start again. "I didn't report it."

Dr. Ambern winces, but her face remains calm and impassive. With a slow nod, she pushes her chair back and climbs to her feet.

"You've showered."

Feeling cowed, like a kindergartner in trouble for talking in class, you duck your chin to your chest and nod.

"It's okay, Delilah," she promises you. "It's okay."

When you look up, she is standing on this side of the desk, leaning her hips against it, and watching you

"I just..." You squint against the onslaught of emotion and shake your head. "Ben was gone. And it happened...in our room. I didn't think anyone would believe me."

"Okay."

"And it wasn't like…" You shrug and draw a deep breath. "It wasn't…violent. He didn't…"

"Was it Ben?"

"No." Stricken with horror and disgust, you stare at Dr. Ambern, shocked that she would ask.

"Delilah, it happens. Did he—"

"It wasn't Ben."

"Was it someone you *invited* to your room?"

"No."

"Then it was rape." Her voice is firm, and though the confirmation validates you, it is confirmation that you were raped, and the thought is unsettling. You swallow hard and strain your head to the right, trying to avoid her gaze. "Have you told Ben?"

"No." You sneak a peek at Dr. Ambern, worried that she is judging you, but you see only compassion on her face.

"Delilah, have you talked to anyone?"

You only shake your head.

"Okay." Dr. Ambern nods. "Here's what we're going to do."

Relief washes over you. You've handed the problem off to someone else, an adult, someone in charge who knows what to do.

"We're going to do an exam."

Dread settles—hard and heavy—like an anvil in your belly. Of course, she needs to do an exam, but the idea of lying back on the table and putting your feet in stirrups and opening your legs to someone's touch makes your heart hammer in your ears.

"And then we'll do a blood test. Okay?" Dr. Ambern's arms are folded over her chest, but you imagine that in just minutes, she will have her fingers inside your body, and you shiver with revulsion. "We're going to do a pregnancy test. And we're going to test for HIV. Okay?"

Of course, this is protocol. Even without a medical degree, you knew Dr. Ambern would order blood work for those very reasons. But it is so much harder to hear a voice of authority say it.

"Okay."

"We'll do the pelvic exam today." Dr. Ambern lowers her arms and rests her hands on the desk at her sides. "And we'll draw blood for the HIV test today, but we'll need to repeat the test at six weeks, three months, and again at six months."

The testing and waiting period sounds like an eternity, but on the other hand, if you're already dead inside, how can it matter?

"Are you still taking the pill?"

Because it feels too intimate to discuss birth control for recreational sex with your husband—especially after the wanton activities you engaged in the night before you were raped—you avoid her eyes and answer with a curt nod.

"Okay." She nods. "We're going to draw blood today to do a pregnancy test. That will eliminate any possibility that you were pregnant before the rape."

Perhaps at some point, you will appreciate that Dr. Ambern believes you without question, but your skin crawls each time she says the word *rape*.

"Do know the date of your last period?"

"Um." You sigh and purse your lips in thought and remember you'd had a period about three weeks ago. Jordan had a soccer game the night you started, and you had to psyche yourself up to go because you didn't feel well. "I think it was about three weeks ago."

Dr. Ambern nods.

"Okay." She takes a step forward and squats at your

side. "We'll work through this together, but you need to talk to someone."

Up close, you see the flecks of gold in her brown eyes. You notice a small scar just above her eyebrow. The feathery lines of her lipstick where she needs to repair her lip pencil and then reapply the color. The color, you guess, might be called praline.

"In this situation, Delilah, it's best to start prophylactic therapy—"

"What does that mean?"

"I'm going to put you on an antibiotic to treat all STDs. Chlamydia—"

You cut her off with a sharp nod as another wave of terror bowls you over. You haven't even considered other sexually transmitted diseases; your concern has been HIV.

"We can also consider prophylactic—"

You cringe again at the word *prophylactic*, and Dr. Ambern stops talking.

"What? Consider what?" you ask, eyes closed to ward off the verbal blows, spoken in her soothing voice.

"Post-exposure prophylaxis. It means taking antiretroviral medicines to prevent becoming infected. And I think you should consider a vaccine for hepatitis B."

Your eyelids are heavy when you lift them, and tears streak your face.

"Okay." You swallow hard and then struggle to take a deep breath. You had thought the terror of the moment was over when the stranger left you alone in the room and greeted someone just outside your closed door. You were wrong, and you wonder if maybe it was a mistake to come here without Ben.

"I'm going to give you some literature when you leave.

Okay? And you need to take the time to read through it. You need to see a therapist, or you should consider a support group."

The thought of slicing yourself open to bleed the details of your assault makes the hairs on the back of your neck stand on end. You shiver and shake your head violently, but when Dr. Ambern touches you—you stare, speechless at her plain, unadorned fingertips on the back of your hand—and murmurs your name again, you mumble yes.

Not because you will do it.

But because you won't. And you don't want to take up more of her time today.

"Okay. I'll step out for a few minutes. You know the drill."

"Do I need to take everything off, since—?" You shrug when she looks back at you from her place at the door.

"Did he touch you anywhere else?"

Cheeks burning with shame, you nod silently.

"Bruising?"

Because your chest is wound too tight to breathe again, you tug your turtleneck—this one is black—down for her to see your bruises.

"Did he touch your breasts?"

Eyes on the floor, you nod.

"Did he break your skin?"

"No."

"Okay. From the waist down." She nods. "Go on in when you're ready. I'll give you a few minutes."

You won't be ready. Who would ever be ready for this kind of exam? Yearly appointments are uncomfortable, and even when you were pregnant and coming monthly with the reward of a baby at the end of the nine months you weren't thrilled to be here. You never dreamed you would see a doctor for this.

Your legs feel weak as you make your way over into the exam room Dr. Ambern uses most often. There is a folded paper sheet on the end of the table. With extreme care—because you want to be in total control of something or maybe because you need this to be as silent and secretive as possible—you set your purse on the padded seat under the window. Sick inside at what is to come, you unbutton and unzip your jeans. The sound is ridiculously loud in the small room, but you know it's all in your head.

With your eyes on the floor as you push your jeans down over your hips, you see the stranger shrug out of his coat. Not wanting the replay, you lift your head and study the various posters of the female reproductive system on the walls. You step out of your favorite, well-worn loafers, lean to tug your jeans off one leg at a time, and fold them neatly to put next to your purse.

It's harder to take your underwear off. On the other hand, the thought of Dr. Ambern tapping on the door and coming inside while you are in the midst of undressing urges you into action. Thumbs under the elastic waistband, you throw up a little bit in your mouth as you ease them down and then tuck them under your jeans. Dr. Ambern won't look at your clothing, but you are remembering how the man found your thong—the one you'd worn just for Ben—in the bed and taken it with him.

You sit on the end of the table with the paper sheet over your lap, the sides tucked in around you. She'll move them when she comes in, but for now, this feels better. While you wait, you study the posters again. For a moment, you let yourself pretend you are here because you suspect you're pregnant. With Ben's child. Maybe a girl this time. Neither of you had ever drawn the line at two children; but you were blessed with two healthy, easy pregnancies; and now, though you would have welcomed another baby, you both believe you're too old for it.

The fantasy doesn't last, though, because your eye catches the collection of literature Dr. Ambern mentioned. Sure, there are pamphlets about birth control and teen sex and STDs, but there are also several right in front of the plastic shelf about domestic violence and sexual assault.

You jump when Dr. Ambern taps on the door. She steps into the room and closes the door. You swallow hard, worried that you might get sick.

"Do you do this a lot?" The words come out, even though you know she can't answer you. She can't tell you how many assault patients she's treated. It's confidential. Even if she isn't sharing names, as a doctor, it would be wrong for her to share anything of the sort.

What you really want to know is that she gets what you're feeling right now. That you're scared to lie back and let her look at you. You're exhausted from not sleeping last night, but you're wired, too, and you probably won't sleep tonight. You need to see this part through—the exam and the blood tests—so you can put it all behind you and move on.

You might be sick.

"Delilah, are you sure you don't want Ben here with you?"

"No. I don't want Ben to know."

"Do you really think you can keep it from him? That he's not going to notice something's wrong?"

You shrug, but you refuse to engage in the conversation, mostly because you know she's right.

"He should notice. And you need to tell him." Dr. Ambern pulls the stirrups from the end of the table. "Your husband is your number one support, Delilah. And if you don't tell him, this could affect your relationship."

"I know."

Dr. Ambern offers you her hand and tells you to lie back. The tears finally streak your face as you lie back and she guides your feet into the stirrups. She turns on the exam light, but you squeeze your eyes closed rather than look at it. You hear the snap of latex gloves and reach to cover your eyes with your hands.

"Okay, Dee. You're going to feel my hands. I'm looking at your inner thighs now, okay?" Her voice is warm and quiet, soothing, except for what she's saying and what she's doing as she talks.

You were wrong.

You want Ben here with you.

CHAPTER 3

"I wanna see your pictures," Khloe St. John says to you, but you avoid her eyes. Jordan just carried four-year-old Naya through the kitchen on his back, and Khloe and Genevieve are still smiling after them, but you can't. You haven't looked either of your sons in the eye since you got home the day before yesterday. Naya's shrill giggles used to make you deliriously happy, but tonight, they shoot through your body like a million little knives, and you sit completely still—body pulled in as small as it can be to avoid rubbing up against anyone else's happiness—and wish you were invisible.

"I didn't take many." Your throat and your voice are a little scratchy, and you wonder if you did scream, though you don't remember that. Is your throat scratchy and achy because he curled his fingers around your neck and applied pressure as he drove inside you hard enough that today you still feel bruised? Or is it because you haven't spoken much since it happened, as if when he left he stole both your dignity and your voice?

Or maybe it's just that your throat is jammed with all

of the emotion you are afraid to let loose? The woman who cleans your house was just here yesterday, and so she won't be back for two weeks, and besides, you doubt she could get an entire body's worth of shame and pain and fear out of the white and silver granite countertop.

"Dee." Khloe rolls her eyes at you, because you always take hundreds of pictures when you travel with Ben. "Where's your phone?"

"I didn't," you argue half-heartedly. Your phone is buried in your top dresser drawer, turned off, and tucked away in your silks and lace.

"You okay?" Genevieve tilts her head now and narrows her eyes as she stares at you. Panic surges through your body, all the way to your toes, and you stir to life and offer them a bright, Delilah Nicholson smile. Khloe buys it first. The look of concern on her face is there and gone so fast, you decide you imagined it. Younger than you and Genevieve by more than ten years, Khloe is either terribly naïve or a die-hard optimist. At different times in your friendship, you have believed both things. Tonight, you believe she is terribly naïve, and you wonder what she would say if you confessed to what had happened.

Why is it a confession? You did nothing wrong. You opened the door, because you thought Ben was—

"Dee?"

You stir again and reach for your wineglass. Sip the expensive, dry red wine and arch your eyebrows expectantly at Genevieve.

"I'm fine." You nod, and thank God, your voice sounds normal. Gen's concerned stare lingers for another moment, but then she looks away. Inside, you slump in relief, but not on the outside. You don't dare let your guard down again, lest they decide you truly are hiding something from them.

"Mom?"

You know you shouldn't hide this. Genevieve and Khloe are your closest friends, and you should lean. You've trusted them both—still do—but this is different, and if you don't tell anyone, it will go away faster.

"Mom?"

You jump when Matthew nudges your shoulder. The glass is still in your left hand, the one with the luxurious diamond ring Ben put there years and years ago, and you jump so hard, wine spills over the top. Horrified, you stare at the red liquid on your fingers, the red spots on the counter.

"Dee." This time, Gen rests her hand on your upper arm, and you lift your gaze from the spilled wine to Gen's intense gray eyes.

"Hmm?"

"Mom, can I go? Do you care?"

A shiver creeps up your spine when you hear Matthew's voice so close.

"Where?" you ask, but the word sticks, and it sounds small when you speak. You turn away from Genevieve, but you still can't meet your son's eyes.

"To Alli's party."

You want to say no. No parties. Because even though you and Ben have taught your boys right from wrong, bad things can happen at parties. Bad things could happen to Matthew. Or Matthew could do bad things—

"Dad said to ask you. He said he doesn't care."

Pain stabs you right between your eyes, and you lower your head. Flashes of the stranger bursting into your room are so real in your mind that you forget you are safe, in your house, with your friends, hundreds of miles away from where it happened.

You press the fingertips of your right hand to your forehead and then slide them down the bridge of your nose. Tears that you cannot cry burn in your eyes.

Have you taught Matthew that no means no? Of course you have. You and Ben are good parents; you're civilized, polite people. You—

"Mom."

"Yeah." You nod and finally look at Matthew. You let your gaze skate over him quickly, because you can't stand that he might see it when he looks at you. The fear. The shame. "You can go."

His grin throws you back sixteen years to an ornery two-year-old, and a noise breaks free from your lips. It's half laugh and half cry, and you know Gen and Khloe are watching you, and Matthew leans in to kiss your cheek. You bristle, but you force yourself to brush your lips over his cheek and offer him a smile.

When he's gone—the keys to his F150 jiggling in his hand—you draw in a deep breath and swallow violently hard. Everything you wanted to throw up when the stranger left you—everything you wanted to vomit and couldn't—is in your throat right now. Because your friends watch you closely, you slide off the stone-colored leather stool and make a show of wiping up the spilled wine.

You imagine the spots of blood you saw on the bathroom floor in the hotel room. From your torn fingernail. The one that you have since trimmed down, but still looks ugly. When the counter is clean, you turn away from your friends to toss the dishrag to the sink. Your fingers are sticky with wine, and you remember the stickiness between your thighs.

"Naya has a boyfriend," Khloe says, and you feel a wave of disgust. Why must parents tease their preschool children about boyfriends and girlfriends? Why is everyone in such a hurry with life? Even with their children's lives?

Not thinking, you shift the glass to your right hand and lift your other to your lips to lick the wine away. And then you remember the stranger again. The way he had pressed his open mouth to your neck. He had done that, hadn't he? Sucked on your skin? Nipped at the tops of your breasts?

At the very least, you fought him with your hands. You broke a nail off your right hand; there are marks on your left hand, as if you fought and scratched at him. The fact that you touched him with the hand you nearly licked just now makes you feel violently sick.

You rest your hands on the counter and lean. Duck your head and breathe. You have to breathe. Death, at this point, might be welcome, but not this way. You have to breathe, because you don't want to suffocate with the memory of his hand over your mouth, his fingers gripping your neck.

"Delilah?"

The harsh sound of a barstool scooting back over the dove gray tiled floor is jarring and unwelcome, but you can't move. You are barely breathing, and when Gen steps so close to you that her thigh and her hip brush against you, a soft moan of protest slips out. You shuffle half a step away.

"What's wrong?" She whispers this, and she rests her hand on your shoulder gingerly, as if somehow she knows how much touch hurts you.

"I...um..." You clear your throat and shake your head and inhale courage enough to stand and look at Gen. Khloe still sits at the kitchen bar, but she looks concerned, and you might smother.

Interesting that they have seen that something is wrong when Ben has not. Ben, who lives with you and sleeps with you. Then again, it's rare for life to slow down enough for you to really look at Ben, and you wonder for a moment if you would notice if something was wrong with him. If your husband was acting funny, acting guilty or sick or afraid, would you notice?

"I'm not feeling well." You shake your head again and lick your lips, and you remember that the stranger's hand was on your mouth, and your shoulders heave with the nausea that hits you in the belly like a vicious front kick.

"Okay." Gen nods, and she's so sincere and so selfless —always has been—that you feel guilty for lying to her, and you wonder if she would be so gentle, so giving if she knew the truth. "Sweetie, why didn't you just tell us? Why didn't you and Ben cancel?"

Ben is the most social person you know. Yes, he's busy with work, and it seems like he's a million miles away most of the time, and you have to repeat what you say to him twice, sometimes three times, and at times, it makes you ridiculously angry. But he's a good man, and he's fun, and he loves to entertain friends and to spend time with friends, and so, of course, you couldn't cancel the dinner party that had been planned for two weeks before you were raped.

You can't just cancel life because you were raped.

"It's okay," you mumble, because you can't go into why you are sick and what feels bad or why you haven't told Ben that you aren't feeling well. You turn back to the sink and dump your wine, because you can't possibly drink it. Your hands tremble when you rinse the glass out, and you pray that Gen and Khloe don't notice.

"Were you sick? In Colorado?" Khloe asks as you shuffle back to the bar and slide onto a stool. You stare at her blankly, because of course you weren't sick in Colorado. You were there three days, and you felt fine when you arrived there. It wasn't until—

"I think it started there," you answer quietly, and both

of them are still watching you so intensely that your palms are starting to sweat.

"Maybe you should go to the—"

Before Gen can say doctor, you cut her off with a sharp shake of your head. Dr. Ambern had been so tender and gentle, and it has crossed your mind a hundred times since you walked out of her office that you're thankful that your first ob-gyn—Dr. Roushe—retired not long after Matthew was born. He was all sharp edges and gruff and arrogant. You hated seeing him, but you were young when you started seeing an ob-gyn, and you didn't stop to think that you had a choice in your physician. It never occurred to you that you had the right to feel comfortable or *comfortable enough* during a physical exam. Thankfully, Dr. Ambern replaced him, because you wonder now how you would have survived that appointment with Dr. Roushe.

But you don't want to talk about it. About not feeling well or seeing your doctor or the fact that after the exam, you dressed in solemn silence and slipped out of the huge medical building all in one piece. That once safely inside your Highlander, you'd locked the doors, rested your forehead on the steering wheel, and let the tears fall. Your body shook as you cried it out, and when you got home finally—two hours after you'd left your house—you stood under a blistering hot shower to scrub the memories—all of them—away.

What if Ben walks in and overhears the conversation? If Ben asks you what's wrong, and he really listens to you try and deny that something is wrong, that you must have just picked up a bug, you won't be able to lie to him.

"I'll be fine," you assure Gen and Khloe, and you wish that Khloe would continue her ridiculous story about Naya having a boyfriend. Anything at all to take the spotlight off you.

"Were you able to get out at all?" Khloe seems to take your word for it that you'll be fine. "Where were you guys? Denver?"

Whenever you go to Colorado, everyone assumes you're going to Denver. When you say you live in Illinois, everyone assumes you live in Chicago. When you say no, it's supposed to mean no.

He said he wouldn't hurt you.

He killed your soul.

Genevieve is sitting at your side again, only she's closer now. Still not touching you, though. Her hands rest on the counter, and you see her right hand twitch like she wants to nudge you. When she clears her throat, you look back at Khloe and remember she asked where you and Ben were this week.

"Aspen," you answer in a hoarse whisper.

"Was it pretty?" Genevieve asks you, and you nod, because Colorado is a beautiful state, and the views are breathtaking, no matter where you are and which way you look.

"You should have stayed at the Stanley Hotel," Khloe says with the laugh that you used to think was cute, but at the moment only infuriates you. Perhaps the Stanley Hotel would have been preferable, but again, you can't say that, so you bite your lip and keep your mouth shut. "Do you think it's really haunted?"

"From what I've read, yes," Genevieve answers. Khloe loves ghost stories and gory movies, and Genevieve loves to read nonfiction stuff, which includes a lot of historical information, so she probably knows everything there is to know about the Stanley Hotel.

What she doesn't know is that you don't have to be dead to leave your soul behind. Is Room 741 haunted now with *your* soul? You hope Khloe never learns that some things haunt you more than paranormal activity. Like normal people. Doing a normal activity. With the wrong person. For the wrong reasons. Without consent.

"That would so cool to see." Khloe gulps her wine, and you want to remind her that it's expensive, and she should sip it, and does she want to end up drunk before she goes home? But then you remember, she'll say it doesn't matter because Oliver Haywood—her new boyfriend—is driving tonight.

You wonder if she feels safe with Oliver. They've been seeing each other for a few months. Khloe is generally careful about who she allows to be around Naya, so you assume she does trust Oliver. Still. What if Khloe drinks too much, and Oliver takes her home later? What if he wants sex, and Khloe says no? Will he respect her? Will he say goodnight and call her in the morning?

You realize your eyes are glued to Khloe's hands now, wrapped around the stem of her glass. You are imagining her hands on Oliver's body, although the face you see in your mind belongs to a stranger.

"The Stanley's in Estes Park," you tell them, and maybe Khloe knows that and was just suggesting that while in Colorado, you and Ben should have gone to Estes Park to spend a night in a haunted hotel.

"You really didn't take any pictures?" Khloe's disappointment is a knife in your heart, and in your head, you see your phone tucked away in silk and lace. It crosses your mind to throw all of it away, the silk and lace—black, red, white—all of it, because you don't feel sexy, and what if you never do again?

You shouldn't.

Feel sexy.

Ever again.

After the dry heaves, after curling up on the cold, tile

floor in the bathroom the morning it happened, you climbed to your feet. Seems like you smeared blood on the wall in the alcove with the toilet—when you pressed your hands on it for traction to stand—but Ben didn't notice it. You were torn about what to do. For long, long moments that felt like days and weeks, even, you had stood helpless, cold, and small in the bathroom, with the ridiculous lights glaring down on you. Intellectually, you knew that you should call someone.

The police. You knew you should report the incident. The assault. And yet, you couldn't make yourself do it. You couldn't lift a foot to go back to the bedroom, back around the foot of the bed where the stranger raped you, to get your phone. You couldn't breathe, let alone talk, and you had no proof.

No signs of forced entry, because you were in a hotel room. You opened the door of your room and let him in. You were careless and stupid. *Your mistake.*

Skin clammy and sticky from tears and snot and sweat and his semen, you poured yourself a hot bath, something you have never done in all the years you and Ben have traveled. You have never been comfortable with the idea of sitting and bathing in a tub where strangers may have done the same.

When you peeled the nightie off, your nude body in the mirror caught your attention. Ben believes you are sexy. Before, you may have agreed now and then, on a good day. Since the morning you were raped, you've felt ugly and disgusting. You stepped closer to the mirror and stared disbelievingly at the bruises the stranger left on your body. For not hurting you, he certainly mottled your skin and your head and your heart.

You placed your hand with the bloodied fingertip on your chest, on the bruise the size of a man's finger between your breasts. Faint markings ringed your neck already, though you knew then they could have been much worse. Bruises circled your wrist where he initially grabbed you, and maybe your thighs were scraped and bruised. You could not bring yourself to look.

In case Ben would ever see the way the stranger marked you—you wouldn't purposely show him—you did go back out to the bedroom to retrieve your phone. But you kept your eyes off the bed, and you stepped over the sheets and comforter on the floor, and you took the phone back to the bathroom.

You have never been into selfies, though when you and Gen and Khloe drink too much, you do get silly and take groupies. In fact, as you took a picture of the bruise between your breasts, you remembered a picture of you and Gen's husband, Christian, and Khloe. You are sitting in Christian's lap, and Khloe is draped over his shoulders.

As you parted your legs and took a picture of your inner thighs—all without looking—you wondered if that picture with Christian and Khloe looked sexual. It was anything, but. Ben and Christian have been friends for decades, as have you and Gen, and Khloe is just flirty and fun.

You didn't take the pictures for legal documentation. You will never take this to the police. But you took them in case Ben noticed a lingering mark on your neck or arm, just so you could maybe tell him you didn't invite any strangers into your room. Maybe the garish bruises will make him believe you said no, that you fought to free yourself.

There are pictures on your phone. Pictures of the mountains and the streams and the sun in the clouds. Beautiful pictures. Pictures you know Khloe and Gen would love. It's become a thing when you and Ben come home from a trip, your friends gather with you, and Gen and Khloe, especially, gasp with awe over your scenic pictures. You're not a photographer, but Khloe sees the world through the lens of your phone.

You cannot show Gen or Khloe the pictures. Because there's no way to show them everything up until the ugly photos of that morning without them asking what you're hiding. You have never hidden anything from them, and you can't start censoring the photos now.

"I'm sorry." You swallow hard and skate your eyes over Khloe's face, and you are sorry. Sorry that you can't share the pictures with her, because you know she would love them. Sorry that she has a sweet little girl who is going to grow up in a world where men force themselves on women and girls and take what they want. You're sorry that humanity is so base and violent—

"Does Ben know?" Gen's question is like a cattle prod, and you jump again, and your friends know you well enough to know it's more than the fact that you aren't feeling well. You've never been skittish and jumpy, but tonight, you are frightened of your own shadow.

"Know what?" You shake your head, but you stare at Genevieve suspiciously, and then she does touch you. She covers your hand with hers for a moment, and you sit absolutely still when all you want to do is scream bloody murder for her to get away from you.

"That you're not feeling well?"

"No." You shrug and hope you sound nonchalant, and you peek at the microwave to see what time it is. You're exhausted from holding yourself together since the other morning and pretending that you're okay.

"I could call Beatrys," Gen suggests, "and have her bring you some cold medicine when she leaves work."

"I'm fine," you insist, because you don't need more of

an audience while your soul is dead and you're pretending that sitting with friends to catch up over wine is still important, and Beatrys is a beautiful girl who must have a hundred other things she would rather do than deliver Nyquil to her mom's friend.

You open your mouth to ask Gen if she's warned Beatrys about being out late or being out anywhere, really, alone. But it's a stupid thought, because of course Gen and Christian have taught their daughter to be alert when she's alone, just as you and Ben have taught Matthew and Jordan to respect girls.

"Is it your stomach? Do you have the flu, do you think?" Khloe asks, and you throw your head back and gasp for air, because you are drowning again, because the feelings come back to you in waves, like water, and because your friends' concern is holding you down.

"I don't have the flu," you promise and shake your head again.

"Mom!"

Jordan's shout echoes off the walls in the wide-open kitchen and living space. You wish he wasn't here, but just as quickly, you take that back, because where else would he be? You can't wish your sons away, though just now, you don't like them.

They are boys, and they will be men—

"Mom." Jordan is sprawled on the area rug on the floor in front of the TV. The rug cost you and Ben several thousand dollars, and you think the hotel where you stayed was over four hundred a night, and so you should have been safe. *Shouldn't you have been safe?* Shouldn't Ben's job, your job, your financial stability have bought your safety?

It's not like someone attacked you from behind in the parking garage when you were leaving your office. Dear God, how often do you look over your shoulder when you leave the office in the dead of winter, when it is dark by 4:30? You can't even count the number of times you have eyed people warily as you tried not to appear to run to your car in full dark.

To think the man who raped you wore nice jeans and a leather coat and smelled of expensive cologne.

"What, J?"

You took too long to answer him, and now Jordan is climbing to his feet. He's grown a foot taller since this summer, and his arms and legs are long and gangly, and his voice is changing. You wish he could stay your baby forever; in fact, you wish you could go back in time so you could love your sons.

Freely.

Without the taint of bad memories and feelings.

"Can we have popcorn? Naya wants some."

You know this is Jordan's way of asking if Naya can have popcorn, because you don't care if he eats it. Mostly, your boys fend for themselves, especially in the kitchen. You glance at Khloe as Jordan comes into the kitchen, Naya on his back again. On the big screen on the wall, Aladdin is frozen on his magic carpet. Naya wraps her arms around Jordan's neck and giggles when he swings back like he's going to drop her.

"Jordan, be careful!" You snap, though you know Jordan would never hurt her.

You want Khloe to say no, that Naya doesn't need popcorn, because they are going to leave. You want them to leave, all of them. You need to be alone; the company is an iron chain around your neck, and you need them all to go.

When Khloe doesn't say no, you glance at Jordan and quickly look away with a nod.

"Sure."

"Naya, tell Gen and Dee about your boyfriend," Khloe suggests as Jordan grabs a bag of microwave popcorn from the cabinet next to the window. You bristle as Naya's eyes light up and a toothless grin wraps around her ears.

Khloe isn't a bad mom. You've reminded yourself this ten times tonight. In fact, Khloe's good with Naya. *You* are the problem. If Khloe would have said no and announced that they were leaving, you would probably argue that popcorn wouldn't hurt her. You feel hateful and mean, and you know this is just another reason why they should go.

Jordan and Naya take lemonade and popcorn to the living room, and the lingering smell makes you sick. You remember the smell of coffee on the seventh floor of the hotel, and you press your lips together and breathe deeply through your nose.

"Are you pregnant?" Genevieve asks just as the French door opens and Ben leads Christian and Oliver inside. Stunned by what he heard Genevieve ask, Ben stares at you with wide eyes, waiting for you to answer.

"No, of course not." You frown and shake your head. "I just don't feel well."

"You're sick?" Ben asks as he moves into the kitchen proper. He hovers close to you now, and you force yourself to breathe evenly.

"I'm fine."

"But you said you don't feel well."

You squeeze your eyes closed, because now it's not just Genevieve and Khloe that are watching you. Christian and Oliver stand behind Ben, and they all watch you with concern.

"You look a bit pale," Christian decides. You don't tell him that a chiropractor can't diagnose what's wrong with you, and so he need not bother to study you so closely.

"You're not drinking your wine?" Ben glances at your

empty glass next to the sink and then looks back at you. He's a handsome man, but you can't look at him. You tug the sleeves of your turtleneck down over your hands, because on display, it seems more likely that he or the rest of them will notice your bruises.

You shake your head. Your heart is beating wildly now, thumping in your throat and your ears. The room is hot, and under the turtleneck and jeans, you're clammy.

"Dee?" Ben covers your hand with his, and you snatch yours away and scoot your stool back to stand. Your heeled boots click on the tile as you step away from the counter, from your husband.

"Just back off, Ben," you mumble, and you try to draw a deep breath. Maybe it will clear your head. Except you can't. Your chest is so tight, you can't catch your breath. Darkness creeps into the edge of your vision, and when the room tilts just slightly, you reach to steady yourself. Ben offers you his hand, but you let yours drop to the back of your stool.

"Delilah?" He steps toward you again and bends his knees just a bit to look into your eyes. Ben is an IT guy, so he can't look at you and know that you're not really ill. He can't look into your eyes and see hidden truths.

"Are you hot, Dee?" Khloe asks. "Want me to go grab you a t-shirt?"

"No." You shake your head, but your voice is faint.

"It is warm in here. And with a turtleneck—"

"Mom?"

You blink and wonder if you heard Jordan's voice in the melee around you.

"What?" Did you speak? Whisper? Or do you just think you did?

"Matthew asked Alli to the homecoming dance."

Apparently oblivious to the tension in the kitchen,

Jordan is suddenly standing by you, leaning into you, his arm thrown over your shoulders. You smell boy—clean and fresh shampoo and soap, but still all boy—and your stomach heaves. He's shoving his phone under your nose, and with just a glance, you see a Snapchat from one of Matthew's friends to Jordan. It's a picture of your oldest son in a lip lock with the little redhead he's crushed on for the past year, and three days ago, you would have been excited for him and ready to buy him a brand new suit for the dance.

Now, Jordan's body is heavy as he leans on you in a way he's done a million times or more. You blink when you see two phones and two Matthews and two Allis, and you sway a bit under Jordan's weight. Ben reaches for you, but when he clamps his hand around your arm to steady you, you're no longer in the kitchen of your house. You're in room 741 in a hotel in Aspen, and a stranger is threatening you.

"Let. Go. Of. Me." You yank your arm away from Ben so hard that you startle him.

Jordan pitches sideways into the barstool, but Gen sort of catches him. He wouldn't have been hurt, you didn't shove him away, but you know Gen wants to soften the blows yet to come.

"Delilah?" Ben is confused and hurt, but you're still struggling to breathe, and even though you are looking hard into your husband's midnight blue eyes, you're seeing someone else.

"Lemme alone."

"Dee—"

You shake your head so violently hard, you feel a flash of pain down through your neck and shoulders.

"We should go." Oliver speaks quietly, as if you are dead, and he has to tiptoe around you to respect your soul as it leaves your body. A sarcastic laugh bubbles up inside you, because it's too damned late to worry about that. Your soul is long gone.

"Yeah." Khloe agrees, but you feel her looking at you, and you take a step back and bump into the huge SubZero refrigerator at your back. "Okay."

Ben's arm is stretched far now, because you've moved as far from him as you can get, and he's latched onto you again. It's the other arm, so it doesn't hurt, but you don't want anyone to touch you, not even Ben.

"Hey." Khloe sidles up to you slowly. "Delilah, I'm here if you need anything, okay?" She speaks softly as if she's afraid to anger you or startle you. You nod and blink, and you're mortified when the tears you've been fighting all night wet your lashes and then slide over your cheeks.

You hate to keep something from your friends, but you can't imagine telling them what's wrong. Once you say those words, you can't take them back. Once they hear them, they'll never look at you and see you again.

They'll see a victim. A whore. A stupid woman who asked for it. A weak woman who couldn't save herself.

They'll never see the true Delilah Nicholson again, because your soul is gone, and you are dead inside.

CHAPTER 4

"*D*ee." Khloe panics when she sees your tears. She reaches out to you, but you shift away from her. The fridge is still at your back, but she sees the way you flinch and drops her hand. You notice when she glances at Genevieve, who is watching you, but turns away to meet Khloe's eyes.

"Naya." Oliver ruffles Naya's fine, brown hair. She's cute, and one day she'll be pretty like her mother. Your mind flashes to Khloe's ex, but you have nothing to focus on, because you've never met him. He's been out of the picture from the time Khloe found out she was pregnant, and you only met her at FitNess when Naya was eighteen months old.

"Let's go, Naya." Khloe nods and sniffles, and you know she's upset because she's worried about you. You want to reassure her. To tell her you'll be fine, but you can't. You don't know if you'll ever be fine again, and you don't know how long this takes—recovering from this sort of personal violation, and right now, you're so fucking exhausted, you want them all the hell out of your house.

Friends or not, they are not welcome right now.

"Dee." Ben's warm voice worms its way inside your turtleneck and slithers over your skin up to your neck and your ears. "Sweetheart, what's wrong?"

"I don't wanna go home, Mommy," Naya argues. Naya loves you, and most times, she would be hanging from your neck like a little monkey. Thankfully, Jordan was home tonight, and he held her attention. The thought of Naya's little fingers warm and sticky on your neck makes you heave again. She doesn't usually fight when it's time to go home, but tonight, her face twists up in a mean frown, and she appears to be gearing up for a meltdown.

The back door opens suddenly, and you lift your eyes to see your older son walk in. The redheaded Alli is behind him, all smiles and teeth and braces. You've never kissed anyone with braces, and you wonder briefly what it feels like. And then you wonder why they're here, if Alli was having a party.

"Hey." Matthew flashes a grin to the room at large, but he quickly realizes something is wrong. Ben turns to look at him, and you seize the opportunity to get away from him. You pull your arm back to your side and studiously ignore him when he swings his gaze from Matthew back to you.

"Say goodnight, Naya." Khloe picks Naya up, but Naya is twisting and struggling to get away from her. She pounds her tiny fists against Khloe's shoulders and upper chest, and you close your eyes and remind yourself to breathe.

Your chest is painfully tight again. It won't help, but you lift your left arm to press your hand to your chest. You push gently, wishing you could ease the pain. It feels like the contractions you had when you were giving birth, only it's in your chest and your lungs and your heart.

"Delilah?"

Eyes open again, no one has moved, but Khloe. She's handing Naya over to Oliver, who throws her over his shoulder like a sack of potatoes. Naya still struggles and hollers for Jordan, but she is also giggling. The noise takes a chunk out of what composure you have left.

"Dee?"

Genevieve speaks louder this time, and you wince and turn your head just enough to look at her. The room feels small and stuffy again, though really, it's almost cavernous, and Matthew is standing there in front of Alli like he's a offensive lineman protecting his quarterback.

Gen stares at you with an intensity that sucks your breath away again. You fall back against the refrigerator and gasp and that same goddamned sob that happened the other day comes out.

You recoil when Gen takes your hand, but when she looks down and then back at you with one eyebrow cocked in question, you look at her hand on yours. Your sleeve has slipped up and revealed the deep purple bracelet the stranger put on you the morning he raped you.

When your eyes meet Gen's again, she stares at you for a long, uncomfortable moment and then slowly, she looks at Ben.

"Dee?" His voice breaks when he says your name, and you shake your head again, because damned if you're going to say a word right here, right now.

"Mom, what's wrong?" Matthew's voice is much deeper than Jordan's, and when you glance at him, you see a young man, not a boy, not your son. Alli ducks her head when she sees that you're looking their way, but you have no intention of talking to her. Not tonight. That thought makes you sad, because you've always been a hands-on mom, and you've always loved hanging with your sons' friends. Somehow, all through the years, you and Ben have walked the tightrope of parenting and being friends with your boys, and you miss that now.

You might never feel it again, because you can't even look at your sons without flinching.

"What?" Jordan has shied away from you, and he's halfway around the counter now, closer to Khloe than you. He looks from you to Matthew and back to you. "What's going on? What's wrong, Mom?"

"Guys, your mom's not feeling well right now."

You should appreciate that Khloe is taking charge. Maybe she can clear the room, and you'll finally be able to breathe.

"Jordan, you wanna come and stay at our house tonight?" she asks, and Jordan blinks and for just a moment, he looks bewildered and homesick as if he is five and Khloe is asking him to come home with her.

"No. Thank you." He shakes his head.

"Yes!" Naya squeals half in delight and half in protest as Oliver takes a few steps toward the door. Genevieve is still holding your hand in hers, and when you look at her, she looks over her shoulder toward Jordan and Khloe.

"We'll talk to you tomorrow, Dee," Khloe says softly. She follows Oliver to the door, and Naya shrieks now, outraged that they are leaving without Jordan. Matthew steps toward you, fear on his face.

"Delilah," Ben says, louder this time. The room is spinning, and your vision is going black.

"Jordan, go with Khloe," Gen says without taking her eyes from your face.

"Mom?"

When the room goes dark around you and their voices fade as if they are speaking in a tunnel, you slump sideways, and you feel Ben sweep you into his arms.

You thrash against him, but you can't fight him. For a

moment, he doesn't move. He just holds you like he knows something is horribly wrong. Genevieve is still trying to corral Jordan and Matthew into going home with Khloe, and you hear Alli say something to Matthew.

And then Ben is moving. He carries you into your bedroom, but when he lowers you to the bed, you struggle to get away from him. You squirm in his arms and gouge his side with your elbow.

"What's going on, Dee?" he asks, and he sounds hurt and angry and scared. He can't be scared. He doesn't get to be scared. Not when this happened to you.

"Ben, leave me alone." Your mouth is dry, and your whispered words are thick and heavy. You turn to your side and ignore the fact that you still hear your company down the hall, and you're not alone with your husband. "Just leave me alone."

You feel the mattress give when he props a knee on it. Afraid that he will touch you, that he will rest his hand on your arm or your belly, you curl into a small, tight ball and squeeze your eyes closed again.

"Delilah." He doesn't touch you, but he sits beside you on the bed now. He's close enough that you feel him there, his solid shape—his thigh and his knee nearly pressed up against your back—and the warmth of his body. "What's going on?"

You have no words and no energy, so you wait. Wait for him to give up and walk away. From far away, you hear the back door open and close, and you know someone is gone now, but you still hear the murmur of voices, so you're still not alone. You're not sure if it's good or bad that you're not alone with Ben, and thinking about it is like a hammer tapping at the back of your skull.

"Dee. Who did that to you?"

Ben moves—you don't know what he's doing—but the

whole bed shakes as he scoots around and settles again. His hand is suddenly on your wrist, and you feel him inching your sleeve up. It's dark in the room, except for where light from the hallway spills through your door. He can't possibly see the bruises on your wrist or your breastbone or anywhere else on your body, but you still shy away from him and pull the sleeve down over your hand.

"Delilah, goddammit. Talk to me."

But you can't. You ball your hand into a fist and hold your breath while you wait for him to give up.

Does your rapist have a wife? He looked like a guy who would have a pretty wife and maybe two or three perfect children. He looked like he could be a doctor or an engineer or even an IT genius. He looked like someone your husband might rub elbows with on a daily basis.

Finally, your lungs burn so badly, your whole chest feels raw, and you have to breathe. You gasp and then groan resentfully that your body keeps working, doing the things it's supposed to do, when your heart and your head can't get it together. You're unreasonably angry with Ben right now for pressuring you. He's angry; you heard the rough edges in his words just seconds ago, and they make you cower from him, even though your rapist didn't swing at you.

After all, he said he wouldn't hurt you.

"Dee," Ben whispers. "Dee, Genevieve thinks I did this."

A harsh, guttural noise escapes you, and you flop over on your back. Fury makes you blind to the man sitting beside you, but you know he's still there because you still feel him beside you. You hear him breathing.

"*That's* what you're worried about?" you whisper. "What Gen's thinking right now?"

"Dee." He groans, and you know he's miserable not

because Gen suspects he hurt you, but because *someone* hurt you, and you didn't tell him. "Babe. Tell me. Please tell me."

"I can't."

"Delilah." He moves again, and this time, the tension is gone from the mattress springs, and the bed is cold. Flat on your back, head on your pillow, you wait with your eyes closed for his next move. The conversation from down the hall has quieted to just two voices, but you don't listen closely enough to discern who it is.

Please, you think. Please, don't let it be my boys.

You need your sons to be anywhere but here right now. In the darkness, your cheeks burn with shame that your sons saw you fall apart minutes ago in your kitchen. You can't explain this to them, and they'll wonder, and no matter what lies you tell them to placate them, they'll look at you with suspicion or pity.

You can't handle their pity. You don't want them to feel sorry for you. You don't want them to wait on you. You don't want them to take care of you, because you are their mother. It is your job to be there for them, and now, you don't know if you can do that job.

Because as much as you love them, you don't want to see them. Or talk to them. Or touch them.

Ever—

Light floods the room, and you whimper as you open your eyes. Ben has turned on the lamp, and the light shines directly over your face. He stands at your side of the bed, hands on his hips and his head hanging low. He looks haggard and worn, but just minutes ago, he didn't. Minutes ago, when he walked into the kitchen with Christian and Oliver—probably coming to grab another beer for each of them—he had looked almost boyish and happy and carefree.

From your angle, with his chin nearly on his chest, you see dark, angry gashes carved in his face, under his eyes. His face is red, maybe with anger. He huffs out a deep breath and purses his lips, and your eyes roam greedily over the dark stubble over his cheeks and his chin. You've not kissed his thin lips since the morning a stranger burst into your hotel room and changed your life—stole your life—and right now, for just a second, you miss his kiss. Each time since that morning that he's moved close to you with the intention of kissing you, you've turned away and he's caught the corner of your lips, and for him, it's normal because you're busy. In all the years of your marriage, each year seems to go by faster and you wonder now if he's kissed you half as many times this year as last year.

It's too bad that he didn't kiss you more, that you didn't slow down and pay attention to the way he's loved you.

Because what if you can't do it again? What if you can't love him the way you did just days ago?

"Dee—"

When he drops his hands and lifts his knee again to perch on the mattress beside you, instinct kicks in and you crawl backwards to put space between you.

"What the hell happened?"

There's noise beneath you, and you realize your sons are downstairs now. What are they doing in the basement? Are they playing video games while you're upstairs coming unglued? Is Jordan playing one of those shooter games? You hate those games, and you've talked to Ben about them before and urged him to put his foot down.

"Delilah. It's me. It's Ben."

He reaches for you then, and when you scramble to get away from him, he moves swiftly and snatches your arm, just like the stranger did, only he doesn't squeeze you hard enough to hurt you. You tug at your arm to get away from him, but he refuses to let go, and bile chokes you.

Softer handcuffs, but you're still imprisoned.

"Please, Ben?"

That hard wall that you threw up to protect yourself, to hide behind just to survive the ten minutes that stole your soul crashes down now, and you sob as you meet Ben's eyes. A violent tremble rips through you, and you press your free hand to your mouth, but you can't stop the strange, guttural sobbing sounds. You can't stop shaking, and though you feel chilled to the bone, Ben's gaze burns the top of your head when you duck your chin.

"Please?" Your whisper is lost in the sobbing, so you repeat it again and again, and rather than let go of you, rather than backing off to give you room to breathe, he stretches over the bed and slides his arm around you.

"Tell me who did this to you." His voice is raw now with desperation, the anger melted away. He's not a big man, but he's strong, and before, you've always felt safe in his arms. Right now, you're not safe. You're suffocating. You don't even picture the stranger in your head, but it's so real—the panic is so real—it's like he's right here in your bedroom with you.

Forehead and face pressed hard to Ben's neck, part of you revels in the warmth of his skin against yours. But you still can't breathe. His arms are wrapped tightly around you, and you're trapped. Still sobbing, still repeating please and stop, you slide your hands up over the hard wall of his chest and push. With all of your strength, you shove at him, and no wonder you couldn't save yourself and escape the man who violated you. You're so weak you can't make Ben move back. You can't draw a full breath.

"Ben, please."

You can't see him, because you still squeeze your eyes closed. You can't look at him. You can't look at your bedroom and see the stranger here, watching you. Ben finally gives you an inch and you twist just enough to drop your forehead to his collarbone. Exhausted and terrified, still, of his touch—of any touch—you press your face into Ben's dark green long-sleeved t-shirt. At first the smell of his cologne mixed with his soap and the laundry detergent you've used for years comforts you, and you concentrate on breathing. If you don't breathe, you'll die.

You can't suffocate. You will not smother. You refuse to give the son-of-a-bitch the satisfaction. You flinch now at the memory of his hand cupped over your mouth and his fingers wrapped around your throat.

Another long, ragged groan and sob tears out of you, and you hear footsteps in the hallway.

"Delilah, it's Ben."

Your husband's voice—the voice you have listened for, the voice you have loved for years—is a gentle caress on the side of your face. You lift your head and turn reluctantly to look at him. You have to be ugly right now. Your heart and your head are black and charred, and your face must be covered in snot and makeup and tears, and you want to want him to hold you.

But you don't.

"Ben? Dee?"

Ben looks up when Genevieve calls softly from the door. You duck your head, too ashamed for Gen to get a glimpse of who you are at the moment. You have been friends for decades, and she has seen you at your worst.

Until this.

This is a new worst. Genevieve has not seen you broken.

"I'm a phone call away," she tells Ben. Maybe she's talking to you, too, but you refuse to glance her way. "If you need anything."

Ben nods, and you realize he's moving. His hand is moving to your neck, and you swing at him, striking his hand to knock it away.

"Let me help you."

"Please don't touch me," you whisper, and when you hear Gen sniffle, you know she heard you. Does she really believe Ben did something to hurt you? No one could believe that, could they? Ben is a kind, selfless man. He wouldn't hurt anyone.

You wonder if the stranger who hurt you is married, and if his wife's friends think the same of him.

Ben turns his full attention back to you, and Genevieve realizes she's been dismissed. You hear her track back down the hall and say something to Christian. Ben scoots back from you so that you are sitting side by side now, but he reaches—slowly—to take your hand.

Rather than clamping his hand around your wrist, he simply slides his fingers over your palm and waits for you to respond. You can't. You can't close your fingers around his, but you don't jerk away. It takes all of your energy, all of your focus to sit with him this way.

"Someone hurt you."

He doesn't phrase it as a question, so you don't answer. You stare at your hands and work to swallow the hard knot of emotion stuck in your throat.

"Dee?" He nudges your leg with his knee, but he doesn't move, doesn't flex his fingers.

"Yeah." You nod, but you press your lips together to keep more of the ugly, messy emotion from spilling out. The shoulder of Ben's shirt is wet with your mess, and you feel a flash of guilt for that.

"When?"

You struggle to make your mouth say words, but when you try, you sob again and your body shudders.

"Babe, please. What happened? You have to tell me what happened."

"I can't." You shake your head.

"You are my wife." He leans forward, but you back away at the same time because if he's in your face, you won't be able to breathe. "I love you. And if someone hurt you, I need to know."

"Why?" The word comes out on a harsh whisper. "Why do I have to talk about it, Ben? You can't change what happened."

"But, Delilah, let me…let me help you. Talk to me."

You lick your lips and turn your head away.

"I can wait," he whispers. "I will sit here with you all night until you're ready to trust me, Dee."

The word *trust* hits you like a battering ram in your chest, and you gasp out loud. You're supposed to trust Ben, your husband. You used to. It's not fair to Ben that you don't now because some stranger shoved the door of your hotel room open and burst in and raped you.

It's just that you thought it was Ben. At the door. You opened it assuming it was Ben.

And it wasn't.

Ben was probably schmoozing in the conference room by that time. Drinking coffee. Talking golf or NFL with his colleagues. Talking about technology and maybe eyeballing the cute blond waitress who wheeled the breakfast cart with pastries and fruit in for the meeting. Maybe one of them—Ben or his colleagues—was saying sexist things about the waitress' legs or her breasts. It's what men do; you've heard them now and then.

Women do it, too. Women either trade cutting remarks

about the same cute little waitresses their husbands work so hard to impress, or they undress the male servers the same as the men do the women.

Evened up the score, and besides, it was all in fun.

Except that someone was in your hotel room, holding you down with his hand over your mouth, while maybe your husband was just being a man.

"I'm scared, Delilah." Ben squeezes your hand.

You bend the leg closest to him and rest your elbow on it. And hide your face in your hand.

"You don't get to be scared, Ben Nicholson." Hand still covering your face, there are more tears, and your voice quivers. "You don't get to be scared. You don't have that right."

"Where?" He leans close again, and you freeze when you feel his lips brush your hair.

"Colorado." Your mouth is dry, which is ridiculous because your face is wet with tears.

"When we were on the last trip?"

"Yes."

"When? Where was I?"

You remember now how you lifted your hands to fight him off. You shoved at the hard wall of his chest, and he batted your hands away like they were nothing. You grabbed his shirt when he unzipped his pants, and you twisted and yanked at it and pushed, and your fingernail ripped off. You're amazed that in the middle of all of that hell, you felt the burning pain of a nail ripping from your fingertip.

Unable to speak, to put two words together, you shake your head.

"Were you out? When you went for coffee? Lunch?"

You answer with a quick, hard shake of your head, and then you say no, though you don't know if he heard you.

"Where, Dee?"

"Why does it matter, Ben? Why does this matter?"

"Because I have to know. I have to know what happened to you. To my wife."

You lift your head finally, and pain shoots through the back of your neck. You blink at him and you rub your eyes and swipe your hand under your nose. It's a move that makes you think of your boys when they were little, and you hate that their mother is damaged.

"In our room."

"What?"

"It happened in our hotel room." The words are so small and quiet, but the room seems to echo with them, and Ben stares at you, horrified and affronted, and you stare back at him boldly because there's a tiny part of you that knows this is not your fault. You are not to blame.

"In our room?"

"Yes."

"Did you invite someone to our room?" Ben tips his head, and suddenly, you understand what he's thinking. Maybe you invited someone back because—what? You thought an afternoon fling would be fun? But you changed your mind, and he wouldn't take no for an answer?

"No!" You snap. "Fuck you. I would never do that, Ben." Seething with anger, with rage and pain, you kick at him when he reaches for you.

"Okay." He nods so enthusiastically, he reminds you of bobbleheads people try to sell on eBay and in sports memorabilia shops. "Okay. What, then? Delilah, what happened?"

You breathe deeply again, and the air in your room is so cold and sharp, it hurts your nose and up into your brain.

"You had just left." You scoot backwards off the bed.

Your boots don't make a sound on the plush carpet in your room. The sounds of video games come from the basement, and for once, you're glad for them. If your sons overheard these details, you would surely never be able to look at them again.

"When?"

"The morning we left."

Ben, still in a heap of muscle and bone and broken innocence, watches you from the same spot on the bed. You move to the far wall, and you breathe easier for a second.

"Who was it?"

Lips pressed together, you shake your head and shrug.

"I dunno."

"But—I mean. How, Dee? How did it happen?"

"He knocked." You lean on the wall at your back and fold your arms over your chest.

"He—? What?" Ben scooches down to the end of the bed, and you hold your breath, praying he stays there. "Why did you let him in?"

"You had just left," you repeat. "I thought it was you. That you forgot something. I didn't pay attention when I opened the door."

Ben stares at you silently.

"Did he rape you, Delilah?"

You said the word. To your doctor. You told her a man *raped* you. You *thought* the word as the stranger shrugged out of his coat and backed you into the bed. You thought the word *rape*, but hearing Ben say it out loud hurts, like he just drove a tank through your heart and your gut, and you gasp out loud again.

What if he doesn't love you? What if Ben can't love you anymore? Because of this?

"Yes."

You stare at him—emotions welling up inside you, so many and so jumbled, you can't make sense of them. Fear. You're scared. God, yes, you're scared that this might change the way your husband feels about you, and you feel guilty because maybe it's changed the way you feel about him. It's not fair; you can't play both sides of that card, but you can't help how you feel. You can't help the rage that pounds inside you now, the hate for the man who did this to you. If he were here now, you would pound your fists on his chest and his shoulders and you would kick and fight and scream—but you did that, didn't you? You didn't scream, because he clamped his hand over your mouth and threatened you. But you fought him, and he beat you—he won, and now here you are. Staring at your husband, gazes locked as you wait with a tiny niggle of hope low in your belly that he will keep loving you.

"Ben?" Your courage breaks and falls in pieces at your feet. "Say something."

"Goddammit." Ben shakes his head. He climbs up from the bed and paces the room. You're thankful he stays at a distance, because you feel his anger, and it scares you. "You are my wife. You. Are. My. Wife." He throws his hands in the air and then lowers them to his head and clutches wildly at his dark hair. "No one has the right to hurt you." He roars like a bear, and you imagine you feel the house shake. "What son-of-a-bitch did this? I'll kill him, Delilah. I will kill him."

He stalks closer to you, but when you cower from him, he stops abruptly, as if his feet are glued to the floor. His hands are still in his hair, and there's a wild, desperate look on his face. His bloodshot eyes are wide with fear and anger and sorrow, and his mouth—those thin lips you have loved to kiss so many times—is turned down in a grimace, and it breaks your heart that you did this to him.

You didn't do this to him.

The thought stabs you between the eyes like an ice pick.

You try to answer Ben. You try to say again that you don't know who he was, but you can't speak over the mewling, and when tears streak Ben's face, you slide down the wall and think that you've probably just left marks from your dark-wash jeans on the sage green paint, and Ben will have to touch it up.

He'll be frustrated. He's too busy—

"Delilah."

Your butt on the floor, your back to the wall, you curl into a ball again, the fetal position, and you think about the blood test Dr. Ambern ordered yesterday. You could be pregnant. The first time was to eliminate the possibility you were already pregnant. You know you weren't. But you could be pregnant with a monster's child right now. You could be infected with AIDS, and you know that even if Ben thinks he still loves you, he shouldn't, because even now that the worst has happened, more can go wrong.

You hear him moving, and you feel the air displaced as he kneels down in front of you. He hovers there, and he's crying, too, and you hate that he is hurting and that he feels responsible, but there's a part of you that wants to blame him and hate him and be angry with him because you thought he was at the door, because he forgot something.

He's done it a hundred times before. Forgot his phone. Forgot his bottle of water. Forgot his wallet. His key. His iPad. Why couldn't it have just been him this time?

"Delilah, let me in." His voice is gruff, and you flash to

a night three years ago when he had just lost his mom. He was angry before he was sad, and you stood back—one arm over your chest and the other hand over your lips—as he tore through the closet and knocked hangers off the rod and yelled about the insanity of cancer and the lack of a cure after all these years.

When he finally crashed that night, he had slumped in the corner of the closet and tugged at the hair on his head —as he's doing now—and you had lowered yourself to your knees beside him and you said, "Ben, let me in."

Because you know how much it hurts to watch someone you love hurt and how helpless you feel watching them struggle in that pain, you give in.

Slowly. Cautiously.

Knees to your chest, arms wrapped around them, you loosen your right arm and open your hand. His grip is strong and safe, and you squeeze back half-heartedly.

"We'll be okay," he says, and before you can argue, before you can ask what the hell he has to do with it, he continues, "you'll be okay, Dee. I'm gonna be right here. I'm gonna love you. I'm gonna love you through this."

You slump into him when he shifts to sit on his butt and reaches to gather you in his arms. With your free hand, you swipe at your face and nod as you rest your forehead on him again.

"It's gonna be okay," he says again, and maybe if he keeps saying it, you'll believe him, and you will be okay.

"Ben?" You bite your lip, but not before his name slips out. With gentle fingers, he cups your chin and makes you look at him. Too afraid to look him in the eye, you let your eyelids slide closed.

"What?"

With your eyes closed, you don't see him move, but you

sense that he's closer. You flinch when he presses his lips in a soft kiss to your cheek.

"What if…" The breath you take is shaky, but you swallow and start again. "What if I'm pregnant?"

"He didn't use—"

Eyes open now, you shake your head. You should be okay. You take an oral contraceptive, but there are days when you forget it or take it at a different time. You should be okay, but Dr. Ambern had insisted on another blood test to rule it out.

"How do we know?"

"Dr. Ambern said to come back in two weeks, and she would order a blood test."

He nods and puffs his cheeks up in a big, deep breath.

"You went without me."

"I didn't know…" You groan and huff with frustration. "I didn't know how to tell you."

"Dee, you can tell me anything."

"I was afraid."

"Of me? I would never hurt—"

"That it would change the way you see me."

Ben shakes his head, but before he can argue, you lift your hand and press two fingers over his lips.

"I'm scared. And I feel…inside out." You clear your throat, wishing you could say this right. "I'm angry. I'm so fucking mad at the whole world, Ben, including you. And I'm embarrassed." You shrug and wag your eyebrows when he starts to argue. "I'm ashamed. I feel weak." You speak slowly, quietly around the hard knot in your chest and your throat, but Ben watches you patiently. "I feel stupid. I feel so goddamned stupid, and I hate that I feel stupid. Because of this."

"It's okay—"

"Don't." You shake your head. "Don't placate me.

Don't treat me like I'm fragile, Ben. I have to still be me, or there's no way I'll get through this."

You stare at him boldly, and warm tears slide over your cheeks. Finally he nods, and he kisses your cheek again.

"You're still my Delilah. No one can take that from you."

CHAPTER 5

*Y*ou don't want to die. The thought comes to you over the weekend, when you still don't want to live. You could have died in your hotel room, and somehow the fact that you didn't is important. You were violated in the worst possible way a woman can be violated, and you survived it.

There are always national news stories about women or girls who have gone missing, and the whole country holds its collective breath while law enforcement searches. Mostly, everyone assumes they are searching for a dead body after the first forty-eight hours have gone by. Some girls, some women are attacked by savage monsters who mutilate their bodies and leave them out in the cold, away from their homes, their loved ones.

Maybe there is a reason that you survived. Other than the fact that your rapist looked like a normal guy.

Ben still sleeps beside you, but he gives you plenty of space in the king-sized bed. You keep your back to him, and you curl into a ball around an extra pillow, and you lie awake and listen to him breathe. When he is asleep, you slip from your bed and tiptoe to the living room where you snuggle on the couch under an old, comfortable fleece throw.

The darkness that presses in outside your windows is absolute in the back of the house, and your nerves are stretched thin. Late night TV has become your best friend, because you can stare at it blankly, and you don't have to think. Ben finds you in the mornings, awake but bleary-eyed, and tousles your hair with his fingers and tells you to go back to bed.

You nod without looking at him, but you wait for him to get a drink of water and head back to the master suite to take a shower before you move. Even though you keep the sound muted, the room feels deadly still when you turn the TV off. Your side of the bed is cold, but you snuggle under the blankets and wait for them and your long, flannel pjs to warm you. The sounds of Ben in the shower are familiar, and you think of mornings in the past when you joined him and the two of you lingered under the hot water.

You've called Anna, at the office, to let her know you would be working from home. You are partners, but not exactly friends, so you didn't explain why you won't be in the office for an undisclosed amount of time. You can do ad work from home, and she knows it, and so she didn't question you. Simply said she hopes everything is okay.

You watched the weekend creep by through your bedroom window. Gray daylight blended slowly into night skies and then dawn and a tease of sunshine and back to the slow darkness gathering, tiptoeing up to you like a stranger with a pillow in his hands to suffocate you.

You dreamt that. After Ben left for work Monday, you dozed in your bed, careful not to stretch and end up on his side of the bed. You slept fitfully, and you dreamt that when the man raped you, he held a pillow over your face.

You woke up gasping for air. Anger pulsed in your neck and your fingertips, and when you dreamt it the second time—Monday afternoon, because you didn't get out of bed—you woke up determined you would not die.

On Tuesday evening, Ben serves you hot chicken soup and homemade bread from Genevieve. Your stomach squeezes at the thought of trying to eat, but Ben looks so hopeful when he sets the tray up for you, that you can't tell him no. You wonder if Ben told Genevieve what's going on or if she is just donning the caretaker role because she knows something is wrong.

The soup is good. You sip it from the oversized mug, but you put the mug down when you notice Ben looking at the bruises on your wrist. They have faded some, but you think you will see them there forever.

"Did he call you by name?" Ben asks. He sits on his bent knee at the foot of his side of the bed. He wants to be near you, but he knows you want space.

"No."

"Did he say anything to you?"

He asked you that before, if the man said anything to you. Friday night after Genevieve and Christian finally left, Ben had asked you questions. So many that you felt badgered, and finally, he had stopped and offered you a blunt, tragic apology.

You want to understand how he feels. What would it be like to watch your spouse drown in the aftermath of a personal attack? It's impossible for you to imagine, because Ben is a man, and he's much stronger than you, even though you do stay fit and healthy. He's bigger than you, and besides, it's not terribly often you hear things about men being victims of sexual assault.

It might happen, but it's hard for you to wrap your head around the thought.

"He said…" You fiddle with the spoon on the tray. There are noodles and carrots in the broth, but if Ben wants to talk about the assault, you can't eat. "He said he wouldn't hurt me, if I kept my mouth shut."

"Wouldn't hurt you," Ben repeats in a tight voice.

"I mean." You shrug. "He didn't. Did he?"

Ben gives you a sharp look when you whisper those words.

"He did, De—"

You nod and close your eyes. Wrist resting on the tray, you lift your fingers to stop him.

"He did. He hurt me." You have to be able to say those words. No, he didn't batter you. He didn't kick you. He didn't cut you; you don't know if he had a weapon with him. But he hurt you. You have bruises on your body to prove it. You have tight, sore muscles from the way you tensed up, like when you see in the rearview mirror that someone is about to hit you.

And, most importantly—you remind yourself—he raped you. He came into your room, uninvited, and forced himself on you. You don't have to qualify the assault. You don't have to pretend it's nothing because he didn't beat you or cut you.

"Did you see him? Before?"

Ben is obsessed with finding the man. With having him arrested, if he can't get his hands on him to kill him. On Saturday morning, when you were on the couch, he left the house dressed for a run. He came home three hours later, a sweaty, bedraggled mess. He had gone to the gym to box out the demons—your words, not his.

"No."

"Like at the bar? Or anywhere on the hotel campus?"

"No—"

"Do you think he was a guest there?"

"Ben, I don't know," you insist. "I don't know. There's no security in the elevator bank, so he didn't have to have a card to get on the elevator or get to our floor."

"So you don't think he was?"

"I don't know!" You groan and twist uncomfortably, careful not to overturn the tray.

"I'm sorry." He sounds miserable and broken. "Try the bread. It's delicious."

Your hands shake when you pick up the thick slice of bread and pluck a small bite of it to stick in your mouth.

"How're the boys?" you ask, because while you don't want to see them, you feel guilty for hiding away. They are both old enough not to need Mommy around all the time, but it feels wrong that four days have gone by that you haven't stood close enough to them to smell their boy smell or tousle their hair or throw your arm around their shoulders for a quick, stolen squeeze.

Friday night, they had left you alone. After Gen and Christian were gone, Ben had sat with you on the floor for what felt like days. He hadn't smothered you with hugs or kisses, but he had been desperate for answers, for details you didn't want to share. You heard the boys the following morning; after Ben was up and sent you back to bed from the couch, you heard the three of them in the kitchen. Matthew was the most concerned, questioning Ben over and over about what was wrong with you.

Matthew is more sensitive than Jordan. He's older and more mature, though he's still young. But he's always been more reserved and sober, where Jordan has always been the comedian.

Ben had told them that you're sick, and Matthew had asked immediately if you had cancer. If you had just found a lump or if you'd seen your doctor already, and lying in bed, you had stuffed your face in your pillow to hide your cries. You're not sure that Ben's reassurances that you don't have cancer, that it's just the flu, did the job. Each night since then, your sons have lingered at your bedroom door and timidly said goodnight and that they love you.

You haven't said it back. You haven't said *I love you* to any of your guys since the morning in your hotel when your life changed.

"They're good," Ben tells you now. You relax back into your pillow, the bread still in your hands. There will be crumbs in the sheets now. You jerk at the image of the hotel bed, the sheets and the comforter twisted and falling on the floor. The stranger's hand hard between your breasts as he jerked his body in and out of yours.

"When's the dance? Matthew needs a new suit."

Ben nods. "Two weeks," he says. "I can take him. But I don't want you to miss it."

"I can't go." You shake your head. The thought of taking Matthew out in the Highlander—just the two of you—and trying to make conversation renders you breathless, browsing the suits at any of the stores you and Ben frequent, dealing with a salesman, strikes you with panic.

"Give it time."

"I can't."

"Delilah, this is Matthew's last homecoming." He pins you to the headboard with his stare. "You'll regret it if you miss it."

"He doesn't need me." You lower your gaze to Ben's hands. "It's something for you to do with him." Before Ben can argue, you continue, "Besides, he has prom in the spring. And Jordan will have to do all of that."

The words sound harsh and cold. Not something a mother would say about her children. You rub your knuckles over your heart and sort of wish you could take them back.

The fact that you sort of don't wish that, because mostly, you mean them makes you feel sick.

"They're scared, Delilah."

You hold the eye contact as long as you can stand it, but when it feels like Ben is seeing into your brain and digging into the secrets you now keep, you jerk your head a bit to the left and stare silently at the wall.

"They know something's wrong."

"You told them I was sick."

"They know I'm lying."

From the corner of your eye, you see Ben shrug.

"If you were sick, you would be curled up on the couch all day. In your robe and blankets. You would be watching movies on the Hallmark channel. The boys would be waiting on you."

They would. When you are sick—and you don't get sick often—the boys treat you like a queen. When they were little, they wanted to snuggle with you, but you tried to keep them away in case you were contagious. In recent years, they've teased you about the sappy movies and delivered warm brownies from the oven and grabbed a new box of tissues for you.

"They know you don't want to be near them." Ben's voice is gentle, but it crashes into you like a tidal wave and almost bowls you over.

"I don't want them to look at me and think about what…" You chance a glance at Ben and see him nod.

"I know," he says quietly. "Baby, I know none of us can understand what you feel right now. But you know you are my world. And you know those boys worship you. You've raised them to be compassionate."

"They're old enough to understand—"

"Don't take it out on them." Ben shakes his head.

"Please. If you have to be angry, take it out on me. Let your sons love you."

You sink back into the pillows again and drop the bread back to the tray. Ben's right, of course. You can't just disappear into yourself and never talk to your sons again. But that doesn't mean you know how to get past it. You don't know how to talk to them—to explain what's wrong or just bury it and move on.

Ben stands to pace the room. You watch him suspiciously, because he's gearing up to something. One hand in his pocket, he lifts the other to knead the back of his neck.

"Maybe it would be easier for you if you found someone else."

"Have you thought about counseling?" After he speaks, he stops pacing. At the foot of the bed, his eyes blaze with indignant anger as he stares at you.

"No." You refuse to consider counseling. You can't talk about what happened with someone who will repeat what you say and ask how you feel. How the hell would anyone feel in your situation? You won't do group therapy, because sitting in a circle and regurgitating the details of what happened in that hotel room feels the same as peeling your clothes off and asking for more of the same.

"You need someone to help you, Delilah."

"I don't need help, Ben. I'll be fine."

He tips his head, and his eyebrows jump in disbelief.

"You've disowned your sons, and you just suggested I might be happier with another woman." He shrugs. You hear the anger, the disgust in his voice.

"It just happened," you remind him. "I just need time."

"You can't wish it away, Dee. You have to work through it."

You drag your teeth over your lower lip and stare at

him silently. Irrational anger makes you want to lash out at him. But you have no energy, so you simply wait him out.

"Have you been googling rape survivor stories?" You speak quietly, but your words are loaded with negative energy. Ben's midnight blue eyes flash with helpless rage.

"What am I supposed to do? We can't live like this. You need—"

You nod and look at his side of the bed. "I told you to find someone else. I don't know if or when I can—"

"I know you're angry," he interrupts you. "Be angry, Delilah. I assume that's a necessary part of healing. But don't you dare make this about me. I'm not some goddamned kid hanging around so I can get in your pants again. I love you."

When his voice breaks, you feel a pang of regret in your chest. It sucks your breath away and leaves a hole in your belly.

"I love you, and the only thing that matters to me is you. You and our boys."

Your throat is so tight, you can't possibly breathe, let alone speak. What you said to him—finding someone else —was wrong, and you knew it as you said it. You and Ben have loved each other through the ups and downs of life, and just because this is hell—this is as down as you can feel —doesn't give you the right to question his commitment or his love.

You breathe through your nose, and you sniffle and roll your lips inward. You owe Ben an apology, but you can't speak. Even knowing you owe him an apology, you aren't sure what would come out of your mouth if you could speak. The venom inside you is tricky and dangerous.

Realizing that you're not going to answer him, Ben sighs, and he sounds exhausted. He drops his hands to his sides and moves to your side of the bed. You avoid his eyes as he takes the tray with the half-eaten meal, but when he walks out of the room, you watch him. In his dress shirt and trousers, after a long day at work and an impossible conversation with you, he looks defeated.

As bad as you feel for him, for what you're doing to him, you don't want to be bothered. With another sniffle, you turn on your side with your back to the door and close your eyes.

This bed is your sanctuary.

It is also your prison.

You don't open your eyes when Ben comes back a few minutes later. You can't fake sleep, but you refuse to acknowledge that he's standing behind you.

"Why don't you take a shower?" he suggests. "I think it would be good for you to get up for a while."

Face half buried in the pillow, you shake your head no.

"How about a bath? You can soak for a while. I'll change the sheets."

"Why do you love me, Ben?" The whisper is harsh. "I don't deserve you."

CHAPTER 6

"*I*t happened in Aspen."

The steady buzz of conversation and Dean Martin's voice surround you, but you barely whisper the words. It's not that you worry someone else will hear you. Paradise, your local trendy coffee bar is always busy, no matter the time of day, and while everyone is usually friendly, no one ever attempts to overhear or insert themselves into your conversations. You simply don't have the courage to say the words any louder, and now that you've said them—now that you've opened the door a crack—you hold your breath as you wait for Genevieve and Khloe to react.

Ben had cajoled you into a hot bath last night. He had helped you from bed, but you shrugged him off impatiently, insisting you aren't an invalid and won't be treated as such. Your cross words didn't seem to faze him. He had helped you get settled in the bathroom. Started your bath water. Brought you clean pajamas and underwear. The black silk in his big hand had been a magnet to your eyes.

When you froze, paralyzed at the sight and the memory of the stranger with your thong, Ben had lowered his gaze to your panties and then looked back at you apologetically. He's touched your lace and silk thousands of times in your married life, sometimes in heated, sexy situations and others when he's doing the laundry. But just then, seeing your intimate item in his hand and thinking of the stranger shoving your thong in his pocket made you shiver with revulsion.

He had wanted to ask, but he didn't. He set your things on the counter, stepped close enough to press a chaste kiss to your forehead, and then he'd backed out of the room. You had hesitated to undress in case he came back. You've been careful not to be naked in front of him since it happened, but you're not sure if it's because you feel violated and threatened or if you don't want Ben to see your bruises and feel impotent in his rage.

The tile floor was cold on your feet, and the tub filled behind you. You'd considered crossing the room to lock the door, but you didn't. If he came back, he came back. If you had any hope of healing and moving forward with your husband, you had to let him see you naked at some point. Feeling like you were playing roulette, you slipped out of your pajamas and climbed into the tub.

Your body has been sore, but you aren't sick. There's no lingering weakness like when you are recovering from the flu. Your head and your heart hurt, but physically, you could put your gear on and run miles. You've cowered in bed because you can't face people, your sons, your friends, not because you are so physically damaged you can't move.

The jets in the whirlpool tub sprayed hot water on the sore muscles, the ones that have been stiff since the struggle in the hotel room. You relaxed in the tub and let the familiar dove grey and white room soothe you. When Ben knocked on the door, you jerked upright in the tub, heart slamming up into your throat.

"Dee?"

"What?"

You whispered, so you knew he didn't hear you. You wanted to be brave, to be ready for this, but even in the hot water, goosebumps kissed your skin.

"Can I come in?"

Can he come in? you wondered. He's asked, and he's knocked and allowed you absolute privacy since the night you told him what happened.

"Yes." You spoke louder, and he heard you because the door opened just a crack. You hunched forward in the tub and circled your arms around your bent knees.

"I won't bother you." Ben had peeked his head in, but with your face resting on your knees, you saw that he wasn't looking directly at you. "I just…Khloe sent you something. I wanted you to see it."

His eyes moved over the walls and met yours for a second, but he'd been careful not to make you uncomfortable.

"It's okay." You cleared your throat. "You can come in."

"What happened, Dee?" Khloe says now, and you blink your sweet, naïve friend into focus. Genevieve sits closest to the wall, Khloe beside her. You are alone on your side of the tall table. By choice.

The Dean Martin song switches to something by Frank Sinatra. In the far corner of the room, there is a black tree decorated with skulls and witches' hats and purple lights for Halloween. Khloe has been talking about how excited Naya is to go trick-or-treating. Life goes on as you struggle, still, to breathe.

You still might drown.

Gen and Khloe are both watching you with concern, but you can't find the words to tell them what happened. To stall, you lift your heavy green coffee mug and sip from it. The liquid scalds your tongue and your throat, and you wonder if it would be so terrible if you couldn't speak again.

When you put the mug back on the table, you keep your fingers around it and rub your thumb over it. Your nails are bitten down to the quick, but they match the rest of your appearance. With today's turtleneck—navy—you wear old, worn jeans, black Uggs, and you pulled your hair back in a messy knot just before you left the house.

You open your mouth to speak, but you still can't find your voice. Tears burn your eyes when you lift them to look at your best friends. Khloe's face is arranged in a deep frown. She's concerned, yes, but she hasn't guessed what you are going to say. Genevieve, though, watches you with a sad expectation. You say a little prayer that she doesn't truly believe Ben would ever hurt you.

"I was raped." You're not sure if you said the words out loud, if you simply thought them, if you mouthed them. You meet Gen's eyes, and whatever, however, you communicated it, she heard you. She flinches and sobs quietly. Khloe reaches across the table and brushes her fingers lightly over the back of your hand. It hurts the way your skin hurts when you have the flu, the way it hurt to move over the sheet after the stranger left you that morning.

You lift your other hand to dab at your eyes. Since it happened, you haven't worn makeup, but you don't want to sit here in a public place and draw attention to yourself.

"Oh, Dee." Genevieve slumps forward and rests her elbows on the table. She hangs her head for a second and before you can think that she can't do that, that she can't steal your emotions, she lifts her head again and meets your eyes. "I was so afraid you were going to say that."

You give her a small nod and rub the saggy, bruised skin under your eye with your thumb.

"How?" you whisper. "How did you know?"

"Just." Gen shrugs. "You've been so skittish. So small."

Small. That kind of sums it up. You were living large and happy, and life smacked you down, and now you realize how insignificant you are in the big scheme of things. You could write a book about happiness made of glass, shattered with a feather.

"That's not you, Delilah," Khloe whispers.

"Maybe it is now." Your voice is hard, because Khloe just dug deeper inside you and yanked up another of your fears. What if this is the new you? What if you don't just lose Ben and the boys, but all of your friends, too?

If you've lost yourself and you become someone new, every relationship you have will have to reset. What if they don't stick? What if the new you is abrasive and unlovable?

"Does Ben know?" Genevieve asks you.

You snort sarcastically and pull your mug closer to you. Rather than look at your friends, you stare at the coffee.

"He does now."

"You told him the other night?" Genevieve asks at the same time Khloe asks, "Why wouldn't you want him to know?"

You blink at Khloe in disbelief.

"I just." You shrug and shake your head. "I feel different now. And I don't want...I didn't want him to know."

"How do you feel different?" Khloe pushes.

"I don't know, Khloe, but I do."

The words sound angry, even to you. Pain flashes over Khloe's face, but she doesn't cower away from you with hurt feelings. You sigh, relieved you will not have to spend time smoothing ruffled feathers.

"We don't know, Dee," Genevieve reminds you. "We want to help. But we don't know what you need."

Genevieve's gentle reminder floors you with shame. You lower your gaze to the coffee again and hunch your shoulders defensively.

"I feel…" You lick your lips, and though you know you are going to cry, you make yourself finish your thought. "Broken."

Both of them look miserable, and you remind yourself they are miserable because they care about you.

"Damaged."

"You're so strong—"

You cut Khloe off with a fierce look. "I don't know how to be strong. I don't know how to get out of my head. To put it behind me."

"What did Ben say?"

You rub your eyes for a few moments, but when you lift your head, you cast your gaze around the room. Nothing has changed. The purple lights on the Halloween tree still twinkle. Dean Martin sings again. There's a small crowd up by the counter, waiting to order. The smell of coffee is bold and heavy in the air.

You gag on the memory.

"He's so angry," you whisper. "And so helpless. He punched a hole in the storage room Sunday night. Jordan told me."

That had been hell. Jordan, at your doorway to tell you goodnight. Jordan—usually joking and smiling—shifting nervously from foot to foot, afraid to ask you. Afraid not to.

Mumbling that he'd seen Dad put his fist through the wall in the storage room next to the furnace.

You hated lying to him. You hate the lie you told. You and Ben have fought through the years. You've fought passionately. You've packed your bag a time or two with the intention of leaving—at least for a while—and always, he's asked you to stay. As you would, if Ben stood at the back door with a bag in hand, intending to leave you. You have never truly wanted to be separate from him.

But you lied and told Jordan you and Ben had had an awful fight. You assured him everything would be okay. Possibly another lie to placate him after the first.

"Do you know who it was?" Genevieve asks you.

"No."

They watch you without comment for a moment, and you know both of them have that same need to know that Ben did. Some people might need to know out of curiosity. Some of your friends who aren't as close to you as Gen and Khloe might need to know so they could claim your tragedy as their own and rush in to be your rescue.

Ben, Genevieve, and Khloe are your family. They want nothing more than to put you back together for your sake.

As pure as their motivation is, their questions are still not totally welcome. No one can put you back together. If you will ever be the same Delilah Nicholson again, you have to be the one to piece yourself back together.

Khloe glances at her watch, and you rub your eyes again and then smooth your hands back over your messy hair.

"Do you need to go?" you ask hopefully, because if she says yes, you can swallow the story of the hotel room and the next time you see them, you can pretend to be over it.

"No. Naya has a play date after school today."

You nod and draw a deep breath. With their eyes on

you, and your eyes on your coffee—because you can't watch pity and relief (it wasn't them, after all), as much as they care, you would assume there is an element of separation for them—paint their faces, you tell them what happened in Aspen.

CHAPTER 7

*M*atthew refills your tea glass, but he's careful not to get too close to you when he sets it on the table. He and Ben went shopping today after school. Ben had asked again if you might like to go, but you begged off. Though you've ventured out of the master suite—even met your friends for coffee—the boys still think you are sick, maybe just beginning to recover. You've pushed your pasta around your plate enough that it looks like you've eaten, but you barely touched it, and the look Ben gives you says he noticed.

You've lost weight, and your jeans are loose on your waist, but you've explained to him that you have no appetite. You haven't been able to look Matthew in the eye tonight, because you are sick inside that you didn't go with him to find something for homecoming. Ben even took him to the florist to look at corsages for Alli, and you are touched because it's sweet and a bit old-fashioned.

Most likely, Matthew can't discern the guilt you feel tonight from the shame you've felt since you were in Aspen, so the fact that you've barely looked at him probably doesn't register. Which adds to the nasty emotional cocktail fizzing in your belly.

"Show me your suit," you say now, and you avoid Ben's eyes. When he'd pressed the matter this morning, reminded you that time flies and you will regret missing out on the shopping spree, you'd put him off until finally you had come unglued and ripped at him with verbal fangs and claws. Probably, the boys heard you when you screamed—shrill and harsh—to back the hell off.

Ben's crestfallen look had been an arrow in your heart, and you'd caved and you cried. Always the crying, when before you had so much more control.

"I can't, Ben," you finally whispered, eyes squeezed closed. "I can't do it."

"He's your son, Dee. He would never judge you."

You didn't argue that point, but you lifted your chin and stared at him boldly and told him you couldn't possibly browse the men's department. That you didn't want to deal with any man in any store, whether he was as polite as God or as treacherous as the devil himself.

His resolve had collapsed in on itself then. He had reached for you, but the thought of a big bear hug from a man who only wanted to protect you was too much, too heavy. You'd backed away and watched him silently until he gave up on that, too.

Matthew hurries out of the kitchen with as much dignity as a high school senior excited about his home-coming date can have. You ignore the pointed look Ben gives you across the table and listen to Jordan tell you about his world history assignment.

Ben wants you to tell the boys what happened. Not the details. But he thinks they deserve a bleached version of the truth. You're not ready even to have that argument with Ben, so you simply ignore him when he mentions it.

On Tuesday, when he drew the bath for you and then came back with the flowers Khloe sent, you finally showed him the bruises. Or rather, you didn't hide them. You had lounged back in the tub, your stomach a ball of barbed wire, and closed your eyes. He had set the flowers—a beautiful fall arrangement that had touched you and then enraged you, because it brought to mind funerals and you didn't want to die anymore—on the counter.

He was sock footed, but you could still hear him moving over the tiled floor. He'd started to walk out and leave you alone, but you knew the moment he stopped. You knew the moment he'd looked at you and seen the damage, because he'd gasped out loud in pain.

Somehow—you're still not sure where you found the courage—you'd opened your eyes to meet his gaze.

"Delilah, baby, I'm so sorry." His broken whisper was sincere. You'd nodded in response, but there was nothing you could say. Ben sank to his knees beside the tub and reached for your hand. For several long, silent moments, he held your hand and you cried. Together.

Your eyes fly up over Ben's face when Matthew returns with his suit. It's that new trendy royal navy, and you know your son will be incredibly handsome. He shows you the new white dress shirt and the blue tie with thin copper lines in it.

"What color is Alli's dress?" you ask with a nod of approval. Matthew stands in front of you, the suit hanging from his outstretched hand.

"It's that color," he says and points at the copper in the tie. "She said she thinks this will work."

"Was she with you?" You can't hide your surprise, and more importantly, you can't hide the jab of pain, jealousy that Alli—a high school kid—might have been part of what is your job, your experience with your son. Ben is watching you. You swallow the words—*yes, dammit, Ben, you were right. I regret it already.*

You stood at the front window earlier today watching for them to come home. But you stood to the side, where you were hidden by the burgundy curtains, as if someone outside might see you. Before, you cried at simple things: happy endings, death, a particularly harsh argument with Ben. Now you cry at everything, and tears slid over your face as you watched the sun light a crisp, fall afternoon.

When Matthew was a freshman, he went to home-coming with a bunch of his buddies. Ben had teased him about getting a date, but you were ridiculously happy that your son was living life and doing the things kids should do. You made an afternoon of it, shopping for a new suit and burgers and fries once your mission was accomplished. The guys had hammed it up for their group photos, and you and Ben had been there with the other parents, and you'd spent the evening around a bonfire, sipping hot chocolate spiked with Bailey's Irish Crème, hunched into your LL Bean winter jacket, your brown and red plaid scarf soft around your neck. When the boys came back from the dance, Matthew's ruddy cheeks were red with exertion, and he was sweaty, his tie loosened around his neck. He'd danced, he said, though not with any girls.

You and Ben had gone home alone—Jordan was at a friend's house—and made love as if you were the teenagers, newly and crazy in love.

"No," Matthew says now. "Alli didn't go. But she texted me a picture of her dress, and I sent a picture of the tie."

You can't look at him or Ben as relief rolls over you in waves. You want to like Alli, and you wouldn't. If she was there shopping with Matthew when you weren't, you wouldn't like her. As stupid, as childish as that is, it's true.

Your cheeks burn with shame. It's familiar by now, and you wonder if you could just wear the shame as your blush.

"Can I see the picture?" You clear your throat. "Of her dress?"

"Yeah." Matthew shrugs and nods.

"He looks good in the suit," Ben tells you, and you glance at him.

"Did you get a picture?"

When you shop with Matthew, you always snap a quick picture of him when he's trying the suit on. He grumbles, but you do it for memories, and you also send it to Ben—who is either at the office or sometimes out of town. Ben always responds with a smiley face emoji.

"No." Ben winces. "I'm sorry."

"It's okay," you mumble, but a small part of you wonders if he didn't take a picture on purpose. If it's his way of reminding you of what you're missing since you're holding back from your family. You have a flash of memory of the way Ben had caved and come undone just the other night when he saw the dark marks on your neck and the bruise between your breasts.

He loves you. He wouldn't hurt you just to prove a point.

He hadn't looked. Once he saw the bruises and held your hand while he cried with you, he ducked his head, climbed to his feet, and left you alone in the bathroom. Alone and relieved. But a little bit lonely, too.

You know Ben won't hurt you. But you can't imagine ever feeling comfortable enough to be intimate with him again.

Desire is gone. Your body feels nothing when you think about the things you used to do with your husband. If anything, the thought of Ben's hands on your body, his penis inside you is repulsive, and you can't tell him that, because no matter that he saw the bruises, he only saw them on your skin. He can't possibly understand how deep, how permanent they feel. If you said what you think when you remember making love with him, you would hurt him.

As his wife, you can't do that. You don't want to hurt the man you love.

Loved.

Afraid that if you look at him now, Ben will see the doubt, the confusion in your eyes, you rest your elbow on the table and cover your eyes with your hand. You've been up most of the day, out of bed, though you lounged on the couch most of the afternoon. Khloe texted you several times, but after the first few, you stopped responding. You don't give a damn about workout routines and the file folder she dropped in her office or that she took Naya to pick out her Halloween costume.

Realizing that you didn't care enough to ask what costume she chose made you sad, and you'd dropped your phone to the floor and turned your face to the back of the couch and slept. And when you'd slept so much, you were wide awake, you squeezed your eyes closed anyway, and ignored everything.

Everything.

Even Jordan when he came home from the bus stop and lingered in the kitchen to grab a snack. Of course he wanted to talk; both boys have always been chatty after school. Matthew has always tended to tell you about something his religion or history class discussed, but Jordan usually laughs his way through a story about somebody laughing so hard in the cafeteria that they end up snorting their chocolate milk.

But Jordan had given up when you didn't lift your head or greet him.

You've lost weight, but the guilt you carry now and

maybe forever more than makes up for it. What if one day nothing fits, because you're so bloated with all of these feelings? What if you can't swallow or can't breathe and you suffocate after all—

"Do you think the tie works?"

When Matthew speaks to you, you clear your throat and lift your head to look at him. He holds his phone out to you, so you take it—careful not to touch him when you do—and study the picture. The dress hangs from a door— presumably Alli's bedroom door and for a second you're paralyzed with the fear that Matthew has been inside her room, maybe inside *her* and if they break up, if Alli chooses she could point her finger at your son and say he forced her to do things she didn't want to do—and it's pretty, but it's hard to tell what a dress—or a suit—will look like when it's on a hanger.

"Yeah," you answer with a slow nod. You're not sure you would have gone for copper with all that red hair, but again, it's hard to imagine it on Alli and maybe she looks beautiful in it. "You guys are gonna look great."

"Evan's parents are having a big dinner for everyone before the dance. In the barn."

Was that the new way a girl could assault a boy? Pointing the finger and making untrue accusations? Did every male on the planet have the capability to throw a woman down and take what he wanted? Was your son like that?

"Sounds like fun, Matthew," you mumble, but your heart's not in it, and your sons are smart and perceptive, and they know something is so wrong. And yet, you're helpless to do anything about it. You're helpless to feel better, to get over it, so that you can get back to being their mom.

"You and Dad are invited," Matthew says, and your

eyelids are so heavy, they close and you don't want to open them again. Not today.

"Like, to take pictures," Matthew continues, "but you know, to stay for dinner. And the bonfire."

The word brings to mind that first homecoming when you and Ben had come home alone. You're powerless to stop the way you glance at your husband, but you can't hold the stare, because it's too intimate. You feel raw and exposed, knowing he's remembering that night, too.

You lower your gaze to the table. Matthew and Ben are watching you, but Jordan is fiddling with his fork. His plate is clean, but he hasn't moved. You wonder if there's more. Ben picked up dinner on the way home; you've not cooked since before you went to Aspen. Food tastes like sand to you, so you don't see the point. Everyone in your house knows how to fix basic meals, so you don't care.

Or, at least, that's what you tell yourself.

"Will you come?"

The word *come* makes you flinch, because you think of the hotel room, and the look on the stranger's face as he came inside your body. Another reason you're not sure you can make love to Ben ever again. You don't want to watch his face and see someone else.

"To the dinner?" Matthew pushes, and you rub your forehead and remind yourself to breathe. "All the other parents are going. Max and Mel will be there."

Max and Mel Sutton are good friends of yours. Their son Trevor is one of Matthew's best friends. You and Mel —short for Melodie—used to be room mothers together when the boys were smaller. Max is a hunter, and he's always trying to talk Ben into going deer hunting with him. You love them both, or you used to, and you've shared some crazy times with them, and that's what comes to mind right now.

You can't imagine hanging with them now, and you really can't fathom leaving the house again. Ben insisted you get out yesterday and meet Genevieve and Khloe for coffee. He reminded you that they love you, and they're concerned, and you were sick of Ben pushing it at you, so you went.

But now you've told your story. Your husband and your two closest girlfriends know the damaging truth, and you never have to talk about it again. As far as you're concerned, you never have to walk outside again.

"Matthew." You dig your thumbs into your eye sockets and press hard enough to see kaleidoscopes of colors.

"Of course we'll go," Ben tells Matthew, and you're sort of relieved that he spoke for you and sort of angry, too.

"Are you guys getting divorced?" Jordan speaks up for the first time in a few minutes, and his out of the blue question renders you speechless. Rather than look at him, rather than reassure him everything is okay, you close your eyes and cover your mouth.

"No."

Ben's steel voice leaves no room for doubt, but even you understand your son's fear. You've never shattered like this; you've never been such a mess, and you guess your sons have told their friends that something is wrong. Kids talk. Both boys have friends whose parents are divorced, and maybe they've said this is how it starts.

You remember that just two nights ago, you suggested to Ben that he find someone else. You can live here until your dying day, but you can't promise Ben that things will ever be the way they used to be.

Maybe this *is* how it starts.

"Right." Jordan throws down the word defiantly. You open your eyes in time to watch him push his chair back.

The sharp bark of the legs of the chair on the floor makes you jump. "You both suck."

He throws down his napkin as he stands to leave the table. You glance at Ben helplessly.

"Sit down. Now."

You want Ben to handle this, but you aren't sure this is the right way. The iron-fist, because-I-said-so method works in certain situations, but maybe it's not right for what's going on right now.

Jordan drops back into the chair and sprawls his legs out in front of him. He stares at the table with a fierce frown, all teen angst, mad at the world.

"We're not getting divorced," you say quietly. Jordan flicks a quick glance at you, but he looks back at his plate. Matthew is still hovering near you, but not close enough to touch.

"You're not sick." Jordan says it hatefully, and the heart you thought was dead breaks a little.

"Guys, Mom's going through something right now." Ben takes charge, and while you want to let him handle it, you bristle at his words. *Going through something.* Going through something could be that you're having a bad period. That you're dealing with insomnia. That you're just feeling blue, because sometimes you do just have a few blue days, and then you're back on your feet. Going through something could be that you and Ben are fighting, could be that someone cheated, could be that you lost a big account at work.

Going through something sort of belittles the hell out of the real truth, and you hold your breath, struggling to decide if Ben meant to do that or if he's just trying to downplay the truth for your sons' sakes.

He's angry about what happened to you, and he's angry that he can't retaliate. Angry with himself that he didn't protect you, which is stupid, because you're a grown woman, and you don't expect or want to be protected every hour of every day.

He's sorry for what happened.

But if he thinks being raped is *just something you're going through*, maybe he's no different than any other man in the world. And he's supposed to be the man who loves you. The man who will fight every demon there is to save you, to bring you back to yourself.

If being raped is just *something you're going through*, it sounds like something you did to yourself. Like it's your fault.

You desperately want to confront him. To ask him if he really believes that. That rape is like throwing your back out and if you tend to it lovingly and use a heating pad and get lots of rest, you'll be fine. Good as new in a few weeks. Maybe he thinks the trauma you feel is all in your head, as in made up, not emotional and mental anguish. You want your boys to know this isn't *something you're going through*.

You open your mouth, but the words don't come. When you sob out loud, all three of them look at you expectantly.

"Mom?" Matthew sounds like he's five and he's frightened because you just broke a nail and cussed in front of him.

"I'm not *going through something*," you argue, but your voice wavers and you sound scared and small, and you hate that about yourself. "Something is wrong, yes. But it's not your dad. And it's not our relationship."

From the corner of your eye, because you refuse to look at him, you see Ben's brow furrow a bit.

"I'm sorry, guys." You sniffle and shake your head. "I'm sorry. I want to get better, but I don't know. If I can."

"Delilah—"

"I promise you." You stand on trembling legs. Touch Matthew's shoulder and then play with Jordan's hair. "I promise you both Dad and I are okay."

Okay.

You were careful with your words. Okay is just sort of a promise that things won't be terrible.

CHAPTER 8

*Y*ou caved on Saturday afternoon and promised Matthew that you would go to Evan's house for homecoming pictures and dinner and the bonfire. In the three days since then, you've stewed over how to break that promise. You had no intention of going; you'd given in to the guilt that presses down on your shoulders and makes you smaller. Maybe you were afraid that guilt coupled with the memories of the thing that happened would make you so small, no one—especially your boys—would ever see you again. Maybe it was the way Jordan has watched you since the night he asked if you and Ben were going to divorce. He's been moody and quiet; his gaze has been sharp and suspicious.

You sleep a lot, but because of Jordan, you are learning to act. Before this is over—and you have no idea if it will ever be over or if you will just become a permanent liar— you could win an Oscar. If you had had that award in Aspen, you could have swung it at your attacker's face and saved yourself. The thought has given you pause more than once since it first crossed your mind.

Are you capable of violence? Inflicting harm on a man to protect yourself? You'd tried, but if you'd had a gun— something more certain to hurt him—could you have pulled the trigger? If someone was threatening your sons, you would point and shoot without thought. Even if someone was threatening Ben, you would shoot. So why is it so hard, so bad to believe you could shoot to save yourself?

Over the weekend, you ventured out to the patio to placate the guys. Ben had started a fire in the pit, and he had brought you blankets and laid them over your lap where you curled up in the lounge chair. Matthew brought you hot chocolate, but Jordan played hard to get and avoided you most of the day.

You tried to read for a while, but you couldn't focus. You never finished the Kate Carley book, and you had no interest in starting anything else. Maybe it feels like a dare. Maybe reading fiction is inviting crazy things into your life. You'd rolled your eyes at yourself and collapsed back against the chair. The trees in the back offered brilliant oranges and yellows and reds, and the sigh of the wind through the rainbow was peaceful.

When Ben came out to check on you later, when he asked what you were thinking about, you lied. Instead of admitting that you were wondering if the man who attacked you was married, if he had a family, you said you were thinking about when the boys were still small enough to trick-or-treat. You willingly put your hand in his when he reached for you, but he had only given you a gentle squeeze and then left you alone again.

Rather than read and to get your mind off the man— what would he say to his children, if he had any—you surfed the Internet on your iPad. Your keywords were *assault* and *healing*. You read stories of women being beaten and raped and left for dead, and you felt guilty for wallowing in self-pity when it could have been worse. You read stories of women who were drugged at bars and date raped, and you read stories about women whose husbands or partners raped and battered them.

When you turned the iPad off—the battery at 29% and your heart drained to nothing—you felt worse. You almost laughed out loud at the thought that a support group could help you. If you opened your mouth surrounded by women like this, would they laugh you out of the room? Tell you to get a manicure to fix that broken nail and deal with it?

The time outside exhausted you, and you slept in on Sunday. Again. You missed mass again. You don't tell Ben or the boys, but you don't care. You're not sure God exists or that he listens, because God wouldn't let bad things happen. And maybe, you're referring to the other girls and women it's happened to rather than yourself.

Your sleep is riddled with dreams, and so when you climb out of bed later—Ben has checked on you no less than five times—you're in a bad place in your head. You jump at the smallest of sounds: the freezer dumping ice from the icemaker, Jordan's shout when the Bears score a touchdown, the ring of the landline. It's Khloe on the phone, and when you shake your head at Ben, Jordan notices.

So Monday, you make yourself climb out of bed to see the boys off to school. Ben was supposed to go out of town this week. Two days in Des Moines. He cancelled because he worries about you. He had promised you it wasn't a big deal that he missed the meeting, so you tell yourself not to let it bother you.

You fix pancakes and eggs for them, and Matthew and Ben thank you with sweet, sincere smiles. Jordan—your baby—mumbles a thanks that sounds defiant and angry. He eyes your pajamas and robe with disgust, and more of that heart you thought was dead breaks.

It's not fair, you want to say. You're trying. You'll never go fast enough for Jordan, but you're trying. Ben sees the way you wipe your eyes after the boys leave for school. He steps closer to you with the natural urge to hold you, comfort you, but you shake your head and move away from him.

When he leaves, you go back to bed. You had intended to clean the kitchen. To shower and dress before the boys are back home. But you don't make it in time. You don't sleep, so much as doze here and there, only to jerk awake each time you think you hear something. You should have set the house alarm, but you don't move to do it now.

Ben fixes dinner, and you join your family in the kitchen for grilled chicken and salads. You skip the pota-toes, but you usually do. Jordan ignores you, but Matthew keeps talking to you about school and the dance and the after party. A zing of terror shoots through you at the thought of an after party. There'll be alcohol there. You know it. And Matthew is a senior. You're not sure what kind of supervision there'll be, and you worry about what could happen.

After dinner, you desperately want to go back to bed. You're not sleepy, but you're tired of pretending things are normal. Especially when the lack of normal is so obvious. You—and what you're *going through*—have become the elephant in the room. The stares—all of them: angry, curi-ous, concerned—are heavy and unwanted and exhausting. And this is just your family, in your own home.

Because of those stares, because knowing your baby is so angry at you is like a toothache, you power up your laptop and pretend to work a bit while the boys clean the kitchen. Maybe slipping your reading glasses on with your robe and pajamas makes you look a little less than a mess and so Jordan will forgive you a little.

You and Ben are not fighting, and you want to point that out to Jordan. *Look,* you want to say. *Look, here's proof. There's not going to be a divorce. We're not fighting. We're getting along fine.* But it's deeper than that. You and Ben have always been demonstrative. In fact, the boys often groan and roll their eyes when they catch you snuggling on the couch or kissing in the kitchen. You're a touchy-feely mom, and you've always been the kind of mom who demands hugs and steals them when they aren't immediately delivered.

Since Aspen, you've been none of those things. You shy away from any physical contact. It's obvious to you what happened—you feel like you wear a scarlet letter on your chest. But your boys go through their days, eyes on you, as if they are trying to solve the mystery.

"Delilah," Ben says when you are in bed later, "you have to tell them something."

You know he's right, but you can't tell them anything, and you can't tell Ben you know he's right, because then he'll push you.

"I see Dr. Ambern again on Friday," you tell him, and it's the day before Matthew's homecoming dance. Even if you somehow got out of bed Friday morning feeling ready to leave the house again—you haven't, not since you met Genevieve and Khloe for coffee last Wednesday—seeing Dr. Ambern and reliving the whole damned thing again will suck the energy and the determination from your heart.

He sighs, but he doesn't say anything. He's waiting. He wants you to need him, but you don't want to need him. You need to find your strength, and if you continue to lean on him, if you continue to hide, you'll always be less than the woman you used to be.

"Will you go with me?"

Tears slide over your face and into your hair.

"Of course."

A mix of relief and self-hatred washes over you. You turn to your side, facing away from him, and close your eyes. The sheets aren't fresh, and the bed is not welcoming, and you hate the man who did this to you.

You hate the woman you've become.

In the morning, you get up with Ben. You make coffee, and you turn on the oven waiting for him to finish in the shower. You'll bake biscuits—canned, but then you were never a baker before, so you cut yourself some slack there —for breakfast. When you hear the shower shut off, you give Ben another ten minutes. He's at least partially dressed—trousers and undershirt—when you carry a cup in and sip from it.

"What're you doing up?" he asks with a small smile. "You can sleep in for a bit."

Your eyes meet his in the mirror, but you look away quickly because you both know you don't need more sleep. Your bed has become your fortress and your prison.

"Jordy hates me, Ben."

You hadn't planned on saying that. It's been in your head, your heart, worming its way around inside you like a parasite, but you hadn't planned to say it to Ben. He's a man, and he thinks when you talk about something bothering you, you need him to fix it. When maybe, you simply need him to listen. It hurts you that Jordan looks at you the way he does, but Ben can't fix it.

"Honey. He doesn't understand what's going on."

"Me neither," you whisper. Tears course over your cheeks again, and you swipe angrily to dry them. "I don't, either. I don't get why, Ben. Why did this have to happen?"

"I don't know." His voice breaks, and he turns to you, his face contorted with pain. "I would take it all away from you if I could, Dee."

"But you can't," you insist. You set your cup on the counter and rub your eyes. "You don't understand that you can't take it away. You can't do anything to make this better. To make it go away. To make it hurt less."

"I do know that—"

"Everything is different now. Everything." You push your hair back from your face and study him with a mix of hunger and regret. "I'm scared. The other day on the patio was terrifying. I did it for Jordan, but it was horrible. I don't even know if I can walk into the grocery store again. I'm afraid that he knows who I am, and that he'll find me and do it again. And I'm afraid that he didn't know me, that it was just random."

You swallow hard and lick your lips. Ben stares at you; anguish makes his eyes dark and fierce.

"If it was random," you continue, "who's to say it won't happen again?"

"Delilah." He groans and drops his head back, blinking to fight his own tears.

"I'm scared that my sons will hate me. They do hate me. I look at them, and I'm scared of them. What if they did this to someone? What if Alli teases Matthew, and he pushes her to—"

"That's not gonna happen." Ben cuts you off with a stern look.

You shrug. "How do you know? How? Don't you think every parent thinks they're doing it right? It still happens."

This time, you sniffle and rub the tip of your nose. "It still happens, Ben."

"So does good stuff," he reminds you. "Good things. Good people."

"I'm not gonna have anything good left," you whisper. "I'm so scared of losing you and the boys. I can't do this, I can't heal fast enough to hold onto you."

"I'm not going anywhere." He reaches for you, but as if he remembers suddenly that you don't want his comfort, he drops his hand to his side and stares at you wistfully. "Ever. I am not going anywhere, Delilah."

"I want you to hold me." Your heart—the one that died but still breaks—falls so hard and fast inside you that it steals your breath away. You gasp and sob and take a step toward him. "I miss you, Ben."

He nods, but he doesn't move.

"I miss you, too, Dee."

Heart in your throat now, you slide a baby step toward him and lift your hand to him.

"I know you won't hurt me," you whisper. "But I know you won't ever understand this, either."

"You can let me try," he reminds you as he takes your hand.

He waits you out, waits for you to move. To protect you? Or because you've pushed him away one time too many? His body is still hot from his shower. You move in close to him, press against him and wish his warmth would take away your chill. He's hard and soft in all the right places, your body pressed to his side. He's safety and strength, and he's loving and soft when he slowly circles his arms around you and rubs his chin over your head.

For long, silent moments, you stand with him. Whether you're waiting for everything to feel better or maybe worse, you can't say. He doesn't press you to move, to hurry along.

"I love you." Your words are barely more than a whisper. "I know I haven't said that in so long. But I do."

"I love you, too." He kisses your forehead, and something breaks inside you. You press harder to him and smooth your hands up over his back. Ben hugs you back cautiously, as if you are a mad dog that he might frighten away.

He hasn't shaved yet, but he smells clean and fresh. His skin is soft and warm. You're a long way from better, but you have forever, you hope. Nerves trace a chill up your spine, but you press your lips to his cheek as you back away.

"Wait for me," you whisper.

"Always."

You nod and step back from him. Nothing feels better, though, because as much as you want Ben to wait for you, you don't know what tomorrow will bring let alone a week or month or year.

"What about the boys?" His voice is gruff, the words quiet and uncertain.

Your gaze flies to meet his, but he's looking down at the floor. You have socks on, but you curl your toes in reflexively to hide from him. He kneads the back of his neck with his right hand.

"No."

"Delilah, you have to tell them—"

"I can't sit down with two teenage boys and say I was raped. Every time I hear that word, every time I think it, I want to vomit. I don't want them to think that. I don't want them to worry—"

"You don't want them to think of you that way. As an object. A victim."

"No." You shake your head when you meet his eyes. "I don't. Is there something wrong with that?"

"They're not just two teenage boys." He sighs, irritated with you. In the pockets of your robe, you fist your hands to hold onto the tender moment that seems more like your imagination now. "They are your sons. They love you. You are the one making them strangers. You're the one who's going to make them see you differently."

Ben's words are like knives under your fingernails. What if they're true? What if he's right? And it's your fault?

"When you said that the other day…" You breathe deeply and gear up to tell him how wrong what he said was. "When you told them I was going through something…"

He nods and shrugs, and maybe he doesn't mean to look indifferent, but to you, he does.

"I'm not going through something, Ben. That makes it sound like I'm having my period. It makes me sound weak and whiny. You made me feel like I'm being petulant. Like this is all my fault."

"It's not what I meant to do…I just…they need answers."

"But is that it? Is that what you think?"

"That it was your fault?" He frowns, and the indifference is now anger. "No. Of course not."

"But do you think there's an expiration date on this? Do you think it's okay for me to feel bad but when X days have come and gone, I should be through it?"

"Delilah."

"He barged into our room. I was in the nightgown I wore for you. He put his hands on me. My face. My neck. He put his penis inside me, Ben, and he moved until he got off." You rub your eyes again. "You can't possibly know what that did to me. You cannot know. You will never know what that did to me."

Ben huffs out another sigh, but you can't read the emotion on his face this time.

"If you can't get it, how are an eighteen-year-old and a fourteen-year-old going to understand it?" You wait for him to say something, but he's silent.

"They don't need to know the details." He moves after long moments of quiet; the exhaust fan hums in the background. "But they need to know you were assaulted. Give them…give us…the chance to support you. You want to heal—"

"You can't make this right." You shake your head. "None of you can make it right."

"Goddammit, Delilah, I know that. No, I don't know what it did to you, but I do know…as a man…that I would never violate a woman like that. And I love you, and Matthew and Jordan love you. And I'm not asking to be your hero. I'm asking you to let me and the boys love you and support you."

"It feels like you want to rescue me, and I don't want to be a damsel in distress."

"Then be a badass woman who fights back and wins. But Dee, let us have your back. Trust us to have your back."

CHAPTER 9

The first pregnancy test had come back negative, as you knew it would. But this time, you're nervous. Ben stands like a sentry behind the lab tech who draws your blood. You want to whisper to him to stand down, because the damage is done. On the other hand, you had cowered when a burly-looking guy held the elevator for you.

You wonder how much more of your confusion, your indecision Ben can take. You feel dangerously close to the end of your own rope, and you can't blame him for his impatience.

The two of you sit in Dr. Ambern's office, side by side. She asks how you're coping, and you shrug her off and say fine, and all the while, Ben gapes at you like you're suddenly speaking French. When she glances at him and then looks at you pointedly, you almost cry. Tears burn your eyes, but you bite your lip, determined not to sob out loud.

"Ben?" Dr. Ambern tips her head at him.

"She's agitated." His words are quiet and apologetic, but no less damning. "Up and down. More down."

"Understandably." Dr. Ambern nods. "Delilah, have you contacted a therapist?"

"No."

Your doctor's sigh is reminiscent of your husband's.

"Talk therapy can help you with the process."

Talk therapy is for weaker persons, you think, but you don't say it. Or maybe it's for people who suffered far worse than you did. Do.

"Are you sleeping?"

"Not at night," you admit.

"She sleeps all day."

"Ben."

You asked him to be with you because he wants to support you. Because maybe you recognize you need it. But now you feel like they are ganging up on you, and you want him to be on your side.

"Would you take something?"

You frown, not sure what she means.

"I can write you a prescription for an antidepressant," she offers. "Something for anxiety."

You want to say no. Taking drugs to be happy feels the same as being raped and being afraid. An external, unnatural force controlling you. You could self-medicate and clean the wine refrigerator out, but you haven't done that, either.

"Dee?" Ben reaches over the arm of your chair and touches your elbow. "What do you think? Will you try it?"

You say yes, but it's a little bit like the yes you gave Matthew about going to Evan's house tomorrow night to do homecoming pictures. You can say what they want to hear, but it doesn't mean you'll do it.

You're still not sure how you'll get out of the picture

thing tomorrow night, but you have to. You can't imagine standing around and rubbing elbows with people who will be rehashing tonight's homecoming football game or worrying about so'n'so's kid making out with that one boy or whether the kids would have preferred this beer over that. It's all meaningless, and some of it feels like promoting bad things, which makes you physically sick.

You drank when you were in high school. So did Ben. And you both turned out okay. You had sex the first time when you were nineteen, and Ben was seventeen his first time, and again, you both turned out okay. So maybe your worries about tomorrow night are silly. But you still can't get excited about going. You especially don't want to hang out with Max and Mel, because you don't feel crazy. You don't know what you'll do if Max grabs you for a bear hug or pats your ass the way he's done a hundred times through the years. It's always been fun and games, and Ben laughs and cozies up to Mel, and it's no big deal.

Except if Max touches you tomorrow night, it'll be a big deal. You don't want to lose your shit in front of Matthew and his friends and their parents. You won't forgive yourself if you embarrass your son.

Dr. Ambern scribbles something on her prescription pad and tears the paper off and hands it over the desk to you. You hesitate, but the weight of Ben's stare forces you to move, to take the paper. You feel smaller when you sit and hold it in your hands.

"Please think about seeing someone," Dr. Ambern says urgently. "Barry Holtman is excellent."

Your heart sort of throws a hitch at the mention of a man's name.

"He's a good therapist, Delilah," Dr. Ambern says when she sees what must be sheer panic on your face. "I also urge you to look into a support group."

"No." You ignore Ben's intense stare and shake your head.

"In case you change your mind," Dr. Ambern says as she writes something on another pad of paper. This one is plain, less official, and you have the unkind thought that maybe it's because this sort of treatment or therapy is witchcraft, and she can't be tied to that. You don't say it, though, because she's trying to help.

And Ben would be disappointed in you if you were vicious to someone other than him.

"There's a support group for sexual assault survivors that meets every other Thursday evening. Here in the clinic. First floor. Barry heads it up. It would do you good, Delilah."

Again, when she reaches over the desk to hand you the paper, you take it, but you don't comment. Dr. Ambern reiterates the purpose of the blood draw today and reminds you both how important it is to be safe, if you are intimate right now, because of the threat of HIV. Your eyes blur with tears as you zone out; Dr. Ambern's flowy script on the papers you hold wavers.

Does she really believe you could make love with Ben right now? The threat of HIV or any STDs aside, *could* you make love with Ben right now? You're not afraid of him. Not really. You've been with him so many times through all of the years together, you know each other's moves by heart. Sex has been sweet and tender, angry and fast, frantic and crazy. But never violent. You know he wouldn't hurt you.

But you're afraid of *something*. Flashbacks, maybe? Would you thrash at Ben? Try to hurt him as nothing more than reflex? Or are you afraid of feeling desire when you shouldn't after what happened? Feeling selfish for wanting that intimacy? Shame for thinking you can turn Ben on after what happened?

"Thank you, Dr. Ambern," you hear Ben say, and you swallow all of your thoughts and guilt. As you lift your face to offer them a brilliant fake smile, you blink away the tears. Neither of them buys your act, and you think you're damned if you do and damned if you don't.

Ben drives you home and then goes to work. Two days in a row now, you've showered and tried to dress in something less ghetto or even zombie-like. Yesterday, after you had that moment with Ben in the bathroom—when you let him hold you for a moment—you wore leggings and a cute light blue tunic. You twisted your hair up in a soft knot, and though it was messy, it didn't scream depressed. You didn't leave the house, and you didn't make any phone calls for work, but you did actually crack the laptop and do some ad design.

It felt meaningless to you. You didn't—and still don't—give a damn if Farrow Dentistry takes on any new patients, but you'd seen the flicker of joy in Jordan's eyes when he glanced at you after school. That one second was worth the effort, though when you went to bed last night, you were exhausted from holding yourself together all day just to give Jordan a moment of normalcy.

You had smiled at him and asked how his day was, but you didn't hear his mumbled answer, and he wasn't up for conversation. He had scurried through the kitchen and down the hall to his room like a mouse fleeing a barn cat. He's still put out with your breakdown, and the mom in you understands that.

The woman in you—the one wronged—doesn't.

When Ben leaves, you push up your sleeves—today you donned expensive jeans and a maroon sweater and you even put mascara on, though by now you might have cried it off—and dig in to the pantry. It looks like you've been absent for months, like a starving army invaded and plundered it, so you decide to clean. The mindless organization might be good for you.

Before you would have turned music on. You have eclectic tastes, and you will listen to almost anything. The day at the coffee shop in Aspen, the day before the incident, you were listening to something folksy and comfortable. You haven't played music at home since then. You're afraid it will distract you from any noises you need to hear.

You wonder, as you set a box of crackers on the counter, if you should get a dog. A German Shepherd, maybe, trained to guard your home.

A barking dog might warn you of danger, but it would probably make you pee your pants with fear.

Conceal and carry, maybe.

Again, you wonder if you could shoot to defend yourself.

Could you kill someone if you had to?

Do you wish him dead?

"Dee?" You jump and cut loose a desperate yelp when someone behind you says your name. The Pringles can in your hand hits the floor, and your heart pounds painfully hard in your chest.

"I'm sorry." Genevieve gushes with regret when you fall apart right in front of her. Slumped over the island counter, you rest your head on your arm and focus on your breathing.

You didn't hear her come in. You had assumed Ben set the alarm.

"It's okay." Your whispered words are a lie, and she

knows it. Khloe slips in behind her, and this time, you hear the quiet squeak of the door and the way it squeals and clicks when she closes it. "I thought Ben set the alarm."

"Can we stay for a while?" Khloe asks now. She hovers behind Genevieve, like she's afraid of you.

You don't want them here. You had to leave the house this morning. It wasn't just seeing Dr. Ambern. You had to walk into the clinic amidst so many other faces. Step onto an elevator with strangers. Sit in a waiting room full of women of all ages. Some pregnant. Some with partners. All of them glancing at you as one does when waiting for an appointment. No one stared at you; no one gawked and wondered if you were there because you're old and starting menopause. No one wondered if you had a mammogram today. No one suspected you were there for a follow-up after the initial visit because of sexual assault.

No one thought twice about you and who you were.

And you were still scared to be in public, afraid to be touched or judged.

If Ben hadn't gone with you, you might have cowered in the Highlander and never made it inside the sprawling four-story clinic.

As of right now, you haven't come up with an excuse to skip out on the homecoming stuff tomorrow night. The thought of going, of dressing like a human being and putting on makeup and hugging old friends and pretending to be normal scares the bloody hell out of you. You're already exhausted, and you have a good twenty-four hours before you're on stage.

You want Gen and Khloe to leave. If they did, you would slink out of the kitchen right now. Crackers and Pringles and pumpkin seeds and canned goods strewn all over the kitchen, you would crawl into bed and hide.

"Yeah." You shrug, because what if they get tired of

trying? Gen has sent baked goods and meals and soup over for you. Khloe sends flowers, and she texts you the silliest things that annoy you.

But they make you laugh.

Last night, she admitted she couldn't find her car in the grocery store parking lot, and even though you rolled your eyes—because you didn't care—you laughed softly as you put your phone down.

"I love you guys," you whisper as Gen swings two plastic bags obviously laden with some type of food up to set on the counter. Khloe carries two bottles of wine, which is silly, because you and Ben have more wine than you know what to do with. Both of them jerk in shock and turn to stare at you, wide-eyed and silent. It hurts you to see how badly you've hurt them by putting them off.

"You know that, right?" You can't look at them now. You can't make eye contact, so you stare hard at your thumb as you smooth a spot on the granite counter—your nails are still ragged and gross—and hate how uncomfortable this whole thing is for everyone.

"Dee." Gen's shoulders slump, and she tugs her hands from the handles of her bags. "We know."

"I just." You frown and shrug and glance at them. "I know I'm being impossible."

"You know we love you, right?" Khloe tilts her head and arches her eyebrows.

You nod and rub the corner of your eye.

"I never thought this would be so hard."

"Of course, it's hard—"

"No." You shake your head and lean against the counter. You fold your arms over your chest and try to find words to say what you mean. "Even after that. You thought it was Ben. I let you think it was Ben that hurt me, and he would never—"

"I didn't believe that."

"You did," you insist with a nod. "You did, Gen. And I let you, and God love you for being willing to love me and protect me, but he wouldn't hurt me like this. You know that, Genevieve."

She nods, but she doesn't speak.

"That killed him. That you would look at me and assume that."

"Delilah—"

"No, I know." You rush to reassure her. "I know. But I let you believe it for a second. I hurt him. I can't let him hold me. I don't want to be close to him. Jordan is angry. He thinks we're tiptoeing around a divorce. I can't tell them. I don't want my sons to look at me and see some stranger doing those things to my body. Ben doesn't get that—"

"Delilah."

Khloe touches your hand. You look down at her fingers on the back of your hand.

"It's okay." She licks her lips and says it again. "This is new for all of us. And it's...it's gotta be unbearable for you. And it's harder than hell for me and Gen to sit on the side and watch you hurt like this. But it's okay."

You take a deep breath and blow it out long and steady.

"I need help," you admit, and you feel a stab of guilt that you can say this to Khloe and Genevieve when just hours ago you denied it to Dr. Ambern and Ben.

"Well." Gen tried to laugh, but it sounded suspiciously like a cry. "You've got a fitness guru and a professional seamstress here on a house call. Khloe can get you in shape, and I'll sew you back together."

"I wish it was that easy."

Khloe moves and turns back to pick up one of the bottles from the counter behind her.

"How about a little of this?" She brandishes a bottle of Boone's Farm wine as if she is offering you Dom Perignon. If nothing else, it makes you smile.

"And I brought…" Gen reaches inside one of her bags and produces a plate of pumpkin and crème cheese cupcakes. You laugh and dab at your eyes again as she peels the Saran Wrap from the plate.

"They're still warm," you gush like a child finding a lollipop. "Oh my God, you guys."

"I have chocolate, too," Genevieve says as she pulls another plate from the other bag.

"I shut you out."

"Not gonna get rid of us that easy." Gen shrugs. "Khloe, get some glasses."

"Do we really have to drink that?" you ask with a shudder, but really, you can't wait for Khloe to pour the cheap wine, and you can't wait to sink your teeth into a cupcake. Genevieve's baking is superb, her pumpkin and cream cheese cupcakes your favorite.

"We used to get drunk on this stuff," Genevieve reminds you.

"In the good old days."

"No." Gen shakes her head. She turns her head and gives you that steely gaze that means business. "Those were good old days. Two weeks ago were good old days. We'll get there again, Delilah."

Before you know what you're doing, you reach for her. She holds you as desperately as you throw yourself at her. Her arms are tight around your back, and when she kisses your cheek you don't flinch.

"I hate this," you whisper.

"I love you," she answers. When she steps away, Khloe

hugs you, and you feel the same strength and comfort. You and Gen went to school together. You know secrets about her, some that matter, and others that don't. She knows all the same about you. You met Khloe just a few years ago after a spin class. She was young and scattered and chasing a toddling Naya around the fitness studio.

You picked her little girl up and told Khloe to go work out. You sat inside the Pilates studio where Khloe could see you reading to her baby, playing with her toys. You had recognized her desperate, frazzled look as one you wore when your boys were smaller.

Two weeks later, she was working as a fitness instructor as a second job because her ex had stiffed her with Naya and no money. You never offered cash, because you knew it would insult her and you had so much more to give with time and love through the years.

"I'm sorry, Khloe," you say to her, and it crosses your mind that you're still not getting it right. One step forward with your friends, but you still haven't made nice with your husband or your sons.

CHAPTER 10

*M*atthew looks so grown-up and so handsome in his suit that it moves you to tears. At least these tears are explainable and normal. It hits you as he stands in a line with six other guys and seven girls that he is a senior, and this moment—the crisp fall night and the turning leaves and the suits and ties and the girls in home-coming dresses—will never come again for him or for you. You bite your lip to keep from crying over that, because Ben had told you so, and it chafes that he was right.

Alli is pretty. The dress is gorgeous. But it makes your stomach hurt. She wears open-toed shoes with stiletto heels, and the dress is skimpy. Her smooth, pale thighs beg for attention, and the neckline is nonexistent. The material is cut deep, and she can't be wearing a bra, and Matthew has been treated to sneak peeks at her small, proud breasts already tonight. You know because you have, too. Everyone here has, and you wonder how her parents—how her dad—can let her walk around like that.

Then again, most of the girls here tonight look like they're years older in experience than the boys. They're all gorgeous, and they all look ready to walk the runway, and you want to ask them what the hell they're thinking. How can they be comfortable showing so much skin? For one thing, it's chilly already, and it'll only get cooler as the night goes on.

Ben stands close to you as you take pictures, and you wonder what he's thinking. What are all the grown men thinking about these young girls strutting around in tiny dresses? You dressed sexy—or you wanted to—when you were their age, but that was a long time ago, and sexy then was different. While you wanted to be flirty, you wanted attention, you would have been embarrassed to dress this way.

Some of the boys are leering at their dates, and you try to be sly and watch Matthew. He looks completely smitten with Alli, but he's not grabbing her ass or intentionally staring every time she leans over a bit too far. Still, touching her breasts will be as easy as putting his arm around her. You wonder again if they're having sex, and when the thought horrifies you, you wonder if it would have bothered you so much just a few weeks ago.

Part of you wants to grab all of the girls and herd them inside and insist they cover up to protect themselves. But on the other hand, you wonder why that's fair to them. This is the style, and while you don't love it, you understand that girls want to be in style. Girls want to be pretty and fun and flirty. None of them should have to cover up if these dresses are what they choose to wear.

When your head starts pounding, you hand Ben your phone—you've cleared the private pictures off of it—to take the rest of the pictures. All around you, there's happy chatter and music playing from speakers artfully hidden behind huge pots of mums. You've known this group of people for years, but right now, you are hundreds of miles away. What were you wearing when you were at the coffee shop? The day before the incident in your room, what did you wear to the coffee shop to work?

Well, you certainly weren't wearing a dress that barely skimmed your thighs. You wore jeans and a sweater. Skinny jeans, tucked into heeled boots. A sweater with a cowl neck. For warmth. For style. Are you supposed to apologize for that? If you had been wearing a skimpy dress and that man had spotted you there while you sipped your coffee and tapped away on your keyboard, did that mean you were to blame?

Did you do something to ask for it?

No.

You didn't.

"Dee." Ben's fingers slide over your back in such a light touch, you barely feel it through your jacket. You glance at him, your eyes move over his face, but you don't see him.

"I can't breathe." You shake your head.

"It's okay."

No one can hear him. People are everywhere around you, but you and Ben hold that intimate eye contact that you've had for years. Before you can nod or argue or move, someone snatches you from behind, and you gasp in surprise. You see your panic mirrored on Ben's face, but Max's voice in your ear is at least familiar.

"Where the hell have you been, Delilah Nicholson?" He growls and kisses your neck as he has many times before. You tense in his arms, but you stare at Ben with big eyes. By the time Max turns you around to hug you for real, you've schooled your features into a mask of calm, but your heart is thudding in your chest.

"Hey." You give him a quick hug and step back from him as soon as he loosens his hold on you. You need Ben to rescue you, but at the moment, his arms are full of Mel.

You watch for a second as his hands slide over her back, and you're thinking that he hasn't had sex in weeks, not since that night in Colorado, and you wonder if his body is responding to Mel. You've never been jealous of the hugs and friendly kisses between them, but tonight, it doesn't feel right.

You turn your attention back to Max, though his intense stare makes you just as uncomfortable as watching your husband hug another woman.

"What's going on?" Max still wears that big, friendly smile. "You guys haven't been to any games this year."

You cast a quick glance at the kids, some of them still preening for pictures, and look back at Max. This is why you didn't want to come. You can't tell them why you haven't wanted to get out of the house. But you can't fool them with lies, either.

"Hey, Dee." Mel slides away from Ben and hugs you. Max and Ben do the bro shake and slap on the back as Mel kisses your cheek hello. "What's been going on? Trev said you've been sick."

You swallow hard and flash an insincere smile.

"I have." The lie is like sand in your mouth, and you wish you had a drink. Anything to wet your throat and make the words slip out easier.

"Are you okay?" Mel drops the bubbly attitude and gives you a careful stare. "Anything I can do?"

You open your mouth to answer her, to assure her you're fine. That lie sticks. You appreciate her offer to help. But you don't want to get involved in this conversation. Definitely not here, and probably not ever with Mel and Max.

"Thanks," you say quietly, but you shake your head and tone down the smile to be more believable. Mel studies your face for a moment, as if she's trying to decide what she's going to say, and you hold your breath waiting for her to ask you something personal. The two of you have discussed a few personal issues, but you are not close to her like you are to Gen and Khloe, and if she asks something you can't answer, you will feel violated.

Again.

"Hey. What the hell is with these dresses?" Max's voice cuts into the private moment between you and Mel. And though you're still stranded, and you just want to go home, you're relieved when Mel looks away, toward the kids. "Never seen so much ass at a high school dance."

You cringe at the crass comment, but you keep your mouth closed.

"I bet somebody ends up pregnant tonight," Mel agrees with a nod.

This time you do react. You curl inward a bit, like Mel sucker punched you. You could be pregnant right now. You could be carrying a stranger's baby. It's not likely, but a month ago, you would have said being raped by a stranger in a swanky hotel room wasn't likely.

Ben moves close to you and stands at your back. All the times before when he's done that, at a bonfire or a football or soccer game, you've been grateful to him for blocking the wind. Tonight, you think of that moment the other morning in the bathroom when he said he had your back.

"Here's what I love," Mel says. "They dress like that. On purpose. And whip our boys into a hormonal frenzy. And then when the boys get handsy, they cry rape. I'd bet money that happens sometime tonight, too."

You flinch again. Because you worry about that, too. You worry that Matthew might put his arm around Alli. His fingers have nowhere to go but inside her dress, where he will technically be touching the curve of her breast. You worry that after the dance, they will make out, and in the morning, if Alli decides she doesn't like Matthew or they get in a fight, she might point the finger at him and say he forced himself on her.

As a woman, you would want to believe her. How could you not believe her after what you've gone through?

As Matthew's mother, you would hate her. Blame her. Want to hurt her.

This day and age, everything kids do has the potential to come back in the years that come and hurt them.

Ruin them.

You huff out a deep breath and lean into Ben.

And then there's the possibility...if Matthew and Alli do make out, what if he misreads her? What if she thinks she wants to have sex, but she's uncertain, and Matthew coaxes her into it?

You know without a doubt he wouldn't pin her down and force her. Nor would he ply her with enough alcohol to get her drunk and take advantage of her. But what if she teases him and entices him and changes her mind, and Matthew thinks he changes it back?

"You hungry?" Ben's voice is soft as he slips his arms around you and clasps his hands over your belly. There's nothing sexual in the gesture. He's trying to protect you from your thoughts.

"No." Your voice throbs with a sarcastic laugh. "God, no."

"Let's get a drink."

You nod, and Ben tells Max and Mel that you're going to grab dinner. They nod, and say they'll catch up to you in a minute, and then Ben takes your hand and leads you away from them.

"I shouldn't have come," you whisper.

"Babe, did you see Matthew tonight? Watching you? Yes, you had to be here. He needed you to be here."

You nod, because you did see him. You have noticed the way your son keeps checking to make sure you're still here.

"I'm a mess." You stand with your back to the group of parents in the barn, where a big dinner buffet is spread over several tables.

"We'll go as soon as they leave for the dance."

Your eyes meet Ben's. "Thank you."

"Delilah?"

"Hmm?"

Ben leans into you and presses his lips to your ear so everyone around you will think he's just kissing you.

"I talked to him. About this."

"Me?" Your heart hits the floor so hard, you cry out in pain.

"No. About Alli. About that dress."

You squeeze your eyes closed, because you can't remember when you went from worrying about scraped knees and bike wrecks to date rape and teen pregnancy.

"Okay."

"He knows how to handle himself."

You stare at Ben silently, eyebrows arched in disbelief. You're more worried about how he'll handle Alli, but you don't say it. You don't have to.

"Are they having sex?"

"He says no."

You nod and try to breathe. You wish the kids would leave, head to the dance and whatever comes after, just to get the night over with.

Just to get this moment over with.

"No means no," Ben says quietly.

"Maybe that's not enough."

"Babe, he knows. He's a smart kid. He's not gonna do something stupid."

"She might as well be naked."

There's not a lot more to Alli's dress than there was to the nighty you were wearing when you let the man into your room.

"Yeah. We talked about that. About what she was gonna look like in that dress."

"Okay." You nod. You have to let it go. You have to trust your husband. Your son.

Ben picks up a paper plate and fills it. He nods at the stack for you to do the same, but you can't. Seems like filling a soup bowl with a splash of chili or tossing a few chips on a plate would draw more attention than just not eating, so you simply hover near him while he gets his own dinner.

You sit at the end of a picnic table. Ben leaves you there to grab drinks. When he returns with two longneck bottles, you take one and twist the top off. The beer is so cold, the bottle hurts your fingers, so you set it down and pull your gloves from your pockets. Ben watches you put them on. There's something on his mind. You watch him warily as he wolfs down a brat.

"I hate it when he kisses you like that." He says it as he takes a drink from his own beer. You watch his Adam's apple bob as he swallows. You're pretty sure it's never bothered him before. Max has even laid kisses square over your mouth, and years ago, there was an accidental tongue touch in one of those kisses. You had all laughed, and then you'd laughed more when Mel had offered Ben a kiss of his own.

But you know what Ben means. Because even though none of it ever bothered you before, everything about it felt wrong tonight. It's one thing for Max to hug you. For Mel to launch herself at Ben for a quick hug. But Max had put his mouth on your neck tonight, and Ben's mouth has not been anywhere south of your face for weeks, and it bugs you that Max feels he has the right to touch you.

When Ben flicks his dark gaze to you, you lower your eyes to his hands.

"Me, too."

"We never just all announced it was okay to hang on each other's spouses," Ben continues. "So why do we do that? Why do we allow it?"

You lick your lips and huddle closer to him. You're chilled to the bone by the damp weather and the bizarre events in your life.

"Are you attracted to her? To Mel?"

"No." Ben's answer is so simple and so honest, you don't doubt him.

"I want to want you again, Ben." Chin tucked to your chest, you look at him sideways. "I'm sorry I can't yet."

"Delilah—" He starts, but Matthew calls for you, and you both turn as he approaches, Alli trailing, but their hands clasped together.

"We're taking off," he says, and you nod and smile, and look at everything but his date. She's cold; not only do you see her shivering, you can see her small, hard nipples clearly through her dress.

"Have fun," you say quietly.

"Thanks for coming, Mom." Matthew leans over to drop a kiss on the top of your head. You wish there was time to go over this again, the whole don't drink and drive, don't do drugs, safe sex talk. But there isn't, and Alli watches you with big eyes. You remember that not too long ago, she saw you go to pieces in your kitchen, and you feel even more exposed than she is.

"Be careful." Ben gives Matthew a nod and a stern look, and Matthew ducks his head and nods and mumbles a goodbye to Ben. You watch them walk away, toward the limo Evan's parents rented for the group, and you pray that whatever you have failed at, parenting is at least your one success.

The house is unnaturally still when you and Ben get home. Jordan—as usual—is at his friend's house. Homecoming in grade school means nothing, except that there are sleep-overs with junk food and video games when the older siblings go to the dance. You unzip your coat and flinch at the sound it makes. Ben flips on the decorative lights that hang over the island counter, and your eyes catch on the empty Boones Farm wine bottle by the sink.

"Was I ever that skinny?" you ask Ben with a sharp laugh. It's not funny; you're not amused. But you need to talk, to dispel the silence, and to brush off the sick feelings you have after seeing the flesh on display earlier. Tonight was an orgy of teenage hormones, and you suppose it's normal. The same way it was normal when you were younger.

It's just that times have changed, and you haven't.

Well.

Times are edgier, and society pushes the envelope.

And maybe you have changed. Maybe you've taken a step back from that electric life. Because it burned you once, and now you're afraid.

"Lots of bony shoulders and ribs," Ben mumbles.

You shrug out of your coat and toss it absently over the counter.

"Lots of nipples, Ben." You stand before him at a loss for something to say. For something to feel.

"You were skinny." He gives you a cheeky grin. "But you had some nice curves."

"Had?" You cock your head and sort of smile.

You're trying. God, you are trying to be lighthearted.

"Still do." Ben touches your cheek. Traces his fingertip over your skin.

Both of you are thinking about the night of Matthew's first homecoming. The night you unzipped Ben's jeans before you made it inside the house. You can't do it now. As sad as that memory makes you, you can't imagine unzipping Ben's jeans and reaching to touch him.

"She's right, ya know." You shrug. You stand in the kitchen in a five thousand square foot home, with only an inch between you. But you can't move. You don't want to back away, but you can't close the last inch. "Mel. Someone could get pregnant tonight. Someone's gonna push—"

"Won't be Matthew," Ben insists. "You have to let him go, Delilah. This is part of growing up. He has to learn to think when he's in a situation like that."

You nod. Of course, Ben's right.

"I know." You close your eyes when Ben cups your face in his hand. His thumb caresses your lips soft as a feather. You bite your lip when you remember the man in your hotel room snatching your chin in his fingers and forcing you to look at him. "I know. But it's hard."

"It is," Ben agrees.

"Ben, what if I'm pregnant?"

"Dee, you know it's not likely. You've been on the pill for years."

"But what if I am? What then?"

"What do you want?"

"I can't have…" You shake your head frantically. "I can't have a baby from that."

"I don't want you to." He strokes his thumb over your

lips again, and this time you feel a flutter of desire in your chest and your belly.

"You would want me to abort it?"

He breathes through his nose, and his nostrils flare and then he sighs. "Yes. But…"

"But what?"

You would never have considered an abortion before. You're pro-life. But now you wonder. What would you do? How could you possibly carry a child that he planted inside you?

But how could you just get rid of a baby?

Could you shoot someone to defend yourself?

"Dee, I will support you. Whatever happens. I don't want to raise a kid that comes from a man who raped my wife." His eyes are drawn to your lips. "But…I will. If you want to have it. Because it would be your baby, too."

Your breath whooshes out in relief. If you are pregnant, you won't raise it. But Ben's words, Ben's generous heart is your undoing.

You don't know who moves first, but suddenly his thumb is gone from your lips. He lifts his other hand to cup the other side of your face, and his thumbs frame your mouth. His kiss is soft and sweet, just the press of his closed lips over yours.

You scream inside your head; you need him to back off. But you remember to breathe, and you smell Ben's subtle cologne, and you move slightly. Your lips brush his. His lips are thin, but they're soft. The rub of your sensitive skin over his makes your fingers tingle. You flex them but squeeze them into fists, because you can't touch him.

"I love you." His words slide over your mouth, and his breath is warm and familiar. You're holding your breath again, but you remind yourself that his hands are on your face, and though your mouths are touching, he hasn't moved. He hasn't tried to pull you closer. You feel that tingle in your fingers again when your lips touch his and you feel the rough stubble on his chin, and he likes it, too, because he rubs your lips yet again in a chaste kiss.

"Do you blame me for this?" you whisper against his mouth.

"No."

"Sometimes women can—"

"No."

Your raise your hands and rest your hands flat on his solid chest. He doesn't react.

"The girls tonight were dressed—"

"In the styles that are available to them," Ben finishes for you. "A little provocative, yes. But it's what they had to choose from. Maybe pop culture is partly to blame for the way the world is now."

"What if he was watching me? I worked in that coffee shop, and I didn't pay a bit of attention to anything—"

"It was broad daylight. You were in a public place surrounded by other people." Ben flexes his thumbs now, and they tickle your skin. "Stop, Delilah. It's not your fault. I don't blame you."

"Genevieve left her cupcakes here," you say after a few moments of intense silence. "Want one?"

The slow grin that crosses his face tugs at your heart, and you share a quiet laugh.

"I do." He nods.

But neither of you move, and then you're kissing again. His lips caress yours patiently. Wanting just a little more of him, you open your mouth and wait. His fingers slide back into your hair, but he still doesn't pull you close. He gives you the space you need. Eyes on his, you drag your teeth gently over his lower lip and moan softly when he does the same to you.

It feels new to kiss him like this, so deliberately aware of the texture of his skin and the stubble on his chin and the slow, easy nip of his teeth on your lip. When you part your lips more, your tongue just touches his, and the warm, velvety slide is still patient and tender. You think of making love with him, and how sometimes, it's like this, and desire unfurls in your belly.

But this is nice.

Just this.

You've always loved kissing Ben, but you wonder now if the two of you forgot how to do it the right way. The way that makes your toes curl and your heart sing. These soft, open-mouthed kisses bring tears to your eyes, just because it's sad that it took something so tragic to slow the two of you down.

"Do you want a glass of wine?" He draws back just enough to look into your eyes. "With your cupcake?"

"I do." You grin and nod. But Ben tips his head and presses his forehead to yours. "You're my world, Delilah."

You nod and move your hands from his chest to cover his over your face.

"I do love you." You can barely get the words out, but he hears you. Another second passes, and then he kisses your forehead and backs away from you. Your heart is galloping in your chest, but this time, it's desire, and as you watch him reach for a bottle of wine from the counter rack —this one is not Boones Farm—you fight a wave of panic and self-loathing.

There's nothing wrong with wanting to be with your husband.

He hands you a glass of the cab and watches you sip from it.

"Genevieve gets brownie points for these," he announces as he sets his own glass down and reaches for the plate of chocolate cupcakes. You would prefer to eat pumpkin and cream cheese, but Ben is wild about the chocolate ones, so you will share one with him.

"I wonder how Christian isn't fat and round." You laugh as Ben holds the treat up for you to take a bite of it.

"Have you seen his racquetball game?" Ben tips his head and arches his eyebrows as you bite into the chocolate and then lick your lips to make sure you got all the frosting. "That's how he's not fat and round."

You stand together in the dimly lit room, and he gives you another bite of the cupcake and then pops the last bite in his mouth. You watch him chew and then swallow a drink of wine. He lifts his hand and rubs his thumb over your mouth again. Your lips are sensitive from the kissing a few minutes ago, and you feel that little jolt of desire again.

"Ben."

"Hmm?"

"I need to get some help." A little bit ashamed to say it, you duck your head to avoid his eyes. Ben tilts your chin up and flicks your lip again with his thumb.

"Frosting." His voice is thick with emotion. He licks his thumb and looks you in the eyes. "Please, Delilah. Do it. For yourself."

CHAPTER 11

*E*ven though you were finally able to admit to Ben that you need professional help to heal from what happened, it takes you days to actually take the first step. You're working from home, and you've conducted a few business calls, but you're not rocking much fashion beyond leggings and tunics and the messy bun. Some days, you only do that much about ten minutes before Jordan gets home from school, and you do it only to placate him.

He talks to you more these days, but his anger is still there. You know if you scratched the surface, he would explode and bring it at you, so you tiptoe around him and stop just short of bending over backwards to please him.

Matthew's homecoming experience was apparently okay. He told you that he and Alli danced a lot. There was an after party back at the barn, but Matthew had no additional comments about it, so you are left to your own wicked imagination. He and Alli are officially dating now, so things must have been good. Three people were picked up for underage drinking and driving, and you listen without comment as Ben uses those arrests as teaching moments for both of your sons.

Your first step is not calling Barry Holtman, as Dr. Ambern urged you to. Nor is it filling the prescription for the antidepressant. You're not ready for that. Instead, late in the evenings, when the boys have gone to their rooms if not to bed, you curl up in the corner of the couch when Ben is sprawled out in the recliner watching TV, and you read the informational pamphlets Dr. Ambern gave you. You read them more than once, and you tell yourself you have to digest the information, although you know that the next step—in any direction—terrifies you.

It seems that one of the most important steps in recovering, in finding strength and healing, is saying out loud that you were assaulted. You lift your eyes from the paper in your hands, because you don't want to admit that to anyone. Saying it the few times you have has been huge and exhausting.

It's not that you need to tell everyone, because it's your business.

But the people who love you should know so they can be supportive. Your parents are across the country; your mom lives in Texas with her husband, and your dad is in South Carolina, twice divorced. You have no intention of telling them. Nor would you ever call your brother and say those words to him.

But maybe your sons should know.

Still, it feels wrong to consider telling them. In fact, the thought makes your skin crawl. The very idea of sitting them down and telling them that you were assaulted makes you throw up in your mouth. Young boys don't need any sexual images of their mothers in their heads, especially something that involves violence. And you worry, too, because kids do talk.

What if they're upset and confused about what you tell them, and they share it with their friends? You don't want all of Holy Trinity Junior and Senior High to be discussing what happened. Matthew might be a senior, but Jordan has another four years there. Besides that, talk can cross school lines and all of Springdale could know what happened to you within twenty-four hours.

All because you laid something much too dark and heavy on your sons' shoulders, and you expected them to be mature enough to handle it.

At the very least, you need to be able to say it to yourself and believe it. You need to be able to look in the mirror and say out loud that you were assaulted. You were raped, and it's not your fault.

Tall orders, you decide, and you pile the pamphlets together and tell Ben goodnight.

When Jordan comes home from school on Wednesday, you are studying the clinic's layout in the yellow pages of your phone book. Maybe Dr. Ambern is right. You still haven't filled the prescription, but you've made the decision to see a counselor. The problem is you can't get past the idea that the counselor your doctor recommended is a man, so for the past hour, you have studied the yellow pages looking for other options.

There are several counselors and therapists listed. There are three psychiatrists listed. There are both male and female names, but the more you've studied the names, the less certain you've become about the idea. You've tried to picture yourself sitting across the desk from a woman and talking to her. A well-dressed, professional woman.

The thought makes you as anxious as thinking of speaking to Barry Holtman.

The issue, you think as you close the phone book and sneak a glance at Jordan, is that you don't want to talk to a stranger. You can't fathom sitting and telling a stranger about a stranger barging into your hotel room and shoving you back on the bed and raping you, because you wouldn't be able to read a stranger's reaction. A calculated, professional-mask would remain that way whether that person believed you or not. Whether he or she pitied you, whether he or she truly wanted to help you overcome something tragic in your life.

But you can't talk to someone you know well, either. Ben will remind you of that.

"How was your day?"

You watch Jordan as he slinks around the kitchen putting together a snack. He seems to be debating an apple or nachos. Maybe the apple would be the healthier choice, but at the moment, you think a plate of nachos sounds better.

"Fine." He shrugs his bony shoulders, back to you, as he finally reaches for a plate. You notice his long, slender fingers as he sets the plate on the counter and picks up the bag of tortilla chips he has already taken from the pantry. He's grown again lately, but you aren't sure when it happened. His soccer season is in the spring, but he works out with some of his teammates now, during the off-season. You watch the flex and bunch of his biceps as he moves and wonder how strong he is.

What if that guy had hit you? Beat you? What if he had blackened your eyes and broken your jaw?

An uncontrollable shiver climbs your spine, and you breathe deeply to ward off the panic. Jordan has given so little, barely acknowledged that you're trying to get back to normal. The littlest things you've done have been so over-whelming, it hardly seems fair that he is still sullen and angry.

He jerks his chin toward the door when Matthew comes in.

"Hi, Mom." Matthew flashes you a smile, and you have never favored one son over the other, but at this moment, you're grateful for Matthew's love when Jordan seems so intent on denying his.

"Hey." You swallow the sharp edges of panic and put the phone book back in the drawer where it was.

"Dude." Jordan eyes Matthew as he puts his plate of chips and cheese in the microwave. "What's up with Trevor, man?"

Jordan's tone is a little bit harsh and a little incredulous, but it's Matthew's reaction that has you curious. You watch them silently, hoping maybe they will forget you are standing there. Matthew sets his backpack on the counter and shoots daggers at Jordan with his eyes. But you're his mother, and you notice the way his shoulders have tensed up, as if he's in fight-or-flight mode.

"It's not true," he mumbles. You wonder what isn't true, because Matthew sounds angry. What's going on with Trevor? You haven't talked to Max and Mel since the night of homecoming. You haven't *thought* about Max and Mel since that night, because you have mixed feelings about seeing them and that makes you feel guilty. No, you aren't as close to Mel as you are to Gen and Khloe, but you are friends, and you feel badly because you blew her off last weekend. While you and Gen go back to the days when you were in school together, you and Mel go back to the years when your boys were very small, and you raised them together. The time Mel kept Matthew all weekend for you because Jordan had an emergency appendectomy comes to mind now. Maybe you could have kept Matthew at home with you, but Ben had been gone that Friday afternoon when Jordan had called you from school. In a panic, you asked Mel for help. She hadn't missed a beat, offered to pick Matthew up and take him home for the weekend.

So, you clammed up when Max bear hugged you and nuzzled your neck. In your head, you know that's because of your current state of mind. Never before have either one of them made you feel funny. With a deep, calming breath, you wonder if you should call her. Feel her out and make sure she's not feeling the other end of your guilt. Make sure everything's okay. You can buy yourself some time before you have to think about her again.

A glance at the cordless phone across the room makes your palms sweat. Too soon. You're not ready to socialize, but you do know you have a limited time to hide out before people start asking what's going on with you. Before your friends decide they don't have time to worry and move on.

Jordan takes the plate from the microwave now and half drops and half throws it to the island. He blows on his fingertips as he shoots Matthew a funny look. Disbelief? Humor?

"Micah Oenning says it's true." Jordan raises his eyebrows. "And Lanie Stotts."

"It's not true." Matthew lunges at Jordan and shoves him up against the counter at his back.

"Whoa, whoa, guys."

Normally, you would get right in the middle of them. Put a hand on each of their shoulders and gently push them back. They fight but not often. When they were little boys, when Matthew was in kindergarten and Jordan was a toddler, Matthew wouldn't think twice about smacking his little brother or knocking him over. As he got older, he seemed to realize there was too much difference in their size. Maybe he worried that he might hurt Jordan.

It occurs to you now, as you cower at the island, that Jordan has filled out enough that he could hold his own in a fistfight with Matthew. Chills climb your arms and legs, and you smooth your hands over your long-sleeves now before the chills can sink into your spine and take over.

Just across the room, Matthew leans into Jordan, the threat of true anger evident on his young face. Jordan stares at him innocently, and in the back of your mind, you think Jordan is goading him.

You wouldn't cry out. When the man threw you down on the bed, and then he warned you to be quiet, you had wanted to scream for help. You wanted to cry. But you wouldn't give him the power, and you bit your tongue to keep your mouth shut.

But you fought him.

In the aftermath, you forgot the way you kicked and thrashed on the bed as he took what he wanted.

"Don't be a dick, Jordan," Matthew says now. "You know it's not true."

You don't often come down on the boys for their language. They don't say much in front of you or Ben, but you're not naïve, and you assume boys still say terribly inappropriate things to each other in the absence of adults. Just as they did when you and Ben were younger.

Just as you and your friends did when you were kids.

It's not even that Matthew chose the word *dick*, and the images the word brings. You didn't see it, thank God. In case there was a chance of seeing his erection before he drove it inside you, you had squeezed your eyes closed and twisted your face as far to the left as you could. When he was done and he pulled out of you, you had immediately curled to the left, crying eyes closed. Not to get away from the sight of his limp penis, but because you were dying.

Because you wanted to die. To close your eyes and shove everything away.

But you feel like you're supposed to say something now. To Matthew for manhandling Jordan and calling him a dick. Not because you think if you give this inch here, either of the boys will take a foot there and start throwing the f-bomb around. But because it's your duty, and Jordan surely will call you on it if you aren't doing what he thinks you are supposed to be doing.

"Guys." You stay at the island, because your head is a jumbled mess of images and emotions. Bruised skin and heart. The guy's leather coat. The way he shrugged it off, as if he had all the time in the world to hurt you. The pressure of his hand over your mouth, his fingers pinching into your skin and down into your bones, as he told you to be quiet. The unwanted penetration. You don't want to get close to your sons while they fight. They won't hurt you; they've never thrown a punch once you've stepped in. If you walked over there right now, they would huff and puff with testosterone and rage, and then they would slink off and burn off the anger somewhere else. An hour later they would be back in the kitchen talking about basketball scores.

You don't want to get close to them now because your body is hard with tension, and your brain keeps telling you there's danger in this room. Danger means you need to protect yourself. Danger means you fight so you don't get hurt. Your brain keeps telling you to fight back faster this time, because you sure fucked up the self-defense last time.

"Matthew, get away from your brother right now." Your hoarse voice carries over the island, and finally,

Matthew backs away from Jordan. If looks were lethal, however, Matthew could kill him.

Jordan rolls his shoulders like an indignant jock in an old 80s movie. The jock who just had a scuffle with the not-so-tough hero of the movie who ends up getting the girl. You watch your son pick up the plate and sidestep Matthew to get out of the room, his face drawn in a mean, unforgiving frown.

Matthew turns to you when he's gone, and the unguarded fear on his face is a knife in your heart. Something is wrong.

Something is wrong with your son.

And you can't fix it. You can't comfort him. You can't do anything. Because you can't move.

"He didn't do it, Mom."

You watch Matthew's lips move, and you hear his voice. But you can't process what he's saying. Jordan? Is Matthew talking about Jordan?

"What?"

He did do it. Someone shoved his way into your hotel room and threw you down on the bed and raped you. It's been nearly three weeks. Even if you went back there—the thought melts your bones with terror and you slump back to the barstool—and talked to hotel management and reported it to the police, nothing would come of it. Except more torture for you. No arrest will be made, because you don't know who the man is. You don't know if he was a local or a tourist or someone there on business. You don't know if he was a guest at the hotel where you were staying or if he just wandered through, looking for a victim. You have no names, no pictures. No rape kit. No DNA. Nothing.

Hotel management could tell you it was just a figment of your imagination. Or maybe anyone you spoke with—

any hotel employee or anyone with the police department there—would suggest that it might have happened just as you described it, but that maybe it was your fault. Maybe you had already had a tryst with this guy, and maybe what happened in your room that morning was a case of mixed signals or you leading him on and then changing your mind.

Either way, that part of your story ended in Aspen.

The rest of it is up to you. The healing and the recovery and getting on with life.

"We were all right there. Nothing happened."

"What happened?"

"Nothing!" Matthew snaps at you. You don't recoil at the energy or rage in his voice. You're still miles away in your head, and even though you're remembering the soft silvery gray comforter on the bed and the slate tile floor beneath your toes and the feel of the stranger's cold zipper teeth scraping up your leg and inner thigh, you don't feel that flash of fear. Not the one that whips over you in an almost consistent pattern like the lights of an emergency vehicle. And not the bigger, sharper one that seems to grab you by the neck and squeeze so hard you think you will suffocate. Your head hurts right now. A dull thud in the base of your skull. You sat down well over an hour ago to choose a counselor to get this ridiculous process started, and your thinking time has been hijacked, and you stare at Matthew wishing he could offer you a way out of your head.

"I don't know what's going on." You shrug and tuck the loose curls behind your ears. Maybe the clip that holds your hair is making your head throb. You reach back and take it out and shake your hair loose. Ben loves it when you do that, especially when the two of you are alone. He says it's sexy, but you feel tired and worn, and you press your fingertips to the puffy skin under your eyes and wait for Matthew to speak again.

"Sophia Marten told everyone at school that she made out with Trevor at the after party."

This is important. Matthew is truly upset, so it's important that you pull yourself together for a minute to listen to him. You have to be present for this conversation. No letting your mind wander to Ben and the way you used to make love. No letting bad memories yank you away from your safe, cozy kitchen. No crying, because you've been selfish and needy with the tears, and your son is looking to you for strength.

You think back to the homecoming pictures. The group shots. The seven boys. Seven girls. The niggling feeling you'd had that night that there could be trouble. Too much bare skin. Too much testosterone.

Homecoming.

Even the word is heavy with expectations. The parents all preening over how gorgeous their kids are. The perfect tie choice and the snazzy suspenders. The stilettos and the heavy makeup. You as parents dress them up like miniature adults. How can you not expect trouble?

You didn't have sex after either homecoming you went to, junior or senior year. But you remember drinking like a fish and cussing like a sailor, all to impress your date. Your stomach sours when you remember that you didn't have sex, but he did slide his hand under your dress, between your legs. Maybe he thought he knew what he was doing, but you didn't feel anything good. In fact, it kind of hurt. He expected a blowjob. Probably, if the party hadn't been busted by your friend's parents, you would have done it.

"I thought Trevor was dating Becca."

The last time you saw Trevor before homecoming—the night before you left for Colorado—he was dating Becca

Cunningham. And had been since the first day of their sophomore year. When he was here that night—if only you could rewind time and go back to that night—he and Matthew were talking about colleges. Becca plans to attend the University of Illinois, and Trevor has been accepted at three universities, all a long drive from Champagne, Illinois. You left the room, because you thought the guys wanted to talk. Trevor seemed upset about losing Becca if they went to different schools.

"He is."

"Then who's Sophie Marten?"

"Sophia," Matthew corrects you. "She's a sophomore—"

"Why was there a sophomore girl at your party?"

Matthew gives you an exaggerated shrug. "There was a group of them there. One of them likes Evan."

You take a deep breath. Matthew stands at the opposite end of the island counter. He rests his elbows on the counter and buries his face in his hands. While he's not looking, your eyes stray to the clock on the microwave. It's after four. Ben could be home around five, but Ben can work until midnight when he wants to. Thankfully, he's been more attentive to you and the boys and the house these last weeks, and he's been coming home earlier. Still. That leaves you with fifty-three minutes to be in charge and no desire to listen or talk to your son.

All of the thinking today has worn you out. The thinking about counseling. Reading the names in the yellow pages, over and over again. You turn your hands over now and notice the black on your left index finger. It's not from mascara or eyeliner, because you aren't wearing any. Has to be from the print on the page. You wonder if you've smeared ink on your face. Your eyes bounce from your left hand to your right, to the fingernail you've cut evenly and filed. But you still see it jagged and bleeding.

You're tired from thinking about counseling. The actual act of sitting in a chair and making eye contact with a stranger and relating cold, hard facts about what someone did to your body. You're tired from looking at your boys. You had planned to make dinner. You had big plans to make lasagna, and because you knew that wouldn't happen, you considered making a simple tater-tot casserole. Now even that seems too much.

You made your bed this morning. Sort of. You used to be obsessive about precise tucks and folds. But now, you can't bear to look at the bed, because it's the perfect back-drop for all of your regrets, whether your regret is the rape or all the times before it happened that Ben made love to you and you didn't appreciate it as if it was something special that you could lose one day.

It would be easy to tug the comforter and the top sheet back. Khloe thinks you are weird for using a top sheet. It's a waste of time, she always says with a laugh, whenever she happens to see you folding sheets or making a bed. Before you only rolled your eyes and shook your head and told her she was a hopeless kid. Now, you wonder if that top sheet is a small layer of protection from the monsters that lurk in your room or in hotel hallways or if it's something you could slide under and eventually use to strangle someone.

Or yourself.

Matthew catches you in a yawn. Embarrassed, you cover your mouth with your right hand. Earlier, before you started looking for counselors in the yellow pages, when you were staring at your laptop screen and getting zero work done, you had closed out the graphic you were designing—it's currently the letter R and nothing else and you don't care—and searched the Internet for information about antidepressants and anti-anxiety medications. The paper with the prescription Dr. Ambern wrote for you is in your purse. You haven't looked at it yet. It's tucked inside the paper with the notes she had written in her neat script about counseling and the group therapy session time and place. You have pulled your billfold and your phone and your Chapstick and your lotion from your bag, but you manage to ignore those papers every time you reach inside for something.

You don't know what medication she prescribed. But nothing you researched today is appealing to you. You don't want to become dependent on swallowing pills to get by. To get out of bed in the morning. It's not about the money or insurance. You just don't want to need it. It makes you feel weak.

The potential side effects listed scare the hell out of you. Nausea. Vomiting. Headaches. Dizziness. Sexual dysfunction. Trouble sleeping.

You've got it all anyway. Why would you take medication to add to those symptoms?

"So why is this girl saying this stuff?"

You ask because you need to hurry the conversation along. Your eyes are glassy from fatigue now. You hope Matthew doesn't notice.

"I dunno." He shakes his head in disgust. "I mean, her friend has a thing for—"

He said that already, right? That one of the sophomore girls had a crush on Evan?

"Did Evan do that? With a sophomore girl?"

Matthew rolls his eyes at you like it's a ridiculous question.

"Evan and five other guys were racing four-wheelers out in the fields all night."

"In the dark." You tip your head to clarify, but Matthew only nods.

Your stomach balks at the question of what Matthew and Alli did at the party, but you won't ask.

"Was Trevor with Becca?"

"For most of the night."

You can't quite swallow that and walk away, so you wait for Matthew to explain. He sighs and turns to the refrigerator as if he's decided he's hungry. You watch him open the door and check his options, but you wish he would get on with the damned story. Rumors and people who spread rumors make you angry, but you're too tired to be angry, and this one doesn't really concern you.

"What?" You finally prompt him, remind him you're waiting for him to continue. He chooses the hummus, closes the door, and then reaches for the tortilla chips Jordan left on the counter. "What does that mean?"

"Trevor was on the four-wheelers for a while."

Which means Matthew was, too. You arch your eyebrows expectantly.

"Becca and the girls were by the fire. They went to the bathroom. We were in the barn. I mean." Matthew shrugs helplessly. "It was just a party, Mom. Trevor didn't touch that girl."

You can't imagine that he did. For one thing, you know Trevor as well as you know your sons. For another, he's not stupid. He wouldn't mess around with someone else when his girlfriend of two and a half years was at the same party.

"Okay." You nod, hope your voice is soft and concerned, because it sounds dangerously flat and bored to you. "It's okay. The girl probably thinks Trev's cute. She wanted to go back to school and sound cool."

"She lied."

"I know." You nod again. "Give it a few days, and it'll all blow over. Something new will happen."

You stand for a moment and watch him the way you watch a grill to make sure it lights before you walk away. You need for him to be okay and go do his thing so you can do your thing, which is pull the comforter and top sheet back and slide into bed.

CHAPTER 12

By Friday, you still have not called to make an appointment with Barry Holtman. Or any other counselor. Ben asks each night when he gets home. Right after how was your day and right before that tired sigh. Wednesday was so bad, so hard, you didn't manage to climb out of bed yesterday until after noon. You were still in your pajamas and robe when Jordan came home from school. He had taken one look at you, and you noticed the sheer heartache in his eyes, and then he'd hidden it behind disgust and left you alone in the living room.

You pretended to be asleep on the couch when Matthew came home a little later. Ben hadn't bothered you, but you heard the three of them in the kitchen while they ate a crazy dinner of hamburgers, corn from the can, and freezer burnt oven fries. Jordan had refused to ask anything about you, about what was wrong, but Matthew had asked Ben if you were depressed. He asked if something had happened on the job, and Ben had stumbled his way through a vague answer that left you feeling guilty and stupid.

Today, you got up determined to be normal. To be
Jordan Nicholson's mom. But you cut yourself shaving
your legs, and the trickles of blood down your shin
reminded you of the blood on the wall in the hotel bathroom from your fingertip. Ben had already showered. He
was in the kitchen, but you cried under the showerhead, so
the tears were washed away. Just in case he would have
come back in for something.

Once out of the shower, you felt a little better. You took
a little extra time pampering yourself, and you insisted that
yes, your heart was in it. And it mattered that you rub
moisturizer over your legs and your stomach and your
neck. Your bruises are faded to an unbecoming sour apple
green. When you wore the tunics, you were careful to cover
the bruises with heavy makeup. Ben did a load of laundry
last night, so your black turtleneck was clean this morning.
You went heavy on the makeup in an attempt to look like
yourself, but when you inspected the finished product this
morning, you saw a ghoul in the mirror.

It fooled Jordan enough, though, when he came home
a while ago. When you asked how school was, he told you
he aced his science test. You didn't know he'd had a test,
but you fake your way through the conversation, and
judging from the twitch in his lips, you did okay. He didn't
bless you with a full smile, but it was something.

You're making lasagna for dinner, and after agonizing
over it for far too long, you pour yourself a glass of wine.
Genevieve calls you while you are mixing the eggs and
ricotta and salt and pepper. When she asks what you're
doing, you don't say making lasagna, just dinner. She does
it all from scratch, and you do yours from a box, and you
don't want to feel like a slacker. Not after all the work it
took you to get out of bed and look normal today.

She asks if you would like to go to lunch next week.

She and Khloe would like to see you. She lets that hang, waiting for you to make an excuse. They probably want to know how therapy is going, and the thought of telling them it's not going at all almost makes you say no. You don't love the idea of leaving the house, either.

"I'm not sure, Gen," you tell her. You want to say that right now it's hard to plan. That you never know how you will feel one day to the next, and if you know something is expected of you, you will spend every minute from now until that lunch happens worrying about it.

But if you tell her that, she'll remind you that you don't like surprises. You don't like for anyone to spring plans on you at the last minute. You never have, and now it's worse. You need time to prepare. You need to plaster on makeup to prepare to be seen, and you need time to prepare yourself mentally and emotionally, except you don't really have any idea how to do that.

She says okay, it's okay, but you feel that damned guilt settling in on you again. You used to laugh about it, the Catholic guilt you've carried since you were a kid. Now, though, you have the guilt, but you have doubts about the god you used to pray to, because you don't know why that god would allow such bad things to happen.

Far worse things have happened to far better people than you, but now that you sort of understand the crippling grief and fear that one morning in your life can bring you, the question has become personal to you. You can't pray when you doubt anyone is listening. Besides that, you don't know what to pray for. Healing? Revenge?

You've looked at websites that sell guns.

You wish you had the courage to get out of the house and sign up for a self-defense class.

You wish a lot of things, but you have no hope for them to come true.

Matthew doesn't come home tonight. He texted you earlier to ask if you care if he goes out with friends. You said it was fine, and you wondered—but you didn't ask—how Trevor was doing. Presumably, the rumor mill has moved on, or you think Matthew would have said something last night to Ben.

Could you have shot the man who raped you? If you had a gun that morning, would you have used it? If you had been anywhere else, if you'd been dressed in more than that slinky nightgown you wore for Ben, could you have fought harder? Kicked him in the balls hard enough to get away?

Ben has a meeting in New York next month. You were supposed to go with him, but when he broached the subject last weekend—he was tender and hesitant—you told him you have no intention of going. Your heart was in your throat as you watched him cancel your flight. Sitting at the island counter, sipping a cold beer, he had misread the panic on your face as sadness and promised you it was okay. The two of you could use the ticket on another trip; you could do a weekend getaway in California or Florida. The idea of a trip—the beeping as people scanned their boarding passes, the clicking of the keyboard as the clerk at the front desk of a hotel checked you in, the smell of coffee on the seventh floor of a hotel, a pristinely made king-sized bed—makes you shiver uncontrollably.

That was the point at which you confessed to Ben you needed help.

Another week has gone by, and you haven't reached out to anyone.

The only ray of sunlight is the fact that you are not pregnant by a monster.

Before Aspen, when Ben came home, he would stand behind you in the kitchen and press his chest, his middle close into your back. You would laugh, and when you threw your head to do that—to cut loose with the joy and love you felt inside—he would bury his face in the curve of your neck and kiss you there. Your face would go warm with the sweet and dirty words he would whisper to you then, and he would close his arms around your waist as a promise of what would come later.

Now, he tiptoes around his own kitchen, afraid to jar his fragile wife.

You hate being fragile. But each time you push yourself to be the old you, shame and terror scorch up your throat, and that hard rush of pain makes you gasp to breathe, and then Ben knows you're not okay. He knows you're still broken, and he just watches you from afar. And then that burning pain goes so cold inside you, you're numb.

"Hey."

You had jumped moments ago when you heard the door alarm beep, because you hadn't heard the garage door open. When you turn away from the sink, you find Ben standing at the island, in the same spot where Matthew had stood just the other night. Ben wears navy trousers today and a light blue shirt. His tie is navy with a lighter blue and white diamond pattern. The blue compliments his eyes, and you want to tell him that. You want to tell your husband that he looks good, but you're afraid to.

"Hi."

"What're you fixing?" His eyes twinkle, and he takes a step toward you, but he stops there. Strains to see the glass baking dish. Your heart hurts a little bit because he stopped. No, because he knew to stop. It's been almost a week since he's touched you—since those soft, intimate kisses you shared right here in the kitchen, right before the wine and Genevieve's cupcake. You want that back, that soft tender moment.

But you're afraid to ask.

There's no room for fear in a marriage. But there's no room for Ben inside you, not now, because of all of that damned fear.

"Lasagna," you answer, and the playful grin on his face makes you laugh softly.

"Oh, damn." He nods his approval. "That sounds good. I am so hungry."

"Me, too." You are hungry, which is sort of surprising. But you know, too, that by the time you sit down to eat dinner, the hunger will be gone, and you will feel full and miserable.

"Have an okay day?" His voice is gentle; he slides his hands into his pockets and studies your face.

"Yeah." You nod.

"Good day?" he suggests hopefully.

"Sort of," you answer. It's been an okay day. Quiet. You got some work done earlier. Dressed to make Jordan happy, you sat at the table with a cup of coffee, and you worked on the R you started on the other day. You finally finished a rough design for Ridley Electronics, and you don't love it. But you finished something.

Today that's what matters.

That and the hair and makeup and dinner for your husband and one of your kids.

"Talk to Gen today?" He leans back on the counter and crosses his ankles. The way he asks tells you he talked to Gen today, too.

"Yeah, she just called a few minutes ago," you tell him with a nod at the cordless phone. "She asked me to go to lunch with her and Khloe next week."

When he doesn't respond, you look at him and then back at the dish.

"I told her I wasn't sure, Ben." You choke the words out as you pick the dish up.

"Is that ready to go in?" He shifts out of the way of the oven and pulls the door open for you. "Gen said she called your cell twice, and you didn't answer."

You slide the dish onto the oven rack and then close the door. Part of you is irritated that they call each other now just to talk about you and your progress. Or maybe, your lack of progress. Part of you is grateful it still matters to them. They haven't given up on you yet.

"Oh." You look around the kitchen, but you don't see your cell. The memory of that shameful, lonely morning in the hotel bathroom—you taking pictures of your bruises with your phone, to document (for yourself and for Ben) what happened—nags at you. It makes your head hurt, but determined to be normal, you will the memory and the headache away. "I think my phone's in my purse."

In fact, last night, the battery was at twenty-three percent. Maybe by now it died. You forced yourself to work all day, which meant ignoring your phone. Your purse is in the bedroom, so even if the battery didn't die, you wouldn't have heard it vibrate when Gen called.

You swing your gaze back to Ben's, and you stare at him boldly, so he knows you aren't lying. You're ready to open your laptop to show him what you did today. But he just smiles and nods and then turns to pour himself a glass of wine.

When he leaves the kitchen, you turn your attention back to dinner. You mix a salad of baby spinach and tossed romaine. Add mozzarella cheese. And then you slice a loaf of bread to tuck in the oven. Eyes on the sharp blade of the bread knife—you're wondering again if you could use a weapon like this...except it's a bread knife, not a weapon...to defend yourself—you still just miss cutting your finger. A surge of adrenaline leaves you feeling breathless and weak in the knees.

Once you put the bread in the oven, you sip your wine and think about Ben in the bedroom. He's changing clothes, and he'll be back in a minute. But rather than wait for him, you set your glass down and hesitantly go looking for him.

Your heartbeat pounds in your fingertips, and just for this moment, your steps feel lighthearted, like you are dancing. That smile he'd left you with had rocked you, and you're sort of excited, like you want to slide into his arms and rub against him. But you're also nervous about it—not that Ben will push you and take advantage of your ten seconds of interest. But that you'll chicken out and only be able to stare at him as he pulls his jeans on and buttons them.

What if it's harder for Ben to wait when you think you want him and then you decide you don't? You don't want to tease him. You just want to talk yourself into loving your husband. You prop yourself in the doorway as he moves around in the closet. He's hanging his slacks now, already in jeans. When he turns and sees you there, your heart climbs up your throat and when you can't speak because it's in your mouth, you only smile. He grins as he unbuttons his shirt and shrugs out of it.

You hold your breath when he stands there—five feet away from you—in his undershirt. He'll leave it on, because the house feels cold. But you imagine him peeling it off over his head, and you imagine his smooth soft skin and the hard plane of his chest. The night before the thing in the hotel room, you had kissed him there. You had straddled him and dropped sweet, staccato kisses over his collarbone, and then hungry for him, you had pressed your open mouth to his chest and sucked his hard, flat nipples into your mouth.

You miss that. You're not sure you could ever do it again, but you miss that connection with him. The physical connection, but the mental connection, too. The sexual awareness that crackled around the two of you like lightning. As parents, you've always been able to fold it up and put it away and be responsible. But when you were alone together, or when you had plans to be alone together, every touch of your skin on his threw sparks and made you both want more.

He tosses his shirt in the dry-cleaning pile and then tugs on a long-sleeved thermal tee, the color of oatmeal, and even though it's not that blue that compliments his eyes, the color makes his eyes and dark hair pop. When he moseys across the room toward you, you suck in a quick breath, sink your teeth into your lip, and slide your hands in your pockets.

"You're so beautiful." He lifts his hand when he stands before you. You don't flinch when his fingertips brush over your cheek. "Do you know that?"

His voice is gruff with emotion, and you have that feeling again that your mouth is full of your heart and maybe sadness and love and wistfulness, so you can't speak. Instead, you lower your eyes to his lips and shake your head silently.

"The lasagna is going to be delicious." He drops his hand to his side. You hope it really will be good, and not just because it's been so long since you fixed dinner, since there was any sense of normalcy in the house.

"I hope so." Still overcome with emotion, your voice is no more than a whisper.

"Maybe we can watch a movie later?" Ben tilts his

head and shrugs a shoulder nonchalantly. You nod enthusiastically, because you want to spend the evening with Ben.

"Matthew's with the guys," you tell him. Ben nods and
steps closer to you.

"Jordan home?"

"Yeah."

"Did he notice?"

You want to argue, to tell Ben you didn't put all of this
effort into making your son happy. But he knows better.

"I don't know."

"Delilah," Ben says. He cups your chin, but he's careful
not to put pressure on your skin. His eyes are wide and
bold as he stares at you. "I know you're trying."

You lift your hand and curl your fingers around his
thick forearm.

"I haven't called anyone yet." The confession slips out,
and you flinch, waiting for him to get angry. On the other
hand, it's a relief to have said it, because it would have
nagged at you all evening if you hadn't.

"I wish you would." There's no trace of anger in his
face or his voice.

"I know." You squeeze his arm and let go. "I just…the
idea of telling a stranger…"

"Baby, the idea of telling someone you know is worse."

You lift your gaze to meet his and lick your lips. "It
would hurt you. It would make you angry—"

"Not at you."

"I know." You nod. "But you would be angry, and not
being able to do something for me, makes you feel helpless.
And…"

"What?" he whispers.

"How can you find anything about me sexy if you
know what he did to me?"

"I want you just as much right this second as I ever

have," he promises. "But I can wait. I can wait until you're ready."

"I don't deserve you."

"You would love me through the same," he reminds you.

You would. Yes, you would. But you can't imagine a scene in which Ben is physically harmed or violated, and that you are weaker and that it happened to you makes you angry.

The overhead light is on, and the room is anything but cozy at the moment. Dinner is in the oven. Jordan is in his room. Ben strokes his thumb over your lip and then slowly, he leans close enough to kiss you. It is the same soft and intimate kiss that he gave you last weekend. When his tongue kisses yours, you taste promise and maybe hope.

"Let's check on dinner." He draws away and shrugs his lips.

"Ben."

"Hmm?"

"What if I want more?"

His face is a tight mask of control. He reaches with his left hand and links his fingers with yours.

"I do, too." He nods. "Delilah, don't think for a second that I don't want to make love to you. But we don't have to rush it. Let's have dinner. See what happens. Let me kiss you again later…"

That damned smile of his squeezes your heart.

"I mean…I don't know if I can." Already you are backtracking, and that old, familiar sinking feeling consumes you. "I don't know…I just…I remember how good it was. The way you loved me."

He nods.

"It's okay, Dee." He rubs his thumb over the back of your hand. "It's okay."

CHAPTER 13

*D*inner is perfect. Or at least as perfect as it can be when you are sitting in the dining room with your husband and your son and that big, ugly bad thing you tiptoe around. Ben and Jordan talk about school. It rubs you a little bit the wrong way that Jordan directs most of his words at Ben, but what do you expect? You've been mentally absent since it happened. He does look at you from time to time, and he talks to you, too. It still stings, though, that these days Ben is the better, more attentive parent, and as much as you want to argue your case, you know that tomorrow might bring the despair that has smothered you since Aspen.

Tomorrow, hell.

The dark feelings are gathered in the shadows in the corner of the room, and all the while you eat—the lasagna is delicious—and sip your wine, you feel them encroaching on your family time. Twice, Ben catches you staring absently at your glass. He nudges you gently under the table, and somehow you ease seamlessly out of the shadows and maybe Jordan is none the wiser.

When you've finished eating, Jordan asks to be excused. It's Friday evening, and the tired you feel at the moment is a good, comfortable tired. It's not heavy and consuming, pressing down on your eyelids and demanding that you sleep. It's cozy and sweet, and Ben has been regaling you with tales of when he and his brothers used to shoot hoops on their driveway. You're laughing, and you want to hear more, and so, you tell Jordan he's excused. Long-limbed and lanky, he straightens in his chair, downs the rest of his lemonade, and then climbs to his feet. You look up at him as he pushes his chair in and tosses you a carefree smile.

You feel an overwhelming desire to say something. To tell him you love him. To apologize for how you've failed at motherhood since your last trip. Maybe to promise him that you'll do better. But those shadows creep out of the corners and into your peripheral vision, and you know better than to make a promise like that.

Instead, you smile at him in return. Luckily, he's still a kid, and he's out of the dining room before he sees how fleeting your smile is. When he's gone, you take a deep breath and duck your head.

"You okay?"

"I am." You nod. Ben doesn't rush to clear the table. He doesn't push you to talk. You drag your fingers back through your hair and rub your neck and finally, when you can breathe again, you lift your face to look at him.

"Is it just me? Or has he grown?" Ben tilts his head and looks at Jordan's empty plate. The kid had polished off two big servings of lasagna. You lost track of how many slices of bread he had after three. When Ben looks back at you, you shrug and nod.

"I think he's grown again," you agree.

"It just comes over you out of nowhere. Doesn't it?"

Embarrassed to talk about the way you can't cope with

what happened, you lower your gaze to your own plate, where a third of your original serving is now cold and unappealing.

"Sort of like waves," you mumble. "Like powerful tidal waves rolling over me, and for a minute, I just can't breathe."

Ben shifts on his chair and reaches for his glass.

"Did I ever tell you about the time I slam-dunked a shot to win a game of Pig?"

"No, and I don't believe you." You peek out from behind your hair and laugh softly when his eyebrows jump in disbelief.

"You don't think I can dunk? I'm tall—"

"You're not that tall, babe," you argue, "and you're not light on your feet."

"I might have been thirty years ago."

The snort of laughter surprises you. You sit back in your chair again and watch him. He shrugs, the grin he wears a reminder of the kid you met when you were nineteen, and he was twenty-one.

"The best part of the story is that Dave tried to dunk and missed the whole backboard. He ended up sprawled out over Mom's hedges."

You roll your eyes, but you can't help but laugh.

"Dave never won a game," he goes on. "Mike painted an L on his forehead one night when he was sleeping."

"Stop it." You shake your head, but you're happy, and you're bigger than the shadows, the dark feelings at the moment. You reach over the table for Jordan's plate and stack yours on top of it.

Ben's eyes twinkle with amusement, and his smile fills you as you work together to clear the table and do the dishes. Your stomach hurts a little bit from laughing, and once you feel the bad thoughts looming, but you focus on

Ben's voice and force yourself to breathe through the anxiety. Matthew comes home with Evan and Trevor with him, but they disappear to the basement. You wonder, when you hear the music blare and the sounds of video games from downstairs, about Trevor. If the rumor stopped. How Becca handled it. You wonder if Matthew told Ben about it, and you consider telling him, but you don't. It will change the vibe, and you feel good right now, and maybe that's all you can do at the moment. Maybe all you can do is right now. Why invite the bad thoughts back in?

When you finish the dishes, there's been more traffic up and down the steps. At this point, you don't know for sure who is here and who left. Ben turns the TV on and hunts for a movie while you wipe the dining room table off and turn the lights out. Together, on the couch—opposite ends —you sip another glass of wine and search for more to laugh about.

Instead of a movie, Ben finally chooses reruns of an old TV show. It's okay, because it's mindless, and you're tired and don't want to think. You don't want anything scary, and you don't want anything with sex, and you don't need any drama. When the doorbell rings a bit later, you find you've scooted down the couch a bit, your foot is propped in Ben's lap—you can feel his junk at your heel, but you don't think about it—and he's massaging the arch of your foot.

You assume another of Matthew's friends is at the door, so neither you nor Ben hurries to answer it. When Matthew doesn't come upstairs, though, and the bell rings again, Ben stands—your toes brush his fly, and you curl them away—and goes to see who is here. Still lounging on the couch, you breathe deeply and close your eyes. It's been a good night. Who knows what tomorrow will bring?

If you'll sleep tonight. At least you've relaxed tonight with Ben and Jordan.

After a few seconds have passed, you realize Ben hasn't come back to sit with you. You hear his voice, though, and there's murmured conversation down the short hall to the entryway.

"Ben?" You sit up and look over the end of the sofa. From where you sit, you can only see the heavy, oak door open at an acute angle and Ben leaning against it. He's talking quietly, so someone is there. You sit up and twist to see further, but you can't make out who it is. Maybe it's Genevieve and Christian, you decide, so you gather yourself and your wits, and you climb to your feet and pad down the hall behind Ben in your socks. You haven't been outside all day, but as you near the open front door, you feel the cold, damp air pressing in. The shiver that rolls over you is all about the feeling of winter trying to steal inside your house—it's not even November yet, for Pete's sake!—but when you come up behind Ben and see Mel and Max on the porch, an uneasy feeling settles into your clothes and seeps into your bones.

Ben is inviting them in, and so you step back as your friends come inside. Max mumbles a greeting, but he is uncharacteristically quiet. Mel, looking small and slight tonight, eyes you silently as Ben closes the door. Your stomach twists at the thought of them lingering too long. Ordinarily, the four of you could hang out and talk until dawn about everything and nothing and laugh yourselves sick while you're at it.

Tonight, the memory of the way Max had grabbed you and kissed you the other night and Ben's comment about how he doesn't like that sticks in your windpipe. The memory of seeing them on homecoming night drags you back through the rough week you've just had and the week before that, and you have to blink and look around the room suddenly to make sure you're home.

Safe.

You are accidentally pressed to Ben's side, seeking sanctuary maybe, and you see in the way he looks at you that he knows the darkness is creeping out of the corners and coming to roll over you and suffocate you. He slides his arm around you and pats your hip gently, but he's careful not to hold you too tight.

Ben offers them something to drink, and you're off. Max follows him back down the hall to the kitchen, conversation easy but quiet. The fierce look on Mel's face nearly knocks you off your feet. Her bloodshot eyes are wide and accusing in her pale, tired face.

"What gives, Dee?"

The meanness melts into sorrow, and you take a step back from her. Your shoulders are laden; you don't have time or energy to comfort a friend.

"What—what you do mean?"

"I called you four times today. Texted you this morning."

You open your mouth to answer her, but you stop. She's upset about something, and if you tell her that your phone battery is probably dead, she won't believe you.

"I asked you to meet me for coffee this morning." She pushes her bottle blond hair back from her face, and it makes you realize you missed a hair appointment. You didn't even bother calling to cancel. Noelle, your stylist, hadn't called your cell, but maybe she had called your landline. You haven't listened to voicemail since you came home from Aspen.

"Oh, Mel." You flinch.

"I just assumed you would go, so I sat at that little table where we always sit, and I waited over an hour."

"Melodie—"

"I drank three cups of coffee, and I watched that one mom with the twins? The one we watch sometimes? And I kept looking at my phone. Checking the time. Looking to see if you texted me to tell me you couldn't make it."

"I'm sorry." You sniffle and tip your head and wish you could explain this to her. That you don't like your phone anymore, and that you don't like being with people anymore, and you want her and Max to go, because a few minutes ago was the most normal you've felt in several weeks. That calm is gone, though. Even if Max and Mel leave right now, the darkness has crept out of the corners and clawed its way inside you.

The way the stranger in the hotel room forced his way inside you.

A deep, hard shiver racks your body, and you have to fight to swallow the bile and the lasagna and the hate that you suddenly need to spew.

"Don't do this to me, Dee," she whispers. "I need you now."

You stare at her silently, wondering what she thinks you are doing *to her* and why she needs you now. There's a stabbing pain between your eyes, and you're tired and irritated, and you want to throw your arms up in a tantrum and tell her to leave.

You can't. God, but you want to come unglued, but you can't. Going to pieces right now could expose the new you, and it will hurt your friend.

"I saw Gen at the grocery store tonight," Mel continues. She swipes at her eyes and then drops her hand to her side and stares at you accusingly. "She said she had just talked to you. That you guys might do lunch next week."

Mel and Gen know each other, and might be friendly, but you are their connection. You blink at Mel's words. It's surreal to imagine them chatting in the produce section of the grocery store. It's damning that Gen mentioned your conversation just after Mel believes you stood her up.

This morning when you got up, you made the bed, but you folded a fleece throw and laid it on the end on your side. You could go lie down now. You wouldn't have to pull back the comforter. You could lie down and pull the fleece blanket over your feet and bury your face in your pillow.

You could make all of this go away.

"I haven't looked at my phone all day." As if your body wants to betray you, you can't make the words come out any louder than a whisper. Even before you see Mel roll her eyes, you know she won't believe you. It's a ridiculous excuse, and you want to take it back, but why would you? It's the truth. Waves of darkness threaten at your feet, and then suddenly, Ben is there beside you.

Careful not to jostle you, he takes your hand and tugs gently. At the same time, he turns to Mel and nods for her to come to the kitchen with him and you. Max stands at the end of the island counter where Matthew stood the other night. His fingers are circled around a tumbler that holds a shot of bourbon over a single cube of ice.

Mel forgets for a moment that she's upset with you. She climbs up on the barstool by Max and nods when Ben holds up the bottle of pinot that you've been drinking. You watch him splash some in a long-stemmed glass for her, and you feel a prickle of selfishness. She's taking your wine now, after robbing you of your first sort of normal evening with your husband since your life changed.

"So, what are her parents saying?" Ben has switched to bourbon now. You flick your gaze from the tumbler in his hand to his empty wineglass on the counter by the sink. It's not a big deal when he drinks bourbon; he's never been a mean drunk. He gets quiet and tired, and if anything, it means he will snore louder tonight. Which technically shouldn't bother you, because you still spend most of those wee morning hours on the sofa.

It does bother you, though.

Max's sigh is long and heavy. Mel watches you turn to look at him as he shoves the heels of his hands up into his eye sockets. He looks tired, too. Maybe it's the time of year. It's October. Daylight saving time has not ended yet, but you are getting closer to that day. Seems reasonable that you won't leave your house once winter descends.

"We haven't talked to them, but they've both talked with the police."

Glass at your lips, you choke on the wine you try to swallow.

"Who talked to the police?" You look at Ben in a panic, even though you know Max and Mel aren't talking about you or what happened in Aspen. It's too close to you, though, and you need to back away from the conversation, from your friends.

Ben moves casually, and his closeness comforts you.

"Matthew didn't tell you?" Mel's question is crisp and cool.

You eye her without comment, the conversation between you and Matthew rushing back at you like a train.

"He told me…" You start and stop, all the things he said coming back to you. But what you're wondering about are all the things he didn't say. And why he didn't say more. Were you engaged in that few moments of quiet conversation with your son? He had caught you yawning. Had that kept him from saying more? Or had he said what was on his mind and walked away?

"Matthew told you?" Ben looks down at you, the surprise obvious on his face.

Mel's sigh melts into a sad, mournful moan.

"He told me some girl went to school the Monday after the dance and said she made out with Trevor at the after party." You shrug and ignore the way the words *made out with* make the hairs on the back of your neck stand on end. Chilled, you set your glass on the counter and rub your arms vigorously.

"Yeah." Max nods. "That's about it. Until here we are."

You flick your eyes from Ben to Max and back to Ben again. Your head is pounding, and the lasagna is churning in your belly. Ben reaches to touch you, just a gentle squeeze on your upper arm.

"You guys know Trev," Mel whispers. But you don't look at her. You can't. You hold eye contact with Ben as long as you can. When he arches his eyebrows, you realize you're holding your breath, and you let it go with a tiny sob. "You know he didn't do this."

Breathing isn't working, and you jump off the barstool and give Ben a gentle shove out of your way. You run to the master suite and barely make it to the bathroom. Bent over double, you grasp at the toilet seat and slam it up just in time—catching your fingers in the process—to vomit the first dinner that tasted good since you've been home. Your hair sticks to the back of your neck now as you retch. Your legs shake, and you squeeze your eyes closed, because you feel like you are in that hotel in Aspen.

"Delilah? You okay?"

If you had energy, you would jump when you hear Mel's voice right behind you. You snatch a tissue from the box on the back of the toilet and wonder why the hell Ben let her come after you. You haven't let Gen and Khloe witness these lows; you sure as hell don't want Mel or Max to see you fall apart like this.

"Where's Ben?" You flush the toilet and dab at your

mouth, but you keep your back to her. She rests her hand on your back and reaches around you with the other to hand you a glass of water.

"He's in the kitchen," she murmurs, and you know she wants to soothe you. "I told him I'd check on you"

You rinse your mouth out and spit and still hesitate to face her.

"Trevor didn't rape that girl, Dee."

She says it as you slowly turn toward her, but another wave of nausea rolls over you. You catch your breath, and then at the same time, you remember you should breathe, and you hold your hands up to ward her off and back her up.

"You can't possibly believe he would do that." Her whispered words are harsh and desperate, and you don't believe it, but you wonder how the story changed from what Matthew told you the other day.

"I don't," you insist. Mel finally backs out of the small alcove, and you push past her and gulp in fresher air. The air in Aspen was cold and fresh, and your mountain views were beautiful. But you can't ever go back. You can't ever go back to Colorado.

You will never get on a plane.

You will never book a hotel room again.

You will never be normal.

Never.

"Do you have the flu?" She perches on the edge of your whirlpool tub. You look away because you see yourself there, and Ben kneeling on the floor, holding your hand, and crying with you.

"I'm fine," you mumble and shake your head, but she doesn't get the message. You peek at her in the mirror over your sink as you put toothpaste on your brush with shaking hands. Chin tucked to her chest, she's not looking at you, but you still resent that she's in your space. She's been in your bathroom before. Many times. Once to look at the new faucets you had installed a few years ago. Once to show you a picture saved on her phone of a pair of shoes she'd ordered for Max for Christmas. She's stood in the middle of this room and the closet while you've changed clothes or tried on a new dress. She's sat on the floor and talked to you about her job while you've scrubbed the shower.

But right now, she's in your space. You brush your teeth and wonder if you should have said you do have the flu. Would that make her leave?

"Are you pregnant?"

The question hits so close to the worries you've kept silent about that it strikes you square in the heart. You gasp out loud, but the water is running, and she doesn't hear you. You brush quickly, the bristles probably tearing your gums up because you're in a hurry to get back to Ben. You hold onto the sink with your left hand and cry out in pain when you jab your gums with the brush.

When you rinse and drop your brush back in the holder, you see in the mirror that she is watching you expectantly. You grab the towel and wipe the counter off, but she stares without apology.

"What?"

"Are you?" The words are a bit more aggressive this time, like she's wielding them like a weapon and poking at you.

"No."

"Then what's the matter with you? You believe it, don't you?"

"I don't believe it, Mel. I don't believe it."

You don't. But just now, you will say anything to get her the hell out of your space. Thank God Ben has been so good about helping out with keeping things clean. If he had left it to you, the house would be disgusting and unfit for any visitors.

"Why didn't you even tell Ben?"

She's crying now. Her words have softened; she no longer brandishes them like she's going to attack you. But tears slide over her face, and guilt slices you open. She's your friend. She's always been your friend. And something is wrong.

"There's a lot…" You swallow hard, because again, you know before you say it how it's going to sound. But it's the truth. If you can't offer her the whole truth, why can't she be satisfied with what you can give? "Mel, there's a lot going on here right now."

She stares at you silently for a moment and finally nods. You watch her rub her face to dry her tears.

"Tell me," you suggest now. "Matthew said Sophia somebody said she and Trev were kissing at the after party. Making out. He said it didn't happen. I figured the girl had a crush on Trev, so she told a lie to make herself look cool at school. He's older, and he's popular. And he's cute."

"Matthew said it didn't happen?"

"Matthew said that some of the guys were racing four-wheelers. Which I'm not happy about," you add as an afterthought. "And that a few sophomore girls showed up at the party. Not with anyone, not like…as someone's date. He said one of them has a thing for Evan."

You struggle to remember what else Matthew said. It makes the pounding in your head worse.

"He said Trev was on the four-wheelers for a while. I'm sure he was, too, but he didn't admit that. He said Becca was there." You shake your head, at a loss for more details. When she continues to stare at you with wide, hungry eyes, you're bombarded with a rush of guilt. "Mel, he said nothing happened. He said there was never a time when Trev was with this girl alone."

"Trev says he wasn't alone with her. Said he and Becca were by the bonfire, and he was going to go race the four-wheelers. He kissed Becca and got up and bumped into the girl. He wasn't even sure who she was the night it happened. Said excuse me and went to the field with the guys. Becca says the girl and her friends sat by the fire for a while, giggling and whispering. They had Solo cups, but she said if they were drinking, they were on a one-cup plan. One of them did make a play for Charlie Orton, but he shot her down in front of her friends and three senior girls, including Becca, and two senior guys."

"Then what's the worry?"

It's not as if someone grabbed Trevor and manhandled him into the darkness behind the barn. Not like someone shoved his pants down and shoved his penis in places Trevor didn't want it. Not even like someone got him drunk and then got handsy with his penis.

Mel sniffled and blinked more tears.

"She told enough people at school that she made out with him. He's eighteen. She's fifteen. She told enough people. She told the wrong people. She told Nick Braun."

Your flinch at that name is bone deep. Even your stomach shivers. Nick Braun is a senior. Matthew and Trevor used to play soccer with him, but they'd stopped hanging out with him several years ago. He's a bully, but he's never bothered Matthew, so you haven't given him much thought through the years.

"He said it all back to her but suggested that maybe Trev raped her. And she decided yeah, maybe he did."

"But there are witnesses who say nothing happened," you remind her.

There are no witnesses that can prove you were raped,

but there are witnesses that can prove there was no rape at
Evan's after party.

Maybe you should have screamed. Could he have hurt
you badly in the time it took for someone to come to your
rescue? Of course he could have. There was a hotel door
with an electronic lock between you and civilization.
Maybe hotel staff could have helped, but maybe he would
have beat you black and blue or pulled a knife before that
happened.

"The school officer called Max the other day. They
wrote up a report."

"With no evidence. Eye witnesses that say otherwise."

Mel nods. You're struck with how ridiculous this is.

"Max called an attorney. They've warned us not to talk
to anyone."

And yet, here they are, horning in on what was an okay
night for you, talking to you. And you assume Max is
talking to Ben.

"I'm sorry, Mel," you whisper. "I just…when Matthew
told me, I assumed it was a stupid rumor thing that would
just go away."

"Max has it all mapped out. According to what Trev
has said about that night and the friends who have talked
to Max—"

"Did Matthew? Talk to Max?" You hold your breath.
You don't know what you want her to say. Yes, of course,
you want Matthew to stand up for his friend. But this
couldn't be happening at a worse time for your family. The
last thing you want is to be dragged into anyone's spotlight.
With harsh lights, you might combust under a magnifying
glass.

"He told Max he never saw Trevor anywhere near
this girl."

You nod, but the immediate feeling of relief settles into unease inside you.

"Max has the whole night mapped out from the things Trev has said and what other people have said. He was never around the girl."

Okay. That doesn't seem so bad. But Mel is still crying, and you're still fighting to breathe. And the girl is still lying.

You flinch at the thought.

If you had told someone the truth about what happened to you, someone other than your husband, someone else could have just had that thought about you. You have no proof that you were raped. Pictures of bruises that are now fading, that could have been inflicted by anyone, including Ben. Proof that you were assaulted, but not proof that it was the stranger who barged into your room.

What if something did happen? To the girl pointing her finger at Trev?

"They're taking it to the state attorney." Mel looks at you helplessly, and when you don't move immediately to comfort her, she ducks her head and covers her face. The shake of her shoulders as she cries there on the side of your tub takes you back to the hotel room when you had cried and tried to pull yourself together to call Dr. Ambern.

Trevor has spent so many nights in your house that if there were a common law of adoption, some might consider him partly yours. He's a good kid. Matthew has some friends who have veered off the straight and narrow through the years; Matthew and Jordan aren't perfect. Jordan had developed an affinity for the word *bastard* when he was ten. No harm, no foul, but you hated that phase. Matthew got a speeding ticket last summer. You caught him sneaking in one night after hanging out with the guys. Trevor was out that night. Trevor packed his bags once when he was nine or ten, intending to run away. He went nose to nose in a shouting match with Max over an error at shortstop.

Neither of them is a bad kid.

But maybe that girl isn't, either.

You don't believe Trevor would hurt anyone, and it sounds like a no brainer situation, with that many witnesses saying he was never around the girl. A wave of irritation rolls over you. Why can't Mel just muscle up and weather the rumor?

But what if someone said something like this about Matthew? Or Jordan?

"Mel." You cross the room and sit down near her, but the tub faucet is between you. "It'll be okay."

She doesn't respond; she doesn't react in any way. With your head back in that bathroom in Aspen the morning you were raped, you hold your breath for a second, and then move closer to her. Your thigh is pressed up against hers now, and gradually, she leans into you.

CHAPTER 14

*Y*ou don't sleep. Even on the couch, you toss and turn, physically uncomfortable. The couch is twelve years old, and your bed is big and warm, and tonight it irks you that Ben is snoring loud enough in there to wake the dead. You're still irritated with Max and Mel for showing up and robbing you of your first okay night and maybe the kisses you and Ben would have stolen later if you had been alone. You wouldn't have made love; you know that without question. But maybe you would have curled into his arms and let him hold you.

You're angry with the girl. With Sophia Marten. Why would she walk into school with such a whopper story? From what Max was saying to Ben earlier when you and Mel joined them in the kitchen, even people Trevor isn't close friends with say they never saw Trevor near Sophia. Trevor wasn't inside the house at any point through the night. He was in the barn, but then so were half of his classmates. It occurs to you, as you stare through layers of darkness at the vaulted ceiling, you don't know exactly what the story is, what Sophia even said. You should have asked Mel, but earlier, all you wanted was to get Mel and Max out of your house.

Your neck is stiff, so you scoot down to the middle of the couch, but the middle cushion is a bit uneven. You sigh when Ben snorts loudly from the other room. You hear him turn over in bed, and you wonder if this is the new normal for your marriage. It's early, though. Early in the aftermath of your recovery. You're still in hiding; you hate leaving your house. You can't choose a counselor. Sexual intimacy might be the hardest part of your recovery. You have no idea what to expect.

Mel hadn't really warmed up to you, even after you talked in the bathroom. She probably sensed your hesitation to get involved. At this point, there's nothing you can do about it. There's been no call to action on Trevor's behalf, and you keep your fingers crossed that it all is dismissed before you might have to do anything—if anything can be done.

You put yourself in Mel's place. Imagine how sick you would be lying here and waiting and wondering if the police will show up to arrest Matthew for something he did not do. Would you be patient with Mel if she were in your position?

You can't pose that absurd question in this scene, because Mel doesn't know what's going on with you. And she's not in your position now, and if she were and she chose to keep it from you, you wouldn't know where she was coming from. A feeling of dread tingles just below your skin as you consider telling Mel what happened. She wouldn't tell anyone else. That's never been your worry.

It's just that in the beginning you didn't even want Ben to know.

Now, you wonder if Mel would believe you if you told her the truth.

When you doze off after four, you dream about Matthew and Trevor kicking a soccer ball back and forth in the backyard. They had played when they were little, but Matthew lost interest in sports, and Trevor decided he wanted to focus on basketball. But when they were in kindergarten, they played in a league, and they were so cute. You have a framed picture from those days on your dresser. Nick Braun is with them, because when they were little, they played on the same team.

In the dream, Trevor keeps drawing his leg back to kick, but the ball keeps moving away from him. He finally plops down on the ground to cry. In reality, he had plopped on the ground once years ago in your backyard. He'd kicked the ball high enough to hit your kitchen window. The window didn't break, but his next kick hit Matthew so hard in his stomach that it knocked the wind out of him. Trev had been inconsolable.

In reality, you gave him a quick hug and gave both boys warm cookies straight from the oven. In the dream, you simply sit with him and pull him into your lap and put your arms around him. Matthew watches you suspiciously, jealous of the comfort you offer Trevor.

Ben is in the kitchen when you open your eyes just after eight. You lie still for long moments, trying to piece together your dreams and your fitful sleeping. The dreams moved from the innocent soccer game in the back to the hotel room in Aspen. The man from the hotel had called you dirty names—and he didn't, not once, in reality—and fingered you. You awoke drenched in sweat after that dream and turned the TV on. Apparently, you had fallen asleep again, with black and white reruns to soothe you. Andy Griffith had seemed safe, but damned if you didn't go right back into that dark dream world where Matthew was behind bars.

You smell coffee, and you blink, scared that you are back in the dreams. But Ben is moving around the kitchen, making breakfast. You're not hungry. Your throat feels raw from the violent vomiting the night before and the way you held everything else down.

"I have to tell them," you say as you swing your legs off the couch and sit up. Ben looks at you from across the room. Still in the flannel pajama pants he's had since dinosaurs walked the earth and the adorable bedhead you've known and loved for years, his face is dark with beard stubble, and his eyes are sleepy but sweet.

"What?"

"The boys." You swallow hard and nod and then stand, but your first step is hesitant. Fear makes you weak, but it's the right thing to do. For one thing, if you decide to tell Mel, your sons need to know first. Besides, even if the girl who invented a story about making out with a senior and then let someone twist her words around to possibly annihilate a young boy's life, even if she made it all up, this is serious. This is a big deal.

This is a teaching moment. And who better to tell your sons what kind of damage one person can do to another person's life than you?

Ben pours coffee. His fingers brush yours when he hands you the cup. You sip from it and watch him cover a yawn with one hand and rub his hair with the other.

"That's really something," he says as he turns back to the skillet where he's scrambling eggs. "About this girl and Trevor."

You nod, but when you don't speak, Ben looks at you over his shoulder.

"You think he did it?"

"No. Not at all." You shake your head.

"Our boys wouldn't do that."

"No." You stand at the kitchen window and watch a brisk wind rustle the leaves on the trees out back. "No. Neither would Trevor."

"Max is so angry."

"I would be, too."

You wonder if someone did touch the girl. If someone might have hurt her. Before the party. After the party. If anyone has tracked every step she took that night, the way Max has mapped out everything Trevor did.

"Delilah."

He hovers behind you. Your hands are cupped around your mug, but you look at him over your shoulder. Slowly he moves to press against your back and rests his hands on your shoulders.

"I'm sorry about last night." His voice is gentle, but his words rub you the wrong way.

"Whatever." You shrug and duck your head. "We weren't going to have sex anyway."

You say it on purpose. But when Ben's hands on your shoulders grow heavy and he squeezes you gently and drops his hands away from you, you don't feel the satisfaction you had anticipated.

"I know that." He still stands behind you, close enough that you feel the warmth of his body.

"You can't just claim me back, Ben," you mumble. Part of you has to say this. You're suddenly so full of venom that you have to get it out, even though part of you hates yourself. Ben doesn't deserve for you to attack him; he's done nothing but love you since your nightmare started. "I have to get my shit together first."

"Delilah." He sounds more hurt than angry, but you're not done yet. You turn to stand facing him, careful not to bump his body. The counter is hard and cold at your back.

"I have to heal, and I have to be able to offer myself to

you." You stare at him boldly. "You can't just…fuck me. And claim me back as your wife. And not another statistic—"

You have no idea where the words come from. It actually makes sense, and you see from the way Ben absorbs the words and flinches and hangs his head that maybe he really hears you and he gets it. But you could have been more careful with how you told him.

But why should you have to be more careful? Nothing that's happened is your fault. Why do you have to be poised and silent and grateful that your husband has been good to you since you were attacked? Why shouldn't you be allowed to bear your teeth and your claws and be outraged at what happened? At what the rest of the world has the nerve to expect of you?

Why does anyone else get to write your plans for recovery? This happened to you.

"Is that what you think?" Head still hanging, you watch Ben's shoulders rise and his chest expand as he takes a deep breath. "Really? That I thought after we watched some TV and drank a little more wine, I was gonna hold you down and claim you?"

Uncomfortable with his anger, you look away when he lifts his head and blasts you with a heated, angry expression.

"When have I ever treated you that way? When, Delilah? I've never done anything but love you. Respect you."

You lick your lips and turn to set your mug on the counter. Your hands are shaking; you're afraid the coffee will spill.

"We fight—"

"Yeah." He nods. "We do. But even then, I've never treated you as a possession. You know that."

You sniffle and barely tilt your head in a nod.

"Even when sex is crazy between us, isn't it because you want it? Like it that way?"

You do, or at least you did—sometimes—but talking about it right now sends a shiver of disgust from your shoulders to your toes.

"Dee?"

"Yes."

"Baby, I'm sorry." His voice breaks, and you gasp and sob when you brave it and look at him and see tears in his eyes. "I'm so sorry. I want to be the man you need right now. I want to do everything I can for you. I love you. I want you to…be you." He's pleading now; desperation arches his brows, and his thin lips—the ones you needed to kiss you just last night—are bogged down in grief. "But I don't know who that is. I don't know who you need me to be."

Your heart hurts. Your chest aches so badly, you think God or someone has his fist wrapped tightly around you. Maybe in vengeance. Maybe to protect you, to keep you from falling apart. Hot tears slide over your face, and even if you could find your voice, you don't have a clue as to what to say.

"I'm trying to be here with the boys," he continues. "I want you to tell them, because they love you, and that love will help you. And I don't want you to tell them, because I love you, and it is fucking torture to see you like this. I want you to be with Gen and Khloe. I want you to give a damn about Max and Mel and Trev. I know you're worried about the girl, and I get that you're overwhelmed. I know sex is going to be complicated, and I want to promise you I will get you through everything."

"I do give a damn," you whisper as you swipe your

hand under your nose and then your eyes. "I care about Max and Mel and Trev."

"I am here. For the long haul." He ignores you. "I am here. Push. Push me however fucking hard you need to. But don't you dare think you know what I'm thinking."

"What does that mean?" You roll your lips inward and duck your head.

"That means I wasn't planning to fuck you last night. That means that five minutes ago when I put my hands on your shoulders and said I was sorry for last night that I didn't mean I'm sorry we didn't get to burn up the sheets and tear down your walls."

You cringe at his word choice.

"It means I enjoyed last night. And I thought you did, too. And I'm sorry that Max and Mel were here and intruded on a good night for you."

You want to argue. They didn't intrude. They're your friends. Trevor could be one of your sons. And yet, how many times through the night did you think that very thing? Why did they have to intrude on a sort of normal night?

Wiped out now, you nod. Your head is heavy and stubborn, but you lift your chin and meet his gaze.

"I'm sorry."

He nods. "I know."

"I just…" You draw a deep breath through your nose, and the smell of coffee almost makes you gag. You don't even remember a coffeemaker in your hotel room, but apparently there was, because someone on your floor was brewing it when a stranger was doing you. "All of this… these feelings. They bottle up, Ben. They make me fucking crazy."

"That's why Dr. Ambern suggested a counselor," he reminds you.

You reach out to him and curl your fingers around his hand when he offers it to you.

"What's the most embarrassing thing that's ever happened to you?"

Ben draws back as if you're speaking gibberish.

"Um." He frowns. "The time I ran out of gas on the way to the airport."

You shake your head.

"What? That was embarrassing as hell." He shrugs.

"Something personal."

"Hmm." He considers your question and finally he gives in and meets your eyes. "I don't know, Dee. I guess I hate it…when I can't…"

"What?"

"Get it up."

You stare at him, surprised by his confession. "What?"

"There've been a few times lately."

"Ben." You squeeze his hand. "It's when you're drinking. And it's only happened a few times."

"I'm not as hard as I used to be, either."

"But—"

"Dee, you asked me what embarrasses me," he reminds you. "Those are the nights when I've…tried to…"

Make up for it with oral sex.

You nod. You've never complained about more oral sex. You never ripped on him for whiskey dick. It never seemed like that big of a deal.

But apparently to him it is.

"Okay. Well, imagine taking that embarrassing thing in to a doctor's office and discussing it with her."

Ben groans. "I get it, Delilah. I get what you're saying. But this is different. This is something that happened to you—"

"But it's very personal, Ben. Very intimate. I've told

you. I've told Gen and Khloe. I told Dr. Ambern. I had to put my feet up in stirrups and spread my legs for her to do a pelvic exam." You let go of his hand and dab at your eyes again. "Hard enough on any given day. Kind of… scarring…after what happened."

Ben opens his mouth to say something, but you shake your head and touch your finger to his lips.

"Don't say I know. Because you don't."

He stares at you silently for a long moment and finally, he gives in with a nod.

"I'm sorry." He sort of just mouths the words, and then you don't know who moved first, but you're in his arms. Pressed against him shoulders to toes, he is warm and solid. When you fling your arms around his neck and hold on, he slides his arms around your waist.

Maybe this is how you will allow him to claim you back as his. And maybe eventually that will help you heal and you can offer yourself to him because you want to, not because you feel obligated.

"I love you." You turn your face to his neck and squeeze your eyes closed.

"I love you, too." His voice is gruff, and the longer you allow him to hold you, the closer he pulls you to him.

When you draw away, you glance at the skillet where he was scrambling eggs, relieved to see he turned the burner off. Rather than scorched eggs, they will be served cold.

"Do you really want to tell the boys?"

Before you can answer, you hear the slap of bare feet on the tile floor. The loud squawk of a barstool being dragged on the tile makes you shiver.

"Tell the boys what?" Matthew asks.

CHAPTER 15

You turn your head and blink at Matthew over Ben's shoulder. Elbows on the counter, he's rubbing his eyes and then he shoots his fingers back through his unruly dark hair and makes it stand on end. He blinks at you and then looks hopefully at the skillet Ben has forgotten. You have that feeling now of someone launching a soccer ball into your belly and knocking the wind out of you.

Maybe you considered telling your sons, but you hadn't thought it through. You didn't plan out exactly what you would say, because if you're going to tell them you were assaulted, you need a game plan. You need an outline. Nothing extremely detailed. No sub-points, no examples. Just bare bones facts. If you haven't planned out what to say, you might accidentally say the wrong thing. If you haven't practiced what you plan to say, you might end up overcome with emotion and then you might break, and while this could be a teaching moment for your boys—

It would be devastating for them to see—

What they've been living with since you came back.

You step back from Ben's embrace and fold your arms over your chest. It's a defensive move, but you're cold, too, and you hunch your shoulders and shiver and look over your shoulder for that coffee mug you put down a few minutes ago.

You've been a train wreck since you and Ben came home from Colorado. You can't simply announce to your sons, as an afterthought, that something bad happened in Aspen. But you don't have to say more. They don't need details; you will not give any. They don't need to know where or how it happened. It will be enough for them to know it happened.

And yes, at the moment, you have to tell them.

They need to understand what this personal violation has done to you. And maybe if he knows this much, it will ease some of Jordan's worries about you and Ben. Still, your heart is a hummingbird in your throat, and your knees are suddenly weak.

"Is Jordan up?" Your voice is little more than a whisper, and when Matthew shrugs and shakes his head, you can't help the swell of relief that climbs up through your belly and chest.

"Did you fix breakfast?" Matthew turns to Ben. Spotlight off, you sink against the counter in relief and look back at the cup of coffee again. You haven't been able to drink a full cup since that morning in the hotel room, but for some reason, you keep trying. Maybe for Ben, maybe for yourself. You need to find a way back to the woman you used to be.

"Um." Ben moves away from you to examine the contents of the skillet. "I can start over. These are probably only half cooked. Getting cold, too."

"Well, I meant Mom."

When you peek at him, Matthew is looking at you hopefully.

"When I heard you out here, I was hoping you were making cinnamon rolls."

You swallow a mouthful of guilt. Hard to remember the last time you did anything special for the boys. Still, it makes you feel good that Matthew came sniffing around looking for a special breakfast treat.

"Sorry." You shake your head slightly.

"Want some eggs?" Ben asks as he crosses the room to get more eggs from the refrigerator.

"Whatever." Matthew ducks his head and scrubs his fingers back through his hair. "Trev's pretty upset."

Just like that, the burn is back in your belly. You and Ben exchange a look, and you ignore the quick arch of his eyebrows. You can't decipher it anyway. First he wanted you to tell the boys about the assault, and now he seems to be against it.

"You think he did it?" Matthew misreads the silent communication between you. "Really?"

"No, we don't." Back to the room, Ben assures Matthew as he cracks more eggs into a bowl to scramble them.

"Mom?" Matthew looks at you so quickly, you don't have time to school your features into a calm mask. God only knows what Matthew sees when he looks at you.

"I don't believe Trevor would do that, no."

"But?"

"But nothing." You shake your head and push off the counter to stand. Your hand trembles as you dump your coffee into the sink. When you look up, you see Ben watching you over his shoulder.

"Why'd you do that?"

The smell of coffee on the seventh floor of the hotel isn't a detail you've shared with him. You've shared very few details, as a matter of fact, and now isn't the time you care to start.

"I didn't want it," you mumble, and the meaning of those words rocks you on your feet and takes your breath away.

"Do we have any bacon?" Matthew asks Ben.

Ben studies you so closely, he doesn't answer Matthew right away.

"Mom, I'm gonna need new shin guards." Jordan's voice joins the noise in the kitchen. Still standing at the sink with Ben watching you suspiciously, as if you are going to plunge the good silver down the garbage disposal next, and the smell of coffee and the seventh floor of the hotel stuck in your head, you feel your shoulder and neck muscles tighten with fear.

"Why?"

Ben tells Matthew there's no bacon, and Matthew groans with frustration, and Jordan repeats his announcement about shin guards. None of them has heard you ask Jordan why he needs new shin guards, and you wonder as you stand with your fingers gripping the edge of the sink— knuckles white with desperation—if you were really talking to Jordan.

Maybe you were asking the stranger why he chose your room. What was it about Room 741 that drew him there? Had he seen you at the hotel? Followed you and learned your routine? Or was it just a random guess that he would find a woman alone, too shocked and maybe too weak to fight him off?

Or maybe you simply wondered out loud why God or the universe or fate had allowed it to happen.

"It's cracked," Jordan says again, but his voice is much closer this time. Ben and Matthew are discussing whether or not there is sausage in the freezer, and Ben reminds Matthew that even if there is, it'll have to be thawed before Ben can fix it. You turn your face to the left and find Jordan nearly close enough to press his nose to yours. His buzz cut hair is much tamer than Matthew's; it's smooshed a bit here and there from sleep, but there's just not enough there to be messy. His face is contorted and angry, though, and when he speaks again, he sounds huffy. He nudges your arm with his hands and nods for you to look. He's holding the damaged guard out to you, but before you can respond, he's griping again that he needs a new pair, and he needs them today, because he has soccer practice this afternoon.

"Okay." You answer him quietly, because in the chaos, you're trying to find your center and hold on. Ben and Matthew have decided to put the sausage links in the microwave to thaw them out, and now Matthew has moved on to pancakes.

"I need 'em now," Jordan is saying, and he nudges you again, and this time the cracked plastic on the guard scratches your wrist. "Can we go now? I want to get—"

"Stop." You give him the look, the one that used to stop both boys in their tracks and shut them up. When Jordan opens his mouth to argue, you remind yourself that he's been pushing your limits and your buttons now and then, and while the current climate in the house might have added to his occasional teenage storm and angst, he's not railroading you now because you're weak.

You aren't weak. You've let a stranger control you, control your life. But the men in this room are your family; they belong to you, and the only way they can understand what you're feeling is for you to tell them.

"I said stop, Jordan!" Your sharp voice silences the kitchen. When you turn to face the room, arms folded over your chest again, all three of your guys are watching you: Ben with trepidation and your sons with dismay.

"Dad, I just need—" Jordan stops in the middle of his plea to Ben. You stare at your youngest silently, fury and fear at war in your head and your heart. Your heart pounds maddeningly hard and slow now, drawing out every beat as if it might be your last. No one moves.

"Zip it." You arch your eyebrows and look Jordan around the island and into a barstool.

"Dad, my guard's cracked. I have practice—"

"Your practice isn't until two," you interrupt Jordan. "We'll get the shin guards, Jordan."

He drops the cracked guard on the counter, and his hands disappear into his lap.

"So." Matthew swallows so hard, you hear it from across the island. "What did you want to tell us?"

Jordan looks at Matthew, his face suddenly a mask of horror. Your knees tremble when he looks back at you.

"You are getting divorced." He narrows his eyes first at you, and then he flashes Ben a mean scowl.

"We're not getting—"

"Whose fault is it?" Jordan continues. "Who do we have to live with?"

"Jordan Michael." Ben's voice is stern, but his eyes are hot with anger.

"We're not getting divorced," you repeat. "But I have to tell you guys something."

"Delilah," Ben murmurs, but you shake him off.

"Are you sick?" Matthew's voice is broken, a little bit sideways.

"No." You draw in a deep breath when you feel the burn of tears in your eyes.

"Then, what is it?" Matthew presses you, but he's as quiet as Jordan has been aggressive.

You look at Ben. You've lost that three minutes of courage you had, and you're not sure this is a good idea. But you've said too much to wave it all away now. Ben sets the whisk he used on the eggs on the counter and moves closer to you.

"You don't have to do this." His whisper slides over the skin on the back of your neck when he stands behind you. He hovers close enough that you sense him there behind you, but he doesn't touch you.

"I do." You nod, but your voice breaks, so you clear your throat and look back at the boys. "When Dad and I were in Aspen…"

Matthew lives and dies with your words; his frown is deep and concerned. Jordan watches you coolly, though he keeps his mouth shut.

"I was assaulted."

"What does that mean?" Jordan tips his head. "Like, what? Someone hit you? Like in a coffee shop or something?"

The word coffee makes you flinch, but you shake your head.

"Someone mugged you," Jordan guesses again.

"Shut up, Jordan." Matthew turns to his little brother with a look of disgust on his face.

"What?" Jordan shrugs. "I'm just trying—"

"Mom was raped," Matthew tells him, and those words in Matthew's voice are cold fingers around your heart. When he looks back at you and meets your gaze, you answer with a small nod.

Matthew wipes his eyes and ducks his head. Jordan watches him curiously for a moment and then looks at you. You aren't sure what hurts more: Matthew's emotional reaction or the fact that Jordan looks right through you to see Ben.

As if you don't exist.

"Was it—" Matthew starts and stops. "Did he—"

"You don't need to know anything else." You lift a hand to wipe your eyes and then press your fist to your forehead just above the bridge of your nose. "I thought you should know because..." You take a deep breath and shrug. "I know you guys know something is wrong. And I don't want you to think it's anything between me and Dad."

Jordan stares just over your shoulder a moment longer. Your thighs and your belly and your shoulders tense again when he slides off the barstool and disappears into the pantry. Tears streak your face, and you hold your breath as you wait for him to say something. When he emerges with a granola bar sticking out of his mouth and heads without comment back down the hall to his room, you can't hold in a small cry of despair.

"I'm sorry," Matthew mumbles. "I'm sorry, Mom."

You nod, and even though his words comfort you, they aren't quite enough to take away the sting of Jordan's rejection.

CHAPTER 16

The results of your first HIV test come back negative, but knowing that it's only the first of many is more exhausting than it is a relief. You don't meet Ben's eyes when you relay the news, because it feels especially humiliating to share the results of your first HIV test with your husband.

Humiliating, like when strangers barge into your hotel room and hold you down so they can get off on owning you for ten minutes.

You aren't sure if the entire thing lasted ten minutes. You marvel at that thought as Ben navigates the streets to take you back home. The memory is like a time warp in your head; it might have been five minutes, or it might have been a half hour. You just don't know. You were sure you hadn't fought him, but your body said otherwise in the days following the attack.

There have been times when you and Ben devoured each other in mere minutes, and you wonder as Ben steers toward the house and Alanis Morissette croons through the

Kenwood speakers why rape could take longer. But there have also been times when you and Ben have made slow, tender love and dragged it out for hours, and it seems unfair that something that shattered your life so completely could take just a few minutes.

"What're you thinking?" His gruff voice startles you, but you don't react. He is frustrated with you, because you still haven't called Barry Holtman. Or anyone else, for that matter. If you want Ben to believe you are recovering, you need to play your part.

"That I might fix corn chowder for dinner."

It's not what you're thinking, but you had decided earlier this morning to do that, so it's not a complete lie.

"Delilah."

You look at Ben now, across the console of his Lexus SUV, and arch your eyebrows expectantly. *What?* You hope your face is saying. *What's wrong?*

"Jordan got sick after practice the other day."

After he disappeared with the granola bar and left you hanging—no acknowledgement whatsoever—after your shared confidence, he had texted Ben from his room and told him he didn't feel like going to practice. You stepped in and insisted he go. The tragic event was in the past, and it happened to you, not Jordan. You wouldn't allow him to wallow in feelings he didn't know how to express.

"Coach ran them, but Jordan pushed himself," Ben goes on.

You want to tell him it's dangerous; he should be watching the road while he drives, not you. But he would know you're being a smartass, that you're deflecting and trying to distract him from the issue. You shouldn't have told them. You shouldn't have told your sons about the assault.

Matthew has been quiet, though he's been attentive

and helpful. Each night since you told them, he's dried the dishes and folded any basket of laundry you carry to the kitchen and don't get to immediately. He's done his homework at the counter, and he's talked more about college and a little about Alli. He's been careful, though, not to bring up Trevor and his situation.

The only communication you've had with Jordan since that morning is a few grunts in response to your questions. He has talked to Ben, though, enough that you get the impression that he's punishing you for being raped.

Apparently, Ben was right on both sides of the coin as far as your sons are concerned. Telling Matthew was the right thing to do. He's been so helpful, so giving, even if he is struggling to understand all that the word rape implies, especially in regard to his mother. But you shouldn't have told Jordan. He's too young; he's just at the wrong age to carry this kind of burden, and now on top of all the teen drama that was just beginning, he's angry and sullen, and he mistakenly believes you asked for it.

At least that's what you assume.

"I don't know what you want me to say, Ben." You are weary of this conversation. If you could just erase the past month and go back to the morning when you and Ben boarded the plane to fly to Aspen. You would kiss Ben and pat his shoulder and tell him you love him and send him on his way. Alone.

And then the rest of this nightmare would be gone, and your little boy wouldn't hate you.

"He's struggling."

Head turned away from Ben as he slows the car to drive the winding roads in your subdivision, you admire the flaming red leaves on the trees in your neighbors' yards. It was late September when you went to Aspen, but the progression of autumn as evidenced in the foliage leaves you a little disconcerted.

You nod; obviously Jordan is struggling. But again, you simply don't know what to say to Ben.

"His teacher called me yesterday afternoon," Ben announces as he pulls the SUV into your drive. The words turn your blood to ice, and your lungs freeze with dread. Did he tell someone what happened?

"And you didn't tell me?" You swing your gaze back around to look at your husband, frustrated with him, with your son, with the whole damned world.

"I'm telling you now!" He throws his hands up in defeat. Rather than remind him he had all last evening to talk to you about this instead of now when he is leaving for work and you will be at home by yourself for the rest of the day, you press your fingertips to your forehead and close your eyes.

"He got in a fight with someone," Ben continues.

You wait for him to go on, because he seems to be enjoying the telling of the story. As if the more he can drag it out, the more he's punishing you for telling Jordan in the first place.

"About what?"

You assume the fight was somehow related to Trev, which in your head feels related to you, and you wait for Ben to throw the blame at you. Either Jordan won the fight easily, or it was interrupted quickly. He hadn't come to the dinner table with any bruises or scrapes last night.

"He and Dylan Wild got into it about the lead singer for Shotput Monkeys."

"The what?"

When you look at Ben in disbelief, he answers with an exaggerated shrug.

"Their teacher caught them before it got much past

shoving each other around. Jordan had his fist cocked and ready to go."

You're still wondering who the hell the Shotput Monkeys are and why Jordan would fight about them.

"Jordan started it."

You nod but stay quiet. Ben turns the car off, and the two of you sit in silence for a moment.

"He's angry, Delilah. He's angry, and he doesn't know what to do with that."

You swallow hard and look at Ben without a word. He's dressed for work. A dark olive green dress shirt and beige trousers. No tie today. With his shirt open at the collar and the shock of thick, black hair that dips over his forehead, he is casual cool and terribly hot at the same time. You wonder if he's attracted to any of the women in his office. You know that he's not the type of man to harass a woman on the job.

But you, apparently, are the type of woman to tease your husband with hot and cold emotions, and at the moment, you want him inside you with your ankles locked around his waist.

Because you need to claim him.

You need to remind him that even though you aren't yourself, he belongs to you.

The thought twists your stomach into a knot. It's wrong to want sex as a means of possession, isn't it? And yet, for a second, you consider climbing across the console of the SUV and straddling him.

Maybe if it weren't eight in the morning.

Maybe if you were normal.

Then again, if you were normal, you wouldn't have an aching need to remind him he is yours.

"I couldn't tell Matthew and not Jordan."

"I know." Ben, oblivious to the sexual thoughts

exploding in your head, pinches the bridge of his nose and nods, his face haggard with exhaustion.

"I know he blames me, Ben. I don't know what to do about it."

"I don't think he blames you, Delilah. He just doesn't…hell, he's probably just getting the feel of his own body. He doesn't get sex and all the nuances and the boundaries—"

"He better damned well know the boundaries, Ben."

"You know what I mean." Ben gives you a pointed look. "At his age, he's adjusting to so many changes. The whole puberty thing. He's noticing cute girls, and he's got morning wood, and he's probably exploring that. He knows no means no, but rape is a big concept for a kid."

You drop your head back to rest on the seat and close your eyes.

"Why is it hard to understand? No means no."

"Again, yes, he knows that. But he doesn't understand how devastating it is for you. You have to give him time to think through this."

"I don't want him to think about it."

"Well, you can't untell him. So he has to process it. Maybe he's not angry with you. Maybe he's angry with himself because he didn't protect you."

"That's ridiculous, Ben. He's a kid. And he was hundreds of miles away."

"And he's a boy, and his mom was assaulted, and he's angry."

"Do you hate me?" you whisper after a moment or two.

"Why would I hate you?"

"For telling him."

"No."

When you hear the seatbelt click free, you open your eyes to look at Ben.

"You don't have to come in." Your voice is flat. You pop your seatbelt and open the door, all before he can respond. But when you stand at the back door and dig through your purse for your keys, Ben is suddenly behind you and reaching around you to unlock the door for you. He follows you inside, but once there, you feel awkward and trapped and you just want him to go.

You need to be alone.

"Call me when you're on the way home," you tell him, and he nods, and you say this every morning. But he doesn't leave, and you don't move, except to touch him. Your hand moves, and your fingers brush his neck in the open collar of his shirt.

By comparison, you feel messy and frazzled. You wear jeans and a gray turtleneck, though your bruises have faded now. The sleeping pill you took last night made it hell to climb from the couch this morning. You raced through a shower, pinned your damp hair up in a messy bun, and touched your eyelashes with a mascara brush.

Ben is delicious and heading off to work in the real world. With real women. Younger women. Women who are cute and sexy and fun. Women who can have conversations with him that have nothing to do with therapy or HIV antigens.

Self-loathing chokes you, and so you press your fingers to his lips to dismiss him and then turn to walk away. He follows you, but when you reach the bedroom, he slips away to use the bathroom. You're still standing there when he's finished, but when he reappears in the bedroom and your eyes meet, neither of you speaks.

You don't know what you're doing, but you step closer to

him. You rest your hand on his shoulder and breathe a sigh of relief when you feel him settle his hands on your hips. You shouldn't do this, but you can't stop your other hand from curling around the back of his neck. Your fingers from combing up through his thick hair. Your lips from touching his.

The kisses are lazy and soft, and the intimate slide of his tongue over yours is nice. He seems content with this, but there's a part of your body that wants more. And then there's the part of your brain that wants to remind him that he belongs to you.

And the part of your brain and your heart and your soul that is damaged and can't keep track of where you are and who you're with and what you want and don't want.

"Dee, are you sure?" He pulls away when you move your hands, and you stare at your fingers on his buttons, rather than look him in the eyes. "There's no rush, babe."

There isn't. But there is. Because every day that you let go by without some form of intimate, sexual encounter with your husband might be a little push toward someone else. Someone willing to offer Ben a little slice of heaven.

"You'll be late," you whisper, unsure if you're saying no, you're not sure or saying yes, you want this and it's going to make him late for the office.

"It's okay." His voice is gruff. He dips his knees and lowers himself to make eye contact. Okay if you're not sure or okay if he's late, you wonder, but you don't speak. Your fingers tremble as you unbutton his shirt.

"Do we have condoms?" you ask as you part his shirt and push it over his shoulders. He nods as he shrugs out of his shirt and walks you backwards a few steps at a time toward your unmade bed. You wonder as you slide your hands around his back and under his t-shirt why he has condoms. For you, if things progressed to this before you felt completely safe from the HIV threat? Or for him, if your marriage bed stays frozen, and he looks elsewhere for entertainment?

"Dee, we don't have to make love," he says, but when you nip at his neck, you hear a familiar low hum in his throat. "Let me just kiss you."

You're not sure if you can do this, and maybe it's unfair that you started this when you did. But you are aroused, and you do want to be with him, and you're scared. Right at this moment, you're more scared of losing him than the memories of what happened in the hotel room.

Your hands smooth and mold his back, and finally, he steps back and grabs the collar of his undershirt and tugs it over his head. You drink in the hard planes of his chest and the muscles in his arms.

"I love you," he reminds you, but you don't answer him. You explore his chest now with your fingers. Careful not because you're afraid you will hurt him, but because this is a little bit new to you, and you're nervous. You hate that some stranger robbed you of the pleasure your husband's body can bring you. The outrage brings tears to your eyes.

"Dee—"

"I'm okay." You shake your head and trail your fingers down over his stomach. His erection is big and proud, but when he sees that you're looking at him, he tries to adjust himself. You close your fingers around his hand and pull it away.

You want to feel his skin against yours, but you're not ready to undress. Ben senses your hesitation, and rather than forcing it or drawing attention to your uncertainty, he kisses you again. Sweet and soft, but so deep and so intimate, you taste his hunger. Hands roaming over his shoulders—though skittering lightly—you allow him to ease you back on the bed.

"Am I hurting you?" he whispers when he is lying over you, his erection pressed hard to your core.

"No." You frame his face and look into his midnight eyes. "You're not gonna hurt me."

"You haven't—"

"Ben." You rub your thumb over his lip. "It's not going to hurt. Physically. I'm okay. The abrasions…bruises…it's all okay."

You feel his chest expand when he takes a deep breath, but he still slides to lie over your side rather than between your thighs. Still fully clothed and still not sure if you want to be, he kisses you again, and there's nothing but Ben and you. He's gentle, but he leads, as if he knows that you're a little uneasy. His erection pressing into your hipbone is uncomfortable, but you don't squirm, because you don't want him to stop. Not yet.

He nibbles at your lips and then he trails sweet kisses over your face and your neck and flicks your earlobe with his tongue. You hear a sigh of relief when his warm fingers make his way under the tail of your shirt, and when you realize the sigh came from somewhere deep inside you, your eyes fill with tears again.

Fingertips caress your bra, but he hesitates.

"Did he touch you here?"

"You're not gonna hurt me."

"Did he?"

At least he's not forcing eye contact.

"Sort of."

"What does that mean?"

"Ben."

"Were you naked? Did he make you undress?"

"No."

"Delilah—"

"Either we do this, or we talk about that." You push

firmly on his shoulder to make him look at you. "I can't do both at the same time."

"Do you want me to touch you?"

"Yes."

"Will you stop me? If you change your mind?"

"Yes."

Rather than undress you, Ben navigates your body by memory. His fingers roam reverently over your bra and when you cry out in protest, he appeases you and unhooks it. It doesn't hurt, but you knew that it wouldn't. He plays with your breasts, gently pinches and tweaks your nipples, and you feel like you've come home.

The bedroom is sunny and warm, and Ben slides lower and pushes your top up enough to kiss your belly. You nod when he looks at you for guidance and lift your hips for him to ease your jeans and your panties down.

You're not going to come, even if he intends to kiss you there, even if he is patient. There's not enough time, and you're not ready. This is for him. You want him inside you because you want him to remember the way you fit together, and you don't have all day.

"Get a condom," you hear yourself say.

You watch him move gracefully from the mattress to his feet. He unbuttons and unzips his slacks, but when he hesitates, you look up to meet his eyes.

"Are you sure?"

You nod, though already you want to stop him. He drops his trousers, and your eyes slide down over his nude body and linger on his thick, heavy penis. He won't hurt you; he's never hurt you. You've always fit together perfectly. Still, you have to take a quick breath for courage when he reaches to take a box of condoms from the nightstand.

He takes one from the box and then kneels on the

mattress between your legs. The air on your bare skin is cold, and Ben's eyes on you make you feel exposed.

"I can wait," he reminds you.

"Do it," you tell him. He holds your gaze as he strokes his hand up your inner thigh. You bend your knees and open your legs further when he touches you. Just his thumb, barely touching your sensitive skin. You're not wet; you're not blind with arousal, and he knows you well enough to know that.

But his gentle fingers feel good as he rubs your thighs and your hips and finally slides them inside you. Your eyes meet again, as he draws a tight circle over you.

"I'm not gonna come, Ben," you tell him honestly.

"Dee—"

"I'm okay." You cover his hand with yours when he tries to move. "But I'm not gonna come."

"We can do this instead. Let me play."

"I want you inside me."

"Delilah, let me do this first—"

"Later." You nod. "Tonight."

"I can't just shove my dick inside you."

You give in, because it won't be comfortable if you aren't ready, and the last thing you need is to clam up when he enters you. Ben knows how to touch you to get you ready. He knows your body, and he knows when to stroke and when to give you more pressure, and he knows the spot inside you that makes you pant and beg and cry all at the same time.

But you can't watch him watch you. Not now. You close your eyes and enjoy his attention. It's pleasant, and it's a relief to you that maybe one day you can find the passion, the desire for this, the need to come at the touch of his fingers and the press of his body inside you. Still, you know it's not going to happen now.

He knows that, too, because you've been together far too long to lie to him, to try and fake it. He tells you again that he can wait, but you shake him off and reach for the condom. Your heart races but not with desire when he rolls it over his penis. Where just moments ago, he was beautiful, and you wanted to want him, the site of his throbbing purple erection now almost makes you gag.

You guide him in, hands on his hips, and your body stretches to fit him as he eases inside you. It doesn't hurt; in fact, the thick pressure feels good. You move with him, and it's slow, and Ben whispers to you and asks you to keep your eyes open, because he needs you there with him.

You do; you hold his gaze as he slowly grinds against you, sliding in and out in a torturous, languid rhythm. If things were different, this would be incredibly sexy and you would have come when he touched you with his fingers, and you would come again now. But you can't, because you are back in the hotel room, and the man inside you is not Ben.

"Babe." Ben grits his teeth and tries to control himself.

"It's okay," you promise him. "Ben, it's okay."

"But I want you to—"

"Come, Ben." You angle your hips more and squeeze him inside you and hear his grunt of approval. "Please. Come inside me."

"Delilah—"

"I can't." You cup his chin in your hand and rub your fingers over his parted lips. "I can't, Ben. It's okay."

You're still working your hips, pumping hard against him, and you raise your head to kiss him, and you whisper again that it's okay. It is okay. You're not in pain, and you hadn't expected an orgasm the first time you made love to him anyway. You feel sexy and powerful when you feel the ripple of pleasure in Ben's back muscles. Your hands slide over his hot, sticky skin, but when his body goes tight like a bow, and he grinds against you one more time, and you feel his orgasm tear through him hard and fast, you can't look at him. You can't look at his face, because twisted and distorted in pleasure, he is a stranger to you.

CHAPTER 17

*E*ven when he pulls out and lies at your side, his leg thrown over your thigh and his arm over your upper body—still covered by the turtleneck—you can't look at him. This should be familiar; all of this with Ben is the way you've loved each other for years. But at the moment, you are back in that hotel room. You're cold, and your body aches—maybe some sort of phantom pain because Ben did not hurt you—and you feel like you might vomit. You pray that Ben will get up in a second and dress and leave for work, so you can sulk to the bathroom and wash up, and then crawl back into bed.

And sleep.

Maybe if you sleep long enough, this will one day fade like a childhood nightmare eventually loses its power.

"Are you okay?" He doesn't lift his head to look at you, and for that, you are grateful.

"I'm fine," you say quietly, but you know you can't lie to him.

"You're not." This time he does move. He slides his hand back over your belly, still touching you through your shirt, and lifts his head to kiss your cheek. "You're not fine."

"Ben—"

"What the hell was that, Delilah?"

His eyes are dark and angry as they devour you. Feeling exposed again, you try to turn away, but he catches you and cups your face in his hand.

"What do you mean?" Your whisper is almost choked off by your heart stuck in your throat.

"Why did you just rush that?"

"I didn't rush it. It's been a month—"

"Delilah—"

"The boys are gone. We're home." You shrug, hoping you sound nonchalant.

"And I have to leave to go to work," he reminds you.

"I know."

"It could have been better—"

"Jesus, Ben. Thanks."

"Dammit, Dee." He sighs and finally peels himself from your body. You can't look when he climbs off the bed and disappears into the bathroom. You lie still on the bed, your head still in Aspen, remembering the way the stranger came back to slap your ass before he walked out of the room. The way he greeted someone as your door closed behind him.

The sound of his voice.

The toilet flushes, and then water runs, and you still don't look. But you feel Ben's presence when he comes back into the bedroom.

"I didn't mean it like that," he says. "I just meant…"

You take a deep breath and turn your head his way. He stands just inside the bedroom, still nude, his hands propped on his hips.

"We should have waited. We could have gone slower. More kissing. More…touching."

Embarrassed to be spread out on the bed, your bottom half naked, you finally sit up and look around for your pants.

"We had to get it over with," you mumble.

"What?"

Your jeans are piled on the floor. Ben watches you dress. He waits for you to explain what you said, but you don't. You can't. You don't want to.

"Dee?"

"Are you upset that I didn't come? Is that it?" you ask when you finally turn to him.

"Are you kidding me?" He tosses his hands up in frustration. "I'm upset because that felt wrong. Because we rushed through it. Because you look haunted, like I was the one that did this to you in that hotel room. All I'm saying is that I could have waited. I would rather have waited for a quiet evening. Or a weekend morning. When we could have taken our time."

"I still couldn't have…" You shrug and shake your head. Your cheeks are flaming hot with shame, and you wish with all your heart that he would just go. "So why does it matter? How that first time…after…happened?"

"I feel dirty, Delilah—"

His words pierce you. The pain is outrageous, as if there is a hole in your lungs, and you can't breathe, and you can't move. The tears are so instant, you can't fight them.

"Wow." You nod and duck your head. "I just wanted to remind you…" You have to stop talking for a moment, because there's a knife in your throat. "I wanted to remind you that I love you. That you're mine. And instead…I reminded you that your wife is damaged. And instead of enjoying sex with me, you feel dirty."

"That's not what I said."

"You did. You said you feel dirty."

"Because you weren't ready for that. Because you manipulated me into fucking you because…why? Because you needed to remind me that I'm yours? Is that what you said?"

"You're a good-looking man. And you're happy. And healthy. And normal." You swipe at your eyes. "You leave this house every day, and you see all kinds of women. Some that you work with closely."

"What? And that means I'm gonna cheat?"

You sob softly and shake your head. "I can count the times I've left the house since it happened on one hand. I'm a wreck. I look disgusting. I can't get through a day without breaking down. And someone else touched me where only you are supposed to touch me." You shrug and push the pieces of hair that have escaped from your messy bun back from your face. "Maybe I would cheat on me. God knows, you have to be sick of this."

Ben stares at you silently, but you notice the hard set of his jaw. He's angry, but he's desperately trying to control himself.

"I keep telling you I love you. I'm here. I will do anything you need me to do. I will wait until the end of time, and then I'll wait some more."

"I needed you to get me past that." You meet his gaze.

"And I would have gladly done it any other way." He drags his hand down over his face. "I didn't realize you thought I was a selfish bastard who would cheat on his wife when she's dealing with something so difficult."

"It's been a month—"

"I can jack off in the shower if I need to, Delilah." He

shakes his head. "I'm not gonna cheat. And I don't appreciate what we just did. What you just did to me."

You're at an impasse. You hurt him, and you know it, but he hurt you. And it wasn't ten minutes ago, in your bed when he hurt you. It was two minutes ago when he said he felt dirty. One thing the two of you will never get past is the fact that someone forced his body inside yours. No matter what you do, you can't change that. A stranger came between you, uninvited, but it still happened.

Before you can think of anything to say, he turns and goes back to the bathroom. Your eyes move slowly over his nudity. The solid sound of the door closing in your face is jarring.

He showered, so by the time he left again—with a quiet goodbye and a chaste kiss on your cheek—the overwhelming urge to curl up and sleep the day away had eased. Instead, you stripped the bed and threw the sheets in the washer, all the while thinking about the sheets on the hotel bed. You made coffee, and you parked at the table in the kitchen and forced yourself to work. Amidst the emails you read and returned, the phone calls you made to clients and to Anna to check in, and the bit of designing, your heart rate returned to normal. You didn't forget what had happened in Aspen or earlier in your bedroom, but after a while, you weren't obsessing over it, either.

Now, after a couple of hours of concentration, you take a break and wander the kitchen weighing dinner ideas. It's cool outside, and the skies are thick and gray. It looks like snow, but there's no winter weather in the forecast. Just rain, but even rain will be cold and miserable. Seems like a good night for chowder and cornbread.

You play music while you brown the burger and mix the cornbread. Your usual choices—anything from Maroon 5 to Frank Sinatra—seem to cause pressure and pain between your eyes, and eventually, you settle on an instrumental station. You've never had any strong feelings for or against classical music, but for now, it's calming.

When your doorbell rings, you catch yourself before you can groan out loud. Perhaps it's UPS, but then again, you haven't begun to shop for the holidays, and you haven't looked online to purchase anything since you've been home. Probably Gen or Khloe or both of them. You feel a weight lift from your shoulders as you make your way to the door. Maybe you won't share specific details about the morning disaster with Ben, but hanging out with your friends for a while will lift your spirits. Maybe some laughter and conversation will rub the rough edges away and make you appear more approachable to Jordan this afternoon after school.

You pull the door open with a smile on your face—relieved that your friends will take your mind off the morning—but you're shocked speechless to find Mel on your porch instead of Gen and Khloe.

"Wow." Mel nods. "Now I know."

"Now you know what?" You tip your head curiously.

"I've been wondering since this whole nightmare began where you are. What I would be doing to support you if our roles were reversed, and if maybe I would want to keep my distance or if I should be offended that you've disowned me."

"Mel."

"You looked like you were expecting company." She makes a show of looking back over her shoulder to see if anyone else is coming and then turns back to look at you.

"And then you saw me on your porch, and you completely shut down."

This guilt is heavy and unwelcome, and yet, Mel has a point. She's the last person you wanted to see when you opened your door.

Well.

Maybe not the *last* person you wanted to see.

Your chest tightens, and you shiver involuntarily. You just opened the door without checking to see who rang the bell. You struggle to get a breath, and your fingertips tingle.

"C'min, Mel." You reach for her, and she stares at your hand suspiciously and finally, she takes it and steps inside. You lean around her to close the door and find her crying when you swing around to face her again. "Did something else happen?"

She shakes her head, but she refuses to look at you.

"No. But." She crosses her arms over her chest and huddles into herself. You know the move. She wants to be smaller; she wants to protect herself. "You have no idea how hard it is to wait around for something to happen. Max and I don't sleep. I keep wandering into Trev's room to watch him sleep. I don't know if I…"

"What?" You want to know what she was going to say. What she's thinking. How she feels. If their waiting to see what happens next with Trev and Sophia is as torturous as you and Ben waiting for the final word on the blood work Dr. Ambern has ordered.

"Do you want me to go?"

"No." You reach for her again and take her hand when she unfolds her arms. You don't want her to leave, but you dread this conversation. You hate that you've hurt her again, and you know she'll be upset when you tell her what's going on in your life that has made you so negligent with your friendship. "No, I don't, Mel. I'm sorry. There are just…things…"

"What things?" she asks as she sets her purse and keys on the island.

You're not ready to get into it, so you wave her question away.

"Do you want some coffee?"

"Do you mind?"

"Of course not." You eye the pot, but there's only a dry rust-colored ring in the bottom. Before you start another pot, you check the soup simmering on the stovetop.

"I watch Trev sleep at night," Mel says now. You glance at her to see that rather than sit, she's propped her hip to lean on the counter. "And I wonder what will happen if they arrest him."

"But there're witnesses who say it didn't happen."

Mel shrugs when you lift your eyes to hers. "There are. But you would think that would have kept it from going as far as it has."

You pour water into the coffee maker, hit the brew button, and then lean on the counter at your back. She has a point, so you don't argue.

"I just wish there was a graceful way for that girl to back herself out of the lie."

You agree, but you bristle at the streak of rage inside. You don't believe Trevor would hurt anyone. There are witnesses that say nothing happened at the party. There is no evidence to prove that anything did happen to the girl.

And yet, when a woman is raped, it is on her to prove it happened. It's her body that is violated. Her pain. It's her life, her soul torn apart by society. It's either her fault, or it didn't happen at all. Even though you believe in Trev, you blanch at the unfairness of rape, the horror that lingers even after the act is committed.

It's very possible that the girl claiming Trevor raped her told a little lie to be cool at school the following Monday. Trevor is a good-looking, well-loved guy. No doubt making out with him at a party would level up a sophomore girl. It's possible that little lie got twisted around into a huge misunderstanding. Maybe the girl worried her parents would find out about it and be angry with her. Maybe she realized amping the story up to a rape story would buy her even more attention.

Whatever the case, the whole mess makes you twitchy and hot and nauseas.

"Do you think he did it?" Mel whispers now.

"Mel, no, I told you I've just been…busy."

"No. I'm asking you." Mel shakes her head and refuses to look at you. Her voice drops to a whisper. "As a mom, as a woman, do you think he did it? Do you think Trev raped her?"

"Do you?"

"No. I don't," Mel answers immediately. "But I'm scared, Delilah. I mean…what if he did?"

"He didn't." You take a deep breath. "Even without the witnesses who say nothing happened, I wouldn't believe it."

"He could get five to ten years in prison," she sobs. "For being at a party. With his girlfriend. Hanging with his friends. Enjoying senior year."

"I'm sorry." Your words are small and terribly inadequate.

"Becca's parents are torn on it. Her mother believes him. Her dad isn't so sure."

"And Bec? She believes him?"

Mel nods.

"No one comes around anymore." Mel licks her lips as she finally caves and meets your gaze. "Matthew's been there for Trev, but none of the other guys come around. Even our friends have suddenly become busier than bees. Max and I can't even talk to each other anymore. The tension is so ridiculous, we got in a blowout last night about salad dressing."

It hurts to be reminded that you aren't the only person who is suffering. To be reminded that you are acting selfishly. That your friends need you. The fact that you just a week or two ago made a judgment call on your friendship with Max and Mel and decided you weren't close enough to share what's going on. To reach out for support.

Mel had a breast cancer scare after Christmas. She told you. She confided in you. The memory of that talk over coffee leaves a bitter taste in your mouth now. The smell of coffee in your kitchen makes you gag.

"Mel." You swallow hard and look away. "I was raped."

She doesn't speak right away, but when the silence goes on too long you have to look at her to see what she's thinking. Rather than concern or outrage on your behalf, her face is cold and impassive.

"Mel?"

Your use of her name gooses her into movement. She purses her lips and nods and then without a word, she picks up her keys and purse. Helpless, you listen to the thud of her boots on the tile floor as she moves back to the door.

"Mel? What are you doing?"

She freezes just inside the door, but she doesn't turn around. You move, follow her, but you stop a few feet away from her. Heart in your throat, you wait for her to say something. Ben's words from the morning come back to you. He felt dirty. Maybe Mel wants nothing to do with you, either. You hadn't realized the taint of rape was so contagious.

"Makes sense." She speaks softly. Her shoulders lift in a deep breath, and she drops her head back for a second. You take in her silky long hair and wonder if you will ever be able to put yourself back together again to look normal. Presentable.

Pretty.

For Ben.

"What does that mean?"

She pivots slowly, almost on her toes, and fixes you with a cool stare.

"You don't want this mess. Not if you're one of those women."

What women? Victims? Is that what she means?

"What?"

"College?" She dips her right shoulder. "High school?" A flick of her eyebrow. "Lemme guess. A homecoming party. No, wait. Prom. Right? Was it your date? Or a classmate?"

Unable to stand there and take her cold sarcasm anymore—she might as well be finger quoting her words to make sure you catch that she's being facetious—you take a few steps closer. Tears streak your face, but this time you let them go.

"Aspen. About a month ago," you say quietly.

You see the color fade from her face. She stares at you in silence, but this time, it's not malevolent.

"Ben?" she tries again, but the edge is gone from her voice. In fact, she sounds like she might cry again.

You don't dignify that snipe with an argument.

"I don't know who he was."

"Dee."

You sniffle and swipe your hand over your face. This

time, it's you who folds her arms over her chest as an act of self-preservation.

"He shoved me down. And he raped me. And he came inside me, and so, Ben and I were waiting for my HIV test results. We just got the first test result back, but I have to have it done again. Three more tests, actually."

Mel narrows her eyes at you. "You can buy HIV tests over the counter."

Her callous answer rips through you like a knife.

"Would you trust your health—your husband's health—to an over-the-counter test, Mel?"

Mel stares at you silently.

"You don't believe me," you say with a bitter laugh that turns into a sob. "That's why I didn't report it. Because I knew no one would believe me."

"So you believe Sophia Marten. Because of some sisterhood or something."

"No." You shake your head slightly. "I don't. I know Trev. I'm just telling you what's going on in my world and why I haven't been there for you."

"Was it…" Mel looks around your entry hall, as if she might find sentences or words to steal and feed to you. "Violent? Did he hurt you?"

You nod. "Yeah. He did."

Mel stares at you without speaking.

"Do you need proof?" You shrug. "Is that it? Do you want to see the bruises?" You flip the neck of your shirt down, and it breaks your heart that she looks. The way she flinches hurts in a different way. "I know. They've faded a lot. But I have pictures of them if you need to see them."

"I don't need…" Mel licks her lips and frowns. She's angry. At you? At herself? At the world? You get it. You are, too.

"I fought him. He caught me off-guard. It was probably over in ten minutes, but that ten minutes sabotaged my whole life."

"Trevor didn't do this, Delilah. My son did not rape that girl. He loves Becca. He's a good kid. He's kind. He's smart. We taught him right from wrong."

"I don't think he did it," you insist. "Mel, I can be this woman, this woman who was…victimized. And still believe in your son."

"Can you?"

"I know that there are men who harass and assault women." You press your fingertips to your lips. "Unfortunately, I know that from experience now. But I don't think all men are rapists, and I know Trevor isn't that kind of kid."

The coffee maker beeps to remind you it's finished. You remember, too, that you have chowder simmering on the stovetop and a bowl of cornbread batter waiting to go in the oven.

"Why didn't you tell me?" Mel cries. "Delilah, I lean on you all the time. Why would you do this alone?"

CHAPTER 18

*M*el follows you back to the kitchen and sets her purse down again. You stir the chowder, and you think that if it were Gen or Khloe standing here with you, both of them would help themselves to coffee. The realization that you've been a bad friend is heavy on your shoulders, and the guilt and the smell of the soup and the coffee make you ill.

"I just told the boys last weekend," you say quietly, dread winding through every inch of your body, settling in the pit of your stomach. Mel will be furious when she finds out that you've told Genevieve and Khloe but not her.

You peek at her as you move from the stovetop to the cabinet to grab a cup for her. Yours is still on the table from earlier. It's nearly full, but it's cold. You nursed your way through one cup after Ben left, but like the sex earlier, it left a bad taste in your mouth, so you'd ignored it.

She won't be furious, you decide when you see her face. Her downturned lips are chapped; her eyes are kind and sad for you. She'll be hurt.

"How did that go?"

She murmurs her thanks when you hand her the cup. Sips from it, and you have that flash of memory again. The smell of coffee on the seventh floor of the hotel.

"I don't know," you admit. You dump your room temperature brew and pour another cup, one you will probably not be able to drink. Mel climbs up to sit on the end barstool as you go back to pouring the cornbread batter into a pan. "Matthew was...concerned. Very upset. He talked with me for a while." Head down, you raise your eyes to meet hers. "And he absolutely does believe Trevor. He was with Trev except for the four-wheeler rides."

Mel starts to say something, but you shake your head.

"I know. I'm sure Matthew did the four-wheelers, too. My point is that unless the two of them were on one together out in the fields, that's the only time they weren't together."

Mel breathes deeply and rubs the bridge of her nose. You watch her close her eyes.

"What about Jordie?"

"He's angry." You sigh and shrug as you consider what Ben suggested earlier. Maybe Ben's right. Maybe Jordan is angry about what happened, and maybe he feels that he let you down somehow. He shouldn't, but then you know you can't tell anyone what or how to feel about anything.

But maybe he's angry with you. Maybe he doesn't believe you. Maybe he thinks that whatever happened is your fault.

"Why is he angry?"

"I don't know." You straighten and swipe the back of your hand under your left eye. "I feel like he blames me. Maybe he thinks I asked for it."

"No woman asks to be assaulted," Mel argues. "I hate when people say that."

"I do, too," you agree. "But I'm just trying to figure out what he's thinking."

"Did you…" Mel huffs a big, deep breath and tips her head when you look at her. "Did you tell the boys…how it happened?"

"No." You squat down in front of the oven and tap the screen to preheat it. Mel doesn't say anything. "Ben had just left the room. It was the morning we left. Someone knocked. I assumed it was Ben. Opened the door." You shrug.

"Oh, God."

"I don't want the boys to know the details. It's humiliating."

"I understand."

"I haven't been able to leave the house," you mumble, careful not to look at her. "I've gone to the doctor. To the lab. And I did homecoming pictures. Met Gen and Khloe for coffee."

From the corner of your eye, you see your words hit Mel and tear through her. She flinches and nods slowly and closes her eyes.

"You told them."

"They were here." You start talking, suddenly desperate to defend yourself, your silence with Mel. "Right after we got home. They were at the house. We had already planned a get-together. I hadn't told Ben. I couldn't keep it together."

"You didn't tell Ben."

"Not at first."

"Why not?"

You hold the cup of coffee, but you only sip from it and then brace yourself as it slides down your throat.

"It's humiliating. I told you that."

"He's your husband."

You shrug. "Still. Hard to just open your mouth and say those words, Mel."

"So you told them all at the same time?" Mel asks hopefully.

"No." You sigh. "I told Ben that night. And then told them over coffee."

"And if this hadn't happened with Trev, you would never have told me."

"It's not easy to talk about," you remind her.

"Yeah. I'm sure it's not." She dabs at her eyes, but it's obvious she's not wearing any makeup. "I'm sorry that you felt too humiliated to tell me."

"Please don't do this," you whisper. "I'm sorry. I didn't purposely decide to keep it from you. If Genevieve and Khloe hadn't seen me acting so skittish that night, I wouldn't have told them."

She presses her lips together and nods. But her eyes are glassy.

"I've been trying to work from home. Because I panic when I'm outside the house. I got kind of sick the other day when a guy got on the elevator with me and Ben."

"You said you don't believe every man is a rapist."

"I don't," you say simply. "But I can't just flip a switch and be over it."

"Does Anna know?"

"No." You turn your back to Mel and start running water to do the dishes. "The guy who raped me could have been Ben. Or Max. Christian."

"What do you mean?"

"He looked...normal." You stare at the water filling the sink and realize you didn't put any soap in it. "If I'd seen him on the street, I'd have said hello or at least smiled at him. He was a nice-looking guy."

Mel is quiet while you squirt detergent under the running water.

"And that makes me wonder if he saw me on the street. At a café where I was working the day before. If he followed me. And that makes me feel like I did something to invite it."

"That's ridiculous, Delilah." She sounds disgusted. "Nothing you did asked him to attack you that way."

You nod and shrug. "I know. But this is my world now, Melodie. I question everything I did. Everything I do. I'm scared to go out. I'm afraid to be home by myself. I can't have a normal conversation with Ben. The boys. I don't sleep at night. I have…flashbacks."

"Are you seeing anyone?"

You shake your head and rush on. "Ben and I haven't been intimate since…that morning. I'm scared that he's going to lose patience with me. That he'll find someone better. Someone normal."

"Ben's not going to punish you for needing time to heal."

You think about this morning, but you grind your teeth together, determined to keep it to yourself. You can't bear to see pity on her face if you tell her that Ben did make love to you this morning, that of course it wasn't pleasant, and that he left you after telling you he felt dirty. Sharing something that personal would be even more humiliating. For both of you.

"Guess we'll see," you mumble.

"Ben loves you, Delilah."

You whip your head around to look at her, desperate for validation. If someone else believes he loves you enough to get you through this, maybe it's true.

"I keep thinking about…him."

"Ben?" She frowns. Drinks from her cup, which

reminds you that you still haven't knocked out half of this cup.

"No. The man who raped me."

"Why?"

"I just. I wonder if he's married. If he has children. I wonder why me, but really, I just wonder *why*."

"Just because he looked normal, doesn't mean he's not a nutcase, Dee. Normal guys don't go around assaulting women for fun."

"I know." You nod again. "I do. Intellectually, I know that. But I can't make my brain stop the wondering. The questions. Can't make my heart stop wishing it was different."

"Imagine." Mel's voice breaks, and the second syllable is a whisper. "He's free. To do anything he wants. And my son could end up in prison."

"It's not gonna come to that, Mel," you insist.

"How do you know that?"

You dry your hands and turn to look at her. She is small and broken, this larger than life woman you've known for so many years. The waiting is excruciating; it would be better to just plunge in and fight if it comes to that. You imagine Max and Mel and Trev live silently and still, paralyzed with terror, in their house.

It's no way to live.

"Even with all of the kids at that party, saying nothing happened, there's a big group at school saying he did it. That he's that kind of guy. People are whispering and pointing their fingers and the hell of it is, nothing happened. And Sophia Marten." Mel shakes her head. "The kid is in so deep with this lie. I just…I don't know what to think."

You nod and rub your face. Push the escaped pieces of

hair—you fixed the bun earlier, but it's messy and loose again—back from your face.

"I keep asking myself if I had had a weapon in that room, could I have used it? Could I have defended myself?"

"I sure as hell hope you're telling yourself yes."

You blink and give yourself a mental shake.

"I don't know. I want to say that I would. But I don't know."

"Do you mean something to hit him with? Fight him off?"

"I mean a gun. Could I have defended myself with a gun? Could I do it here at home?"

"A gun wouldn't make a difference in Trev's situation."

"Of course it wouldn't." You shake your head; it wasn't what you were suggesting.

"I pray, Delilah."

"For Trev."

She nods. "And for the girl. I don't know the answers, so I pray and I hope someone's listening."

You don't tell her that you've wondered where God was when you were in Aspen. Then again, maybe God can't rescue everyone, and he passed you over to focus on Trev.

CHAPTER 19

You and Ben are polite but distant for the next few days. It hurts; your heartache has bled into your body, and you climb from the couch each morning with new aches and pains. Your world has been turned upside down, but suddenly, upside down is the new normal, and you're lonely and sad. Matthew talks to you about school, about Trev, about all the normal things. He tells you one day after school that he wants to get Alli something special for Christmas, and the reminder of young love nearly brings you to your knees. When you and Ben treat each other with courtesy rather than passion and indifference rather than love or anger, it makes it hard to remember your own young love affair.

Matthew's rumblings about Christmas gifts remind you, also, that the holidays are coming. Your family is small and spread out; you don't always see either of your parents. This year, it's okay with you. You can't imagine seeing any of them when you are struggling just to survive each day. You will host Thanksgiving dinner, and Ben's dad will be here. Khloe and Naya will come for dinner, and of course, you'll invite Oliver. Gen and Christian will come by later for cocktails.

By this time of the year, you usually have the house deep-cleaned, windows washed and floors mopped. You will need to plan for the meal and get to the grocery store eventually to pick up the things you need to make dinner, but the thought freezes you. How will you be able to walk into a crowded grocery store and navigate every aisle to pick up what you need?

You can't. Not without Ben. And odds are, if you ask him now, he will either go with you grudgingly, which will only be worse for you. Or snarl at you and tell you to get over it.

He wouldn't. He would never say that to you, and you know it. But you're still hurt by what he said the other day, and rather than tell him that, you've chosen to nurse that hurt and pout about it.

You've texted Mel a few times since the conversation. She's answered you, but she isn't any better, because things in her house aren't any different, either. You imagine her and Max and Trev tiptoeing around each other, and you wonder if Becca and Trevor are still seeing each other.

Ben hasn't kissed you since the morning sex disaster, and at first it was okay with you. The sad thing is that everything up to his climax had been okay. You had felt a bit of panic when he rolled the condom on. Not that it would hurt. But you just had a quick jolt of panic, just a reaction, and then he was inside you, and it was okay. For a short time, it was good, even though you knew you were too keyed up for Ben to take you over the edge.

It was the way Ben had seized and the look on his face as the pleasure hit him. Not that you envied him what you couldn't have. But that it took you back to the way you were pinned to the bed and a stranger moved inside you and over you and finally, finished with your body for his disgusting purpose, he had ejaculated inside you because you were still helpless to fight him, to stop him.

You wish you could make Ben understand that, but you can't. Not without complete honesty. He thinks he wants to know, that he can be supportive of you if he knows exactly what happened to you that morning. But it will eat at him like acid in his veins until there's nothing left of him but bitter rage.

And you know that the only reason that knowledge could make him so angry is because of how much he loves you. Doesn't make any of this any easier, though. When you've grown tired of watching Ben and your boys live around you—without you—you think again about counseling. You can't tell Ben the details; you can't hurt him just so he will comfort you, and maybe you won't have to tell a therapist details. But if you could just talk long enough to sort yourself out, if you hear your own voice long enough, maybe you'll remember who you are.

If you can remember who you are, maybe you can like yourself again.

Love yourself.

And if you love yourself, you can love Ben freely again.

On a Thursday afternoon, five weeks after your life changed so drastically, you find yourself at the kitchen table. Your eyes are on your laptop screen, but your fingers rest on the back of your phone. You just spoke with Anna. She has been happy to work this way—her from the office and you from home—though she has to be curious about what's going on. You're finally zeroed in on your clients through work hours, so you are accomplishing things. But you've put Anna off anytime she's asked if you can meet with any particular clients. You called her because you felt you owed her an explanation, though you hedged and lied through the conversation. You had simply said you were dealing with a health issue, not life-threatening, but something serious.

She had been friendly and warm, and again, you had to swallow a mouthful of guilt for lying, for keeping secrets. You and Anna have a good working relationship. You don't spend a lot of time together outside of work, but you do enjoy her company. The concern in her voice made you question yourself and how you read people. The fact that you don't trust people, people that might consider you a true friend.

You shake the thought off as you pull the phone book toward you again. You don't have to tell Anna. It is your truth, and you have no obligation to share it with anyone. While it was wrong of you to string her along as long as you had, it's okay to keep your darkest secrets to yourself.

Just as it's okay to keep the horrid details of that morning from Ben. He would love you, and he would hold you, and you crave the comfort his love would bring. You need to cry in his arms. Maybe over and over again. But you can save Ben from the horror of that morning and still burrow into his arms and let his warmth thaw the ice inside you.

You scan the list of therapists in the yellow pages again, but of course, there are no new names listed. Heart crashing in your ribcage, you stare at Barry Holtman's name and number long enough to make your hands sweat.

The thought of Ben spurs you into action. Ben, the other day, after you manipulated him into making love to you. The way he'd thrown his arm and leg across your body possessively, protectively. That the first thing he said to you, after, was to ask if you were okay. That he'd known you lied when you said yes.

Ben, before that morning. The knowing stroke of his

hand on the back of your thigh. The brush of his lips over the back of your neck. The way he looked at you when your bodies were intimately entwined. His mad desire to pleasure you, to please you.

Everywhere. All the time.

Your hands tremble, and once you've dialed Barry's number, you put the phone to your ear and wipe your free hand over your thigh. The receptionist answers on the second ring, and you're not prepared to speak so quickly. You catch your breath as she identifies herself as Jan and the office as that of Barry Holtman. It takes you two tries to speak up, and at first, your voice is soft and unsure. Jan is patient as you spit out in fits and starts that you would like to schedule an appointment with Barry. You tell her Dr. Ambern referred you, and she is warm and friendly as she takes your information and schedules you to come in the following Monday.

For several long moments after you hang up, you sit at the table, certain that you're going to be sick. You concentrate on your breathing. Deep, cleansing breaths, until finally you know your stomach has settled. But when you lift your hands to your face, you're surprised to feel it wet with tears. You want to feel relieved that you've taken this step, because you want to bridge that gap that the stranger wedged between you and Ben. But you're terrified of being in a clinical setting, sharing the details of the worst morning of your life with an absolute stranger.

It's true that each time you've said the words, each time you've shared the confidence—first with Ben and then with your friends and the boys—it's been okay. No one has pointed fingers at you and accused you of lying. Even Mel wants to support you, and she is in the middle of her own hell with her son in a miserable situation. No one has abandoned you and your friendship. Jordan still looks through you most of the time, takes all of the things he used to discuss with you straight to Ben. But he's a kid, and you give him a pass because you laid a big weight on his shoulders.

Still. Each time you've shared the secret—even with people you love—you've relived the humiliation and the pain. It feels like rape again. You certainly identify with those women who are afraid to report an assault to the police, even those women who have absolute proof. Once it happens, simply saying the words out loud is like an invitation for the rest of the world to look at you, to rape you over and over again. How can you ever heal if that wound is never allowed to close?

Exhausted and overcome with dread and fear and grief, you fold your arms on the table and lean over to rest your head on them. The house is quiet, but the silence roars so loudly around you, it hurts your head.

If only you had paid more attention when you opened the door of your hotel room. If only you had looked through the peephole, called out to ask if it was Ben.

If only…

Tears streak your face, and you close your eyes now. Your modern kitchen in the beautiful home you share with Ben and your sons reminds you that everything has changed. The cool gray and white décor feels stark and cold, and you wish Ben was home.

With you.

You hadn't meant to manipulate him, to hurt him. It had seemed like a good time to get that first awful experience after the rape out of the way. Both boys gone, Ben looking so handsome, and you clawing at the past, needing to expand it and drag it into your future. Because the limbo, the present that you are living in is killing you.

Jordan comes home first, and though you have moved

from the kitchen table and you've washed your face and you look human, though maybe not like yourself, he offers you a stingy smile, grabs a granola bar, and disappears to his room without a word. You've finished your work for the afternoon; there is always something more to be done—you're grateful for the job security—but after the phone call and the ache that set in, you can't concentrate on anything more. You've started dinner; you're making taco pizza, one of Jordan's favorite meals.

You miss your happy kid. You miss the way he used to joke with you all the time. The noise had pierced you the night Jordan was teasing Naya when you first came back from Aspen, but now you wish you had recorded the two of them talking and giggling together. You would play it back when you're alone and lonely.

When Matthew comes home, he lingers in the kitchen with you. You talk with him about school and the goings on with his friends. He wolfs down an apple and a cookie, and you hear his phone vibrate with texts dropping in. But he leaves it face down on the counter while he hangs out with you. Finally, feeling guilty because he's babysitting you when he clearly has other things to do, you shoo him out of the kitchen and tell him to do some homework or answer texts or something.

You're both laughing as he snags the straps of his back-pack in his hands and heads down the hall to his room. But when you hear his door close, you collapse against the counter with the sink at your back and cover your face with your hands. You've reached an all new low if your teenage son—your college-bound son—is hanging out with you just to humor you, babysit you because you're too pathetic to pass an hour or two alone.

Within minutes, classic rock blares from Matthew's room. You draw a deep breath when you hear Bachman-

Turner Overdrive's music down the hall and wonder what Matthew is really thinking about you, about what happened. He's been supportive and mature, and right up until this very moment, you've taken that at face value. But he's still just a kid, and he might be talking Ben's ear off about things, too.

It hurts to feel left out in your own home. Always before, you have been in the thick of things, perhaps more so than Ben. You've worked since the boys were small, but you were still the more available parent at home. Ben used to coach Matthew's soccer team, until Matthew decided he wasn't interested. He coached Jordan's team when he was little, and now that Jordan plays in a very competitive league, Ben goes to all the games and cheers him on. Ben helps both boys with homework if they ask.

But you've been the parent at home when the boys come home from school. You've been the parent to work on the fly and take calls via Bluetooth, while shuttling Jordan from school to practice or games. You've been the parent at home when the school bus drops Jordan off, so you've been the parent who gets the afterschool kid, hyped up on school tales and bus ride shenanigans. You've been the parent to provide snacks and an ear if an assignment has one of the boys confused or if there're any friendship issues, though admittedly, those are few and far between with boys.

You've been the parent to hear about cute girls. Matthew has talked to you about Alli for the past six or seven months, and now that he finally asked her out, you're in a spot where thinking too far into those particulars makes you uncomfortable. But the idea that Matthew might be going to Ben now for those talks, for dating advice, hurts.

Your knees feel weak as you make your way down the

hall to Jordan's closed door. Under Matthew's music, you hear the sounds of a video game. You catch yourself when you see your fist poised to knock on Jordan's door. He doesn't want to talk to you, can't even look at you these days. Instead, you straighten your fingers and press them lightly against Jordan's door.

And you wish that things were different.

What if Jordan can't learn to look beneath your bruises to see the real you?

CHAPTER 20

*D*inner is more of the same. Jordan devours five slices of pizza, but he doesn't acknowledge that you chose to make it for him. You tell yourself it's enough that he enjoyed it, and you shouldn't have to be thanked. But as he turns his back to you and talks only to Ben, gushing laughter about an incident in the cafeteria today, you think it's not his thanks that you want. Just a little bit of that conversation. Eye contact.

Love.

Matthew appreciates the pizza, eats the other half of the one Jordan tackled. He talks to you and Ben about a calculus test he has tomorrow. He mentions that he got an A on a history exam, and again, you are lost because you didn't realize he had a test recently. Because you feel as if you are on suspension already for being a bad mom, you keep your mouth closed and pretend to keep up.

He tells you and Ben that he and Alli are going to a movie over the weekend, and then when he takes his plate to the dishwasher and Ben is at the sink, the two of them whisper and laugh together and you wonder if it's about his upcoming date. You watch the two of them, torn apart with longing. You are relieved that the boys have learned they can count on Ben, they can talk to him, but you miss the talks you used to have with them.

You miss Ben.

When both boys disappear back to their rooms again, you are broken and paralyzed at the table. Ben washes the pizza pans and the mixing bowls, but you feel the weight of his stare now and again. You want to tell him about your appointment with Barry Holtman, but you've buried yourself so deep in your grief, you aren't sure how to bring it up. When he washes the table down and the kitchen is clean, you get up and leave the room without a word.

It's chilly on the front porch, but you step outside and close the door behind you. A handful of stars shine in the distance. You stand with your arms folded over your chest and remember a time years ago when you and the boys stood here on the porch and watched the city fireworks on the Fourth of July. Tears streak your face, but you let them fall.

You haven't done this since you came home. You spent one afternoon out on the patio, but every noise you heard sent your pulse racing in fear. The fear is still inside you, but it takes a backseat to this sudden restless feeling clawing its way up your throat. Your world has shrunk to the tiniest of spaces, and more and more you find yourself suffocating. You're a hundred shades of blue, and these days, the color repulses you. You can't live this way anymore.

When you hear the soft squeak of the door behind you, you don't turn around to see who's there. You lift a hand— the sleeve of your turtleneck pulled down around your fingers to fight the chill—and swipe helplessly at the tears. Ben must be so sick of waiting on you, waiting for normal.

"You okay?" His voice is gruff but quiet.

You nod, but at the same time, you lift a shoulder in a dejected shrug. You're not sure that you are, and you're afraid okay is all you might ever be from now on. When you've lived a blissfully full life, being okay sounds sad.

"Do you wanna talk?"

He hovers behind you, and you wish with all of your heart that he would move closer and put his arms around you. If he believes you manipulated him the other morning, then you need his forgiveness. Trouble is, you haven't apologized, and you have a hard time understanding his pain when you're drowning in your own.

You shake your head no and wish he would go back inside. You came out here to be alone. To soak up the night. To reclaim your home, your territory. It's embarrassing to need something so basic with someone else watching you.

"Dee." He steps closer. Your body tenses up when he settles his hand on your shoulder. "Delilah, I'm sorry."

The knife in your throat is painful, and you want to shrug his hand away, but you want him to hold you, too.

"For what?" Your whisper is thick with emotion.

"The other day."

When you don't say anything, he squeezes your shoulder gently. You sag backwards and sigh with relief when you press into his hard, familiar body. He moves slowly, giving you time to shrug him off, but you don't. When he slides his arms around your middle, you cover his hands with yours.

"It's my fault." You turn your face to his and rest your forehead on his cheek.

"None of this is your fault," he says firmly.

Eyes squeezed shut, you don't answer him.

"I wanted it to be different for you."

"I just needed to get it over with."

"It's not gonna be any easier next time."

The truth in his words settles heavy and low in your belly.

"Ben, you didn't hurt me." You shake your head and step away from him.

"But it wasn't good for you."

You don't know if it ever will be, but you don't say that to him.

"I just wish you wouldn't have pushed it. We have forever to get this figured out."

You duck your head to avoid his intense gaze, but he cups your chin and forces you to look at him.

"There's no cure for PTSD, Ben," you mumble. "And that's why I pushed it."

"I don't follow you."

"I can't be the wife you used to have. I can't be that woman again, Ben. I'm damaged. You're whole, and you're healthy, and you're everything a woman could want."

"Delilah, I love you—"

You hold up a hand to stop him. "I know that. I do. And I didn't mean to…" You shake your head and glance up at the stars. "Suggest that you would cheat. I didn't mean that. It's just…I feel like…I'm not enough for you now. And I…"

"What?"

"I was just overwhelmed. Thinking about you leaving the nuthouse here to go to work. And I needed to remind you that I love you. That I want…things…to be the way they used to be."

"You can't push it, okay? God, I'm inside you, and you feel so damned good, and I'm having an incredible orgasm, and I look at your face and you looked…"

"What?" You lift your chin now to look him boldly in the eyes.

"Disgusted. Sickened."

You sniffle and turn away from him slowly.

"It's not you," you whisper.

"I know." Ben groans, clearly frustrated. "I know that. I just…We need more than a half hour to put things back together."

"I can't live like this, Ben." You rub your eyes and then dry your hands on your leggings. "I can't do this anymore."

"What does that mean?" he asks quickly.

"I made an appointment to see the therapist Dr. Ambern recommended."

"Oh, Dee. Babe." He forgets that he's been careful with you, and suddenly, you're swallowed up in his arms, pressed tight to his chest, face to his neck. "Good. I know you're afraid, and I know you don't want to do this, and I know you hate it when I say I know how you feel. Because I can't. But I'm so…" He buries his face in your neck, in your hair, and he holds on so tight, you wonder how you can breathe. But for the first time since this nightmare began, you can. You breathe deeply and fill your lungs with the crisp night air and Ben's familiar cologne and hope.

"I'm so relieved for you, Dee," he continues. "I just want you to be okay."

"No guarantees, Ben," you remind him.

"I know. But I think it would be good for you. To talk about it."

"Do the boys ask about it?" you whisper, still safe in his arms.

"Matthew has mentioned it. Jordan's been quiet about it."

Backing up enough to rest your forehead on his collarbone, you wince. You want to ask about what Matthew has said, but you know you shouldn't.

"I shouldn't have told them."

"He'll come around."

"I didn't want him to believe it was something between us."

"I know." He kisses your head and strokes your hair back from your face.

"I told Mel."

Ben makes a quiet noise in his throat. Maybe a soft groan. Maybe he wanted to argue that you shouldn't have and thought better of it.

"And?"

"She accused me of lying." You shrug as you step back from him and look up to meet his eyes. "Asked me if it was a college thing. If I believed the girl pointing her finger at Trev."

"Do you?"

"No." You shake your head. "I don't. And I told Mel that. I will stand behind Trev. The same way I would support my own sons."

"Do you think it's going to amount to anything?" Ben tucks his hands in his pockets and tips his head.

"No, but I don't understand how it got this far."

"I'd like to talk to Trev."

"You don't believe him?"

"I do." Ben nods without hesitation. "I just want to hear his side of this. I want to know what happened at that party."

"Were they drinking?"

Ben raises his eyebrows, but he doesn't answer you.

"So, they were." You nod.

"Matthew said he had two beers. Trev had a couple. But he says Trev was nowhere near the girl."

"What would you do if someone pointed her finger at you out of nowhere and accused you of assault?"

Before Ben can answer you, you reach for him and grip his arm, his hand still in his pocket.

"I know you, Ben. And you'd never do that to a woman. But what if someone accused you?"

"I'd fight, Dee. I'd fight to protect my family from that kind of slander."

"But it would kill you," you whisper. "For someone to say that about you. It would kill me."

"But you would stand by me."

"Absolutely." You nod.

Ben arches his eyebrows again.

"I know." You sigh and shake your head. "I know, but it's still not the same."

"Did he make you undress?"

Your heart sort of hitches and drags down to slow motion at the sudden change in direction. Ben had asked you the other day, when you were making love, if the man who raped you made you undress. And so now, you stand on the porch and remember both the disastrous experience you and Ben shared and the violent morning in the hotel room in Aspen.

With your heart slowing down, you fight to breathe, and you can't speak, so you simply shake your head. You stare at Ben, at your husband's familiar midnight blue eyes, but in your head you see yourself opening the door. The silky nightie you had worn for Ben. The thong that Ben had tugged at with his teeth that had been lost in the sheets, only to be found and taken by a stranger.

"Did he talk to you? Did he threaten you?"

You sigh and drag your eyes from Ben's face. The light is on in the neighbors' house—the living room—across the street. You wonder what they are doing, but afraid of where your thoughts might take you, you focus on the stars instead.

"He said…" You breathe deeply and feel pain in your throat. You wish that Ben would let this go. "If I was quiet, he wouldn't hurt me."

"He wouldn't hurt you," Ben repeats.

You nod without comment.

"Did it? Hurt?"

Again, you nod but don't speak.

"Did I hurt you?"

"No."

"What did he look like?"

"Ben." You sob and press your fingers to your lips.

"We could have someone draw him from your description."

"Don't do this," you whisper. "Please? I don't know who he was. Now he's one in millions of people in the country. Maybe in the world."

"He had an accent?" Ben asks quickly.

"No."

"He might be one of millions of people, but he was in Aspen the same time we were. What if they have video surveillance in the hotel? What if they can find him?"

"What if they can't?" You shrug. "You want to find him and…and…and…get revenge. Make him pay. See him punished by law. Whatever. I get it. But if they can't find him, you're still telling Aspen…people you work with…you're telling them your wife was sexually assaulted."

"Delilah—"

"And if we do find him? Then what?" You shake your head. Tears streak your face again, and you taste salt when you lick your lips. "You go after him, and you tell the world that he raped me, and I stand around with all eyes on me."

"But—"

"Some people will believe me. Some won't. Some women would make me their poster child. Some people would vilify me. There's no rape kit. There's no police report. There's no evidence but faded bruises. And my word."

"But it happened."

"It did. I chose to keep it to myself." You shrug. "I don't wanna be raped again, Ben. Please don't put me through it again."

It pains him. Swallowing it and pretending it didn't happen. Letting your attacker get away with it. It rattles his chains, but you stare at him, lips pressed together, and pray that he agrees to let it go. A different woman would have reported it and gone after the man. You didn't. Ben has to accept that to accept you.

His nostrils flare when he breathes deeply, but finally, he nods and reaches his hand out to you. You take his hand and move in to stand close to him again.

"I thought it was you," you whisper. "And I let him in."

"I'm so sorry." He has apologized over and over for what happened, but you don't remind him he didn't do anything wrong.

"I had the silk nightie on that I wore for you," you continue. You wrap your arms around him and press your cheek to his chest, but your head is turned away from his face. "When he pushed the door open, I knew. I knew…I was in trouble. But I couldn't…wrap my brain around it."

Ben holds you. Under your hands, you feel his back muscles, hard and tense.

"He took his coat off."

"Bastard." Ben's voice is small and tight.

"Pushed me back to the bed. Put his hand over my mouth. When I heard his zipper…"

Ben waits silently for you to continue. You swallow hard, ready to vomit now. Your fingers twist his shirt so you can hold on to the present.

"I just…I went away. In my head. It probably didn't last ten minutes. The whole thing."

"How did you get so bruised?"

"I guess I fought him." You shrug. "I don't remember, really. The memories come to me when I try to sleep. I pushed at him, and I ripped a fingernail off. He clamped his hand over my mouth. I guess he put his hands on my neck, too."

"Did he put—"

Still without looking at him, you shake your head.

"No more. Please."

"Dee."

"I can't say more, Ben. Please. Give me that much? A little dignity."

"Did he sodomize you?"

"No." You breathe deeply and finally lift your head to look up at him.

"Was there anyone—"

"No more." You say it again. "Please. I don't want to talk about it like this again."

"Okay." When he nods, the tears in his eyes shine.

CHAPTER 21

*B*arry Holtman is a bespectacled, gray-haired black man with a warm smile. He greets you with a gentle but firm handshake and gestures for you to come into his office. You glance back at Jan—a very plain-looking woman who brings to mind Jane Hathaway in The Beverly Hillbillies—and then twist around to see Ben. He sits in the waiting room, iPad on his lap. But his eyes are on you. He insisted on driving you here, and you are still a little bit relieved he is here and a little bit annoyed that he couldn't give you a little space.

After the conversation on the porch, you had gone inside, chilled by the late October air and the words you and Ben exchanged. You've given him the bare bones of the attack, and it's all you will say. You can't find the words to express the horror you felt when your biggest fear became real. When the stranger's hand touched your breastbone and pushed you to the bed. There are no words in your world to say what it felt like to have a stranger force his penis inside you, to have to lie there and wait for him to be done.

There are no words to say how badly it would make you feel to try and paint that picture for the man who loves you and who has touched your body with love and respect for the past twenty plus years.

Ben turned on a movie, and you soaked in a hot bath. You needed to warm up, and before you climbed out of the tub, you scrubbed your skin pink and raw again, desperately trying to wipe away the taint of the assault and the words you used to describe it and those you swallowed to protect Ben. At least the quiet moments on the porch paved the way for a calm weekend.

This morning, he didn't go to work, though. He insisted he would drive you to your appointment and wait for you.

He looks at you now with the worry a parent wears as he shoos a child into a kindergarten classroom or a college dorm.

Barry Holtman offers you coffee, but you shake your head and mumble no thank you. You cast one last look at the door as he closes it. Your body freezes with fear, but you can't sit here and talk about this with the door open, either. Barry makes his way to one of two comfortable chairs in front of a large, imposing desk. On the desk, you see a framed photograph. Two women, beautiful smiles beaming at you.

"My daughters," he says when he notices you looking. "Avril is married and living in Dayton. She's a fourth-grade teacher. She has five kids, ranging from fourteen down to three."

"Wow." You laugh softly, unable to imagine having a busy career like teaching and raising five children.

"And Anita lives in Springfield, Missouri. She's got a boy. Been in a little bit of trouble, but he's finding his way back."

You process that, process what he didn't say. Anita's not married, apparently. You wonder why. And then you wonder why it matters.

"My wife and I have been married forty-one years," he continues. His voice is warm and soothing. "She runs a ladies garden club. Loves tulips. Says there's over three thousand varieties of tulips. Can you even imagine?"

He says this with delight, though he's definitely soft-spoken. When you look at him, his smile is genuine.

"I know next to nothing about flowers," you admit as you perch on the edge of the chair opposite him. "Except maybe how not to care for them."

"Have a favorite to look at?"

You open your mouth to answer him, but you stop yourself. *Roses* had been on the tip of your tongue, but you wonder now if they are your favorite to look at. Or if you just feel that you should say you love them because Ben used to bring you a dozen every year on your anniversary.

When had that stopped?

"Sunflowers," you answer quietly.

Barry Holtman doesn't question you or call you out for choosing a flower other than those Ben used to bring you. He simply nods, his lips pursed as he thinks. While he doesn't appear to be an aggressive person, he's dressed neatly in gray trousers, a white dress shirt, and a navy cardigan. No tie, his shirt is loose at the collar. He wears a thick gold band on his finger, and a gold watchband peeks out from under his shirtsleeve.

"Favorite color?"

"Blue."

He nods. "Green." He grins at you and rests his folded hands in his lap. "Song?"

"'Fly Me To the Moon,'" you answer without pausing to think. This gets a big grin in response.

"'Round Midnight.'"

"Thelonius Monk," you shoot back at him, and when he nods his approval, you realize you've already sunk back into your chair as if you're here to discuss music with an old friend rather than the dreaded truth.

"I like a little Whitney Houston, too," he tells you, and he draws the most honest laugh from your lips you've heard in nearly six weeks.

"Well, who doesn't?" You shrug. Your purse is at your feet, and you are wearing a familiar smile, though now that you realize you're wearing it, it feels rusty and crooked.

"Dr. Ambern referred you," he says it so easily, so smoothly that you don't startle as you thought you might. Instead, you simply nod and wait for him to ask something harder than a favorite song or color. "How long have you been Dr. Ambern's patient?"

"Um." You blink and shake your head. "I don't know. I guess…I started seeing her not long after my oldest son was born. Maybe…fifteen years? Sixteen?"

"How old is your son?"

"Matthew is eighteen," you answer, and the good feeling leaches out of you. "And my younger son is fourteen."

"Do they know?"

You open your mouth before you realize you don't know what to say. You haven't told Barry Holtman yet why you are here. Does he simply assume it was an assault because Dr. Ambern referred you? Or did she send your medical files?

"Yes."

"How's that going?"

Just like that, the floodgates open, and you're weeping again.

"You strike me as a good mother."

"How would you know that?" you ask. You lean forward to grab tissues from your purse, but Barry snags two from the box on a small round table between you and hands them to you.

Barry shrugs. "You're wearing a beautiful wedding ring. There's a very concerned-looking man in the waiting room, who was watching me closely when you came in. You have strong hands. And your heart is in your eyes when you speak about your sons."

"Matthew seems to be dealing with it," you say quietly, careful not to meet his eyes. "Jordan avoids me like I'm contagious."

"When?"

"About…" You pull in a big, deep breath and feel your lungs and chest expand. "Six weeks ago."

Barry nods. "Wanna tell me how it happened?"

You don't. As nice as the guy has been, you don't want to talk about it.

"My wife plays the piano at church," he announces. "She knows the prayer ladies there. She prays for you. She prays for everyone."

You laugh again, and suddenly, you're talking about the morning in Aspen. Granted, you are relating the story in that bare bones, sketchy way you shared it with Ben last night. You leave out the part about the night you spent with Ben before it happened. About the way Ben made you quiver and beg and cry for more. You leave out the part about the stranger taking your thong and pinching your nipples. You end the story before he slapped your ass and walked out and you heard someone ask for the USA Today.

Even then, you're shaking when you finish talking. Your nose is stopped up, and your eyes burn, and it amazes you that it can feel like this, even when you've told the story this way, detached. As if it happened to someone else.

When you and Ben climbed into the car to leave the house earlier, you announced to him that you would go once and see Barry Holtman and see what you thought. When you leave his office, you feel somewhat calm, and you don't think twice when you stop and talk to Jan to make a second appointment.

Ben is solicitous and eager to please when the two of you go to the car. He takes your hand, and you not only let him, you squeeze his fingers. He's dressed in jeans, but it's not until you are in the car and on the way home that you notice and wonder why. He offers to take you to lunch, so you accept. Over a cup of soup—Ben has a big deli sand-wich with his soup—at the café where you met Genevieve and Khloe that day for lunch, you ask him won't he be late for work. He tells you he took the day off. It's hard for you to swallow, and the soup doesn't settle right. You wonder if he expects sex when you get home, but you tell yourself that's not like Ben.

You talk about the boys over lunch, about the days gone by. Halloween is tomorrow night, and so you remi-nisce their costumes and laugh and choose your favorites. Yours is Matthew as a Billy goat when he was four and Jordan as Spiderman when he was three. Ben likes your choices, but he says Matthew as a vampire at seven and Jordan as Winnie the Pooh his first Halloween are his favorites.

Ben announces that Matthew has been invited to a Halloween party. Your stomach is in knots instantly, but before you can protest, Ben lifts his fingers to stop you.

"He's not going."

"How can any of them think about partying right

now?" You shiver as you sip your iced tea. "How can the parents allow it?"

"I suppose they think it can't happen to them."

You wince, because once upon a time, you thought the same.

"So what's he doing? Just staying home?"

"He asked if Alli could come over."

"Is that any better, Ben?"

"We'll be home. Trev and Becca are coming over."

You sigh, but that sounds better than Matthew and Trevor attending a party where anything can happen or anyone can say anything happened.

"It's kind of sad, isn't it?" you say quietly.

"What's that?" Ben rests his spoon against his bowl and wipes his mouth with his napkin. You stare at the bowl and then his plate, where only one bite of his sandwich is left. If he kisses you when you get home, will you taste pickles on his tongue?

Do you want him to kiss you?

Can you do this the right way?

"That our boys…that the good kids can't go hang out somewhere with their friends and have fun…without worrying about this stuff. Maybe they're no safer than girls."

Ben sighs and nods. "I know, Dee."

"My heart." You shake your head. "I mean, Ben, I know there are boys…men who hurt girls. I'm not naïve."

"I think you know that better than anyone else, Delilah."

You shrug and roll your eyes. "Even before," you say softly. "But it's not fair for a girl to make up a story about a boy and ruin his life."

"Girls want that power, though," he tells you.

"Women need to be strong," you concede. "I'm all for

teaching girls to be strong and self-sufficient. And I'm all for justice for women…like me. But I don't think women having the power to hurt men is any better than the way the world is now."

You hold the eye contact for a long time, and finally, Ben breaks it to take a drink of his soda.

"Matthew said he and Alli made out the night of the party."

Your stomach pitches, and you cover your mouth.

"They had sex?"

"No." Ben shakes his head, but he avoids your eyes. "But they messed around."

"Oh, man." You rub your eyes, careful not to make a mess of the makeup you tried to touch up in the restroom in Barry Holtman's building. You hadn't worn much, and you did a decent repair job even before Ben asked if you wanted to grab lunch.

"Lots of kissing," Ben goes on, eyes on the table. He speaks very quietly, so he won't be overheard.

"Where at?"

Ben looks up at you quickly, but you roll your eyes.

"The barn," he answers with a little grin. "When Trev was on the four-wheeler. Some kissing. Second base."

"Wow." You squeeze your eyes closed and duck your head. "I don't think I want to know this stuff."

"He said he was pretty cool with it, until all of this stuff started with Trev."

"Did he say what Alli says about it?"

"Alli and Bec are friends. He says both of them say nothing happened."

"Did this stuff happen when we were kids? Did kids make out and cry foul the next day?"

"Not very often." Ben sighs. "I think we took more

responsibility for our actions when we were kids. Things have changed."

"I know."

"You ready?" Ben eyes your cup of soup, nearly empty. You can't finish it now, but you take your tea with you when you leave. You and Ben hold hands on the way out to the car, and then at your door, he kisses your cheek.

He won't force it, but you decide on the drive back to the house that he wants you to suggest making love again. You're not sure it's the right day, not after telling him last night the things you did about the rape, and not after your first session with a therapist. He talks about Matthew and Alli and how they will be going to different colleges as he drives home. What strikes you is that Matthew has told Ben where Alli plans to go to school, and that he and Ben have discussed college. He's not decided yet where to go, because you know he would tell you where he's decided. But the fact that he's talked to Ben at all about his plans hurts you.

At home, the house is quiet, and when you go inside, you are reminded instantly of the other morning and how you pushed Ben to make love to you just to try and barrel past the hard stuff. It has to be front and center in his mind, too, but he doesn't mention it as he heads through the living room. You stand at the kitchen island when he disappears into the bathroom, and you haven't moved when he comes back out.

"I think I'm going to mow the yard," he announces. "Probably the last time of the year." He slips by you and leans over the sink to peek out the window. "I'll get some of the leaves up that way, too."

Relief and disappointment hit you in equal measure. You give him a small nod when he looks at you.

"Delilah?" He presses in closer to you, his thigh rubbing yours.

"Hmm?" You nibble on your lower lip as you try so hard to avoid his eyes. He settles one hand on your hip, the other he leaves wide, on the counter.

"I want very much to take you to the bedroom and undress you." He kisses your cheek again and then rubs his face against yours. "I want to kiss you. Touch you. All day. I want you to remember me. My hands. My lips."

Mouth dry, you try to swallow.

"But I'm not going to force it. Not going to push you. I don't want to make love. I don't want to rush you. I'm perfectly happy going out to work in the yard."

"Did you take the day off for that?" you whisper and flick your gaze up to meet his eyes. "To mess around?"

"No." Gentle fingers cup your chin. "I took the day off to be with my wife on a potentially hard day. I took my beautiful wife to lunch. We had an important conversation over lunch. And now I'm going to either work out in the yard and let my wife work in here, or I'm going to lay her down and worship her body and show her I don't see anything damaged about her."

"And what if…she can't relax?"

"Then I'll go work in the yard, and she can take a nap. Or soak in the tub. Or work on a client's stuff."

You feel shy as you rest your forehead on his shoulder. You want to climb into bed with him and see how it feels. But you can't open your mouth to say those words.

"Do you remember—"

Your shoulders go tight with fear, afraid he is going to bring up something about Aspen.

"Relax." He trails his fingertips up your back. "That night in Sacramento. We had dinner. A bottle of wine. You got a little touchy feely in the elevator."

You laugh softly, but your cheeks burn.

"When we got to our room, I laid you down and brought you to tears?"

"Yes."

"I'm still me," he reminds you. "And I still love you. And you…" You close your eyes when he nudges you to make you look at him. "Baby, you're still you. A little sad and hurt and shy, but you're still Delilah Nicholson. And I still love you just the same damned way I always have."

You're supposed to ask how he loves you. This is a game you've played from the beginning of your lives together. Tears streak your face now, and you lick your lips and look at him.

"How do you love me, Ben?"

This time your whisper means so much more than usual. But Ben offers you the same, sweet smile he's given you since day one.

"A little bit more every damned day I'm with you, Dee."

CHAPTER 22

*W*hen the boys get home later, you feel rested and much more relaxed than you thought you would after seeing the therapist. Ben is outside. He's been working in the yard for a while now, and he's out in the garage putting the mower away. The leaves that had carpeted the yard are gone, but there are still dry, colored leaves in the trees, so someone will have to rake them when they fall.

Maybe you will, you decide as you stare out the kitchen window. It's dark, so all you can see is the yard under the floodlights, the shadows creeping in around the edges. But the thought of getting outside to do something fills you with energy.

Earlier, you and Ben did go back to bed. But this time, Ben moved slowly, and he spent more time just kissing you. He had locked your bedroom door, and for a moment, you were frozen at your side of the bed, remembering the heavy clunk of the hotel room door closing.

You wanted to suggest opening the door. After all, it wasn't even noon, and the boys wouldn't be home for a while. But if by chance you messed around and fell asleep, you wouldn't have wanted them to find you half-dressed or less. But Ben hadn't pushed you to do anything. In fact, for the longest time, you lay in his arms, both of you fully clothed. His kisses were warm and tender, and it helped that the stranger hadn't put his mouth on you. Ben whispered to you as he held you, sweet things, and his voice kept you grounded in the moment.

Eventually, you dozed off with your head on his chest and his arm around you, both of you still fully clothed. When you awoke, you were alone with the blanket tucked up around you, and you lay for a long time listening to the drone of the mower outside. Eyes closed, you remembered the tenderness Ben had shown you today, and you were surprised to feel a stir of desire for him.

You spent the rest of the afternoon working, so when the boys are home and Ben comes inside after working in the yard, you don't have anything thawed for dinner. Ben suggests going out for pizza, and you almost balk at the idea. You could remind them all that you just fixed taco pizza last week. You don't want to be out in the thick of things. You don't want to run into someone you know, because you don't want them to look at you and wonder what you've been up to. You don't want to feel those flashes of panic that take your breath away and leave you feeling weak and exhausted.

But Jordan watches you skeptically, expecting you to shut Ben down. You're not a family who eats out all the time, though when Jordan's soccer season is in full swing, you are on the go a lot more often. But it's been a long time since the four of you have gone out together for a fun night. You haven't grabbed a pizza out since you've been back from Aspen. And it wouldn't matter to the boys if you served them pizza six days a week.

You agree with Ben's suggestion, and you hold your breath, wishing that Jordan would say or do something. Acknowledge that you're trying to do better. He doesn't, though. He only rushes to grab his shoes and hurries out to the car.

Pizza night is fine, and though you're somewhat jumpy, you're glad you agreed to come. It's fun, and though Jordan still doesn't say much directly to you, Ben and Matthew keep you in the conversation. The conversation is light and easy; there's an unspoken agreement that no one will talk about the bad stuff in public. None of you wants to discuss Trev's situation outside your home, for his sake, and your situation is so dark, the boys tiptoe around you and never mention it even inside the house.

You do see a few people you know, but you're on the inside of the booth. Tucked away under Ben's protective arm, you're able to engage in conversations and laugh off the comments about not seeing much of you out and about lately. One of the moms from the high school approaches your table. Her name is Jill; her daughter is in Matthew's class. You see from the way she's eyeing you critically that she wants to ask you what you think about Trev. While she is a casual friend, you have no intention of getting into any dialogue with anyone about Trev or Max and Mel. When Jill starts talking to you, asking where you've been, and if you've talked to any of the other senior moms, Ben gets that she's feeling you out to see what you know. Your thighs are pressed together, and you feel him flinch.

You answer her, though. You tell her you've traveled some recently and haven't been feeling well, so you haven't gone out much. She asks if you were at the homecoming get-together to do pictures; she says she thought she saw you there, but then you were gone. Ben pulls cash from his billfold to cover the pizza and—you know—to let her know you're ready to leave and finished with the conversation.

She doesn't get it, though. She leans on the booth, you think a little too close to Ben—if he turned his head now, his face would be in her breasts—and asks if you've heard what's going on. She flicks a glance at Matthew and Jordan. Matthew is watching you closely, but Jordan is looking at his phone.

"I have," you answer simply. She arches her eyebrows and shakes her head. She mumbles something about *can you believe this* and you wonder if she was in theater when she was in school. She's egging this on, doing her best to stir up drama. In teen terms, you wonder if she is Team Sophia or Trev.

She stares at you with big eyes, and you realize she wasn't rattling about believing how crazy things have gotten. She is flat out asking you what you think. And while you are disgusted by her audacity, and you assume she's not the only one out there stirring the pot, you have to let her know what you think.

"Trevor didn't do it." Your voice is calm and firm. Nothing outward gives away the fact that your insides are trembling now.

"So you think that girl is lying?" The mom gasps and leans into Ben, and now her breasts are resting against his head. He's looking at you, and you see the frustration on his face when he leans forward to escape her proximity. This conversation could turn dicey really quickly, and by the time you are in the car headed home, half of the parents in Matthew's class will know what you said.

But Max and Mel are your friends. And Trev is a good kid caught in someone else's lie.

"I don't know what the girl's doing. I don't know her at all." You shrug. Because even though it seems pretty likely that she made up a story to sound cool at school and one lie led to another until she was in too deep to take it back, you do know it's possible someone somewhere assaulted her and she's pointing the finger at the wrong person. "But I do know Trev. He's a good kid. He wouldn't do that."

"Those boys were pretty hyped up that night."

You blink at the woman, stunned that she's pushing this.

"The boys I saw there were having a good time because it was their senior homecoming. That doesn't mean any of them were thinking about raping any of the girls there."

"It happens." The woman shrugs and laughs as she sweeps her gaze around the room, probably looking to see if there's anyone else here she can gossip with. You know damned well the next person she talks to is going to hear your name.

Ben rests his hand on your leg.

It does happen. You are living proof that rape happens. You take a deep breath and cover his hand with yours.

"It does," you agree. You want to remind her that girls push the envelope with their behavior and the skin they display. You don't believe any woman or girl deserves to be assaulted. Ever. But you do think a girl's behavior can give boys the wrong idea.

None of which is relevant in *this* conversation. This isn't a story about date rape. A girl Trev doesn't even know accused him of rape.

"I'm just saying who knows what went on at that party." The mom looks back at you. A syrupy sweet smile crosses her face when her eyes meet yours. "In that barn. I bet there was a lot of naughty stuff happening. Lots of hormones. Trev might have thought it was okay to help himself. Everyone was doing it."

"Trev didn't touch Sophia," Matthew says quietly. "No one at the party saw him near her except when he stood up by the bonfire to go to the four-wheelers, and he bumped into her."

"Really?" Jill turns her attention to your son, and you imagine you hear her sharpening her claws. All you need is this woman deciding to up the ante and throw Matthew's name into the circle. Especially if Matthew did drink and get in on his own little make out session with his date.

"You ready, Dee?" Ben squeezes your thigh and starts scooting out of the booth. Jill moves, but not far enough out of Ben's way. You notice the sparkle of light on her diamond as Ben bumps into her to stand up. Her laughter sounds like a purr, and you wonder when the lines with all of this sexual harassment and assault stuff got so blurred.

"Yeah." You scoot out of the booth, too. The woman touches your arm and rubs her hand up and down your sweater sleeve. Your bruises have faded so that they aren't noticeable, but her lingering stare still makes you uncomfortable.

"Good to see you guys." She flashes you a big smile.

"You, too," you lie through your teeth and return her smile.

"Guess we'll just keep our fingers crossed for Trev, huh?" She shrugs and grins and mumbles goodbye. You stare after her as she returns to her own table, her mouth wagging already. Matthew and Jordan hurry out of their side of the booth, and the four of you traipse back out to the car.

"What the hell was that?" Ben asks as he stabs the key in the ignition.

"That's the jury. They've already decided he's guilty."

It makes your head hurt. You close your eyes as Ben steers the car back home. The night had started out fun, but you're exhausted when you flip the kitchen light on and shrug out of your jacket. You thought Mel was being over-dramatic when she worried that Trev could go to prison, but the possibility chills you now.

There are witnesses who say nothing happened, but apparently their word means nothing up against the fifteen-year-old girl pointing her finger at Trev.

"Mom?"

"What, hon?" You turn to Matthew, a jab of pain in your heart when you notice that his eyes are glassy.

"Thank you."

"For what?" You cup his face in your hands, and it hits you that you have not held either of your sons—you have not hugged them and said you loved them—since you were raped six weeks ago.

"Trevor didn't rape her." Matthew sniffles and tries to jerk his chin away from you. "He wouldn't hurt anyone like that."

"I know that, Matthew." You nod, eyes locked with his. "I know that."

"How can you defend him if…"

You tear your gaze away from Matthew's to look at Jordan. He watches you with a frown, the whole situation too damned much for a kid to process.

"What happened to me is a completely different thing, Jordie," you whisper. "I don't believe that Trevor would hurt anyone like that."

"But how is it different?" He pushes, and the enormity of the situation hits you again. "If she says he raped her. How is it different from what happened to you?"

Matthew watches you closely, apparently waiting for you to answer.

"Guys, maybe Mom doesn't want to talk about this—"

"No, Ben. It's okay." You shake your head. Maybe it's

past time to talk about this. You take a deep breath and try to figure out how to say what you think, what you feel. "First of all, I meant that I can keep what happened to me separate. I don't think every guy in the world is a rapist."

"But we could be?" Jordan arches his eyebrows. "Just because we have penises, we could be rapists?"

"Who told you that?"

He shrugs and lowers his gaze to the floor.

"I suppose some women look at it that way." You back away from Matthew and lean on the counter. "I don't believe that. I just don't believe every man has that inside him. I also don't believe that Trev did anything to this girl. I think she told her friends she made out with him because he's a cute senior guy. And that probably scored her some points."

"Does rape always hurt?" Jordan asks you.

You stare at him silently for a moment, blown away by the question.

"I don't know, Jordan." You finally give him the only truth you can. "Psychologically, I would have to say yes. Physically...I don't know."

"I don't get it." He stares at you boldly. "I know it's wrong. I wouldn't do that to a girl. But I don't get it."

"That it hurts?"

"That it might hurt sometimes. That you and Dad have sex, and it doesn't."

"Oh, Jordan." You flinch and turn to Ben for help.

"Right?" Jordan shrugs and frowns. "You and Dad do it. I mean, I assume you do. And it's fine, but this...this happened to you, and you're...it's like you're dying. It's like you wanna die and forget us."

Ben wraps his arm around your shoulders. You can't stand here another second. You can't listen to your son's questions about rape and sex, and you can't stand the accusation in his voice. The way he sounds angry with you. That he wants to equate that violent act with what you and Ben did that created him, what you and Ben still do.

Except. You haven't. Not since…

"I'm gonna…" You shake your head and turn into Ben for protection. From your own son. "I can't. I can't do this."

"I know." Ben kisses your hair and rubs your back.

You duck out of his arms and make a beeline for the bedroom.

"Good job, dickwad," Matthew mutters.

"I didn't mean to make her mad." You hear Jordan snap. "I just don't get it."

"That's because you're just a kid," Matthew answers. You stand in the darkness in your bedroom with your hand over your mouth. "If a girl's into it, it feels different. Like her body actually feels different. Something you'll never know, dumbass."

"Guys!" Ben's voice thunders through the room. You close the door with trembling hands and slink to the bathroom. Your body trembles violently—thoughts of that morning in Aspen heavy and dark in your mind. You hear Jordan's innocent voice asking loaded questions, and you hate yourself for not being able to give him answers.

Sinking to sit on the edge of the tub, you prop your elbows on your knees and bury your face in your hands. You need Ben, but maybe the boys need him more at the moment. You can't have Matthew explaining this to Jordan, not when Matthew is not much older than his brother and—you hope—has no more true experience with women than Jordan does.

How is it different, you ask yourself now.

It's different because as you told Jordan, you can keep your assault separate from everything else. Now. Maybe not immediately after it happened. You hated the whole world; you told Ben that time and again. But now, you can look at the majority of men in your life and know they aren't going to violate you or other women. You've always believed every incident of assault—violent attacks by strangers and date rape, both—should be approached and judged one at a time. There's too much gray area these days to just throw around blanket statements. You don't believe every woman who claims to have been attacked should be taken at her word; nor do you believe every man who claims he didn't assault a woman should be believed without question.

You swipe at your eyes now and wish that you could have stayed calm out there in the kitchen to say that to Jordan. But his question about how rape hurt you but sex with Ben doesn't had been so unexpected, it had taken your breath away and ripped away all the peace you've found since it happened.

For one thing, you can't sit and look your son in the eye and make him understand that the mechanics of sex work better when the people involved are aroused. That it's a completely different act when you have feelings—especially love—for the person you're with. That you are attracted to Ben and as Matthew stated so crudely, your body is ready for his when you make love. But that a stranger forcing himself on you was a complete violation, and it did hurt, physically and mentally and emotionally.

Jordan is too young to really understand the whole situation. He does know that it's wrong to force attention or touch on someone who doesn't want it. But he knows that because you've taught him that. He has no life experience to draw on here, and that makes you wonder how much experience Matthew has.

You pray that Ben can make Jordan understand why

you're hurt. That if you believed for a second that Sophia Marten really had been raped, you would be out there crusading for her. That yes, a man can ruin a woman's whole life with that one act, but women have that same power over men, and it's wrong on both sides of the equation.

CHAPTER 23

The constant ringing of the doorbell is enough to send your heart rate through the roof. Eventually, Ben carries the bowl of candy to the front porch and sits there to greet Trick-or-Treaters and save your sanity. As much as you enjoy seeing the costumes and saying hello to the neighbor kids, you have no interest in any of it this year, so Christian sits with Ben. They wear goofy hats as costumes—Ben's is an old fedora that pairs interestingly with his faded Dad jeans and pullover navy fleece. Christian—dressed in khaki dress slacks and a green cashmere sweater—sports a White Sox cap. From inside, curled into opposite corners of the sofa, you and Genevieve hear them laughing and teasing the kids who come looking for candy.

Gen sips a cup of tea and watches you over the rim. She's asked how you're feeling, and she's mentioned that she saw Mel. Of course she must know what is going on with Trev. Before you can say you don't believe Trev would hurt a girl, she tells you she doesn't believe he did anything. On a big sigh of relief, you simply nod. As if she senses you are tired of talking about assault and rape and consent and boys and girls and men and women, she launches into an update on Beatrys.

You're grateful that she simply knows what you need, and you drink up the news about her daughter greedily. Beatrys is in college at the local university, but she plans to go away next year. She's pre-med, but her interests are in research and pathology. Gen tells you she was dating someone, but both she and the boy have decided they don't have time for each other and therefore shouldn't date.

But they still study together and nothing has changed, other than what they call it.

It strikes you that this is a little bit of what's wrong in the world, today. Maybe nothing has changed, other than what everyone calls everything. Labels and misunderstandings cause so many problems, and that only complicates bigger problems.

Still, you love Beatrys, and you don't see her settling down before she's forty or fifty, and Gen has long since accepted that she will most likely never be a grandmother.

Matthew and Alli are downstairs, and now and then you flash on the thought of them downstairs and hope they aren't doing something inappropriate. Ben reminded you again earlier that Trev and Becca are here, too, but does that mean anything? It's possible to watch a movie and cop a feel without anyone else knowing. You did the same things when you were younger.

Gen asks after Jordan, if he's trick-or-treating. You tell her he is at his friend's house, and really, you worry as much about him now as you do Matthew and Alli. Jordan had announced even before the incident in Aspen that he was too old for trick-or-treating, but it feels like you've forced him to grow up so fast in the past few weeks. You rushed him through a process that should take a while, and you worry that the rush job was inadequate, and he might have missed something.

Like feelings. You taught him right from wrong, but did you teach him that making the wrong choice has consequences besides those he experiences? Did you teach him that his bad choices not only lead to his punishment but maybe hurting others?

Ben says they talked a long time last night. Maybe they did. You had given up and crawled into bed. Clothes on, makeup a mess on your face, you had buried your face in your pillow and cried yourself to sleep. Ben promises you that everything is fine. Jordan doesn't blame you; he doesn't have any wild need to do things and see what happens or if he hurts someone. He simply wanted to understand how sex can be physically pleasing but rape is not.

The idea of Ben and your sons discussing the particulars of sex and the way a woman's body is aroused—rather than focusing on the birds and bees for boys—still makes your skin flush with shame and embarrassment. You suppose with everything happening right now, it was good for Ben to sit and answer their questions. But you feel raw and overexposed, and you pray with all your heart that the boys can process the information separately from you.

Later, Khloe and Oliver come by, and Naya—dressed as a ninja kitten—storms Ben and Christian and the candy bowl. You and Gen share a smile as you listen from the sofa while Naya gushes to the guys about her fun night, the millions of candies she got, and the piggy-back rides Oliver has given her to get from house to house. It's getting late, though, and when Khloe opens the door, Naya trails her inside. She smiles shyly when she sees you, and then with a big yawn, she climbs into your lap. Khloe winces apologetically and reaches to take her, but you shake your head and wrap your arms around her.

You've missed this sweet, devotional love, and you feel a pang of regret. You closed yourself off from everything—your own sons included—when you came home from Aspen. It's up to you to get back to the woman you used to be, and you thrive on love, so in order to be that woman again, you have to accept the love in your life.

No, you have to do more than accept it. You have to claim it. And give it back.

"She's fine," you murmur to Khloe. Khloe unzips her heavy jacket as she lowers herself to sit on the ottoman by the wingback chair.

"You sure?"

"Yes."

"Where's Oliver?" Gen asks her.

"As luck would have it, he's wearing a safari hat. He thinks he fits right in with Ben and Christian."

You laugh softly and offer Khloe a shrug.

"Where's Jordie?" Naya asks as she snuggles her sticky lips close to your neck. She smells fruity, and you wonder if she's been hitting Skittles or lollipops. You close your eyes and revel in the feel of her warm breath on your skin, the tug of her fingers tangling the back of your hair.

"He's at a party," you tell her.

"Will he be home soon?"

You smile down at her hopeful face. Probably, Naya will be sound asleep by the time Ben goes to pick Jordan up. But you understand how much she wants to see Jordan, because you do, too. You hadn't been able to face the day or either of your sons this morning, so you haven't seen much of Jordan at all today. In fact, you'd seen him for less than ten minutes when he got home and changed from school clothes to jeans and then rushed out the door when his ride to the party pulled up.

"Soon." You nod, but already Naya closes her eyes.

"You doing okay?" Khloe asks quietly.

"One step forward," you admit. "I'm so sick of living like this."

"You can't rush it, Delilah," Genevieve reminds you.

"I talked to Mel this morning," Khloe announces. "Told her to let me know if I can do anything."

"How's she doing?" you ask, because even though you've talked to her a time or two since she was here, you feel disconnected.

It's your fault, and your stomach is heavy. It's more than guilt. You're disappointed in yourself. You're a better person than this.

"I think they're in limbo." Khloe tucks her hair behind her ears. "I can't imagine the waiting around. Wondering what's going to happen."

You squirm a bit in place on the sofa. Technically, you're waiting on HIV results, though you feel somewhat easier about the wait after the first blood work came back okay.

Still. The idea of sitting, holding your breath for days on end, wondering if the police will show up to arrest your son for something he didn't do makes your skin crawl.

Not for the first time, you wonder what the man who attacked you is doing right now. Is he lingering in another hotel waiting to strike another innocent woman? Or is he at home with his wife handing out Halloween candy? Walking with his kids, lingering on driveways, watching over them while they trick-or-treat?

"Is Mel working?" you ask, and you see the quick look Genevieve gives you. She covers it quickly, rearranges the shocked arch of her brows into the smooth, calm look she always wears, and nods in response.

Definitely time to dig yourself out of this hole. Setbacks are one thing, and to be expected, according to Barry. But the wallowing—what had Jordan said? That you act like you want to die?—wasn't going to change anything.

Mel works at a physical therapy office; she does accounting and handles payables and receivables, all the stuff that makes you crazy. You don't want to bother her at work, but maybe you could drive over and see her after hours tomorrow.

You startle when the front door opens again. Naya twists in your arms, but she's warm and sleepy and presses back into you. Khloe and Gen both notice the way you jump, though. They don't react, but it embarrasses you anyway. Christian and Oliver follow Ben inside, Oliver pausing to close the door behind them and flip off the porch light. Ben holds the bowl up to show you it's empty; his face softens when he sees Naya snuggled up to you.

"I'm gonna go get Jordan."

You meet his eyes and nod as Gen and Khloe stand to go.

"Wanna ride along?" He grins, hopeful you will say yes. You want to, but you're not sure leaving Matthew and Alli and Trev and Becca alone is a good idea.

"Hey." Gen leans in and kisses your cheek. "Let's get together next week."

"Yeah." You nod and turn toward Khloe so she can take Naya, who mewls in protest but goes willingly into Khloe's arms.

"Come back to class, Dee," Khloe whispers as she draws you close for a hug. "We miss you."

Your company leaves, and you stand in the kitchen and

watch Ben put the candy bowl—you've always gone big
with holidays, so the Halloween candy bowl is big and
black with orange and purple cats on it—in the sink and
then fish his keys from the drawer. He turns to look at you
and arches an eyebrow.

"Don't you think someone should stay here?"

When he moves to stand before you, you press close
and rest your hands on his chest. He wears a playful smile,
and you swear his eyes are twinkling, and a tingle of joy
touches your heart. You miss this stuff, the sweet, lovey-
dovey way you and Ben have always connected. For a
second, you're tempted to feel anger toward the stranger
who did this. But you swallow that thought and remind
yourself that you have the power to move on. You are still
letting him hold you down.

"Maybe." Ben shrugs his lips. "Maybe I just want you
with me."

He cups your upper arms in his hands and then drags
his fingers down your arms and moves them to your hips.
He curls his fingers into your small curves and with a
gentle tug, he pulls your middle close to his.

"Khloe wants me to come back to class."

Sliding your hands up over his shoulders and around
the back of his neck, you lift up on your tiptoes and press
your lips to his.

"I think that sounds like a good idea." He splays his
hands wide now to cup your backside, and it feels flirty
and fun.

You've experimented with different fitness classes, you
and Genevieve together. Your favorite always seems to be
yoga, though you enjoy Gen's company enough that it's all
kind of fun. You miss it. The time spent with friends, sure,
but the actual physical activity and the stretches and
meditation.

The realization startles you.

"What do you think?" Ben ducks his head to kiss your neck playfully. Nothing he's doing right now is sexual; this is a scene you played out on a nightly basis back when life was normal. Still, there's a tiny flame of desire burning low in your belly, and though you're nervous like a schoolgirl expecting her first kiss, your body is almost weak with relief.

"Maybe I should try it." You arch your eyebrows and lift your shoulders in a tiny shrug. Ben's hands roam possessively up over your back as he nibbles on your neck and your earlobe. You laugh, but you want to ask him what he thinks about other classes. Like self-defense. "What would you think about…"

You hesitate, because maybe it's a stupid idea. Could you defend yourself with a well-placed kick or punch? Or would you freeze? And submit? The guy had threatened you, but if you were better prepared and in better shape—

You're not in shape to run a marathon, but you do stay in shape, so maybe that's not a valid argument—

"Think about what?" Ben coaxes you. He pulls back from your neck to meet your eyes and trails his fingertips over your face.

"I don't know," you hedge now, because you feel self-conscious. "I was thinking about taking some self-defense classes."

The playfulness is gone, and Ben, the protector, is back. The fingers that just touched you gently now cup your chin. He nods.

"I think that's a good idea," he agrees. "I've been thinking about things we can do. Maybe things we can do together."

"You wanna learn martial arts with me?" You can't help the small laugh.

"I will." His lips tip up with the hint of a smile. "But I was thinking more along the lines of conceal and carry permits. Shooting lessons."

"Oh."

"No?" He draws back again and studies you with an intense frown.

"No. Well, yes. I mean…I'm just surprised you mention it." Your fingers are moving over the back of his neck now. His skin is soft and warm under his hair. "I've thought about it, too."

"Okay." Ben nods, all business now. "Let's look into it."

"I'm not sure I could shoot someone, Ben."

"Not even if he was coming after Matthew or Jordan?"

"Yeah. Definitely. But." You shrug helplessly and shake your head.

"You couldn't defend yourself?"

"I don't know."

"After what this has done to you and done to us as a family, you don't think you could defend yourself?" Ben shakes his head, obviously frustrated with you. "Delilah, you're the heart of this family. Someone hurt you, and he hurt all of us. I'd kill the son-of-a-bitch with my bare hands if I could."

When you blink, the tears that burn in your eyes slide over your face. Ben smooths them away with his thumbs.

"We'll think about it."

"Okay."

"You stay here on duty." He kisses your forehead. "I'll be right back."

"Ben."

"Hmm?" He stops at the door and turns back to look at you.

"Thank you."

He nods and almost smiles, but his lips don't quite make it. When he breaks the eye contact and goes out to the garage, you shiver with a chill that has nothing to do with the cool temperatures outside.

CHAPTER 24

*M*atthew and his friends had come upstairs not long after Ben left to get Jordan. You had been curled up in the corner of the sofa again with the TV on. No scary movies, even though it used to be a Halloween tradition. You lived through your own horror. No telling what might happen if you got caught up now in a thriller or paranormal movie. Your eyes were on the TV —a wholesome movie you would have thought was boring just a couple of months ago—but your mind was racing.

You were caught up in thoughts about self-defense classes and conceal and carry permits and the thing Ben had said about protecting yourself. Sadly, no matter what Max and Mel do, they can't muscle up and save Trev, because *the truth* is on his side, and they're *still* waiting for a third party to make a decision about Trev's future. You'd also been worried about what you would say to Jordan when he came home, if he would even give you the time of day.

And, of course, your mind kept venturing down to the basement, concerned about what might be going on there.

Before, you might have ventured down once just to say hi and remind all of them that there was an adult in the house. Maybe they needed that reminder now more than ever, and maybe not, but you couldn't bring yourself to do it.

So when they came upstairs, you were jumpy. Uncomfortable with the girls and their glittery eye shadow and shiny-teenage enthusiasm. Both of them are adorable, and you think they're probably nice girls. You've known Becca longer than Alli, but you think Matthew has a good head on his shoulders, so he has to be a good judge of character. The four of them talked to you for a few minutes about school. The girls were soft-spoken, and the conversation was punctuated with nervous laughter, and you should have been able to put them all at ease. You should have been able to engage with them and talk to them, because you're the adult. But the time they stood behind the couch to talk was miserable. You caught yourself trying to be sneaky and study Trev, as if the current struggle would be painted on his chest or his face. He's still the same good kid, though, and when they all finally left, your heart hurt for him and Max and Mel.

Jordan had been all smiles when he came in, and your immediate thoughts had involved girls and Trev's current issue. The party Jordan had attended was for the whole class, boys and girls, alike. The only saving grace had been that you knew the parents were present all night. You would have liked to talk to Jordan, to ask if he had fun and what they did. If they watched scary movies or played games. But he had called a quick goodnight to you and disappeared to his room.

You tried to hide your hurt feelings, but Ben reads you too well not to have noticed. He tried to placate you, relaying information to you from Jordan. He had a reading test to study for—naturally, he waited until after the party to study—but they had fun. Played some games.

Not enough, and yet, probably all you would ever get.

Your next appointment with Barry Holtman is not until next week, and you find yourself antsy and wishing you could talk to him now. Maybe talking about the party and about Jordan's questions about sex and rape would make it easier for you to process. The irony doesn't escape you. For weeks, you balked at the idea of seeing him because you couldn't imagine talking to a stranger, to a strange man, about rape. Somehow Barry had put you at ease and now you think maybe talking to him about this extra stuff might help.

Until then, though, you try to stay busy. You go back to FitNess, and Gen and Khloe and the rest of the ladies there are so happy to see you, you feel a flash of guilt—again—for your lack of faith in the people who care about you. It takes a bit to settle back into the stretches, and your balance is off, but the weight on your shoulders surely has something to do with that. Maybe the meditation is what you needed most, and it might take you a while to be able to clear your mind and focus.

After Halloween and having the older kids in the base-ment and the ringing doorbell and Naya plastered against you and soaking up your energy, you can't muster the energy—the guts—to go see Mel the next day. Instead, you fix dinner for Ben and the boys. The night out, the one that was supposed to be fun, had turned exhausting and frustrating, and you don't want to relive that any time soon. And as you clean the kitchen later, you wonder if it bothers you so much, how can Max and Mel possibly deal with it day in and day out?

You make yourself go the next afternoon. After a solid seven hours of work—your laptop open on your kitchen table—you pack it all up, touch up your makeup, and then stand in the kitchen indecisively. The boys are in their bedrooms, but you wonder if you should tell them you are leaving. You decide you would rather avoid conversation right now—you need to bolster yourself to see Mel—so you scribble out a note to tell them you will be home in a while. You thawed chicken breasts for dinner, but Ben will grill them, so you don't need to worry about it until you come home.

"What're you doing?" Matthew asks as you throw your purse straps over your shoulder and scoop up your keys. You stare at him silently, irritated that he has come out of his room just as you are ready to leave.

"Going to see Mel," you finally tell him.

His eyes go wide in expectation, and he ambles down the hall toward you. Behind him, light spills out his open bedroom door to the hall. You hear music and wonder if he was studying or if maybe he's been on the phone with Alli.

"Did something happen?"

"No." You feel a stab of guilt. Of course it's reasonable for Matthew to worry that something has happened to Trev. The situation has been ongoing now for weeks, but this is the first time you've decided to venture out of the house to see Mel. "Not…that I know of. I just thought I'd go check on her."

Matthew responds with an enthusiastic nod, but he keeps his eyes down to hide from you. You hesitate to leave now, because you've upset him. You should be reassuring him—both of your sons—that Trev will be okay, that the truth is all he needs and everything will eventually sort itself out. Instead, you're bumbling around and upsetting both of them more than offering them any comfort.

"I won't be long," you say to his back. He moves to

the sink and rests his hands on the counter. No answer, other than a shrug. You hesitate a moment longer, wondering if you should go tell Jordan where you're going. You even take a stutter step down the hall, but you can't do it. You simply can't face your youngest right now. You fear the judgment still in his eyes when he looks at you.

You push away the thought that you're behaving cowardly as you go out the back door to the garage. Your Highlander hovers in the garage, and you feel as if it's watching you, judging you because you have hardly driven it since you were in Aspen. You fight off a wave of anxiety, climb into the driver's seat, and open the garage door.

Frank Sinatra keeps you company on the short drive to Max and Mel's house. His voice makes you think of your first meeting with Barry, and that memory is comforting. You realize when you pull to the curb in front of Max and Mel's big, brick house—it's a gorgeous, imposing sanctuary that has proven to be no safer than yours—you are smiling, and it feels good.

When the smile starts to slip as you head up to the front door, you bite your lower lip to keep it in place. You even push the doorbell button with confidence, but it starts to waiver when you wait on the porch for Mel to answer the door. You shiver a little and huddle deeper into your heavy jacket, and you consider running now before Mel sees you here. You've given it two minutes; maybe she ran errands after work and isn't home yet.

But the door suddenly opens with a violent yank and a low, shrill squeak. Mel stares at you silently when you meet her eyes. She's still dressed in khakis and a sweater from work; still wears sexy little boots that fill you with regret. You used to care about things like fashion and your appearance. At the moment, you feel inadequate and ugly, which is ridiculous because Mel is your friend. And she wouldn't judge you.

Even if her son wasn't being held over a barrel of boiling tar, she wouldn't judge you.

Still, you have to fight the urge to turn and hurry away, back to the Highlander.

"Hey." You arch your eyebrows in question. Without a word, she flings her hand up in a lazy invitation for you to come inside. When you do, you see the cracks in her appearance. She wears makeup, as usual, but up close, you notice the lines in her red-rimmed eyes and the dark circles that tell you she's not sleeping.

"Slumming today, Delilah?"

"Mel." You wince.

"I'm sorry," she mumbles as she closes the door. You watch her when she steps around you and leads you into her kitchen. Like yours, it's spacious, but hers is decorated in deep greens and splashes of copper. The woodwork in their house is cherry with a dark stain. You stand now to study the house and wonder if it feels cozy and welcoming to her or if the darker rooms feel smothering and depressing. Your light colors and white woodwork are bright, but the bright can sometimes feel harsh and cold.

"I'm sorry," you argue. "Gen and Khloe both said they've run into you lately, and I know I've been horrible to you. Not coming around more or showing more support."

"I'm sure being around me and Trev is hard for you."

"Mel, no." You shake your head, but it *is* hard for you. You don't start each day with the thought that you can't be around Max and Mel or Trev. You don't think of the man who attacked you and paint Trev's face over him. You can't begin to imagine Trevor manhandling any girl, and as you told your sons the other night, you can keep the two things separate in your head. But there's some part of your body that reacts to Trev's situation with anxiety and dread. "It's not—"

"Dee, if you were raped, the last thing you want is to be involved—"

"I was raped, Mel." You interrupt her. Your voice is firm, though your heart climbs into your throat. "I was."

"I didn't mean it to sound like that." Mel shakes her head. She ducks her head to her hands and rubs her eyes. When she lifts her face to look at you, you see she's smeared a bit of mascara into the bruises under her eyes. "Even if it was a college or high school situation. Like this. I wouldn't mean to question you."

Your hands shake as you peel the straps of your purse from you shoulder and set it on the counter. Next, you shrug out of your jacket and toss it over the back of a stool.

"I just can't imagine you want to spend your time around us. Dealing with the…" She clears her throat and frowns, as if she is reliving your worst memories. "Do you have flashbacks? PTSD?"

"Something." You shake your head to shoo her question away. You do have flashbacks, and odds are you do have PTSD and will. You know from your discussion with Barry and from your own online research that there's no cure for it. You might learn to manage it, but you will carry that repercussion for the rest of your life.

For instance, you may have an aversion to travel forever. At the very least, you will most likely never travel back to Aspen. You will never choose to stay on the seventh floor of a hotel again.

"Then you don't need to be here." Mel clears her throat and goes back to the other side of the counter. She's apparently dismissed you; she goes back to dicing a bell pepper, her hands unsteady on the huge knife.

"I do need to be here," you say quietly as you slide

onto a stool and watch her. "I need to get over myself. And you need—"

"I need a stiff drink and a beach vacation or a time machine so I could undo homecoming." Mel shoots you a little grin. "And maybe a new job, and some new friends, and maybe to move to the coast or something."

"Why do you need a new job?"

Mel ignores your whisper. "Have you and Ben made love since it happened?"

The direct question is a knife in your ribs. You purse your lips and stare at her for a long, uncomfortable moment. Finally, you look away and answer with a small nod.

"And?"

"It was hard."

Ordinarily, that would have led to crude jokes and laughter. Today, Mel only stares, waiting for more of an explanation.

"It was okay. Until Ben…"

"Why until then? Until what?"

"I just…" You squint to hold back your tears and take a deep breath. "Had a flashback. And we ended up fighting about it."

"Ben? Ben fights?" Mel mumbles. "I'm sorry. I know no one's perfect, but things are so bad here right now. I love Max, but we can't get along for two minutes. Ben just seems so…compassionate."

"He is, and so is Max," you remind her. "The stress you guys are dealing with…" You're grasping at straws to convince her that what she's going through is normal. But there's nothing normal about what she and her family are going through. Nothing normal about the way you and Ben have lived recently.

Well. It shouldn't be normal, and that it's become your normal makes you sad.

"You haven't heard anything?" Your whisper is thick with emotion.

"No." She focuses on the pepper she is cutting into strips, but you know it's just that it's easier for her not to look at you. "Waiting on the state's attorney to make a decision."

"And what's he doing to make his decision? Interviewing people? Getting the truth?"

Mel sobs and drops the knife so quickly, you're moving before you realize it. You assume she cut herself, but there's no blood. Instead, she covers her face with her hands again and cries softly.

"I was putting stuff away in Trev's room the other day. And he was on his laptop. I thought he was doing homework."

Your stomach shrivels up in dread.

"He was reading some guy's blog about prison."

"What?"

You let out a huge sigh of relief, and Mel gives you a pointed look—her makeup smeared even more now. You swallow your apology and wait for her to go on.

"The guy is a married man. Has two kids. And he was accused of raping someone seven years ago. Shocked the whole town. You know the story. Town hero. Everyone loved him. Kids loved him. A woman he worked with accused him of rape when they were at the office late one night around the holidays."

"Trev was reading this?"

"Trev follows his blog now." Mel shrugs. She snatches a napkin from the drawer in front of her and blows her nose. "The guy says he walked his coworker to the parking deck, and they parted ways. The next morning, two uniform cops show up at the door of his office—it's an advertising agency—and walk him out. The woman said she and the guy worked late. That she was up for a promotion, and so even though it was the holiday season and she wanted to get home to her boyfriend, she worked late to finish a project. She claims the guy got handsy with her in the building, and she told him no. Says that when they were in the parking garage, he forced her back into the main building and shoved her into the ladies' room. Covered her mouth with his hand and raped her from behind."

Your stomach lurches, and without an explanation, you turn and dart to the bathroom. You didn't eat much today, but the images Mel just shared with you painted your own memories back to life, and you throw up enough to make your throat burn and your mouth taste nasty.

When you've finished and you've flushed the toilet and washed your hands, Mel is at the door when you open it. She offers you a glass of water, which you take. You sip and swish and turn back to spit in the toilet again.

She doesn't apologize when you finally return to the kitchen. She's moved on from the red pepper to an onion. You set the glass on the counter with a bang and ease onto the barstool again, relieved to get off your trembling legs.

"The guy was sentenced to prison. Served seven months before she came clean and said she made it up. That she was having an affair and her boyfriend had figured it out. So she lied and said it wasn't a consensual thing. That her coworker raped her."

"How did Trev find the blog?"

"I dunno. But last night he was reading a kid's story on that blog—I guess a lot of people follow this guy and comment. This kid is nineteen. And he's a freshman at college. He was at a party. Left with a girl he knows from class. They're friends. They went back to her dorm, and he says they had consensual sex. The girl changed her mind the next morning, and he was questioned and arrested within the next week."

"But, Mel, it's different for Trev—"

"It's not, Delilah." She drops the knife again and looks you in the eye. This time, her eyes are cold and dry. "It's not different. I get that sexual assault happens, and even without seeing you suffering the flashbacks, I can imagine how horrible you feel. I think every goddamned woman in the world can sit for just two seconds and feel the absolute horrible fear and rage that being victimized would bring. We're women. The last thing in the world I want is for another woman to be violated—"

"I know that." You nod. "I agree." Now you're crying, and you dash at your tears.

"But there are women, girls, who lie. For whatever reason. And because it's so horrible for the women who suffer that disgusting thing, we have to believe every woman or girl who claims rape. That girl lied about Trev. And it doesn't matter. The fact that over ten or fifteen kids have told the cops that Trev didn't touch her doesn't matter. If the state's attorney wants to bring charges against my son, he can. And I have to stand here in this goddamned kitchen and fix supper like everything's normal. I have to pretend we're okay."

You cover your face to hide from Mel's rage, from her terror. You are a rape survivor, but you're also a boy mom. And a wife. And this—Mel's hell—could so very easily be yours.

"People who don't even know Trev think he did it. That he's one of those entitled kids. That he was at a party. Boys will be boys." Mel sniffles. You jump when you hear her slam something on the counter. "Not my son. Not my son, Dee. My son cried when Mrs. Madigan died the summer after fourth grade. My son rescued a baby bird in the backyard when he was twelve. My son volunteers for community service. Does he complain about it when it means he has to get up early? Hell, yes, he does. Does he drop the f bomb when he thinks I'm not listening? Yes. He does. Does he watch movies with nudity in them? Yeah, he does. Show me a kid who doesn't. My son would never feel entitled to anything with a girl."

When you look, you see that she's thrown the cutting board to the back counter by the sink. There's a scuffmark on the wall where it hit it before careening into the sink. The knife is on the counter, still, and she is wringing her hands.

"But we don't get a say in what happens. The kids who told the police that nothing happened don't matter. We're hostages in our own home. Every day I go to work, I see Sophia Marten's mom's friend's cousin's brother who lets me know every chance he gets that Trev is a vile, disgusting kid who raped a fifteen-year-old girl."

Remembering your own night out with Ben and the boys, you press your lips together.

"What can I do?"

"Nothing."

"No, Mel, let me do something. Let me help you."

"What can you do, Dee? What? Are you gonna go door to door and campaign for my son's innocence?"

She's right. She and Max can't move; their hands are tied. You certainly can't fix it. Nobody can fix this, other than Sophia Marten.

"Max feels bad for the girl."

"I'm sorry?"

"I mean, he's angry," Mel continues, quieter now. Her whisper is almost mechanical. "He's angry. He's worried about Trev. But he feels bad for the girl. Because she lied and got herself in so deep, she can't get out."

"Have her parents made a statement?"

Mel shrugs and licks her lips as she meets your eyes. "I wanna strangle the kid. I want to put my hands on her neck and strangle her for what she's done to Trev."

You feel a pang in your belly, a shared maternal streak because you would like to get your hands on the girl, too. And yet, you wouldn't. And neither would Mel.

"Sweetie, I know," you say with a nod, "but I know you. You don't have that in you, any more than Trev had this in him."

Mel squeezes her eyes closed, but she nods in defeat.

"Trev's having nightmares."

"About the girl?"

"That. Prison. I keep telling him I'm going to take his computer if he doesn't stay away from that blog. From all the articles about sexual assault and prison. Max says he needs it. Not knowing what will happen is making him sick with worry, and that is his way of trying to prepare."

That makes sense, but you agree with Mel, too.

"I'm worried about him." Mel wipes her eyes again and then pushes her hair back from her face. She meets your eyes again. "I'm worried he'll hurt himself, Dee."

"Trev?" you yelp, and then you look around and wonder for the first time if Trev is here.

"He's depressed. Kids do stupid things when life looks hopeless."

"Is he here?"

Mel shakes her head as she slips into movement again. You watch her as she straightens the cutting board in the sink, but she ignores the scuff on the wall. She carries a plate of chopped vegetables to the stovetop and drops them into the skillet already there.

"He and Max went for a run."

From where you stand, you watch her struggle to get her emotions under control.

"Max is trying to keep him busy. They've been running every evening."

"Good." You nod when she looks at you.

"He and Bec broke up."

"What?" You blink and shake your head, shocked by the latest news. "They were just at the house the other night. Mel, she doesn't—"

"Trev broke up with her."

"What?" Your voice jumps up an octave again. "Why?"

"Because he feels like he's dragging her down with him. He loves her, and he doesn't want her to get hurt by what's happening to him."

"Mel, she loves him."

"I know." Mel shoots you a helpless look. "I'm worried his college acceptances are going to start disappearing."

You watch her for a few silent moments as she continues to prepare dinner for her family. You wonder what dinnertime is like here now. Is it quiet and sad, or are Max and Mel raging at each other all the time?

Part of you wishes you hadn't come. And that has nothing to do with that primal need to avoid the whole sexual assault issue because of the physical way it impacts your body. You hate being a spectator in this mess, and you hate that you are completely helpless to do anything for your friends.

"What can I do?" Your voice is gruff, so you clear your throat and hold your breath while you wait for Mel to answer.

"Go home and let Ben hold you. And let him love you. And love him back." Mel turns to you, dishtowel in her hands, her face a mask of anguish. "Because Max and I can't find that right now, Dee. Max and I can't see each other through this, and it scares me to death that we might—"

"No." You shake your head and move to take Mel in your arms. "Nope. I will go home and love Ben, but Mel, it's been ugly. It's been a struggle. If I can do this, you guys can do this. You can beat this. You have to do this together."

"I'm just so angry," she sobs against your shoulder. "I'm so goddamned angry, and he's hurt. I need him to grow some balls and go after them, Dee."

"But what can he do?"

"I don't know, but I need him to do something. I need him to fix this for our son."

CHAPTER 25

*Y*ou didn't tell Ben last night when you made love that something Mel said had driven you into his arms. You simply burrowed against his warm body when he climbed into bed beside you. When he kissed you, it was a sweet, tender goodnight kiss, but you turned it into more. You moved to straddle him, your open mouth on his neck, but when you sat up to ease your nightshirt off, Ben had stilled your hands at your sides.

"Are you sure?" he'd asked in that firm, but gentle voice. "Because I can wait."

Still a little bit put off by the idea of lying skin to skin with him, you had pushed his hands away, pulled your nightshirt off, and offered yourself to him. Mostly, you wanted this, and the part of you that didn't, wanted to want it. And then there was Mel, tiptoeing around big, ugly words like separation and irreconcilable, asking you to go home and love your husband. Ben's hands were familiar and strong and capable. Things had been slow at first, between your stuttering desire and his stop and start actions, making sure you were with him in the moment.

Your orgasm had been a slow simmer. Twice, you had urged him to forget it, that it wasn't going to happen, but he had been in no hurry. Rather, he had reminded you in whispered words that he loved the feel of your skin on his and the feel of your slick heat around his fingers. He had kissed you, his lips and his tongue reclaiming your breasts and your neck and your shoulders as his, and through it all, you kept your eyes wide open, desperate to ground yourself in your marriage bed.

The sob that escaped your lips was a familiar sound of pleasure pain as the heat of orgasm tingled and throbbed through your body, and when he entered you, this time, the two of you moved together in that delicious, intimate dance from before. When it was over, neither of you moved, except to shift positions. Ben lay on his back, and you curled up with your head on his chest. And you slept together, nude, for the first time since the assault in Aspen.

This morning is full of tender kisses and intimate looks exchanged. You're imagining it, because Ben was never angry or rough, but you feel like his touch when he squeezes your shoulders as you pour his coffee is softer. In his suit trousers and white shirt and tie, he looks devilishly handsome, and you can't help yourself when you grab his tie and yank him close for a kiss.

He hadn't joined you in the shower this morning. Rather, he had stood at the edge of the walk-in, arms folded over his chest and talked to you. He'd looked his fill, and heart racing with desire and maybe a little bit of panic, you let him. But he hadn't joined you, hadn't copped a feel when you dried off and dressed, the way he's done a hundred times or more in the past. You appreciate his respect for your need to call the shots. Now, though, in the kitchen, you can't help but wind your arms around him and rub your lips over his.

The hell of it is, you want him now. The orgasms last night had broken the dam inside you, and you're both relieved that your body connected with his and hungry for more. But it's a workday, and both boys are up and moving for school.

"Mom, how was Mel last night?" Matthew interrupts the kissing, but you don't move away from Ben. In fact, you hang on tight, but you rest your head on his shoulder. Your boys have seen this behavior before; you and Ben have always been the touchy feely kind of parents teens groan about.

When you came home from Max and Mel's, Matthew was gone. He'd left you a scribbled note that he'd gone to study with Alli. When he had come home after nine, dinner was finished, and the dishes had been washed and put away. You and Ben had been watching a movie, so there hadn't been much conversation. You offered him a plate of leftovers, but he'd thanked you and said Alli's Mom had made dinner. That had irked you, but on the other hand, you had fixed dinner for all three of your guys, so it wasn't as if you had wasted anything.

"Yuck," Jordan mumbles. You automatically drop your hands from Ben's shoulders and step away from him. It makes you sad that you've lost your son—temporarily, you hope. You've done nothing wrong, but your youngest looks at you with contempt and disgust, and you're completely helpless.

"No word." Your voice is gruff when you answer Matthew. "It's really…bad there. Like the house is just…" You feel Jordan's eyes on you as you struggle to describe what you felt at Max and Mel's house yesterday. "Oppressive. Like, the tension is so thick, you can't breathe."

"Trev broke up with Becca." Matthew pours orange juice in a glass. You flinch when it splashes all over the counter. You nod when he lifts his eyes to look at you. "She kept calling and texting Alli."

"He thinks he's protecting her," you whisper.

"Alli's freaked out. Worried about her."

"And Matthew's pissed because those phone calls took away from his hook up time with Alli." Jordan grins at all of you. Your hand shakes so badly, you can't pick up your coffee cup. The smell of the coffee hits you suddenly, and you hear someone asking for a USA Today, and the stranger's voice saying I won't hurt you, and you think he did hurt you and your husband and your sons. The son-of-a-bitch lit a bomb and threw it right smack in the middle of your family.

"That's enough, Jordan." Ben sounds exhausted.

Jordan doesn't answer, but you watch him as he moves through the kitchen grabbing a bowl and a spoon for cereal. When he glances at you, you steel yourself for another vicious comment. Maybe he heard you and Ben last night, maybe he heard the bed moving or maybe he heard you moan and call Ben's name. Maybe he'll never stop hating you. But you wish he would at least stop hating the rest of the world. If your son can't love you, you love him enough to want him to be himself again, the happy, fun-loving kid that vanished overnight.

Finally, the trembling has stopped so you raise your cup to your lips. The coffee tastes like regret.

"At the party the other night." Jordan looks at Matthew when he speaks. "Three girls took their shirts off. One of 'em wasn't wearing a bra. And one had tits like—"

"E. Nough." You slam the cup down hard enough that it breaks. Hot coffee pools on the counter, chips of the cup —the handle broken off completely—islands in the dark liquid. "I don't know what the hell has gotten into you, but I have had it with your ridiculous attitude, Jordan. I shouldn't have told you what happened. It's a very private, hurtful thing, and you've thrown it back in my face every day since then."

"Then why did you?" He snaps at you. His face is twisted with ugly rage and hurt. In that ugly, distorted face, you see the little boy you miss so deeply. "Why did you tell me? It makes me sick. I can't stop thinking—"

"I told you because you thought Dad and I were talking about divorce, and I didn't want you walking around with that fear. Because no matter how often I reassured you it wasn't something like that, you didn't believe me. I told you because I needed to tell Mel. After all hell broke loose with Trev, I had to tell Mel what was going on. And I didn't want the two of you to end up hearing from someone else something that should come directly from me."

Jordan seethes on the opposite side of the counter. His face is mottled and red, as if he is trying not to cry. Matthew sits at the island, his head in his hands. Ben stands at the opposite end of the counter, hands on his hips, a scowl on his face.

"And I told you because I thought it might be a good lesson for you. For both of you." You tear your eyes from Jordan to look at Matthew. He peeks at you from between his fingers that now cover his face. "This is the face of rape. This is what it feels like, guys. This is what it does to a woman. To her family."

"Mom—"

You hold a hand up to stop Matthew, because you're not finished.

"Do not ever walk into my kitchen talking about a girl's tits, Jordan. Do you hear me? Do not *ever* do that. You guys think you're so damned mature, so cool, playing with fire like this. Wake the hell up! Trev could do prison time for something he didn't do. For something someone else might have done at that party. For something that might have happened at a grade school party. Do you get that?"

When neither of your sons responds, you take a few steps around the counter.

"Do. You. Get. It?"

Matthew nods. Jordan refuses to meet your eyes.

"You're not mature. It's not mature to walk around talking about women that way, Jordan. It's horribly childish, and just proves that you're much too young to get involved in any sort of relationship with a girl."

"They took their shirts off. No one asked them to."

You stare at Jordan, stunned that he intends to continue this argument.

"I don't give a damn. Maybe someone needs to call their parents. In this house, we do not treat anyone with such disrespect. What if one of those girls went home and told her mom—what if the girl who took her top off and had no bra on—what if she told her mom one of you boys touched her? Even if you didn't. Or let's say that you did. Her mom could report it. And whoever she pointed the finger at—or whoever did touch her—is in the same goddamned kind of trouble Trev is in."

"It's different," Jordan argues. Your knees go weak with the worry that your son did put his hands on the topless girl.

"It's not different." Ben stirs. He tosses what's left of his coffee into the sink and rinses his cup out. "It's not different. I'm not sure you understand this, Jordan. Trevor could do ten years in prison. When he gets old, he's an ex-con. He's a sex offender. That means he's on a list of sex offenders in the state. That affects the rest of his life. Where he works, if he works. Where he lives, because registered sex offenders aren't allowed near children. He's already lost Becca. What other woman is gonna wanna get involved with him when she learns he's an ex-con? That he was convicted of rape?"

"But what if he's not?" Jordan shrugs.

"If Max and Mel get a call today from the state's attorney, and they find out he's not bringing charges against Trev, do you think this is over?"

"If there're no charges, he doesn't go to prison." Jordan's voice is smaller now.

"But he goes to school, and there's still a big group of kids that are going to point their finger and say but what if he did? There'll still be parents out there who think he got away with something. Just the question, the *doubt* could affect his college career. And his professional career. What if twenty years down the road, he runs for political office and someone slinks out of the closet waving a flag saying wait a minute, that dude raped a girl at a party when he was a senior in high school?"

"I didn't touch her." Jordan shakes his head. "A few guys did, but I didn't."

"And just by being present at the party you're at risk."

The thought of young kids—girls or boys—undressing and parading around at a party makes you physically ill. Why are kids in such a hurry to grow up? Where did they have to hurry to? Responsibility. Jobs. Kids. Money problems. Headaches. Why not be kids and have fun for a while? Fun that doesn't involve skin and nudity and touching?

"I didn't think it was that big of a deal." Jordan nudges the cereal box away. "Since they were the ones who did it. Who took their shirts off."

"But all they have to do is say it didn't happen that way," Ben argues.

"And it is a big deal if someone touched them," you

remind them. "No one should be putting their hands on fourteen-year-old girls."

"I didn't."

You might have believed him, but after the third denial, you have to wonder if he's lying.

"This is the way bad things happen." You inch around Ben and lean over to grab the roll of paper towels. Mopping up the spilled coffee, you swallow a wave of nausea. "The girls shouldn't have done what they did. Any boys who touched them shouldn't have done that. Do you guys see what I mean? What could have happened there? What happened at the homecoming after party?"

"So that's not yes? When they start taking their clothes off?" Jordan tilts his head and stares at you intently.

"No. Absolutely not. That's a little false bravado. Maybe they thought it was funny. Maybe they wanted to tease you boys. I'm very angry that they did what they did, but no, that is not consent. A girl can work you into a frenzy—"

"What does that mean?"

You glance at Ben for help.

"Boner," Matthew supplies. You and Ben roll your eyes.

"You might think it's gonna happen, she might be doing things…but until she says yes, it's not consent."

You glance at Matthew again.

"You have no right to force yourself on anyone unless she says yes," you say quietly. "And guys, even then, you never know. I hope to hell you're being smart, Matthew Nicholson."

"How is this like what happened to you?" Jordan asks in the ensuing silence. Matthew squirms on his chair, uncomfortable under your direct gaze. If he's sleeping with Alli after everything that's happened lately, you want to wring his neck.

The thought reminds you of Mel and what she said about Sophia Marten yesterday.

"It's not, Jordan." Reluctantly, you drag your eyes from Matthew to look at your youngest son. "What happened to me is completely different."

You feel his eyes on you as you dab up the last of the spilled coffee. Ben steps up beside you with a wet dishrag as you toss the sopping wet paper towels into the trash.

"I didn't know that man. I'd never seen him. He over-powered me. And he…" Your throat closes off, and you have to pause to find your breath. "He assaulted me. At one point, he had his hand over my mouth, and he also had his hands around my neck. It was violent."

"What Mom's trying to tell you is that none of it is acceptable. Date rape. Forcing yourself on a girl you know at a party. At school. Taking advantage of a girl who's been drinking. Who's passed out. Cornering a woman in a parking deck or in an alleyway and shoving her against the wall and hurting her. It's all rape. And it is completely unacceptable."

"So you do think Trev did it." Matthew swallows hard.

"No, Matthew, I don't. I believe everything Dad just said. But I also think there are times when women or girls point a finger and make a false accusation. And that's just as completely wrong and unacceptable. False accusations —of any kind—have the power to destroy people. Families."

"Same as rape," Ben adds, and you bristle, because yes, it's the same sort of violation. And yet, because of the most basic biological difference between men and women, it's equally as horrible and still not the same.

CHAPTER 26

*Y*our body can't let go of the fury. It explodes inside you, burns up your throat, and turns your hands to claws. You fight the urge, the crazy need to explode in a frenzied rage. Your sons and your husband remain in the kitchen, and it's possible they are watching you as you walk out of the room. You eye the lamp on the end table in the living room and consider how satisfying it would be to launch it across the room through the French door. Maybe you would even beat back the remaining shards of glass and step outside to the patio. In your head, you thump your chest with your fists and roar with rage and howl with pain. All the broken pieces inside you are out of alignment, and the jagged edges rub your soul raw. You imagine yourself wailing in desperation to make your family understand who you are now, after what happened to you.

Because underneath those broken pieces, you are still you. Maybe a bit wiser. Street smart. Maybe jaded. But you are still Ben Nicholson's wife, and you are still the mother of the two boys in the kitchen who can sit and bat around words like *tits* and *boner* right in front of you. Even before your own assault, you would have called Jordan out on his obnoxious behavior and the horrible things he's said lately.

But what hurts the most is being nearly positive that before the assault, you would never have had to call him out on anything of the sort. Because he wasn't that kid. He wasn't a boy to push you to your limits, and now that you are staggering through every day just struggling to survive, he seems to take pleasure in walking on your last nerve. It's your fault that your son has learned cruelty, and you continue to fail to teach him compassion.

In the bedroom, you slip into the closet and step into a pair of black flats you haven't worn in ages. The boys are still at the counter, Ben still by the sink when you return. You avoid their gazes, but you feel all of them watching you as you pack your laptop and your planner—you've always been a control freak who needs a hard copy of her schedule as well as a digital version (fat lot of good that control has done you now)—into your bag. You shoulder the bag and fish your keys from the drawer where you keep them.

"Where are you going?" Matthew's voice is gruff, but you hear a note of surprise, too. All three of them watch you with greedy eyes when you look up at them. The storm inside you rages on, but you give them an impassive face. It's the best you can do to save them from the gut-wrenching mess of emotion tearing you apart at the moment. You're currently choking on emotion, and the one riding highest in your throat just this second is fury.

"Work." You smooth your hands over the seat of your jeans. The idea of jumping back into the daily fray sends your heart racing like you've been running sprints. But you doubt being in the office can be any more infuriating or soul-sucking than it is to be in your home right now.

"Work?" Ben sounds shocked. "Are you sure?"

Slowly—perhaps to them you appear smooth and well put together but inside you are seething and counting to three—you turn to him. When you'd climbed from bed this morning, you might have glowed. Not from sexual satisfaction, though God knows it was so good to be back to that with Ben. But from the intimacy, the closeness you felt to him after the way you made love last night. Now, you stare at him from across the kitchen, though it feels to you as if you're on one side of a chasm in the earth and the men in your life—Ben, included—are on the other side.

"I'm sure."

"But Mom, you—"

Jordan stops talking instantly when you turn silently to look at him.

"I'll be home after five," you announce as you walk out of the room. "Don't call me unless someone's dead."

You hear Matthew bark a nervous laugh, and then Ben says something, but you cut him off when you close the door behind you. The garage is chilly, but it's a relief just to be away from them. To be alone. You climb into your SUV and call Anna as you drive. It almost feels like the past several weeks haven't happened as you cruise your familiar route to work, talking business on Bluetooth.

Except that you have a white-knuckle grip on the steering wheel. You have a hard knot of bitter anger in your belly. The aftertaste of coffee on your tongue because you didn't take time to brush your teeth. The weight of a ball and chain around your neck because your assault has penetrated so deep into your home and family, you doubt you will ever feel content there again. To hell with taking control of your emotions and owning the anger and not allowing that man to hold you down any longer. The aftermath of your rape has contaminated your family, and the residual damage is out of your hands.

As if on auto-pilot, your Highlander stops at a local drive-up coffee kiosk. Nothing fancy. No fancy name—Coffee—and no frou-frou drinks. Just coffee. You end your call to Anna—you had called as a courtesy, so you didn't frighten her when you suddenly showed up at the office—and place an order for a large black coffee. Money and elixir exchanged, you drive away without sipping first. At the next stoplight, you stare at the plain white paper cup and blink away memories of Aspen.

"Fuck you," you say to the coffee and then because it feels good, you say it again. You imagine pouring the scalding coffee over the stranger. Over his face and genitals. You're not a violent person, and given an opportunity, you wouldn't do something so vicious. Imagining it makes you feel better for a moment.

At the office, you kill the ignition and sit for a moment in silence. You need to see Barry. Now. Not in a few days. You need to go to the gym and don boxing gloves and beat the absolute hell out of something. You need to go stand on the bluff overlooking the Mississippi and scream the rage out.

You need someone to understand.

You need someone to get that you want to be normal. That sometimes you are normal. But sometimes you remember the pain—the physical pain and the fear and the grief—and you need to lash out at whoever is nearest. You need your sons to understand how real this is. You need Jordan to get off your back, and you need Matthew to pay attention to what's going on with Trev and what he's doing with Alli, because you're terrified of what will happen to Trev and you can't stomach the thought of the same happening with either of your boys.

Anna greets you with a hesitant smile, and then as you set your bag on your desk, she moves quickly to give you a friendly hug. When she asks if your health is still an issue, you simply tell her you're dealing with it as best you can. Maybe part of your healing is knowing that you can share your story if you want to, but you don't have to tell anyone anything. You control what happens now. As much as you like Anna, you don't care to share any of the past few weeks with her.

Appeased by your reassurances that you are dealing with the situation without knowing exactly what the situation is, Anna seems happy to perch on the edge of one of the chairs in front of your desk and do shop talk. She catches you up on the clients she's dealt with since you've been gone, and you fill her in on the work you've done from home. You tell her you're ready to be back at it full time, that you'll see clients again. You aren't, and you don't want to, but it's time. Either you jump in headfirst or you leave it all behind. Running the business as you have been, with minimal contact with your partner, isn't fair to her, so you tell yourself you'll suck it up and get over it. Maybe, you think as Anna leaves your office with a warm smile, it will do you good to be back in your old routine.

Later, you have to admit to yourself, it's been a good day. You spent some time reading Anna's notes on different accounts. You read a few emails from clients who are pleased with the work the two of you have done. You went over some of Anna's recent designs, and you shot her a quick email to ooooh and aaaah over an ad design she's preparing for Gemstones, a local jeweler.

Sometime through the day, the tension in your shoulders and upper back eases, but you can't pinpoint the exact moment it happens. You just realize while you're on the phone with a woman who owns a small upscale boutique downtown that you feel good. The woman asks to meet with you or Anna to discuss an ad campaign for the holidays, and you feel a flash of panic over the coming season. But you agree to a meeting, and when you end the call, you roll your shoulders and it hits you that you feel good.

In the late afternoon hours, eyes glued to your computer screen, you feel a chill climb your back and up the back of your neck. Immediately, your stomach reacts, and you feel like you might be sick. It's that feeling that someone is watching you, and it brings to mind the day at the café in Aspen. The question of whether your rapist was somewhere in that café watching you, if he followed you that day and then came back to get you the next morning.

Was he watching the hotel? Your room? How else would he have known that you would be alone? What if he was one of Ben's colleagues? What if the man who raped you walked out of your room, hit the men's room to wash his hands, and then joined your husband in a conference room to discuss the latest IT news? Visual reality. Fiber networks. Smart houses.

Slowly, you lift your chin and look around the room. Ben is propped in your open doorway. His hands are tucked away in his hip pockets, and his face is a mask of concern. You stare at him for a moment, so overwhelmed with emotion you can't process what you're feeling or thinking.

"Don't do that," you finally mumble.

"Don't do what?" he asks from the doorway. His hair is tousled and messy, and there are deep grooves under his eyes. The collar of his shirt is open, his tie tugged loose and low. His shirtsleeves are rolled, and your eyes sweep over the bit of his forearms visible between his trouser pockets and his rolled sleeves. He looks like a tired, middle-aged man who might be worried about his wife, but looking at him from where you sit, he's still easy on the eyes, and you're still so in love with him.

"Watch me."

"Watch you?" He finally moves, but he approaches you cautiously, as if the floor is made of eggshells.

"I just…" You lift your hand and wave it at the back of your neck. "I felt someone watching me. And it made me think…" You let your words trail off and shake your head, because you can't say it.

"I thought you might call me." He jiggles his keys in his pocket and draws your eyes to his hips. The fly of his slacks. Seems like it's been much longer than just today since you made love, and even though you're still frustrated with him and even with that chill on the back of your neck from thinking someone was watching you, you crave that intimacy with him.

"I needed a break, Ben." You turn back to the screen, but you feel his stare, heavy and heartbreaking, on the top of your head.

"A seven-hour break?"

"Yeah." You nod without looking at him again. "Seven hours. A day. Two days."

"What does that mean?"

You huff out an anxious sigh and drop your hands to your lap. Tears blur your vision, but you make yourself remember the scene in the kitchen this morning. The way your sons—specifically your youngest—are tearing away at your comfort, your peace of mind. Your mind itself.

"I can't deal with it, Ben," you whisper. The words are so small, you know he didn't hear you clearly. He starts to speak, but before he can ask you to repeat yourself, you shake your head and hold a hand up to stop him. When you finally stand and turn to him, he's wearing a look of fear and heartache. It looks familiar; it's a look you see in the mirror every day.

"Deal with what, Delilah?"

"You guys."

"Me? What did I do?" He tosses his hands up, desperate to find answers, to find you, to hold you. You lift your gaze to look over his shoulder and wonder if Anna is at her desk. This isn't a conversation you want to have, and you most certainly can't have it here.

"I was gonna go by Khloe's when I leave here. Stay there tonight."

Ben lowers his head, ducks his chin to his chest. You watch him breathe deeply; his shoulders lift, and his chest expands big and wide. When he looks up again, his blood-shot eyes are rimmed in red. Sensing that he's going to explode, you slip around the end of your desk and cross the room in four big strides. You hear Anna on the phone as you press your door closed gently and then click the lock.

"You spent the day at work to let me know you're gonna leave me?" he asks before you get back around to your side of the desk.

"I'm not leaving you." You roll your eyes, annoyed with the drama. For a while, the office had been big and spacious, and you had been able to breathe. You'd felt connected to something again, and now that Ben is here and the door is closed, the air is thick and heavy, and you're suffocating.

"Then what in the hell is going on? What did I do? Why did you walk out this morning?"

"Because I needed a break from all the testosterone in the house, Ben. You guys are making me crazy."

"I didn't say anything wrong! I totally backed you up,

and I completely agree with what you said. Jordan's completely out of line with what he's saying. And the idea of him being at a party like that—"

You fold your arms over your chest and stare at Ben, anxious for him to finish his tirade.

"Speaking of which, someone needs to talk to the parents."

"Shouldn't that be you?" Ben asks with a frown. "The girls' parents? Wouldn't it be better coming from you? Than me?"

"Look." You draw in a deep breath. "I came to work to get away from this for a while. I gotta find me again, Ben. Our whole world is wrecked right now, and I'm telling you, if I don't find myself in this mess, I…" You shrug.

"So you're asking me for space so you can decide if you need me or if you need to divorce me?"

"Ben." You sob and swipe at your eyes. "I don't want a divorce."

"Then what is going on? What the hell, Dee? Wasn't last night okay? I thought it was pretty fucking incredible, and I thought you thought that, too. I got up this morning thinking okay, maybe. Maybe we're on the right track. And then you walk out after throwing a coffee mug—"

"I didn't throw it," you mumble, but Ben rages on.

"You don't call me. You don't even text me to let me know you're okay. Now you tell me you wanna go to Khloe's and not come home? I don't get it. I don't get this, Dee—"

You sink into your chair and cover your face with your hands.

"I was so furious this morning, Ben, I wanted to throw things. To break things. I wanted to scream at him. I wanted to backhand him. I walked out in a fucking rage, and I walked out so I wouldn't do any of those things." You sniffle and lower your hands to the desk. Ben leans over your desk now, his hands planted on the top. His fingertips nearly touch your desk calendar that's covered with your handwritten notes. The writing comforts you.

"Because of what he said?"

"Because of what he said. Because I think he was a little more involved in what he talked about than what he admitted. Because he's turned into a horrible hateful child, and it's because I've become a lousy excuse for a mother. Because some son-of-a-bitch raped me."

"You're not a lousy excuse for a mother."

"Jordan never even flirted with being so disrespectful—with anyone—until now. That's on me."

"It's not on you!" Ben argues. You watch him drag his fingers over the desktop to close his hands into fists. "How is it your fault?"

"Believe me, I'm trying to figure it out." You swallow hard.

"I get it, Dee. Jordan and I had a long talk after you left."

"Yeah? Think that's gonna do any good? Like that last talk you had with him?"

Ben grits his teeth and straightens. He stares at you, eyes bright with anger.

"Here's the thing, Ben. You're trying. I get it. You're trying because I'm failing, and I love you for that. But you're not me, and you're saying things to him, to both of them, that aren't wrong. But they're not right, either, and it's all killing me. This is killing me."

"I'm not wrong. But I'm not right." Ben frowns and drops to sit in the chair in front of your desk, the same one Anna chose earlier. "What does that mean?"

"Do we have to talk about this now?"

"When are we going to talk about this, Dee? Tomorrow? Next week? Ever?"

You stare at him silently for a moment. Tears burn in your eyes, and dammit, you don't want to cry here at work. Because you don't want to explain anything to Anna, and if she saw Ben come in and then sees later that you've been crying, she'll make assumptions. She'll think all of your health issues are actually problems between you and Ben. You don't want to tell her the truth, but you sure as hell don't want anyone to believe there's something happening between you and Ben.

Rage is a knife in your chest. Your whole life is now a play with your family and friends privy to your thoughts and your feelings; either that, or you let everyone look and assume and make judgments without hearing your side of anything. How unfair that ten minutes in that hotel room in Aspen has yanked your world out from under your feet.

Your hand trembles as you smooth the curled corner of the desktop calendar. How unfair that Max and Mel and Trev are living in limbo and will be for the foreseeable future.

"I came here to find myself. To find my normal, Ben." Your words are a little chilling, the broken whisper in your office. The throb of pain in your throat, in your chest. "And I was doing okay. And then you showed up. And dragged all the ugly that I need desperately to get away from in here with you. Do you get that?"

"What I don't get is that we finally had a good night together." His voice is low and tight, but his face is a stone mask, as if it's all he can do to hold himself together. "And I don't just mean the sex. I mean a good night. You slept, Dee. You slept well. In my arms."

Pinned under his intense stare, you fall back in your chair and dab at your eyes. He's right. And that's what you were thinking when you got up this morning. Yes, the sex was good. After the assault, you couldn't imagine being intimate, let alone reaching orgasm again. But what had touched you was the intimacy. Curling into Ben when it was over and sleeping soundly, knowing you were safe in his arms.

"And now, you're gonna throw that night out and start over. You're gonna go to Khloe's and sleep alone in her spare bedroom."

"God, Ben, I won't go to Khloe's, okay? I'll be home—"

"Why? Just tell me what's in your head. Right now."

"It's awful," you say softly. You pitch forward and rest your elbows on your desk. You look him in the eye and say the same words again. "My heart breaks for Trev and Max and Mel. And I'm scared to death every time our boys leave the house now, because we can't protect them when they're gone. But, Ben…"

"What?" He leans forward, as if he can reach you from the chair where his ass rides the very edge, poised to jump and rescue you.

"It's not the same." You shake your head. "You can't ever, ever say that to our boys. As awful as it is…the waiting for Trev…it's not the same as being a woman. And being overpowered. And held down. While a man shoves himself inside your body."

Ben's face—that stone mask of control—breaks slowly, bits at a time. Tears leak from his midnight eyes and follow the grooves in his skin.

"Waiting. Making your mind go somewhere else so you aren't there while that man presses and jerks inside you… waiting for him to get off, to get what he came for before you can move again."

"Dee." His voice is gruff, a little desperate.

"I held on for you. Because don't think it didn't cross my mind that if I fought him, he might kill me. If he killed me, I wouldn't be here now." You shrug and arch your eyebrows. "For you and the boys. But I waited it out. For you. For the boys. And this is what's left. This is who I am."

"Delilah—"

"I'm trying to dig deeper, Ben. I'm trying to dig deeper for all of those pieces inside that shattered that day. Because I want to be more than this. I didn't survive that to live a damaged life."

He leans forward and rests his elbows on his knees. Lets his hands hang between his legs. Huffs out several deep breaths. You worry that he might hyperventilate, but you're paralyzed behind the desk.

"I'm doing my best. But you have to acknowledge that it's not the same. You have to understand that. I know that's way too complicated for Matthew and Jordan, and I know the point right now for them is that they have to learn respect. For others. For women. For themselves. But I need you to acknowledge that it's not the same."

CHAPTER 27

This time when you talk to Barry about the assault, you forget to tiptoe, to be cautious. Your recitation of those ten minutes that broke your life is gritty and ugly, and when you're done—when you've vomited the last words—the silence in the room is broken by your sobs. Barry, who has turned on music this time (you had actually nodded your acknowledgement when you heard Sinatra singing ever so quietly), simply hands you a tissue and nods solemnly and lets you catch your breath.

At first, you are ashamed. You want to run, to break through the door instead of taking time to open it and run away. You hadn't intended to actually let your guard down here, and definitely not so quickly. But the house has become a bomb ready to explode, and each day you move cautiously, afraid of what might set it off.

When Barry simply waits you out, you realize you're breathing easier. Deeper. While the sadness, the sting of losing something most people don't know they have—you suppose it's a level of innocence that most people aren't even aware of—still fills you, your body feels like the house in the quiet after a raging storm has passed over. Little ticks and sighs as it settles but the hardest part is over, and now you must go about assessing the damage and making repairs. One thing at a time.

Before you know you are going to open your mouth, you're talking again. Barry listens with an open face, his eyes kind and warm, and you tell him about your son's best friend. You tell him about a boy who used to stay at your house overnight. The boy that wore footie pajamas until he was six, and the boy that shared his cookies with you. The kid who helped Jordan with a big science project two years ago when Matthew was buckling down to attempt the ACT again. The kid who has mentioned studying pre-med, because he wants to help people.

The sharp pains come back when you keep talking. The jabs in your chest when you talk about the way your youngest son has changed. That you're afraid of what he's doing. That you know he's rebelling against what happened to you, and he's misplaced that anger, and now he's taking it out on you. You admit that as much as you love him, you don't like Jordan right now, and surely, Jordan senses that, too.

Barry says nothing. He simply lets you talk until you're hoarse and exhausted. When you've finished that round, he asks if you're sleeping. And this time, your tears are silent. You most definitely had no plans to tell Barry that you and Ben are trying to find the intimacy in your marriage again, that you often sleep on the couch. That you considered leaving last week, even if just for a night.

And yet, you dump all of that, too, and Barry lets you talk. He doesn't fill your head with empty words, platitudes that sound like they're written by people who eat rainbows and stars and have never dealt with any adversity. And yet, you can't help but think them as you sit there in his office.

Sinatra is crooning about trying again, and it hits you that you didn't leave last week. Not even for a night. Ben had talked you into coming home. And when you'd gone to bed that night, you let him hold you. In your fleece pj pants and long-sleeved tee, Ben had pulled you in to hold you against his chest. And you'd slept.

Matthew has been at home more nights this week than not. Twice, Alli came over, but they stayed upstairs to do homework. You didn't mean to eavesdrop, but now and then you heard them teasing each other, and you heard sweet things said that made you think of you and Ben back in the beginning. Jordan has been quiet, and after all of the harsh, hateful things he's said lately, you've decided you'll take quiet.

Barry suggests that you consider filling the prescription for the antidepressant, but you still don't love that idea. When he senses your hesitation, he asks if you're exercising, tells you that might help to exorcise the demons. He also reminds you, as he did last time, that there's a group of assault survivors who meet and talk, and it might do you good to try that. Again, when you shy away from that, he lets it go. However, you do stop and schedule another appointment to see Barry when you leave his office.

Ben is stern with the boys, and you sense there are things being said in rooms where you are not. In undertones, so that you don't hear them. It rankles a bit, and yet, you let it go. You have sons, and they need their father to navigate them through this. Even if you hadn't been in that Aspen hotel room six weeks ago, even if you had come home from Aspen the same woman you were when you left, there are things boys needs their fathers for. Therefore, you trust that Ben is teaching them all the things you—as a woman—need them to know but as their mother cannot talk about. You trust, after the way

Ben broke down in your office—thankfully, Anna was gone when you opened your door later that afternoon— that he will never again say that what Trev is going through is the same horrible thing you're going through. You trust that he is eloquent and compassionate enough to make them get that Trev's ordeal is a nightmare, and your experience is a nightmare, but you're fighting different monsters.

FitNess has helped you some. Not that you feel the need to slim down or smooth the belly or hips away. If anything, you need to put weight on. But that will come in time. First, you have to heal your heart and your mind. Yoga and the spin class you return to go a long way toward that mental healing. Physical exhaustion and the clear mind help you sleep. So does Ben's warm, solid strength there beside you in your bed.

Even though you go to work now each morning and spend a few hours there, you're still anxious and uneasy when you get home. In fact, that part is almost worse. You find yourself double and triple checking to make sure no one is following you on the drive home. You double and triple check your doors once you are safely inside the house. You find yourself double-checking to make sure you've set the alarm. You still jump at every little noise.

Exercise helps, but you miss fresh air. You miss the long walks you used to take through your neighborhood. You hate that you took that freedom, that independence for granted. And each day when you get home from your office, you vow that the time has come to claim it back. Piece by piece, you will put yourself back together.

Dressed in yoga pants and a long sweatshirt—it's chilly, but still mild for early November—that covers your butt, you stand at the front door, eyes on the world outside. You've done this each day you've come home and made that vow, but every other day, you've changed your mind. You're afraid.

Afraid to go outside. To walk. Alone.

You promised yourself today on the drive home that this time would be different. And yet, your chest is tight, and your lungs are locked down, and you can't breathe. Palm pressed to the sturdy wooden door that keeps you safe, you watch out the sidelights around the door. There's no one around, so you should be fine. You should feel safe to go out and walk. There's no one around to talk to you, to hold you up. As much as you like your neighbors, you can't get held up once you make the decision to go outside and walk. You have to get it done. You have to put one foot in front of the other and just keep doing it over and over, until you believe in yourself, in your strength again.

But, on the other hand, there's no one out there. If anyone were to harass you, if a car were to pull up close to the curb and idle next to you and a stranger were to put his window down to ask you for directions to Elmwood Hollow Estates and if that stranger were to reach for you—there's no one out there to witness it. To help you.

It's unlikely. But seems more plausible than a stranger barging into a hotel room to rape a woman before breakfast.

Instead, you pace the house and breathe the stale air that's heavy with regret. But outside, it's brisk and chilly, and the heavy, gray clouds call to you, and you wonder what the timeline is on being a woman again.

You go to the back door and stand for a moment with your hand on the doorknob. What if someone *is* out there? What if you get too far away from home and realize someone is watching you? What if—

"What're you doing?"

You jump when you hear Jordan's voice just behind

you. You glance at him over your shoulder and consider not answering him. But for just a moment, you remember you're the parent, the adult, and you can't behave like a sullen child. You're only perpetuating the behavior you don't like.

"I want…" You clear your throat and avoid Jordan's eyes. "I want to go for a walk."

He watches you for a moment, and though you work hard at holding a poker face, you know he sees through the mask.

"Can I go with you?" he asks hopefully, and you see a glimpse of the kid he used to be. Probably, he is asking to go because Ben has all but hammered it into his and Matthew's heads that they need to be considerate of you. But what if he wants to go to spend time with you? To protect you?

"You want to?" You tip your head and eye him with suspicion.

"I do." He nods, and he flashes you a grin—the sweet, happy grin you haven't seen in so long, it brings tears to your eyes. "Wait just a second. Let me grab my hoodie."

He darts out of the room before you can respond, but he's back in five seconds tops, tugging his black and gray school hoodie over his head.

"Let me grab the keys," you say, and you start to step around him.

"I'll get them." He's gone again and then back quicker this time, your key ring in his hands. He hands them to you, and the feel of his fingertips against the palm of your hand makes something in your chest and your belly flutter a little bit.

Outside, there is a lazy, chilly breeze, and you both hunch your shoulders as you walk. Jordan had closed the overhead garage door, and the two of you slipped out the side door and locked it. You walk in silence; the only sound is the tap of your shoes on the pavement. Cars creep by you; some drivers wave, and others don't. It all feels so normal, it brings tears to your eyes.

You think again about that day in the café in Aspen. Try to see the layout of tables there, the people who were sipping coffee and tapping away on laptops when you were there doing the same. You wonder if the man who attacked you watched you there.

You wonder if it had happened to someone else in that café that morning, if that man had picked someone else as his victim, would you have suspected something? Would you have seen him watching someone? Would you have seen him follow a woman out? Make notes on what she was doing? Would you have stopped him?

If you had had a weapon there in the room, would you have used it? Could you have harmed him to save yourself?

"Mom?"

You glance at Jordan, surprised to hear his voice. You're startled to realize he's as tall as you are now, and you wonder when he grew that last inch or two. You might be shoulder to shoulder, but at the moment, his face is sweet and innocent, and the answer is yes. You could and would have defended yourself if you'd had the proper weapon. Maybe you don't remember those ten minutes terribly clearly, but your body fought him. You had the bruises and the blood to prove it.

You've told Ben you could defend your sons if you had to, and as you watch your youngest struggle to say something to you, it hits you that defending yourself is defending your boys. Your family. You fought him to survive, and you wanted to survive because your family is everything to you.

"What?"

"Maybe you should get a dog." He speaks so softly, you have to lean in close to hear him. "You know. A big dog. To walk with you. When I can't."

And there, under those words you hear all the words your baby hasn't been able to say. He feels bad that you were hurt, that he wasn't there to protect you. Never mind that it isn't his job, it's what your son feels and he's acting out against his helplessness.

"I like that idea." You nod, and you keep walking, and you don't acknowledge Jordan's worry and his unspoken apology, because to do so might embarrass him and push him to act out again.

"I've been researching German Shepherds," he goes on, and you're touched that he's researching something to protect you. For when he's not with you. The same way Ben wants to take shooting lessons and begin the proper procedures to become legal gun owners.

"Yeah?" You glance at Jordan and arch an eyebrow as you walk. "They're pretty cute."

"They're not supposed to be cute, Mom," he says as if he's exasperated, but you catch the grin he wants to hide from you.

"Okay. They're guard dogs, right?"

"Yes. And we could get one as a puppy. And train it...to protect...us."

You wince, because what he really means is you could train the dog to protect you. You hate being vulnerable, being a woman that needs protecting. But then again, maybe utilizing those sorts of things—guard dogs, weapons, self-defense classes, even therapy—is part of being strong again. Smart and strong. Being prepared certainly doesn't equal being weak.

"Okay." You nod again, because you want Jordan to

know you like his idea. That you appreciate his thoughts, his concern.

"I'll talk to Dad. Tell him what I've been reading."

"Sounds good."

"Mom?"

"What, bud?"

"I didn't touch that girl. At that party."

"Okay." You take a deep breath.

"I mean…some guys did. But I was thinking that it was kind of…gross. And stupid. With what happened with Trev."

"That's true."

"And you." He clears his throat. "I know you were hurt. I'm sorry for how I've behaved."

"Oh, sweetheart." You wince again, and this time, you slip your arm around his shoulders. He's not as bony as he was just a few weeks ago. Your boys are growing up so fast, and you've missed a good chunk of time with them lately that you can't get back. The thought makes your body feel heavy and slow. "It's okay. It's not fair that you have to deal with this."

"Wasn't fair that it happened to you, either."

When you look at him this time, your eyes meet. His are glassy with tears, too.

"Dad said he would kill the guy if he ever found him."

"He won't, Jordie. I've never seen him before in my life."

"I know." Jordan nods. "But me and Matthew. We would, too, Mom."

CHAPTER 28

*J*ordan disappears to his room again when you get back from your walk. You want to pull him in for a hug; for the first time since the assault, you need to put your arms around your son and draw him close and love him. But you're afraid to push for more than what he's just given you. The offer to walk with you should be enough, and the conversation shared *is* enough. Still, you stand at the end of the hall and stare at his closed door for several moments before you move again.

Before you left for work this morning, you put pork chops in the crockpot, so dinner's ready when Ben gets home. The four of you sit together at the table, and even though you're quiet—you're observing more than contributing—conversation is easy and almost normal. Jordan announces that he has a big project in his literature class, due just before the holidays. He's not into recreational reading, and he's even less excited about mandatory reading for school. The idea of fighting him through this project, nitpicking him constantly to make sure it's finished on time makes you tired.

Jordan includes you this time, makes sure he looks at you often as he speaks, though he's still skittish about making eye contact with you. Because you have no idea what things have been said between him and his father and his brother about women and sex and rape, eye contact is difficult for you, too. It's okay, though. You'll take what you can get. Mending the broken fences with your family is the most important part of your recovery process. You won't heal without their love.

Matthew talks about Alli, who is worried about Becca. Becca still hangs with them, even when Trev is around. Matthew says they all still have fun, but it's different now. Trev is quiet, and Becca is quieter, and you prop your chin in your hand, eyes on Matthew, but you're thinking about Mel. You wonder how she's doing, and that makes you wonder what's going on between her and Max. If things have gotten any better. Or, if things are worse. You worry about Mel—as flirty and outrageous as she and Max can be, you know they love each other, and neither would hurt the other with infidelity—because they're hurting each other in every other way. The same way you've done to Ben since Aspen. Maybe a little bit of venom is understandable, but there has to come a time when you make the choice to put the fangs away and move on.

Without turning away from Matthew, you peek at Ben. Study the lines in his face, his thick lashes and his thick, dark hair. Your husband has been your superhero, and even when you refused to be the damsel in distress, he promised to have your back and love you in any way you needed him.

When he catches you watching him, he arches his eyebrows as if to ask if you're okay. Right now, you are, so you nod. You have no idea what tomorrow might bring, and you suppose you might live a big part of your life with that cautious approach. But that's okay, as long as you remember to live in the moment and be thankful for each piece of yourself you reclaim along the way.

After dinner, Matthew clears the table, and you're about to tell him to let it go. That you'll do it. But when Jordan opens the dishwasher to load the plates Matthew carries to him, you stay silent. Maybe he's not ready to hug you, maybe he hasn't processed everything just yet, but maybe this is Jordan's way of supporting you, loving you.

You glance at Ben with a small smile, but when he gives you a wide-eyed look and a tiny shrug of his shoulders, you laugh softly and shake your head.

"I have something to ask you, Delilah Nicholson."

You lift your chin from your hand and stretch, all of your attention on Ben now. The clatter of dishes and your sons' chatter are the perfect backdrop to this ordinary weeknight.

"What do you wanna ask me, Ben Nicholson?" You twist your wineglass in circles on the table and finally lift it to sip from it.

"Would you go out with me?" Ben flashes you a grin. "I'm thinking dinner. Drinks. Some dancing."

You tip your head back and laugh, and for just a moment, you can't breathe. That every day feeling of home and happiness overwhelms you, and you have to concentrate to take a deep breath.

"Where in the world are we gonna go dancing?" you ask, but you reach over the table to him. He slides his fingers over your hand and holds on.

"Well, we could have dinner and then come home and dance."

"Yeah?"

"And maybe I could kiss you once or twice."

Your heartbeat hums in your throat as he leans over the

corner of the table to kiss you. His lips are soft and warm on yours, and you remember the night you told him about the morning in Aspen, how you looked at his lips and wished you would have shared more long, intimate kisses with him before, in case you couldn't do it again.

Even though tomorrow is a wild card, right now, you want to do it again. You lift your hand to his face and smooth your fingers over the dark stubble on his cheeks and chin. Ben parts his lips, and you're kissing him like the rest of the world has fallen away.

"Welp," Matthew calls loudly from behind you. "We're done. See you."

"That's gross." Jordan apparently agrees with Matthew that the kitchen clean-up work is done.

"Well, it's really not," Matthew tells him. "But yeah, when it's Mom and Dad…" His voice fades.

"Madden football?" You hear Jordan ask him, and even though your smiling lips are pressed to Ben's smiling lips, you feel a pang of fear that Matthew will turn him down, and the solid moment between brothers will break. Your totally ordinary weeknight will be ruined, and you'll have to start over on feeling good.

"I'll kick your ass."

You consider calling Matthew out for his language, but Ben nuzzles your neck and presses a kiss below your ear, and you hope this time Jordan kicks Matthew's ass.

"You okay?" Ben's voice is a low rumble, his lips still at your neck.

"Mmm." You nod and squeeze his hand.

"You had a look on your face earlier."

"What kind of look?"

"Like you were in deep thought." Ben straightens, but he scoots his chair closer to the table so he's closer to you.

"I was," you admit.

"About?"

"When Jordan and I were walking earlier?"

He nods. You'd gushed to him the second he stepped into the kitchen that Jordan had asked to go walking with you. You would have gushed the details of the walk, but both boys had heard Ben come inside, so they joined you in the kitchen before you could say more.

"He...um." You purse your lips and then sigh, a little tired, a little hopeful. "He told me he thinks you should get me a dog. For protection. Well. He said to protect the family, but I knew what he meant."

Ben nods again. His eyes take a slow stroll over your face, lingering on your parted lips, and finally return to meet your gaze. "He's been researching the best dog to get you."

"You know?"

"Dee, he's been looking into this since right after...you told them...about what happened. It just took him a while to process everything."

You lick your lips and huff out another sigh, frustrated with your own fragile state.

"What's wrong?" Ben rubs his thumb over your lips.

"I hate being helpless."

"You're not being helpless," he argues. "A strong woman is a smart woman. You're too smart to be stubborn about this. I get that you need to slay your own dragons here. But you'd be smart to let us hold the perimeter while you fight."

You turn away from him when your eyes fill. So beautifully said, and so heartfelt.

"Ben, I love you."

"I know, Delilah. Whoever said love isn't enough doesn't know that love is everything."

"Sometimes, it's not—"

"It is. It's me, giving you any and everything you need to survive. And it's you. Being strong enough to accept any and everything I give you. That's what it is. Nothing else matters." He presses his lips to your forehead. "Not in this house."

You nod, but you swallow down the urge to argue. It is what matters in your house. But what about Max and Mel? Crusading not for each other, but for their son.

"Ben." You draw back from him and lose yourself in his eyes.

"What?"

"I've been thinking." You press your lips together, uncertain how to say it, uncertain of what you even want to say.

"Just don't think of leaving—"

You shake your head and lift his hand to your lips.

"I need to do something."

"What do you mean?"

"For Trev. I need to do something."

He watches you for a moment. You see the fight in his eyes. He doesn't want you to get involved. Not because he doesn't believe in Trev, but because he worries it will tear you down all over again.

He leans in so close to you, you feel his breath on your lips. The overhead light in the kitchen is bright, and even though the boys loaded the dishwasher, the kitchen is still messy. From down the hall, you hear a Post Malone song, and your sons trash talking each other, and looking at Ben, you see the exact moment when he lets go of his need to protect you.

"What're you gonna do?" His voice is gruff, and his eyes are glassy, but he squeezes your hand as if to promise he will stand by you.

"I don't know. But I have to do something." You press

your lips together and continue, "Mel said things are really bad for her and Max. Trev's obsessed with a blog about prison, like he's trying to acclimate himself to the idea that he's going to prison."

Ben flinches.

"I know you're frustrated with Max." You search his eyes for understanding.

"I'm not—it's just—when I can't throw my arms around my wife and kiss her just for fun, why the hell should he have that right? That trust?"

"You're right," you whisper. "But this is bigger than that. This is Trev's life."

"I know."

"I survived a sexual assault." You clear your throat. "Good days and bad days, but I did survive it. I...just... feel like it's time for me to act like it."

Ben blinks and tears wet his lashes.

"Okay." He nods. "I know."

"Maybe I can help." You shrug. "Maybe not. But maybe trying to help Trev, maybe that's why—"

"No." Ben shakes his head, his voice hard with anger. "Don't tell me your assault was meant to happen. If you need to take a stand, help Trev." He shrugs. "I get it. But don't tell me this was meant to be."

You don't argue, because even though you've questioned God a hundred times since the morning in Aspen, you don't want to believe your rape was destiny. It was a random assault, and you happened to be the victim.

"Maybe helping him would help me. Why not use what I...use my experience...to help him?"

He watches you silently for several long moments, and finally, he cups your face in both hands. His eyes are glassy, and your own face is wet with tears.

"Okay."

"I'm gonna go see Mel tomorrow."

"And do what?"

You don't know, exactly. But it feels important that you check in with Mel first. That you share your thoughts with her. And suddenly, you need to talk to Sophia Marten. Maybe it's a Hail Mary for Trev, maybe part of you needs to see that she's okay or for her to see that you're okay after your assault, and maybe taking charge and trying to change something for the better, do something good for someone, will make you stronger.

"I'm going to ask for her permission to go and see Sophia Marten."

AFTERWORD

If you are a victim of sexual assault, you can call the National Sexual Assault Hotline for support, information, or referrals.

https://www.rainn.org/

800-656-**HOPE** (4673)

ACKNOWLEDGMENTS

Sending a huge thank you to Heather Leindecker, MSN, FNP-BC for your medical & technical advice. Your willingness to sit down and talk to me or email in-depth answers to my crazy questions is so very much appreciated. I love that no matter what questions I pose, no matter what book plot I have in mind, you are always so excited to be involved and to share your knowledge and experience with me. Any mistakes made in the writing of this novel are my own.

A big thank you to Kim Joyce and Jennifer Naumann for your time with reading bits and pieces and giving me early feedback.

Thank you Kate Carley for a really fast beta read & the honest, emotional response. So happy I went to MBLU in 2016 & made some lifelong writer friends 🖤 You're at the top of the list!

Thanks to Jennifer Probst-one of my very favorite authors-for a very kind exchange in an email (that I initiated) when I was in the beginning stages of writing this book. Your books & your kindness whenever I fangirl are so inspiring and so very much appreciated.

ABOUT THE AUTHOR

As an only child, Tracy Broemmer grew up with a wild imagination. An avid reader from a young age, she spent a lot of time with her nose buried in books and a lot of time making up her own stories. She penned her first book in grade school and hasn't stopped writing since.

Tracy is the author of the Lorelei Bluffs women's fiction series, the women's fiction series the Williams Legacy, and several stand-alone women's fiction novels. She has recently dabbled in contemporary romance and is the author of The Mississippi Queen Trilogy.

For more information, go to www.broemmerbooks.com

A Lorelei Ending, Lorelei Bluffs, Book 9

I Do, Lorelei Bluffs, Book 10

Truth Is, The Williams Legacy, Book 1

Other People's Ugly, The Williams Legacy, Book 2

Omissions, The Williams Legacy, Book 3

Contemporary Romance Novels:

Destiny's Calling: Your Future is Waiting

Wedding Day Shenanigans

Holiday Fling

The Kiss Off

Something Like Love

Love, Nashville, Mississippi Queen Trilogy, Book 1

Forever Duncan, Mississippi Queen Trilogy, Book 2

Always, Jess, Mississippi Queen Trilogy, Book 3

Contemporary Romance Novellas:

Indian Summer, A Novella

Dear Jaclyn Perris, A Novella

Short Stories

Perfect Pictures, The Wine Tasting Series: Traminette